PENGUIN METRO READS
NINE

Shobha Nihalani is the author of *The Silent Monument*. Her
debut novel, *Karmic Blues*, was translated and published in
Denmark. She has worked as a freelance journalist,
copywriter, bookkeeper, English teacher and salesperson.
She lives in Hong Kong with her family. Read more at
www.shobhanihalani.com.

[Author name] is the author of [...] novel [...] and [...] Press [...] and later published in [...] Germany. She has worked as a freelance journalist [...] creative non-fiction [...] theatre and education [...] She lives in [...] with her family. [Read about] an author [...]

CURSE OF THE
KALINGAN

NINE

BOOK ONE
SHOBHA NIHALANI

Penguin
metro reads

PENGUIN METRO READS

Published by the Penguin Group

Penguin Books India Pvt Ltd, 11 Community Centre, Panchsheel Park,
New Delhi 110 017, India

Penguin Group (USA) Inc., 375 Hudson Street, New York, New York 10014, USA

Penguin Group (Canada), 90 Eglinton Avenue East, Suite 700, Toronto,
Ontario, M4P 2Y3, Canada (a division of Pearson Penguin Canada Inc.)

Penguin Books Ltd, 80 Strand, London WC2R 0RL, England

Penguin Ireland, 25 St Stephen's Green, Dublin 2, Ireland (a division of Penguin Books
Ltd)

Penguin Group (Australia), 707 Collins Street, Melbourne, Victoria 3008, Australia
(a division of Pearson Australia Group Pty Ltd)

Penguin Group (NZ), 67 Apollo Drive, Rosedale, Auckland 0632,
New Zealand (a division of Pearson New Zealand Ltd)

Penguin Books (South Africa) (Pty) Ltd, Block D, Rosebank Office Park, 181 Jan
Smuts Avenue, Parktown North, Johannesburg 2193, South Africa

Penguin Books Ltd, Registered Offices: 80 Strand, London WC2R 0RL, England

First published in Penguin Metro Reads by Penguin Books India 2013

ISBN 9780143418856

Typeset in Minion Regular by SÚRYA, New Delhi
Printed at Manipal Technologies Ltd, Manipal

ALWAYS LEARNING   **PEARSON**

The world depends on souls of heroes

—The Mother

PROLOGUE

Kalinga
Modern Bhubaneshwar, Orissa
261 BC

The odour of decaying flesh coiled around the Kalingan's dying body. He heard the piercing cries of circling and swooping carrion birds. Torn limbs lay scattered, some corpses still clutched weapons and others were crushed by the weight of elephants. The air was thick with the metallic smell of blood. It came from his body and those of his clan. Pain, like a thousand spikes, gutted his spirit. If there was hell on earth, then this was it.

The human body is weak compared to the arrogant power of its ego, to its desire to win. The sun and the earth bore witness to such horror of mankind. How shameful, how despicable the human heart must appear to the gods! His throat was clogged, a ball of regret and anger swelling within him. Death hovered. He could feel his breath struggle, holding on to a carcass. There was solace in the skies, he should let go. But he wasn't ready yet. There were others, battered and waiting for death. He sensed their restlessness. They wanted to fight and shout out the battle cry, their lives lingered between this hell and freedom. He heard moans from the dying and then the flapping of wings—the carrion birds were perched and waiting. Their claws sharp like daggers, ready to sink into soft flesh. Stone-black eyes surveying

1

the area—they waited. Instinct as primitive as time kept the creatures patient. Death must claim their meal first.

Aware of each inward and outward movement of breath, he waited for release, and slowly his mind seemed to melt into the stillness of time. The battle sounds roaring in his ears disappeared. His inner senses heightened. With his one good eye he blinked and saw mist swirling in the distance.

The Daya River flowed red. A strange mist rose and rolled towards the hills. There was more to see—a hundred thousand broken bodies spread across the battlefield in the valley. His men, the Kalingan warriors, had fought bravely. He wished he could move this useless flesh and muscle, stand up and lead them to victory. But it was too late. He willed himself to get up, but only managed to drag one arm, a lump of clay, towards his face. He twisted himself on his side, his head half sank into the wet soil. Caked in mud, he saw that his third finger was bent at an odd angle, and a jagged red line oozed blood where his thumb had been sliced. The palm of his hand was covered with cuts and calluses from driving his spear into the enemy. A deep rumbling sound emerged from his throat. He pressed down on the earth, it gave easily. His vision turned dark; there were tiny rivulets of blood dripping down his battered face, and the earth absorbed the liquid, turning a fiery red. The Kalingan felt his strength seeping out but he willed himself to stay alert; he cried out, his hand pressed down, harder and harder.

Deep in his soul, he felt the scream erupt, loud and coarse with anger and tears, he cursed the Mauryans—their king. His spirit was wild with fury. He was not one to give up; the blood of the Kalingan clan that flowed through him had fought the Mauryan dynasty for generations. 'I swear by the Kalingan blood on this earth,' he cried, 'I will get my revenge!' Then he fell on his face. His scream had taken all his strength. He heard the flapping of wings and felt the birds' talons sink into his flesh. He closed his eyes for the last time.

1

Previously, it would take Vayu King hours to get into the zone. But this time within five minutes he felt the power surging like waves through his senses. He focused on it until he was the energy and nothing more. He knew he had the power, and that he was more than just an ordinary human being, meant for a greater destiny. He had been given a new lease on life and it meant something. Vayu was at one with the ancient mystical energy, connecting with a life force, like an antenna tuning into the right channel. He focused on his inner energy centres. The seven primary chakras revolved at amazing speed, and located along the central vertical axis of the spine, formed a single white column of light emerging from the crown of his head. After one of his marathon channelling sessions, he felt such incredible strength that he once struck a five-foot brick wall and cracked it right down the middle. Yes, he had the power! And he was meant to achieve great things, it was in his destiny.

There was an oddity about the present moment. He felt another power in the vicinity, like a buzzing fly that broke the centre of his focus.

His body was still, his breathing controlled, his mind was in a state of deep, conscious awareness. And in the stillness, the subtle sound was clear.

Vayu surveyed his room through the narrow line of his lashes. His futon bed was folded and tucked in one corner, and the rolled up straw mat leaned against the wall. The spent syringe lay some distance from the mat. The sparse furnishings included one small stool and a side table for his basic necessities. The office table and chair were pushed to the corner. The unusual humming sound was perceptible; there was no electronic appliance connected, he always made sure of that. Lead-lined rods circled him like a fence. He used them to trap 'white noise', including random thoughts of others. A crisp fresh breeze of dewy air wafted through the small window, bringing in an odd metallic aroma. Nothing was out of place and no intruder was physically present. Then, in a split-second back-flash, he was aware of what was here. Memories were not a slave to time: a blink of an eye, and an entire scene from the past came to light.

A sensation hit him like a gut-wrenching punch. There was nothing but pure red-hot emotion in that room. His heart raced in unison with the anger that flowed like a wild gushing river, pushing into him harder, it pressed, forcing his mind to relent. This was his destiny, he understood the ancient force was waiting until he was ready.

And he let it take over. Still seated in the lotus position, he felt a warmth in his hands. He looked down at his upturned palm. In the centre, he saw the lines deepen and curve. Blood pooled and like tiny tributaries filled and flowed between his fingers. Vayu didn't shift. He closed his eyes.

The Kalingan finally took over Vayu's mind completely. It didn't take him long and Vayu continued to meditate, to slow down the energy, to compress the anger.

Then his mind was drawn to painful memories from his teen years.

Vayu was fifteen when he'd almost died. He'd suffered terrible aches in his stomach, so bad that they had brought him to his knees. The pain, along with the diarrhoea, vomiting and fever, interrupted his life. His parents had tried everything. He'd lost a lot of weight and would miss school often. Doctors couldn't figure out why—they'd tried all kinds of medication. And most times the symptoms got worse. His father presumed it was black magic at work. He had a gambling debt growing at such a rate that strangers threatened him on the street. His mother, a lawyer, didn't believe in the occult, nor was she aware of her husband's addiction.

Despite medication and other treatments, Vayu became weaker and weaker. One by one, his organs shut down. In a few months, he was in the intensive care unit, hooked up to tubes and machines. His parents wept helplessly in the corner, watching him die.

His guilt-ridden father had tried alternative treatments, crystal therapy and spiritual healers while his mother scoffed at his primitive beliefs. For her, science was God and there was nothing else that could save her son. Then

Vayu's father wanted to try one more extreme ritual: psychosurgical healing. His mother threatened to sue him if he let a barbaric witch doctor touch her son. Vayu could only watch, wishing he would die so they would stop their arguments. But finally his mother relented. She was never the same again, Vayu realized.

Very late that critical night, Vayu saw his father leave. He followed him. It was an odd sensation—Vayu was as light as air, weaving in and out of his room; sometimes he watched from the ceiling. He stood face-to-face, but his father didn't seem to notice his son. Vayu felt a sense of anguish and fear spread through him. He was a ghost floating away from his lifeless body. But somewhere, Vayu understood he still had a chance: his body was still alive, the heart pumping blood.

He wished desperately to be alive. And promised he would do anything in return. Vayu noticed his father moving quickly past the hospital gates towards a car waiting by the road. He spoke to the driver. And the rear window slid down.

There was a thin-framed old man in the car. He looked ancient with wrinkled, dark skin and pale eyes, hair as grey and wild as his eyes. The man turned his head slowly and looked out of the window—at Vayu's ghostly form.

He smiled directly at him.

Then, as if time didn't matter, Vayu was back in the ICU, watching his physical self die. He was hovering in the corner of the ceiling.

The nurse stared curiously at the old man with Vayu's father. She didn't react until they entered the room and shut the door. The man took out a bottle of oil from his bag. While Vayu's mother stared in horror, the shaman spread his hands, palms down, above Vayu's body and began chanting words. As his voice became stronger and more energetic, his hands shivered and shook. He moved the cloth until Vayu's pale skin was visible. Without hesitation, the shaman's hands pressed deep and firm into Vayu's stomach. While the healer kneaded with his fingers, blood surfaced, pooled and spilled out of Vayu's midriff, flowing like a stream down the sides of the bed. Vayu's body didn't react. He was asleep. Or dead.

Vayu's mother froze and then let out a scream. She shouted at the crazy man to stop killing her son. Her husband held her back. The nurse and a security guard were at the door trying to open it. But there was a steel chair holding it in place. The ICU was in panic mode, trying its best to keep down the noise: nurses scattered, alarms buzzed, doctors were called in, two more security guards arrived. But they could not enter the room. They could see what was going on through the square porthole in the door and the glass wall next to it.

Besides the healer, Vayu's father was the only person not affected by the scene. He made sure nobody interrupted the ritual. The spectators watched the horror show, afraid to break down the glass and upset the other patients in the unit. They had already created a commotion in a primarily silent environment.

And then it happened.

Vayu hovered from above and watched with horror as the healer's bloody hands dipped in and out of his stomach and with a final yank, a writhing snake-like object was removed. He inhaled loudly, and the healer muttered more strange words, and dropped the black length of organic bloody mass into his bag. He waved his hands in the air, beckoning at him to return and then he wiped away the blood. Vayu felt a strong forceful wind push him back into his body. The whole process took less than ten minutes.

The healer moved away, allowing Vayu's parents to clean him up. His mother, weeping silently, wiped away the residual blood and noted Vayu's unblemished stomach area. While the focus was on Vayu's midriff, the shaman leaned close to his ear, and whispered, 'You remember your promise, boy . . .'

And then, without another word, he turned away.

Vayu's father unlatched the door and moved the chair, and the shaman walked through the crowd of gaping men and women that parted to let him pass.

The doctors and nurses rushed in. Their first concern was their patient. The police, called in by security, arrested the healer at the hospital gates. Vayu, given up for dead by the doctors, was conscious and asking for water.

Vayu's parents bailed out Master Jon Lubo, the faith healer who'd saved their son. They gave him and his organization—the Lubo Spiritual Healing Agency—their support and donations.

When Vayu was out of the hospital, he went to visit Jon Lubo to thank him. 'You don't need to thank me. You must thank the spirit. You are nothing but a slave to this angry ghost. I am telling you this, and know that it will cost me my life but it's important that you know the power of this spirit. It is going to use you for its purpose,' Jon said, fixing him with those blind pale eyes.

'What spirit?' Vayu asked surprised.

'The one you asked to help, the one you made the promise to,' Jon said solemnly.

'I didn't make any promise to any spirit!'

'You did. And he heard you, when you left your body, when you wanted to live. And this is a warrior spirit— very strong and very angry. He is so powerful he can destroy anyone in a split second; he has been restless for centuries. This one wanted you. He is the one who came through me to heal you,' Jon Lubo explained.

'But what does he want of me?'

'He will let you know when the time is right. Be careful. You are going to become what he chooses for you, you will become one with this entity,' Jon Lubo said.

Three days later the faith healer was dead.

And Vayu had forgotten about the incident—until today. Till the day his destiny had arrived.

2

Lomas Rishi cave
Barabar Hills, 20 kilometres north of Gaya, Bihar

'We have been called to seek the guidance of the Ancients,' Professor Gupta said, sitting on the polished floor. His voice echoed even though he spoke in a whisper. 'Bose sent a message. His mind has been captured. No one has ever known the identity of the Nine. Yet, they found out about him, and now about you and me.'

The interior of the dark cave consisted of a large oval chamber like a scooped out aeroplane without wings. The walls glistened as if they had been cut out of the rock by a giant laser. This was surprising as the cave had actually been built during the time of King Ashoka, over two thousand years ago.

'The Kalingan warrior spirit has become strong,' Dr Kuruvella agreed, nodding as if he had to convince himself of the facts. 'He has found a willing human. The man is an expert in martial arts, has harnessed the powers of the Kala Yogis to destroy the Nine and its source of knowledge.'

'Yes, and he is getting stronger; they have many who have succumbed to the Kalingan energy. And are willing to destroy Ashoka's legend.'

'It takes many to strengthen the Kalingan power and only one human to connect it. That one person in which it dwells, has mastered the mind. There is no limit to his dark powers. It must be destroyed before it finds—'

And then the two men went suddenly quiet. And very still.

A monk had appeared as if from thin air. It was the apparition of Gedun Rinpoche, the monk who was the earthly coordinator of the Council of Nine. Like a wax statue, he seemed to glow in the dark. He sat cross-legged on a slightly elevated rock surface, in the furthest and darkest part of the cave. The two kneeled on the stone floor and bowed facing the burgundy-robed senior monk. It was hard to gauge his exact age.

Professor Gupta waited expectantly. Ever since he received the message from the elderly monk clanging a metal bowl on the street next to his house, he had known that the end was near. He had passed the stooped old beggar many times, without a glance. And when the monk stopped him, the Professor had fished out a few coins to deposit in his bowl. The monk shook his head and instead gave him the message about the meeting.

It wasn't the machines and computers that had the capability of finding the Nine, it was something even more potent—the minds of the Kala Yogis. They used the power of black energy, exploited from natural disasters and phenomena like earthquakes, tsunamis and eclipses. The negative energy generated was a reservoir of such immense abilities, it transcended the ordinary ways of communication through time and space. For now, the best line of attack was defence.

Professor Gupta had read recent reports in newspapers

of gruesome murders, dismembered victims, headless corpses and buried babies—he knew it was the work of the Kala Yogis. The vile side of human behaviour was revealed: abuse and violence in homes, within families, which meant their power was increasing. And they used their strength to control more minds, sowing the seeds of anger and hatred. It was slow poison, but meant to infect from the grassroots, creating small disruptions, disorder and disharmony between neighbours and then discord within families. This mass consciousness of unrest gave strength to their negative powers.

Professor Gupta had faced his fear, surrendered to the will of his destiny. He did not want to be possessed the way they had taken Dr Bose and erased his knowledge. That was the ultimate insult, and humiliation to the Nine. It was a blatant challenge. And Professor Gupta would rather be the martyr than let the Kalingan get to him. Facing the monk, he emptied his mind so that he was nothing more than a hollow vessel. A blank page.

Professor Gupta could tell Dr Kuruvella struggled to face his fears. He carried a gun. Ever since black-cloaked vandals had attacked him, he had developed a fear that wasn't an emotion experienced by any of the Nine. Those black-magic men had eaten the very core of his conscience, destroyed the doctor's willpower, his faith in good over evil. It was a sad state to be in. Dr Kuruvella's eyes were wide and watery in anticipation that something terrible would happen any minute. Blotting the sweat from his

brow, Dr Kuruvella feared death when he should have
been the one to welcome the crossover. He was a respected
scientist and had written dozens of papers on the
interaction of the mind and spirit with the body—he was
the world-renowned expert on the science of alchemy,
head of the faculty for post-graduate studies in sciences
at Calcutta University. Within academic circles, he was a
well-respected and revered man. And in here, he cowered
in fear.

They waited for the monk to solve their dilemma. The
six masters, part of the Council of Nine, were safe for
now. Dr Bose, one of the Nine, was taken, and hopefully
had not lost his mind completely. Professor Gupta and
Dr Kuruvella, the remaining two, were both marked men
and carried the most potent of knowledge that had been
handed down from the ascended masters. It was time to
hand it over.

The monk was small-built, like a young boy, with a
perfect dome-shaped head. He opened his eyes and
studied them quietly. 'The sun shines by day, the moon
by night, the warrior is resplendent in armour and the
Brahman radiant in meditation. But Buddha, the
Awakened One, illumines both day and night by the
splendor of his wisdom.' As he had done before, Gedun
Rinpoche recited from the *Dhammapada*, Buddha's
recitations to his disciples.

'The three unknown have become known. Dr Bose is
possessed and the two of you have been identified. You

are vulnerable. It is time to return the knowledge and live as ordinary men.'

The monk then extracted a small metal object from within his robe. It had a flat square base and four corners converged to a point at the top, like a fat pyramid, but not exactly; grooves and circular lines were engraved all over the object. Resting in the palm of his hand, the pyramid began to glow, showering the cave with golden points of light.

Professor Gupta wasn't surprised at its sudden appearance, whatever happened in the cave defied reality. Even the methods of communication. In an instant, the two men understood what had to be done.

First, the professor accepted the pyramid with both hands. Carefully he positioned the square base against the centre of his forehead, between his eyebrows. This was the location of the *aadnyaa* chakra, the sixth spiritual centre of the body. Wisps of smoky light glowed from the triangular object, as if it was translucent. The light that emanated from within turned it into a shining white beam. The professor shuddered slightly, then he was still. He opened his eyes and returned the pyramid to the monk.

The monk passed a hand over it and then offered it to the doctor.

Dr Kuruvella's hand trembled, sweat oozed from his temples and his eyes turned bright, reflecting the light.

'You've lost your faith.' The monk's eyes glittered like diamonds. 'You bring shame to the Nine.'

'No!' the doctor murmured nervously. Fear rose in the form of black clouds of wispy smoke emanating from his shoulders. The monk's raised hand glided across him, as if wiping away dirt from a screen. Within seconds, Dr Kuruvella's expression transformed from one of fear to that of determination, the black aura disappeared. He held the golden pyramid to his forehead and closed his eyes.

The monk stretched out his right palm. It was time. Dr Kuruvella and Professor Gupta removed the pendants from their necks and placed them in his hand.

The monk looked solemnly at them. 'The Ancients have decided. We have to contact the three who will replace you. One of them is a woman.'

Professor Gupta and Dr Kuruvella looked shocked. King Ashoka's secret society had consisted only of men, as far back as it existed.

'Time brings with it change, and we too must change with the times. Change is part of life. The three are young and immature, but they are destined. They will come here to gain knowledge of the Nine.'

Dr Kuruvella understood. 'We don't have much time before the yogis get to us.'

The monk didn't seem to care. 'The Nine will continue as it has for yugas. There are times of evil, and good overcomes it. And the three will fulfil their destiny. The third is Tara and she will bring the female shakti to the power of the new trinity. There is no need for you to return any more. May peace be with you,' the monk said, and within their line of vision, the professor saw nothing. The cave was empty when the two of them had entered, and it was empty now.

3

Vayu King gripped the man's arm, whipped him over, and slammed him hard on his back. Not one to stay down, the muscled man was up on his feet in a flash. Before he could seize Vayu's shoulder, he felt his legs buckle, and he was flat on the ground again. Vayu stepped back, and waited for Eric, his student, to stand up. He took longer than expected and Vayu held out his hand to help him up. Eric's sheepish expression confirmed that he still had a lot to learn. The other students, watching wide-eyed, whispered disappointedly amongst themselves. They were school-age boys and looked up to the thick-chested buff Eric as the only possible candidate to challenge Vayu. He was the only adult student and visibly the strongest person in the martial arts class to win a match. Standing on the sidelines, around the cushioned floor mats, the students expected Eric the hulk to slam their teacher Vayu to the ground with just one twist of his bulging arm.

Vayu was deceptively small-built, with wide shoulders and stout arms. And the bouncer, Eric, built like the incredible hulk with legs as thick as tree trunks, should have been a clear winner.

'You need to work on your speed and agility,' Vayu explained, standing solidly with feet shoulder-width apart, knuckles on hips, eyes focused on Eric. 'You have to be quick and light like a dancer,' he advised.

The students' attention was distracted by a gentle rapping and then the squeak of the door opening. Vayu's assistant, Phillip Chu, leaned in looking worried. He mimed a phone call with his thumb and finger, repeating the gesture twice, indicating its urgency.

Vayu turned to one of the taller students, guided him by the shoulder to the centre of the floor mat. 'Work on your reaction time, Eric, with Terence here. I have to take this call, I'll be back soon.'

He strode towards Phillip. 'The man said it was serious, sir,' Phillip explained, noticing his boss's frown. 'He didn't want to give his name or call back later,' he added quickly, pre-empting Vayu's next question.

'It's okay,' Vayu said, waving him away. The telephone line blinked red at the reception desk. Vayu picked up the receiver and pressed a button and it turned green. 'Yes?' he answered, when he saw that Phillip was out of earshot, in his cubicle and focused on his monitor.

There was no preamble of pleasantries. 'What is it?' Vayu asked when he recognized the voice of the chief of the Kala Yogis, Refaq.

'I have news, master,' the young male voice said. 'The three have been targeted. One has been dealt with, and the other two are in Barabar Hills. We lost contact after that.'

There was a brief pause. Vayu closed his eyes and took a deep breath.

He spoke in a calm tone. 'This is careless behaviour. You should have got to them before they entered the Hills.' His trained army was a group of Kala Yogis. They were capable and had followed his instructions to a T. He had trained them to incite hatred. It was the power of the people—a propaganda that created its own initiative. Used by politicians to sway mass consciousness, it was capable of affecting voting and attitudes in social psychology. And Vayu knew that the Council of Nine had influenced many powerful nations and polluted the minds of millions for what they defined as 'common good'. If they could do it, so could he. The human mind was a playground for his capacity to influence it—and it was as subtle as air. People had an arrogant attitude of believing they were inherently good. But bad lurked just under the surface, a pinprick away. And people would not hesitate to murder for what they justified was right.

Racial abuse amongst a group of students escalated with the help of Vayu's men to truculent wild killings. A simple act of poisoning the local water supply to a specific slum area, and neighbours, religious groups, turned on each other. Eventually fierce threats by the slumlords led to violence and a few deaths. Others committed the evil acts, instigated by the Kala Yogis passing through those places. These kinds of sporadic events revealed true human nature—at its most barbaric level. Vayu's men created the small pockets of violence.

In some places the bad vibes were curbed. Spiritual behaviour prevailed like cold water over a stoked fire. It was a meek effort. There too, corrupt priests were easy to manipulate. Worship, forgiveness didn't work for Vayu's men. The only way to destroy the goodness was to destroy the holy shrines. Then the accusations and violence reached a bloody level. Vayu enjoyed that the most. People died for a pile of bricks and mortar. In certain areas the purity of the Buddha energy interfered with their capacity. And Vayu had no power in these places.

'Yes, we will find them,' Refaq's voice was calm and controlled. He was the strong, silent type. And intuitive— a mentalist of such genius, he could tell a person's weaknesses by just spending fifteen minutes with him. 'But there is news that the Council is recruiting three more.'

Vayu sighed deeply. 'Work quickly! Find out who these new puppets are. Their powers will be limited, and their minds still scattered by maya. It will be easy to prey on them while they live in this illusory world. You of all people can do this.'

'We will do our best, master,' the voice responded.

'First, find the destination of the two elders. They are useless but I would like to take the pleasure of ending their pathetic lives myself.'

'Yes, I will inform you.'

'Good. Expand the unit. Keep track of the new recruits. Do not approach. Only track,' Vayu ordered and hung up. He paused for a few minutes, stared at the art on the wall, turned his mind blank and focused on the eloquent Chinese brushstrokes. Taking deep breaths, he calmed himself and returned to his class. But his mind wasn't focused. He had to act fast, and now.

The King Centre was a small square room with mirrors extending across one wall and grey paint on the other three. A small black and white framed photograph of Vayu's parents hung on one of them. The floor was all wood and made the room look spacious.

Located on the top floor of a narrow building, Vayu's studio was squeezed between a fast food restaurant and a fitness centre. It faced a row of dirty office buildings across the busy Wellington Street.

When Vayu returned to his class, Eric was pretending to play wounded bad guy facing Terence's swift moves for the benefit of a giggling audience. They stopped when he entered. 'I have something urgent to attend to. I apologize but I must ask you to leave immediately. Please arrange for someone to pick you up. I will make up for this class another time,' he said, clasping his hands.

In less than half an hour the Centre was empty.

Vayu dismissed his assistant and locked the main outer door. He pressed his hand against a portion of the wall next to the wall hanging—it slid aside. From the small square safe, he withdrew a dagger with an enamel handle. It was gilded with pure gold. He traced the edge, feeling the sharp point in the palm of his hand.

Lights off, doors locked, and the studio was a silent room. Vayu headed to his inner office. He removed the floor mat and with the knife he carved a symbol on the floor. It was the Kalingan warrior signal. There were dozens of them etched on the floor, and he added one more. It was a sign for the spirit to take him over. Switching off all electronic gadgets, he unfolded his mat, placed a thin cushion on the floor, and sat down on it cross-legged. The power surged within him in waves. He pushed his mind to connect, but there was an interruption like a sharp jarring sound of metal falling on tile. His eyes snapped open.

He heard the rapping on his door. Harder and insistent. Whoever it was, would die a horrible death. He cursed. Vayu stayed still and willed the person to leave. The rapping continued. His heart began to race—perspiration trickled down the sides of his face, burning hot against his cooling skin. His eyes were red with rage. Vayu stood up rigid. 'You asked for it,' he said as he headed to the entrance. He waited by the door, and heard the knocking again.

'Who is it?'

'Phillip.'

His doormat assistant. What was he doing here? Maybe he was a spy, a little voice in his head said. And burning rage coursed through him like a wild river, firing his blood to a boil. He tried to hold back and was amazed at its strength and the way it made him feel. Amazingly powerful!

Vayu opened the door, and before the man could say another word, Vayu's fist contracted and plunged hard into his middle. Phillip bent over in half. Vayu dragged him inside by the scruff of his collar. He shut the door and pulled the dazed man up. 'What do you want?' Vayu asked in a seething whisper.

Phillip's eyes were wide with fear, he clutched his stomach. Vayu's punch was just enough to cause some internal bleeding.

'What—?'

But before he could say more, Vayu's palm closed around the man's throat. 'Who do you work for, spy?' he thundered, pressing hard on his Adam's apple. Phillip struggled, shook his head and tried to release the iron grip. Vayu knew his lungs would be burning for every breath of air. He held him for another five seconds, and then eased the pressure.

'I . . . I . . . Sir, I just came to get my glasses . . . over there,' Phillip pointed to the low table in the corner. His voice was no more than a squeak.

'You lie,' Vayu said softly. He reached for his assistant's hands, pushed the thumbs back at just a specific angle. He waited. Phillip's voice box was damaged, he couldn't scream even though the pain must have been excruciating.

The Kalingan warrior was always calm; the anger was a rising tide and the true warrior knew how to control and use it as his strength.

'Please . . . let me go,' Phillip said in a hoarse whisper. Squares of light from passing street traffic that stretched across the empty room slid down the walls, briefly illuminating them. Phillip's face was a white mask contorted in pain.

Vayu let go.

When Phillip tried to stand up, holding the wall for support, he inadvertently switched on the lights. The Kalingan roared. Phillip let out a yelp. Vayu smelled the weakening of Phillip's bladder, he grabbed Phillip by the collar and placed his fingers on the nape of his neck and pressed. There was an almost imperceptible sound of bone cracking and the assistant fell to the floor like a puppet with no strings.

This felt so good, the sense of victory was invigorating. Vayu's heart raced at a galloping speed. He switched off the lights and closed his eyes, trying to calm the wild spirit. It took him a few minutes but he managed to get his pulse down to a reasonable pace. When he was calmer, he picked up the phone, dialled a number and spoke.

'I need someone for a clean-up job,' he whispered into the mouthpiece and then listened. His reflection in the mirror was contorted when he smiled and his sunburnt eyes glimmered in the dusky light from the street.

'Yes, I will arrange it. There is news. The two have left the Hills.'

'And I will leave for Calcutta tonight.' Vayu continued to grin at himself as he spoke into the mouthpiece. He raised his left hand, and carefully smoothed down his spiky hair. 'Thank you for taking care of it. Make it look like an accident.'

Vayu returned to his inner office, where the air was free of electromagnetic radiation. He closed his eyes and, in a few seconds, he rose into the realms of consciousness that were beyond his capacity to understand or explain. He was able to tap into a different world of spirit energy. He could see beyond the three dimensions of what the human brain could perceive. Vayu felt like he was the most powerful man, stronger than even the great King Ashoka of the Mauryan dynasty. And once the ancient Kalingan warrior had come to him, there was no limit to the knowledge he had acquired in his life.

He was complete and invincible. When he returned to the world, he felt like the ruler. Like the power of the universe was for him to harness. And he had earned this blessing; he was the one—the saviour. And to achieve that end, he would have to destroy the legacy of the Mauryan dynasty once and for all.

The Kalinga warrior knew his plan: destroy the millennia-old secret society of Ashoka which existed as the Nine and find the one source of their wisdom that contained knowledge of all existing things.

Vayu had power and now he was in control.

And once he acquired the power of the Nine, he would

be stronger than any man on earth. Vayu smiled to himself. It would definitely make him look more attractive!

4

Tara
Deo, 20 kilometres north of Gaya, Bihar

Life was not so much about the minutes that ticked by, but the unforgettable moments that held a person captive in the depths of emotion. If fear were alive, then it was palpable and visible in that one night. She had heard stories of possessed people, or evil spirits lurking in trees waiting for a passer-by to pounce on. It happened, she guessed. There was a God. She prayed when she could. And now she thought it was time to seriously ask God for help. Science had not helped—it was useless when she tried to understand within her capacity. Tara's life had turned into a sequence of one unbelievable experience after another. One might think of madness, but it was the unexplainable that had changed her life.

Forever.

Listening to the cries of agony, Tara, the night nurse, wished she wasn't there in the dead of night alone without help. She was more than a little concerned about what the villagers had to say when they had brought in the comatose man earlier that day. He had suddenly come alive, but not in the way she'd expected. She tried her best to comfort her patient, but he'd continued to writhe as if being prodded by an invisible knife. She tried to wake up the other patients who, oddly enough, slept undisturbed through the shrieks. Tara wondered if she was dreaming, but no, a self-inflicted jab with a pen reminded her that she was fully alert.

The howling man's physical contortions were excruciating to watch. Something existed, something inhuman inside that animal stare. It chilled her to the bone. For a few moments, the sudden quiet rang in her ears, more deafening than the brief pause. The man was panting; exhausted, he let his head roll forward, then very slowly, as if taken over by some insatiable evil spirit, his gaze lifted and cut right through to Tara. He stretched his hands out, mewling pitifully. Tara came forward, and in a flash, he grabbed her hand. Tight.

'Let go!' She pulled her hand away as hard as she could.

He let go, grinning devilishly. His fingers were like ice.

'Why are you doing this? What do you want?' Tara asked, struggling to get away from the insane man. Perspiration trickled down his brow. He watched her like she was prey. Fear raised the hair on her neck.

'We have our reasons to be here,' the voice sounded like two or three old women speaking in chorus. 'We have to extract something from this man.' The laughter was like nails scratching on a blackboard. Was he possessed? Her scientific mind took a back seat as she covered her ears and crouched low until the sounds disappeared.

She wanted to leave. But she wasn't able to think clearly. She took a deep courageous breath and buried the rising dread. She was strong, and would never give in to fear. Although she was being tested to the limit, there was something about the man that made her want to stay and help him.

The night light was just a small lamp in the corner. It wasn't bright enough. She switched on the tubelights. The only people alert were the madman and Tara. The rest were like sleeping statues.

The man tortured himself, rolling his head in circles. Hands folded, she stood some distance away and watched him, thinking hard. And an idea began to take shape in her mind.

Yes, there was one possible way to keep the demon quiet. Tara filled the syringe with a tranquillizer—twice the normal dose. The possessed man dry retched, over and over again, the sounds, animal-like, echoed in the clinic. Then he heaved and threw up all over the floor. Vomit that looked like millions of tiny black bugs, collected in a mound on the floor and a shit-like stench filled the room. Tara baulked but controlled herself. She checked again to see if anyone was awake, but no, the patients were still comatose.

The man lay on his back now and struggled with himself. 'Let me go!' he cried to some invisible being. He grasped his own neck and tightened his fingers around it, his thumbs pressed against his windpipe. His eyes bulged, and his lips were slowly turning blue. Gasping for air, he sounded like a dying animal. Tara stabbed the needle in his arm. And pressed.

And in a flash, he was in her face, his fingers closing round her neck.

'Wait!' she managed to say before her voice was cut to silence. He squeezed harder. Tara saw red spots. Her legs buckled and just when she thought that this was it, that death would claim her, he let go. Tara dropped to the floor like a sack, drawing in sweet breath. She coughed heavily, and waited for the burning inside her to subside. Cool air filled her lungs and scarred her throat. Anger rose like a bubbling force. Tara stood up and looked into the wild man's eyes.

'Don't try that again. I don't scare easily,' she told him firmly and with courage, aiming the sharp point of the needle at him. The tranquillizer was beginning to work. He was losing his edge, getting heavy-eyed. Yes, sleep would do him some good. And her too.

Sweat trickled down his face and stained the white sheets in shades of grey. He smiled. 'Don't try that again or it will kill you for sure,' he said, and fell into a fitful sleep. His left leg twitched and trembled violently. Tara pumped him with more of the drug. And then he was finally still, in deep sleep. Tara was exhausted from the effort. She looked at him for a while and then moved away.

Standing by the window, inhaling a cool draught of fresh air, Tara considered her next move. Outside, it was pitch black. And indoors, patients occupied the ten beds in the rectangular room. Dr Goyel's rural clinic was in the middle of one of the poorest villages in the area. The makeshift dispensary and doctor's office were housed in a whitewashed square block of bricks and cement, equipped with the barest of medical necessities. The only nurse who dared to work in this tiny village was Tara. You had to be crazy to want to be out here in the middle of nowhere, Tara thought. She had been a psychology student, a good one, and could have done well in life eventually as a professor. However, she'd taken up a two-year nursing course thinking that it would help her, give her a more rounded approach to patient care. And because of her inherent distaste for city life, she had ended up in this godforsaken place with a lunatic.

While working on a thesis on the uses of ayurvedic medicine in Indian villages, Tara had attended a passionate lecture by an NGO doctor who had spoken of the importance of a 'hands-on approach' and doing good for the impoverished. She liked what he said. He said that it was best to be in the thick of things to understand the minds of the villagers and the various uses of a cowdung wrap. By the end of the lecture, Tara had decided to leave the security of her apartment, and Karan, her dentist boyfriend of three years. He was upset with her, but when she said it was for a short while, he agreed.

The thought of him helped her relax. He had a dazzling smile and people called him a walking-talking ad for his profession. Tara used to get a little green when she learned that most of his patients were women. Karan was big, like a bear, and his presence alone was enough to make her feel safe. Probably his female patients felt the same way.

One time, she recalled, they were on a holiday together, and when she was strolling alone on a beach, a man had approached her, tried to get too friendly. Karan, like a film hero, had stood menacingly behind her, hands on her shoulders. Tara wasn't afraid any more. Just his large, comforting physique was enough to scare the guy away. She wished he was here with her now. Those images were as distant as a fading photograph.

Damn the stupid mobile phone and the landline for not working. She kept checking but it was a useless effort.

The crazy patient had been brought in the previous afternoon and they had managed to squeeze in an extra bed to accommodate him. When he'd come in, he was not dead, but his eyes were. They were focused on a corner of the ceiling, not responding to any of the doctor's treatments. The villagers said they'd found him like that, sitting in a cave near the hillside. One of the villagers said he was possessed and bringing him to a doctor was a waste of time.

The doctor had an ever-ready insipid smile and then Tara realized it was a habit—his smile was there even when it wasn't necessary. He smiled at the stoic, the

young and the old. And even at the angry women who
thought he was using the needle to scare them. Tara had
become used to it, and even knew from his expression
when he was irritated, despite the smile. And when he
was with the new patient he was irritated at his non-
responsiveness to medication. He didn't believe in the
superstitious talk, and as his assistant and nurse, neither
did Tara.

And that very night the crazy man started his drama.
There was something about the way the villagers shrugged
it off—they didn't bat an eyelid. For them, ghosts were
part of village life. Spirits lived in trees, on their farms, in
their wells. And if you were not careful and walked under
a tree on a full moon night, and worse still, if you were
menstruating, then you would surely have a wicked ghost
take control of your mind and that was that. If a person
ate too much, or was extremely thin, it wasn't the result
of a hormonal imbalance or stomach worms. The farmers
believed that ghosts and evil spirits were at work. And
only the tantrik could exorcise them.

In addition, the power of daily prayer, for reasons of
fear, was what helped them stay on the side of good and
keep evil at bay. Tara took a long, deep breath. And
decided to pray. But before she could even start, the
possessed man began his rant again. Tara bit back a
scream when she turned to look at him. He was sitting
up. His eyes bulged out of their sockets and rolled back
in his head.

Her heart slammed repeatedly against her chest. Then a deathly moan penetrated her skull, raising goosebumps all over her body. The terror was sliding through her and Tara shivered in the heat while he was drenched in sweat.

Just hold out till the morning, she whispered to herself. She prepared a cool compress and tried to place it on his forehead—he calmed slightly. It was clear that the double dose of sedative she'd injected had hardly had an effect. He should have been completely knocked out for at least ten hours. She didn't know what to do. She needed help. Dr Goyel lived half an hour away and to reach him would be difficult. And the compounder who normally would have stayed the night, had left early because of a death in the family.

The doors on either side of the one-storey building were latched from the inside. Tara heard a faint knocking and wondered who it could be. Soon the rapping became louder, more insistent. She rushed to the door but a chilling thought made her hesitate. *What if what's outside is worse than what is inside?* The doors shook, someone was kicking it. Tara shrunk back, uncertain how to deal with this new unknown danger. There were four windows along the walls of the clinic, and only one was open. She glanced outside and saw red points in the darkness. There was no sign of a human being. She shut the window tight and retreated.

A strange misty glow filled the room. Panic grew inside her, spreading through her insides, thick and heavy like tar. Tara waited for something to happen.

But it didn't. Instead the man sat up in his bed.

'Can I have some water, please?' he said. His voice was the barest gritty whisper and his words were clear and controlled. Tara turned towards him, she moved closer to his bed. For a moment, just the mundane task of fetching seemed to ease her a bit.

But as she turned to him, her hand gripped the bed rails so tight that she could feel the cracks in the paint. He looked battered like a refugee from a war zone. The kind she had seen on television. His face was splotched with blue–black bruises and his bloodshot eyes were circled by deep shades of purple. His cheekbones jutted out like those of farmers in a famine-stricken village.

'Some water, please,' he repeated politely, as if nothing was wrong and he was having an ordinary sleepless night. With trembling hands, Tara managed to pour him a glass of water from a plastic jug. Keeping a safe distance, she leaned forward and handed it to him.

'Are you feeling better?' It was a silly question. He didn't answer and drank thirstily, gulping down half the water. Then, he removed a pocket knife from under his pillow and wound it open. 'You better turn your face away, you might not be able to handle this,' he warned her.

Then without a moment of hesitation he pressed the sharp point of the knife on the underside of his foot and cut a straight line from one end of his heel to the other. Tara froze. This was like . . . so crazy that she was either mad or in a bad dream. Tara muttered in her head, *This is not real, cannot be real.*

And then she jerked to action. 'Are you out of your mind?' she yelled, and grabbed the knife from his bloody hands. He pushed her away and continued to carve, as if his foot was nothing but a piece of meat attached to his body. There wasn't a hint of pain on his face.

'Stop it, stop it!' she screamed as she struggled to pull his hand away, prising the knife from his grip. Her fingers were slick with blood, and slipped.

Briefly, he stopped his probing and looked at her. 'I told you to turn away. This will all be over soon. Now stop interrupting me.'

He was back at his heel. Tara's efforts were futile but she pulled hard at his sleeve, begging him to stop. And yet she watched, mesmerized by his surgically precise methods of cutting.

'I am almost done,' he said, without so much as a tremor in his voice. The sheets were soaked with blood and bits of flesh lay scattered everywhere. Combined with the stench of his body, the odour overwhelmed her. With one more determined effort, Tara pulled at his murderous arm. He pushed her away with his bloody hands and said in an irritated tone, 'I told you I'm almost done!'

Tara watched the cutting, now observing every graphic detail. 'Who are you?' Tara asked, resigning to the insanity of the moment. The madman spoke in a matter-of-fact tone. 'I'm Dr Bose. This is all an illusion. I have to do this, you are not to worry. Everything will be all right.' He spoke lucidly, pieces of his bloody foot lay strewn on the bed. And now his probing fingers were deep inside his heel, though not a sign of agony registered on his face. And he called it an illusion—from what Tara could tell this did seem like some kind of depraved magic show.

'I can see this . . . illusion, you are mutilating yourself, and feel no pain . . . it makes no sense. Why are you doing this?' she asked, stammering.

His glance left her cold, not because he looked crazy, but because he looked perfectly sane and intelligent, conscious of his actions. 'There is not much time left. I will explain later but first you need to do something for me.' He continued to work on his heel, pulling the tendons apart, and Tara could hear the small knife hit the bone. Bile rose in her throat, the stench of flesh and blood filled her nostrils. Tara buckled over, her hand pressing her stomach. The bitterness rising in her throat wouldn't come out. Taking deep breaths, she waited helplessly for the feeling to subside. She rose slowly.

Dr Bose was pulling out an object from his foot. It was completely covered in blood and flesh. Turning it over in his hand, he dropped it into the half-filled glass of water and handed it to Tara.

'Take this. It is a precious piece of the chakra and you must keep it safe. The Kala Yogis have got to me.' He was holding the glass. Reluctantly, Tara took it from him. There was a dark lump in the cloudy water. *What is this?*

He continued, 'You must go to the Lomas Rishi cave and then you will understand what to do.' Tara was mesmerized by the contents of the glass. 'Did you hear me? You have to leave now.'

Tara nodded, still dazed.

Dr Bose watched her for a few brief seconds. 'I think it's too late. Don't worry, I will help you,' he said. And in that split second, in one swift move, the mad Dr Bose cleanly slit his own throat. Blood spilled in gushing rivulets down his neck. His wild stare caught Tara's eye. Her pulse galloped, her hand tightened around the glass. And then it was as if she was stuck. Tara was unable to break eye contact. She was paralysed. Inside her head she screamed and screamed. *Let me go!* With tremendous effort, she tried to move her eyes away, but she was nothing but stone. Dread struck and panic flooded her mind and all she could do was watch the blood spill from the madman's neck over his shirt and down his chest, while he held her gaze with those dead eyes. And just as the terror threatened to leave her senseless, she felt a strength slowly building up inside her, squashing out the fear.

And she could move.

Breathing with effort, Tara's attention turned to the object in the glass. She poured out the water and placed the piece on her palm. The smoky crystal-like thing was small and circular in shape, like the wheel of a bullock cart, complete with spokes and a thick centre. She slipped it into her kurta pocket.

No time to waste, just act.

She laid Dr Bose's body flat and covered him with a white sheet. It was just enough to hide the bloody mess. They were coming, she heard the violence on the doors, the slide latches wouldn't hold for long. The Kala Yogis who had got to Dr Bose were going to get her. She rushed to the window, opened it wide and climbed onto the ledge. Then she heard the vicious crashing—they were inside. Tara jumped out. Crouching in the darkness, under the window, she waited for a few seconds and started moving away as quietly as she could. The darkness was her friend, they hadn't noticed her. She heard bold, angry voices but Tara was already on her way, racing into the blackness.

She ran blind, but she could see the path in her head. It was one she had travelled on countless times. It was odd how the brain worked, taking in everyday details without being aware of it, while the conscious mind whirled amidst dreams, desires, regrets and relationships. Tara felt a heightened sense of awareness. And strength. A strange sound whistled in her ear.

And then a male voice. *Hello Tara, I'm Dr Bose, and I have a secret*, it said from inside her head.

5

They were CEOs of Fortune 500 companies and owned many businesses but they secretly invested in the scientific study of the human mind. Under their umbrella group, low-key and off the charts, medical centres carried out research on brain function.

They had developed a new drug that enhanced the power of the mind. And Vayu was offered this perk.

Vayu enjoyed incentives. If life didn't offer incentives then there was no hope, he believed. And with perks came opportunities—opportunities to become powerful. So when a briefcase full of cash was presented to Vayu, he was more than enthusiastic to prove himself. It was an extraordinary request but Vayu was no stranger to the extraordinary. After his near-death experience, he had developed a sixth sense, an extra-sensory perception.

He applied himself diligently. *After all, of what use was a skill if not used to its fullest potential?* Macau was his destination. There were many players in the field. Vayu started as a two-bit small-time gambler, but with his extra-sensory perceptive ability, he was soon playing not with the big league, but for them. In return, he received many bonuses, a free home, cars, women and luxury dining. And what he really did was to fine-tune his powers. He had bigger fish to catch, and bigger reasons to use his power.

The casinos soon discovered he was on a winning

streak and banned him from entering their premises. Vayu didn't care any more. He had made his money, trained and learned. The three months were up and he returned to Hong Kong. He resumed teaching at his martial arts school.

A week later, the Golden Group contacted him. They were not triads extorting money, nor were they skinheads with tattoos or members of any of the organized crime groups. No, these guys were different, more upmarket. Hell! They could have bought up Africa if they wanted to, and made sure no one went hungry!

Vayu was met in his studio by a tall, dark-haired man dressed in a business suit. He asked if he could have a few minutes to discuss a business deal. Vayu nodded and allowed him to enter. The man introduced himself as Mr Chan. Vayu led him to his inner office, they sat down. The man didn't wait for pleasantries. He removed a thick wad of notes from his inside pocket, and without fanfare, as if he was going to offer a cigarette or mints, placed it on the table in front of Vayu.

'This is the rent for the first month—we need your office for meetings,' Mr Chan said. This was about more than simply renting his studio. Vayu picked up the money and fanned himself with it.

'What else do you need?' Vayu asked.

And in the softest voice he heard the word, 'You.'

Mr Chan knew about the power of the Kala Yogis.

The Golden Group had communicated with the spirit

world. Their research scholars had been working on gaining extraordinary human powers. For the Golden Group, wealth alone wasn't enough. The members of the Golden Group desired more than just a man's life, they wanted it all: they wanted the power to own the world— the ultimate aphrodisiac. And Vayu understood the need and the restlessness of the spirits.

Mr Chan explained a little about the Golden Group, and when Vayu met the six tycoons, he knew he was in with the really big fish.

Late at night, the studio converted into a meeting place for the Golden Group. The six men, of different ethnic backgrounds, had one common motive: to push the final frontier, the integration of human spirituality and modern science and technology. They had got hold of maps and evidence of old civilizations that existed thousands of years ago, using technology unheard of today. Nuclear power, anti-gravity machines, communication devices, weapons and much more existed on this very earth.

Vayu's job was just a front. His martial arts classes were no more than practice time to deal with the inane outside world—to show that he was just an ordinary guy with a registered address who paid his bills, rates and taxes and had a job. But he had other plans. And he sensed it was going to happen very soon. The Kalingan spirit was his power. And he had been especially summoned to act and destroy its ultimate enemy: King

Ashoka's men—the Nine. This was his mission in life. He smiled and accepted. Now he was going to get paid to carry out something he would have done for free!

6

Calcutta

Calcutta University was accredited as one of the oldest of modern universities in India. It included a number of Nobel Laureates and had a long list of eminent personalities as both students and professors. It was also rumoured that a few of them were members of the Council of Nine.

Vayu strolled through the main campus sprawled across three acres of land. The faculty of science and technology had over twenty departments—finding Dr Kuruvella and Professor Gupta would prove to be a daunting task, and he didn't want to arouse suspicion by asking every passing student. Vayu had planned ahead. He went to the admissions department to apply for a post-graduate degree in electrical technology and allied sciences. He knew he wasn't going to get in—he wasn't an honours student, and there were probably thousands of students on their waiting list—but it gave him an opportunity to find out more about the locations of the two members of the Nine.

The friendly alumni member offered to take him to the faculty department, but he politely declined. Instead, he decided to find it himself with the help of a map of the grounds. At least he was able to narrow down the location of each target. Professor Gupta taught quantum field theory in the physics department. It was just round the corner, a colonial building painted white and blue. His office was on the first floor. Vayu entered the building and climbed the staircase. He asked a young woman at the reception desk about the professor. She eyed him suspiciously at first. Then, taking in his light complexion, Chinese features, T-shirt, jeans and grey holdall, she concluded that he had been referred by someone. She gave him directions. He thanked her, followed her instructions and knocked on the third door on the right. A plaque on it said: 'Head of Physics'.

Vayu waited. Then he turned the knob and pushed. The door opened easily and he entered. The professor was standing by the window gazing out at the flourishing growth of trees, lost in thought.

'Good evening Professor Gupta,' Vayu smiled, and extended his hand like an eager student. 'Sorry to interrupt you, sir, but I was keen to meet you.'

The professor was tall, in his seventies, with grey hair, and looked smart in his Nehru-collar blazer. Vayu noted the startled expression and the look of distrust on his face. The professor frowned.

Awkwardly, Vayu apologized for the intrusion. He smiled wider, mumbling his reason, and accidentally stubbed his toe against the foot of the table.

The professor's expression softened, 'Sit down,' he indicated.

Vayu's gaze scanned his room. It was dusty and filled with books and piles of papers. 'What can I do for you, young man?' The professor shuffled some papers and, still standing, waited for Vayu to provide the reason for coming all the way to meet him.

Vayu gazed at him and decided to be direct. 'I have come to tell you . . . that I know about Ashoka's men and his secret society and have so far discovered three of you who are members.' Vayu spoke slowly and waited to see his victim squirm. 'I am going to kill each and every one of you.'

The professor froze. Then he stared at him and without warning, he laughed: it was a rich, rumbling guffaw from the belly. Vayu felt wild rage raring to escape. He stood up and faced the professor at eye level.

'Are you one of those conspiracy theorists?' Professor Gupta asked, amused. He seemed unconcerned, an unusual glint in his eyes. 'There is no such thing as the secret society or Ashoka's men—they're all fairy tales.'

Vayu faced him—the fire of fury had erupted and his eyes appeared wild. 'You lie. You are one of them.'

'Very nice of you to think so,' the professor said, indulging his fantasy.

'You have special powers too,' Vayu said.

'I don't have special powers, young man. If that's the reason you are here, I'm sorry you have come to the wrong place.' The professor indicated the door. 'Maybe you should try the head of the literature department; she will be fascinated by your stories.'

'I have the spirit of the Kalingan warrior. He does not forgive easily.' Vayu's face felt like it was burning.

'Tell him let bygones be bygones. I will pray for your spirit,' the professor smiled gently. Then, raising an eyebrow and leaning towards him, he said, 'And his.'

Vayu was confused. The man had no fear or hatred in his eyes. The warrior was in a rage. Before the professor could utter another word, Vayu's hand was at his throat.

'What do you have there?' Vayu pulled his collar apart—his neck was bare. 'No chakra, professor?' Vayu shook his head. 'Not good.'

The professor smiled and stared into his cold eyes. 'I don't need it any more.'

'Let this be a lesson for the others,' Vayu's voice had taken on an animal tone. He growled. And then with a hard twist, crushed the professor's neck. As his body sank to the floor, a dark stream of blood flowed out of the professor's mouth, spreading and staining the scattered papers and files.

Vayu closed his eyes and stilled the energy currents. He wiped his face on the sleeve of his shirt, and then, adjusting his holdall, he exited the room. He whistled as he passed the receptionist, who gave him a bright smile. He sprinted down the stairs and emerged into the bright sunlight and the chirping of birds. It was a beautiful day.

Vayu felt a surge of joy, an immense sense of strength, and he felt connected to the universe.

The Kalingan warrior was happy.

He made it out to the street and flagged a taxi, handing the driver Dr Kuruvella's home address. By now Vayu was calm, his mind focused and his breathing controlled. He had handled it well. Dr Kuruvella would learn of the professor's death and the terror would reduce him to a withering leaf. It would be a pleasure to crush him.

*

Dr Kuruvella, world expert on the science of alchemy, head of the faculty for post-graduate studies in sciences at Calcutta University was also the head of the Indian Institute of Sciences and the Indian Society of Scientific Values. He was still mulling over his Barabar Hills experience with the monk when a phone call interrupted his thoughts. The words of the panicky receptionist chilled him to the bone and he dropped the receiver. His wife and two daughters were in the house. With minimal explanation and maximum rush, he piled them into their car and sent them off to his brother's house. 'Go now, I will explain in detail later!' he said urgently. They understood. And he saw the look of pride in his wife's eyes. She had suspected that he was involved in something noble and big, but now she was sure it was true. The doctor gave her a sad smile.

Dr Kuruvella had warned the guard at the gate not to

let anyone in. Once inside, he waited, a loaded gun by his side.

Vayu paused at the corner where the lane merged with the main road. He saw the family car drive away raising a cloud of dust. The alert guard pulled the gate shut, latched it and checked that the boundary was secure. The two-storeyed colonial-style bungalow was enclosed by concrete and stone walls. There was only one way in or out and that was the gate.

Vayu approached the house. The guard, alert and clearly aware of impending danger, had his hand on his lathi. He came out of his sentry box and stood with his feet shoulder-width apart, ready to attack.

'I am a student of Calcutta University. I need to see Dr Kuruvella,' Vayu explained to the guard.

The tall Gurkha narrowed his eyes, taking in the distinct Chinese features. He shook his head—no one was allowed inside. 'Please go and call his office to fix an appointment,' he said.

'It has taken me a long time to get here. Please, I must see him, it is important,' Vayu explained. He clung to the gate. It wasn't armed with a remote switch. It was just a matter of sliding the latch on the other side, he noted. 'I have a gift from Professor Leung of Hong Kong University. Do you think Dr Kuruvella will like it if you don't let me in?' The gate was just about six feet high and had horizontal grooves—he could easily scale it.

The guard weakened slightly, but stood his ground.

'He is not to be disturbed. Give me your parcel and I will pass it to him.'

Vayu wiped his brow and, bent as if exhausted, he pressed his hands to his knees. 'Actually, can I have some water? I'm not used to this kind of heat.'

The guard laughed. 'This is nothing, you should come in May. It gets so hot that even the flowers look like they are melting.'

Vayu looked at him sheepishly. 'I won't come in May then.' He waited, shifting his weight from foot to foot, wiping sweat from his forehead with a tissue.

The guard weakened some more, but didn't open the gate. 'Okay. You wait here,' he said and returned to his sentry box. He then fished out a bottle of water. 'Drink this, I will call Saheb and see if he will let you in.' He unscrewed the cap and offered the bottle to Vayu. In the split second that the guard's body connected with the gate, Vayu grabbed him by the collar and slammed him hard against the metal. The guard reacted, but not quickly enough. Vayu had already reached into his back pocket with his other hand. He pulled out the carving knife and gutted the whimpering man without hesitation. The guard's eyes widened in shock as he shook violently.

Vayu held on tighter, and stuck the knife deeper. 'You are a careless guard. Because of you the doctor will die. Your soul will wander for many lifetimes.'

When the guard's legs stopped trembling and his clawing hands lost their strength, Vayu removed the knife, wiped it against the man's khaki shirt, and let go. The guard's body dropped to the ground like a sack of potatoes.

Vayu climbed the gate, swung over, and landed comfortably on the ground. Breathing evenly, he was in control; there was a whirling current pushing but he didn't want to lose his temper. Yet. The Kalingan must wait.

Quickly, he dragged the guard and pushed him into his sentry box. The bottle of water had rolled away. Vayu picked it up and swallowed the few sips that hadn't poured out. It didn't satisfy him. He was really thirsty and hoped that Dr Kuruvella would offer him a drink. Vayu made his way to the back entrance. The kitchen windows would be easy to break, but first he tried the back door. It didn't budge. Vayu picked up a stone and slammed it against the window. It shattered, sending shards flying. A splinter of glass hit Vayu on the cheek. He touched it and felt the sliver embedded an inch below his eye; blood was flowing profusely. He pulled out the glass and threw it aside. Hooking his fingers on the sill, Vayu pulled himself inside the dark, quiet house.

He crouched, taking in his surroundings. His senses were as sharp as a lion's when ready for the kill. The house was too quiet for comfort. There was a rolling pin on the side cabinet. Vayu flung it across the floor. There was a burst of gunfire.

So Dr Kuruvella had armed guards inside his house!

They didn't know Vayu's strength—well, now was the time to prove it.

'Don't shoot!' Vayu called out in mock surrender. He stood up slowly, his arms raised.

Only one man.

Vayu felt a surge of adrenalin. A piece of cake. Clad head-to-toe in black, the guard had an AK-47 aimed at him. 'Turn around slowly or I will shoot your head off!' he growled.

Vayu did as he was told. He interlaced his hands behind his head.

The guard grabbed his wrist and before he could say hello, Vayu kicked back, a solid crunch to the knee. The man staggered back, and grunted in pain. Before he could raise his gun, Vayu swiftly turned and landed another hard kick on his chest. Vayu snatched the gun from the motionless body and moved boldly into the house.

Vayu smiled to himself, and winced at the pang from the cut in his cheek. He ignored it. Moving quickly through open doors, he crossed a dining room with a long table and eight chairs, followed by a spacious living room done up with four sofas, three armchairs and a coffee table. There was a winding staircase close to the right wall. He didn't bother going upstairs. The closed door to the left caught his attention. The doctor's vibes were strong. This is where he was. Vayu's senses were heightened, he breathed deeply and sweat poured down his face. He knew exactly where the doctor was hiding.

'Dr Kuruvella . . . I have a present for you!' Vayu said in a sing-song voice, turning the handle and pushing the door wide open. It was a study, its walls lined with books from floor to ceiling.

Dr Kuruvella was sitting behind his desk in his chair, facing the door. He had a gun aimed at Vayu. 'You take one more step forward and I will shoot.'

Vayu grinned. He felt the Kalingan take over his mind—the rush was immediate and felt like a downhill slide on a roller-coaster ride. 'You will not shoot, doctor. That is not your dharma.'

Vayu took two steps forward. Dr Kuruvella was on his feet, gun still aimed at him, but he moved away from the grinning monster. 'Stay back, I'm warning you.'

Vayu took another step forward. 'I just met your friend Professor Gupta. He sacrificed himself for your clan. Are you going to do the same?' Vayu eyed him with a cold stare. His smile now changed into a hard line. 'Make it easier and point the gun at your head.'

This time Dr Kuruvella fired. His target moved swiftly and the bullet missed by inches. 'Bad aim,' Vayu said and surged forward in giant strides. 'It's my turn.'

Dr Kuruvella tried to shoot again but his hands trembled so much, he ended up firing at the ceiling. The concrete cracked and its fragments fell on them. Vayu pushed him towards the wall. The doctor struggled, and tried to shoot at his assailant, but Vayu was too strong for him. He seized the doctor's hand and aimed the weapon to his head. He twisted him to the floor. 'Maybe suicide is the only solution,' Vayu said through gritted teeth. And pulled the trigger. The gunshot was so loud that Vayu felt the ground shake. Books fell from the shelves raising dust clouds.

Vayu staggered back from the impact. The gun slid to the floor. He was breathing heavily as though he had run a marathon. His heart pumped violently and his body felt weak from the effort. He sat down and held his head in his hands. 'Kalingan warrior, why do you do this to me?' he said, shivering in the hot, musty room. There was a dead silence.

You owe me! were the only words he heard.

Vayu stood up, feeling strong and brave again. Whenever he felt weak, some force pulled him up again. He knew it controlled his life. He looked down. From his angle the floor was covered with a bright red spray of blood and brain.

7

London, England

Someone was watching Akash. He didn't realize he was being followed, lost in the music of a Bollywood remix that piped into his ears. Akash moved easily through Burlington, his head bobbing to the rhythm. It was still early evening and his job at the club only started after eight. He had about two hours to kill. Jenny or Karina?

He couldn't make up his mind—both of them had the hots for him, and both had catfights to get his attention. He enjoyed that. It was no fun with just one. Maybe he should suggest a threesome. But Karina had a temper, and he had seen jealousy-fuelled eruptions at the club that bordered on the violent. The other night Jenny had almost wasted a vodka chillini on Karina. Luckily, a few of her friends had held her back. In the big city, DJs were a dime a dozen and popular nightclubs only a handful. He had to be careful with his personal life.

Akash turned the corner and fished his mobile out of his jacket pocket. The street was deserted, except for a van in the corner. He just had to cross at the traffic lights and he would be home, in the warmth of his first-floor flat, courtesy the Q Club. They paid him as much for his DJing abilities as for his appearance. He was already blessed with a handsome face and a smile that any woman would swoon over. And every afternoon, he worked out to build a body to match his face. Dressed in Italian-fit black shirts, Gap jeans and Ralph Lauren alligator shoes, he rocked the club. Shoes were his weakness, and he didn't think it fair that only women were allowed to have the freedom to express their passion for shoes. Men had feelings too, and enjoyed the feel of handsome, soft leather on their feet.

The workout at the gym had got his juices flowing, and he needed some release. If the traffic lights turned red, it would be Karina; if not, then Jenny. He headed for the pedestrian crossing, it was green and ticking. If he ran, he might just make it. Jenny. He slowed his pace. The lights turned amber and then red. He waited, his feet tapping to a distinct beat. He sent her a text message, and ended it with: *cant wait to c u gorgeous* ☺

A young woman stood next to him. She had wide brown eyes, pouty lips and a very tight top under her winter jacket, which she had purposefully unbuttoned for his viewing pleasure. She whisked her long brunette hair and smiled at him flirtatiously. An invitation! How could he resist? He gave her an appreciative smile. He was not in the habit of picking up strangers, but Akash knew class when it stared him in the face. The lady had money. From her leather jacket to her designer clutch, she was easily worth twice his monthly salary. She had sexy glimmering lips and smoky eyes that added intensity to her gaze.

'Hi, I'm Mona!' she whispered demurely. In her butt-firming heels, her lips reached his ears. Akash caught the heady fragrance of Guerlain.

'Axe,' he said, going by his DJ name. DJ Axe—action extreme, he'd add when he was on the mic.

'I know.' She offered her hand, perfect nails glistened burgundy. Akash imagined them caressing his bare chest. 'I come to the club just to watch you,' she added. He smiled wider and shook her hand. The lights turned green. She let go of his hand and started walking across. His phone beeped. He had to make a decision fast. He read Karina's message and caught up with Mona. 'Would you like to have a cup of coffee? I have a racy Lamborghini coffee machine at my place,' he said, willing to take the risk that she would slap him across the face. And he would still get into Karina's hot pants. She had responded to his message with equal fervour: *cant wait to c u—nude!*

Mona gave him a nod and a smile. 'I like mine strong and fast. Only one cup of coffee,' she said. There was a husky edge to her voice.

'Great! I like your style.'

Akash couldn't believe his luck! He was used to female attention, a lot of it. But Mona agreeing to be with him was something else. Even at the gym, sometimes it was distracting. Some women purposely dropped their towels to give him clear views of full cleavages, perfect bodies, but he didn't go to the gym to pick up women, at least not while he was serious about sculpting his own body.

When he turned twenty, he had started to take life more seriously. A severe skin allergy and asthma got him to focus on taking care of his health, eating right. He quit smoking. After going through tests he discovered he was allergic to certain kinds of food. He followed the list. The experience helped him realize that he was not invincible and his body was capable of breaking down. If he didn't do something about it, like eating healthy and exercising regularly, he could be dead in five years.

To him it meant that his good looks would be wasted. As soon as he unlocked the door to his apartment,

Mona strode past him and entered his home as if she owned it. She did a whirl, smiled and turned to him. 'Nice,' she nodded, 'very nice.'

Akash's home was a typical bachelor pad: lots of steel and black leather furniture, a small, bare kitchen, and bottles of booze and crystal glasses. She continued to check out his place.

Akash followed Mona's exceedingly alluring rear. She was sexy, with perfect curves and long lean legs. Her interest in him was a compliment and Akash wanted her real bad. She had already discarded her jacket on the leather sofa. He steadied himself. He felt that at this stage he should offer her that cup of coffee or something stronger. Bloody hell, he needed a shot of bourbon too!

Maybe he should call the club and tell them he would be late, make an excuse of a headache. The club would buy it, he never missed work. She was wearing a fitted gold top that contoured her upper body. Skinny jeans sat snug on her perfectly round ass, and with stilettos, she had an arch that would inspire an artist. As she gazed out of the window, Akash watched her with undisguised pleasure.

'What's this?' she asked, looking through the telescope positioned by the window. It was set on a tripod at an angle facing the sky. It took Akash a very long time, a few weeks actually, to find the Pleiades star cluster. He didn't stop her when she shifted the angle of the lens. *Yeah baby, lean some more*, Akash mused.

He cleared his dry throat and said, 'That's my hobby, I'm a stargazer.'

'Wow!' she said. 'Didn't think you were the type to be interested in astronomy.'

'What type is that?' He was next to her.

'A man with more brawn than brain,' she smiled and raised a perfectly arched brow.

He nodded and leaned in closer, 'Plenty of brawn too.' She turned to look up at the sky, and Akash placed his hand on her back and slid it down slowly.

Mona didn't push him away. Instead, she smiled slowly and gave him a sideways glance. 'Aren't you going to offer a lady a cup of coffee, first?' Her tongue lingered on 'first'. Her lips parted, and she was close to almost touching his chin. He could feel her warm, minty breath. He dropped his hand from her back, and suddenly felt awkward.

'Yes, of course! Unless you prefer some vintage wine?' Akash offered and turned towards the kitchen, but before he could do much else, he felt as if a hammer hit his jaw and everything went dark.

Akash felt a throbbing ache as though a drill was in his cheekbone, and it was working overtime. He tried to open his eyes and squinted at the sharp light. 'Crap. What the bloody hell happened?' he mumbled, blinking repeatedly.

Carefully, he touched his jaw and winced. Slowly he sat up on the sofa, his head reeled, and he thought he would throw up. One minute he was being seduced by the most gorgeous woman, and the next thing he knew she had given him a solid punch that totally knocked him out. Women! Akash groaned in pain. His face was probably swollen and bruised black and blue. He couldn't go to work like this.

'I sent the club a message telling them your mother came to visit,' Mona said, patting him gently. She gave him a bag of ice from the freezer.

'Why did you hit me like that? What do you want from me?' Akash asked angrily, pressing the ice bag on the throbbing ache. 'Take the money or whatever you want and go. I don't have much.'

'Money? Hah! Is that all I'm after?' She gave him a wide smile. 'What about plenty of brawn?'

'Let him be.'

Akash hadn't realized there was another person in the room. The suited man was sitting in Akash's favourite stressed leather armchair—his prized possession! He had bought it at an auction and it once belonged to a very famous actor, the name wasn't coming to him. Shit! He'd probably suffered a concussion or something like that, and lost his memory. His telescope was his other prized possession, already contaminated by the woman's violent hands.

The man spoke in a distinguished voice. 'Akash, there is something you need to know.'

'What? Who are you? And why are you here? I'm

calling the police.' He reached for the phone in his back pocket.

Mona smiled at him. 'You actually thought I would return your phone?'

The male voice spoke. 'Get me a single malt and pour me a double shot, will you please, Mona darling.'

She nodded and helped herself to Akash's bar. Freeloaders!

Akash winced.

'Well?' he asked impatiently. 'What do you want?'

The man was silent until he sipped his drink. 'Hmmm. Smooth. Very good-quality Scotch.' He nodded appreciatively.

'Okay, that's it.' Akash stood up slowly, and felt his head spin. 'I'm calling the police.'

'You don't want to do that,' Mona reached towards him and showed him her fist. Akash sat down.

The freeloader spoke and Akash thought the drink had got to him. 'How would you like to be someone who has the most unusual power, the ability to defy gravity? One minute you're here, and the next you're on the other side of the town. Just like that!' He clicked his fingers. 'And to entrust you with this two millennia-old secret of an ancient past . . .' the old man let the thought drift.

Akash felt as if he was in the middle of an *X-Files* episode and waited for the dream to end. Or was it an elaborate prank? Not his birthday yet. Not Halloween or April Fool's Day. Bloody hell, he was getting a headache trying to figure out what these two were really up to. Damn! He should have just called Karina and had a nice relaxing evening with her. Shit! She must be fuming and probably thinking he was with Jenny. Double shit!

'So what do you think, young man?' The elderly man's voice had a hint of an accent. Akash recognized it. Indian. Akash could tell. No matter how long an Indian had lived in England, you could still figure out that English wasn't his mother tongue. That teeny emphasis on a word gave them away.

'After that whack your girl gave me, I can't think. You tell me,' Akash responded dryly. He wasn't interested in their stupid games, or whatever it was. Then it suddenly struck him—a trap! The word reverberated in his head like a hot record. Akash tried to see the man's face in the low light, the table lamp was off and the fact that he was sitting in the shadows wasn't helping. Wait a minute, the silhouette of the man looked vaguely familiar. Akash had a fleeting recollection of reading about him in the papers, and then it was gone.

Mona smiled. She sat next to her man on the armrest, her fingers intertwined with his. Even in the shadowy darkness you could tell how beautiful she was. *Shit! What had he got himself into?* Akash wondered. Didn't he remember the adage: beauty begets danger, or something like that? He should have used his head, the one that contained a brain, before he let her into his house.

'We want you,' the man said in an ever-so-soft voice

that made Akash grit his teeth and want to punch him in the face. He looked towards the old man, surprised.

'Have you ever wondered why you are interested in astronomy?' he continued in his soothing voice, as if he were speaking to a child.

'Everyone's got some hobby or the other. I'm interested in stargazing. That's all,' Akash said defensively. 'What's the big deal?'

'Never asked yourself, why stargazing? Never self-reflected on the who or why of life and the purpose of your pathetic existence?'

'What's the point of all this?' Akash stood up. 'Either tell me what you want or just leave.'

'This generation has no patience! And no respect for the past. The future looks bleak, Akash. If you don't take what we have to say seriously, there will be chaos. In our time, we knew how to keep secrets. But I don't know what will happen . . . now with this lot, in this era.' He looked up at Mona. She gave him a radiant smile.

There was a pause.

'I need to take a piss,' Akash said aloud. He stood up.

There was irritation in the man's voice. 'Go with him, Mona.'

Akash grinned. 'Yes, Mona darling, come watch me piss,' he said teasingly. But as he tried to walk, his legs quavered slightly. Mona extended her hand but he didn't accept her help, and made his way slowly towards the bathroom, leaning against the wall. He hoped to make it with his dignity intact. Mona turned and waited by the door.

Akash unzipped his pants and faced the toilet bowl. 'So how long have you been with your sugar daddy?'

Silence. The only sound was that of trickling.

'You really didn't have to punch me in the face. I was going to give you a really good time. Probably a rare treat, sweetheart, considering I'm the master at making women scream with pleasure. And this is how you treat me?' He shook his head and tched tched at her. Turning towards her he zipped up. She looked away. He pressed the flush, and stepped up to the washbasin. 'Where did you learn to hit like that? They don't teach that kind of violence at acting school. Or were you sent to a training camp for boxers?' Akash turned on the tap. A large rectangular mirror hung above the basin, and in the reflection Akash noticed her face tighten and turn a deep shade of red. 'I know, you grew up on the streets.'

He washed his hands slowly and looked at himself in the mirror. A distinct discolouring and swelling were visible on his jaw. It was sensitive to touch. Mona was watching him with raised eyebrows and fire in her eyes.

'Is he into kinky stuff? I'm not that kind of guy, you know.' Akash faced her. 'Too bad you missed the most wonderful time of your life, Mona darling. I know how to make a woman feel like she's in heaven. Over and over again.' He came close, his face just inches from hers. Their eyes met. He caught a whiff of her perfume. It was heady.

Akash leaned in closer as if to kiss her cheek, instead he whispered in her ear. 'Oh, by the way, can he still get it up?'

That one really got to her. He shifted slightly. Mona's eyes were mere slits, her face flushed and he noticed her hands tighten into a fist.

'Tut tut, don't get all excited, darling,' Akash said wagging his finger in her face. She grabbed it and bent it till he yelled in pain. Mona opened the door, and with her iron grip still on his hand, he was led back to his seat.

Akash picked up the melting ice bag and nursed his hand. He gave her a grin, and winced at the pain. The throbbing pain was worth the look on Mona's face. No one hit DJ Axe and got away with it!

'Take a look at this,' the man dropped a memory stick on the low table next to him. It was attached to a chain and made a clattering sound on the glass. It hurt his ears.

Akash tossed the bag of ice. 'Why should I bother?'

He paid all his bills on time, he was careful not to get entangled with people heavily into alcohol and orgies and drugs. The Q Club was a favourite haunt, and often he was invited to their parties. Rule No. 1: no partying with guests. And Akash stuck by the rules. Akash had a cool dude image, but outside of his job, he was a straight, serious guy with a secret hobby. He could have had a relaxing time with Karina, instead he got Mona with a James Bond attitude who gave him the wrong kind of a blow job. Akash closed his eyes and waited for the pain and embarrassment to subside.

When he opened them, the man in the suit was standing over him. Akash saw his face for the first time. The recognition hit him as hard as Mona's blow. The face of one of the richest media tycoons in the world—David Dariwal—was staring down at him! The thick white hair that curled around his collar and carefully groomed beard were unmistakable. It was him. He had been in the news recently, his picture splashed on every newspaper across the country. But for the wrong reasons. David Dariwal was supposed to be dead—murdered by the secret Pakistani police for threatening to reveal classified information on their connections with bombings in India.

Akash's jaw dropped; he pointed at the man and said, 'You're supposed to be dead.'

'Yes, and you're supposed to have superhuman powers,' David smiled, revealing slightly crooked teeth. Akash was normally good at comebacks. But nothing came from his lips.

This was a strange day, and he hoped that he would wake up and it would all be over, and he would dismiss these events as a very weird dream.

David sat next to him, Akash shifted, keeping him at arm's length.

Mona smirked. 'He's not a ghost, Akash. He's alive and well. The world had to know he was dead. So they would stop trying to kill him.'

'Ironic, isn't it?' David retorted. 'I have to be dead so they would leave me alone.'

'Who are they?' Akash asked.

David crossed his legs and appeared relaxed, as if he had come to make a social call. He joined the tips of his fingers and spoke, ignoring Akash's question. 'Akash Pandit, age twenty-six, born in India, adopted and moved to Leicester, England.' When Akash didn't react, he continued, 'Adoptive parents: English father and Indian mother, separated when you turned eighteen. You moved out and started working at a local school as a science teacher.' Mona looked at him with wide eyes that said *You don't look like a teacher.* 'Later, you changed jobs, moved to different cities, tried a few places, until London gave you your dream job. Akash Pandit, aka DJ Axe! You enjoy the perks—string of girlfriends, no steady relationships, few friends and a passion for stargazing. Ah yes, one more thing: you don't keep in touch with your family. Have I missed anything?'

Akash didn't respond. He was still wondering where this was going.

'Good,' David said, satisfied by the silence. 'Now that we understand each other, read the information on that stick. Here's my card, call me when all this sinks in. And don't do anything stupid like call the police or Google the information.' David stood up, and very slowly limped towards the door, leaning heavily on Mona's arm. His long jacket hid his slight body, and even though he carried himself tall and distinguished like in the papers, David's shoulders seemed burdened, and his face was lined with worry. He opened the door.

'Wait!' Pain forgotten, Akash shot up and ran towards them. 'Why have you kept tabs on me? I still don't understand the connection, and what exactly do you want?'

It was odd that David Dariwal came to see him—a nobody—risking the chance of someone noticing, and if his life was in danger then what else was he hiding?

David gave him a tight smile. 'There is a memory stick on your table there. I suggest you take a look at it. And then call me. If you value your life and those few silly girlfriends you have, then you will take this matter as urgently and seriously as I have. I repeat the warning because it is important—don't make any calls or speak to anyone about what is on that stick. Is that understood?'

There was a pause.

'Woo-hoo and I'm supposed to be all scared!' Akash laughed. 'Is this another one of your pranks—Bhim and Ken,' he called, looking around, 'come out, come out wherever you are. I've had enough of your jokes.' Akash was used to their games—it was one of the ways of his friends' laidback lifestyles. They worked nights, slept away part of the day and worked out in the afternoons. And to cut out the seriousness of life, they played pranks on each other.

If looks could kill, Mona's sharp gaze would have flatlined him in one second. A very subtle nod from David as he moved out into the corridor gave Mona a chance to get back at him. Before he knew it, Akash was punched, head on, and he passed out again.

It was late in the night when Akash came to. And this time he shouted obscenities, and slammed a few doors. He let the tears of pain roll freely when he looked at his face in the mirror. He grabbed another bag of ice from the freezer and nursed his nose. Feeling light-headed, he realized he hadn't eaten anything after his workout; his stomach growled, warning him that if he didn't consume food he might just pass out again. After a heavy sandwich with a coffee, he popped two painkillers. He called Ken and asked him to cover for him for a couple of days.

Then he switched on his computer, and when it had whirred to the start-up screen, he stuck the memory stick in its socket. And waited. The symbol of a chakra—a wheel with spokes—filled the screen. Akash vaguely remembered seeing a similar wheel on the Indian flag. What did this have to do with him? Glued to the content, he read eagerly and tried to make sense of the information. The secrets mentioned were odd, scientific, and yet magical. And Akash, despite David's warning, clicked on Internet explorer and typed 'nine unknown men', researching the information. He wasn't the type to follow the rules. The old guy might as well understand that now—he didn't want to be part of this or any other secret society. He Googled deeper, but nothing more was forthcoming, and then suddenly he found himself facing the words, 'This is a restricted site'. He used another site to search for information but by then he had lost the Net connection. This had never happened before. He never

ever lost the wireless network even in the worst of storms! Akash leaned back and closed his eyes. There had to be more to all this.

In the dead silence, the quiet ticking of the pipes and the hum of the refrigerator were sounds he was used to around the house. He wasn't lulled by them—a coldness crept over him. He began to sense an odd presence, the feeling of being watched. He jerked up, turned around. There was no one there. Nothing out of place. He looked out of the window. The streetlamps offered a subdued glow on the deserted tree-lined road. There was nothing unusual.

It was probably all in his mind, he thought, and sat down at his desk again. He knew he needed to rest. He stared at the screen. Suddenly, out of nowhere a black spider appeared and bit him hard on his hand, a needle-like bite that stung sharply. He quickly flicked it away from the table, rubbing his hand. The pain was a feverish burning sensation. *What was happening?* But before he could understand, dozens of spiders spilled out from the CD rack, the sound system, the woofers and through the wall sockets, scurrying all around him. The black carpet of deadly insects was heading in his direction. Horrified, he raced to the front door and pulled at the doorknob— it wouldn't budge. Suddenly, the spiders were coming out of the wall, crawling up his legs and down his neck. He brushed them off as fast as he could. He opened his mouth to yell for help—a spider fell out.

Akash found himself sitting bolt upright in his chair. He stared in the semi-darkness, his eyes wide open, heart pounding wildly. At the same time, he heard the impatient banging on his door. So *that* had been one ugly bug dream. He had dozed off! He got out of his seat and looked around—no spiders. It was all a nightmare. His hands trembled, the sensation of the crawling insects clung to him. He could still feel them all over his body. He heard the insistent rapping on his door. He wasn't expecting anyone at that hour. Was it crazy David Dariwal and his fiendish friend again? He looked through the peephole. There was a man, he could only see a wide chest clad in a black T-shirt.

Akash moved away and noticed a large red bruise on his hand, exactly where he dreamed the spider had bit him! The banging startled him. 'Open up, Akash! Your life is in danger!' the urgent voice demanded.

He hesitated, but instinct directed him and he opened the door wide. There was a large Asian man fuming impatiently. 'What is the matter with you? Deaf?' he said, pushing Akash aside as he entered his home. Akash gaped at the intruder. The man had a red smear on his forehead. 'Get a move on! We have to leave now. They are on their way to kill you!' he said, looking around.

'I . . . don't believe you,' Akash said, trying to block his path as he ventured further inside. He grabbed a knife from the kitchen counter.

'Listen to me carefully. I am here to protect you.' He

held up his hands, and walked slowly towards Akash. 'David Dariwal sent me. They will come for you, try and understand that it's dangerous to be here.'

'Prove that I can trust you,' Akash said, holding the knife in a threatening manner.

The man pushed up his T-shirt sleeve. On his upper arm was a tattoo the size of a coin. It was a circle with spokes. It was the same chakra he had seen on the memory stick.

'That doesn't mean anything, anyone can get a tattoo,' Akash said, waving his weapon.

'Mr Dariwal gave you some information. We have a van outside, monitoring your movements. You made a mistake—you searched the Internet, they emit like radio waves, and they found out, you know. They filled your nightmares with spiders. Am I right?'

Akash still held the knife. But he stood stock-still for a second—thinking. He had no choice. 'Then what are we waiting for? Let's go.'

'Take your laptop, your passport, some money,' the man said. He hurried towards the kitchen and grabbed a few knives.

'Give me your mobile!' he called out. Akash reached over and handed it to him. The man threw it to the ground and crushed it under his hardy boots. 'They can trace you with this.'

'That was one of my precious . . .' Akash shook his head. It had cost him an arm and a leg to get that all-in-one mobile. 'What's your name?' If someone was taking control of his life—at least he should know his name for times when he needed to curse.

'Jona,' he replied. 'We have to make sure you reach your destination safely. You are now our responsibility.'

'India?' Akash asked as he picked up his belongings. The thought had suddenly struck him.

'And then to the land of monks.'

Akash looked shocked. 'What do you mean? I'm not ready yet!'

Akash pulled out a bag and stuffed all of his things in his carryall. He slipped David Dariwal's memory stick in his pocket. 'But I guess I don't have a chance to think about it,' he said, looking at Jona's big monk face, barrel chest and strong arms. 'Do I?'

'No,' Jona said, reaching for the door. 'Let's go.'

Akash followed Jona, bending down as he did. Further down the corridor, there was a bald, thickset man with clasped hands. He was in a burgundy robe—apparently waiting for them. Jona moved ahead as they started towards the lifts. Akash turned to look at his home for the last time and was pushed hard to the ground. He heard a whistling sound and a rush of heat singed his cheek. Someone was firing a gun with a silencer attached. Jona was right, he had got out in time or he would have been dead soon enough. The monk crawled towards the door marked with an exit sign. Jona had fallen. Akash nudged him to keeping moving. Then he saw the blood, it was spreading around his head. *Shit, Jona had got shot. He had saved his life!* Akash then realized the seriousness of the situation.

Suddenly, out of nowhere, the silence was broken by a burst of machine-gun fire. Black-clothed men sliding down a rope were sweeping in from the sole window at the other end of the corridor. They looked like the army of spiders in his dream.

'Come on, there's no time to waste!' the monk said impatiently.

'What about Jona?' Akash asked.

'What about him? You've got to move on, you idiot, or you will get us all killed!' The monk said pushing him with strong arms.

The two had not been spotted. They pushed backwards against the exit doors that led to the staircase and once through, ran at full speed. The monk was surprisingly agile despite his robes.

'I'm sorry, I'm sorry,' Akash repeated.

'Shut up and focus,' the monk said to him, gripping his arm. 'Follow me.'

They raced down the stairs, the monk ahead and Akash close behind. They heard glass crashing, a window, and with each sound Akash imagined the devastation in his apartment. Again another damaging burst of sound, and that was probably his telescope; another loud crash, that must have been his expensive coffee machine. They were looking for something. He felt in his pocket, the memory stick was safe. His carryall was strapped over his shoulders. They reached the street. The monk opened the door slightly. A van was waiting for them, the door opened wide like a dark cave waiting to swallow anyone who entered. They jumped in and the last vision that Akash had was of Karina sitting in the corner coffee shop, watching the scene in horror.

8

Minneapolis, Minnesota, USA

Zubin Ghosh liked working with the dead. At the Hennepin County Medical Examiner's office, he often had to prove himself, not because he was more than trained for the job, but because his skin colour stood out like a sore thumb. Distinctly dark-skinned amongst a group of fair-haired, pale-skinned men and women, every day was a test for the death investigator. But Zubin had one strong winning hand—his boss respected him.

'The body's in the dumpster,' the Minneapolis detective cackled when Zubin arrived on the scene. 'Can you handle it?' he asked, looking at his partner and giving him a subtle nod.

Zubin was used to the reserved temperament of the new cops. This one had probably assumed the chocolate-coloured man with the square glasses would be reluctant to investigate the body inside a garbage bin. The cops often ended up being friends with him, eventually. He didn't really mind. He smiled coolly. 'That's my job, detective. I can handle it.'

It was freezing, but Zubin removed his jacket and rolled up his sleeves. From his work case, he pulled out and put on his latex gloves. There were three other cops standing around, looking uneasily at him and then at each other. Spotlights were positioned over the dumpster and a police tape had cordoned off the area. A narrow ladder led up and into the dumpster.

Even though it was pre-dawn, there were a few curious bystanders. The two garbage collectors who had found the body were already at the local police station, being questioned.

This seemed like it would be another one of those violent, unexplained deaths. Zubin had investigated many, and some of them were easily explained, but oddly enough, now there were more and more cases that were still open—because of lack of evidence surrounding the deaths. Zubin had his logic for it, there was an overload of pent-up anger and resentment, and it was spilling out on the streets in the most horrific ways.

Carefully, Zubin climbed inside. He heard scuttling. Rats. He trod carefully over the unsteady surface of discarded cans, food and plastic bags ballooning with decaying matter. A stench rose each time Zubin set his foot down. Focusing on the job, he kneeled down next to the girl's body.

Zubin gasped. What struck him was her beauty—

despite the blood there was an ethereal quality about her. An angel dead in a dumpster! One glassy blue eye stared at him, the other one was swollen shut. From her attire, he guessed she was a prostitute. She was wearing a short skirt, spiky heels and a tight, cleavage-revealing top. The icing on the cake was a thick boa of faux fur that half clung to her body. There was no identification on her person. He checked her forearm. There were needle marks—a drug-induced death. Her head was badly bashed in, the skull had split, and part of her brain was exposed. Flies buzzed around, attracted to the warmth of the oozing thick blood.

There should have been more blood, Zubin deduced. She must have been dumped here after she was killed. The thought sickened him, but he kept his emotions at bay. Times like these he wished he was back in the hospital saving pathetic young lives like hers, instead of seeing them wasted like this. She was so young, and he guessed she would have been a college kid if she hadn't got caught up in drugs. He searched gently around her. There was nothing to bag as evidence.

He noticed on her middle finger a ring set with a little heart-shaped red stone. It was tiny but glistened in the light. *Someone must have loved you very much*, Zubin thought. Where the blood hadn't marred her, wispy blonde hair framed her doll-like face. She had a beautiful complexion, like porcelain. Zubin's mud-coloured skin contrasted sharply with her lily-white shade. Zubin shook his head. *What a waste!* 'Rest in peace,' he whispered and called in the cops to move her. Her glassy eye seemed to follow him as he exited from the dumpster and removed his gloves. The cops were scanning the area searching for clues.

Zubin's cell phone buzzed. He answered.

'What's up?' Barry said.

'You called me, you tell me.'

'The boss is looking for you,' Barry whispered in a conspiratorial tone. 'Just thought I'd give you a heads-up.'

'Why?'

'Maybe you are going to get your ass kicked or you're going to get a promotion. The guys bet it's the first.'

'Cool. Now you're betting on my job?'

'Just for fun. There's only so much one can do during a coffee break in the garden of the dead.'

'Thanks, I'll talk to you later,' Zubin said and hung up. The detective was approaching him. The girl seemed to be just one of many dead prostitutes. Still he would follow procedure and go over the details of the crime scene and the lab results of the victim. Find out what happened, arrest the perp before they stamped 'file closed'. Closure is good, not just for the family, but also, Zubin felt, for himself.

Life in a metropolis was full of excitement: bright lights, fast cars and desires that led to addiction and crime. Most of the ten thousand deaths that occurred in the county each year were natural, which meant the deceaseds' physicians could sign their death certificates. But about one per cent of these cases were accidents, homicides, suicides or unexplained natural deaths and required the medical examiner to establish the cause of death. Zubin was the 'death investigator'.

'Victim is female, in her mid-thirties, fractured skull and left leg, needle tracks on her arms indicate drug abuse, but it needs to be verified,' Zubin reported. 'Appears to have been violently beaten to death.'

They started walking away from the scene. Some of the officers were questioning the bystanders. He saw them shift away uneasily.

'Any ID?' the detective asked. He was bulked up in a thick jacket with fur around the collar. Zubin thought of the dead girl wearing a gold spaghetti top and mini skirt, her black tights were shredded. Hope they've covered her up well.

'None.' Zubin had searched through the dumpster. The police department would run her through the system, the cop informed him. Zubin's forensic team was at the scene collecting evidence, photographs, samples from under her nails, and following the trail of blood outside the dumpster. He would rush for results.

'We'll prepare an autopsy report,' Zubin said. The detective nodded and offered his hand.

Zubin shook hands and got into his car. The detective waved at him as he drove away. It was a clear-cut case of drug overdose and an ill-tempered guy. The cop didn't have to say anything. They had seen cases like this before, and it wasn't priority. Dead hooker. Life in a big city. Happened all the time. Zubin usually wasn't this cut and dry, but the girl seemed to fit the mould of so many young prostitutes who had run away from home at a young age, got caught in the web of drugs, and then needed money to feed the habit.

Lots of people thought working crime scenes was an interesting job. Collecting forensic evidence was one thing, but facing violent deaths every day needed a high tolerance for the grisly. Zubin mused as he switched lanes. Dawn was breaking the mist and clearing the darkness. It was a brand new day. Or was it the same old day—a rerun of the same deaths and murders? Sometimes the cases got to him. There was a department psychiatrist he could talk to. And he knew a few of his colleagues suffered from depression. Living amongst violent deaths day in and day out . . . eventually it messed up a person's mind.

There was one particularly gruesome case that stuck on in Zubin's mind. He didn't think he would ever get over that one. It was such an ordinary day for an ordinary housewife. And then a freak accident had killed her. She had stuck her hand inside a grinder, trying to get it to work. Unfortunately, while it was still plugged in. Next thing she knew, her fingers were minced and in a state of panic, she tried to pull out what was left of her hand. She tripped backwards and banged her neck against the edge of the sink. Death was instantaneous, but the machine continued to grind. The kitchen was a mess. Blood and flesh splattered all over. Luckily, she didn't have any children to witness the horror.

The fresh-faced cop looked pale when he had called it. He hung around outside, retching in the corner. He had probably left his job to work elsewhere. But the memory was difficult to blank out. The sight and overwhelming smell of flesh, bone and blood stayed forever. Only people with iron stomachs could stand there without being physically or mentally sickened by the gory sight. The poor housewife was just doing her chores, would have settled down with a nice cup of coffee and the afternoon soap. And in an instant life was snapped out of her. The husband was devastated. Death that came fast and furious was the worst kind. Zubin didn't think her man would ever get over it either. He switched lanes, switching out of the memory.

Zubin used to be an ER nurse before he chose to become a death investigator. He'd sometimes dated young girls who were nurses, but more often than not everyone was just too tired to socialize. When he switched jobs he didn't go on dates any more—his macabre career wasn't great dinnertime conversation.

Women found him weird because he often talked about death. 'It is fascinating. How much we fight the inevitable. If you think about it, all the research in science boils down to finding the ultimate solution for immortality.' Zubin would then notice his date squirming uncomfortably in her seat. Death made people uneasy and thinking about it made it seem like it was closer than expected.

Zubin broke through the bumper-to-bumper traffic and drove down side streets back to the county morgue. Parking by the kerb was restricted for employees. He liked the convenience of sliding into a wide space, unlike at his apartment building, where he had to drive into the basement and manoeuvre into a tight slot next to a wall. He entered the beige–brown building behind the Metrodome. The elevator led Zubin down to the morgue and he walked out onto a long narrow corridor. Two autopsy rooms occupied the basement floor, through which a back entrance led to a garage—the bodies were transported on a ramp through this unmarked location. It was more discreet this way. Double doors with square portholes separated the sections.

There was one battered reception desk to ward off or prepare any visitors. This wasn't a place to visit, but sometimes it was necessary. Gary, the young attendant, was reading a novel when Zubin entered. He waved a hello before he pushed the double doors and entered the mortuary. The room was cold and the odour of chemicals still hung distinctly in the air, despite the floral disinfectants.

Zubin placed his jacket on a hanger, and put on his lab coat. He entered his cubicle, which was a triangular room wedged in a corner, with a clear view of the autopsy rooms. He shut the door and sat at his desk. On it was a computer with post-it notes on the frame of the monitor. He had a pile of files and more post-it notes on another wall. With just enough walking space, the room had a low bookshelf crammed with three-ring binders, technical manuals and a dog-eared copy of *Sleeping, Dreaming, and Dying: An Exploration of Consciousness* by His Holiness the Dalai Lama, next to the door. Every available space was taken up. Before he could sit down, his PC buzzed, reminding him that he had got an email.

Barry Chusak, senior investigator, slightly thick around the middle, tall, dressed like a cowboy and sporting a ponytail, poked his head through the door. 'Need some coffee?' he asked. Zubin liked him. He was a frank, opinionated person, and a good friend. He often stayed in late, discussing autopsy reports and reviewing open cases.

'Seriously, you need to get out of your closet once in a while,' he said in a drawl.

'Got to deal with this,' Zubin patted and lifted a stack of files with 'urgent' stamped across the top, and picked up a Ziploc bag containing razor blades. 'The boss wants this analysed by yesterday.'

'Speaking of the boss, he called again to see if you were back.'

Before Zubin could respond, the phone rang. Barry raised his eyebrows. 'Speak of the devil,' he mouthed and plucked a white coat from one of the hooks on the corridor wall. He whistled as he wheeled a cadaver into one of the autopsy rooms.

'Zubin, I have been looking for you,' Carl Heiselberg lisped. His trademark cigar must be wedged between his teeth.

'I was called on a case. Anything urgent? By the way, I'll get the tissue sample results by this afternoon.'

'There's . . . someone here to see you. It's important.'

Carl Heiselberg never hesitated! Even when he told the governor to go kiss someone else's ass, he spoke with a steady strong voice.

A sense of uneasiness settled in Zubin's stomach. He had worked for five years and had a team of investigators under him. No mistakes so far. 'What's the problem?' he asked, alarmed.

'Zubin, I think you better come into my office.'

'Now?'

'Yes, right now.'

Sounded serious.

As soon as Zubin reached the first floor where the offices were located, he realized he had forgotten to take off his lab coat and wear his jacket. The others in their office clothes stared at him from their cubicles. He avoided their glances and headed straight for Carl Heiselberg's office. The office area had been renovated recently and the workspace had increased, with uniformly arranged desks and chairs set in rows. The employees faced their monitors and worked silently like drones. He realized he hadn't been up here in a while. Changes were happening around him while he worked with the dead in the basement of the building. Once in a while, the boss would come to the nether regions to check on the cases. Mostly it was emailed memos or webcam meetings through the Internet. The narrow corridors led to offices where the old-style walls were still wood-panelled, the bulbs gave off a soft glow and the floors were marble. Zubin turned into one of the corridors.

Abby, the receptionist, wore a neat bun and narrow-framed spectacles. She smiled at him when he entered. 'He's waiting for you,' she said and turned her attention to her computer. Her fingers skimmed over the keyboard, typing at what seemed like a hundred words a minute. Zubin hesitated for a second, took a deep breath and pushed open the solid oak door.

Carl Heiselberg was short and rotund, and wore tailored suits that fit him perfectly. His ties matched his shirts, and his English leather shoes gleamed with fresh polish. As usual, the distinctly sweet aroma of tobacco assailed his nostrils.

Zubin was wearing scuffed sneakers and wrinkled trousers. Good thing he still had his lab coat on. He hoped he didn't smell of the dumpster. Carl approached him and guided him, like a favourite son, towards the elderly gentleman sitting in an armchair. 'Come, Zubin,' he said, as if he expected him to turn away. 'There's someone here who is eager to meet you.' Carl's voice was light but Zubin caught the slight hesitation in his words.

The man he was so eager to introduce was of Asian descent. He had neatly combed thick hair streaked with grey. From his facial features, Zubin could tell he was from the northern regions of India or Pakistan. He had a straight nose and hooded eyes with long lashes.

'Meet Tarun Vaz. Senior attaché, intelligence unit, from the Indian Consulate, Chicago,' Carl said. He didn't explain more, nor did he introduce Zubin. Instead, he crossed the room to the exit; his cigar was between his thumb and forefinger, instead of between his teeth. Zubin hid his confusion, nodded and politely shook the man's outstretched hand. Carl waved at them, 'I'll be outside if you need me.' Then he shut the door behind him.

Instead of escorting the stranger and Zubin to one of the many conference rooms, the boss had let them use his office. *Odd*. Tarun Vaz must carry a lot of weight, Zubin realized. Bet Barry hadn't thought of this new twist.

'You are confused,' Vaz offered. His smile was formal. 'I'm sorry for the unexpected meeting but this is a matter of some urgency.'

'Urgency?' Zubin repeated.

Tarun Vaz indicated the other armchair. Zubin said that he preferred to stand. He leaned against the lined bookshelf, arms folded, and faced the stranger.

'It is related to your past. Ever since the . . . unfortunate incident with your father, Dr Ghosh, we have had to take care of his responsibilities.' Vaz put on thin tortoiseshell glasses and pretended to study from a file on his lap. He was avoiding eye contact.

'What responsibilities?'

'There was a special branch of biochemistry he was working on—'

'Yes, I know—bio-electromagnetics,' Zubin said, curious about the twenty-year-old news. His father wasn't a scientist any more in any capacity. He was in an old people's home paid for by the research foundation he used to work for.

'He had made tremendous progress in this field. You know that too?' Vaz asked him candidly.

'Yes, I do. So what?'

'Well, there has been a situation where the foundation he used to work for needs your help.'

'I already have a job. I don't need another one,' Zubin shrugged. He waited for the man to get to the point.

'Your father had worked on a project. It was a covert operation involving a private organization that was working on advanced research in a specific area. A few years later, the research work was stolen. But the most valuable detailed information has been preserved at a secret location.'

'What do you want me to do?' Zubin asked.

'You are now needed to continue with your father's work. To take it one step forward, apply it in real life.'

Zubin stepped away as if trying to keep a distance from his past. 'I don't quite understand the project, and why I have to continue after all these years.' He knew about his father's work in the branch of bio-electromagnetics. But he wasn't specialized in the field. Maybe this was about something else. 'Look, if this is some charitable cause or civil liberties matter, I can offer a small donation.'

Vaz gave him an icy stare. 'Don't jump to your own conclusions. The matter is of a serious nature. And you are the chosen one.' He noticed Zubin's confused look and changed his tone. 'I mean this is of vital importance and it is you who knows your father's work best. Your life is not as you see it—you are destined for bigger responsibilities. The sooner you accept it, the better.' Zubin was turning away from the man, when the next sentence made him pause and give him his full attention. Vaz continued, 'Deny it all you want, Zubin, you still cling to the past. Your father may not be the most popular person in your life. But he was a well-respected scientist.'

'The past is part of who I am, sir. I will cling to it if I want,' Zubin responded, keeping his cool.

There was a momentary pause. Tarun Vaz relented. He held up his hand. 'I apologize. Please don't dismiss what I have said.' He stood up.

A memory stick materialized from the file. Vaz handed it to Zubin. 'There is one branch of bio-electromagnetics that deals with bio-energy. Your father knew how to generate potent healing energy.'

Zubin shook his head. 'You actually believe that?'

This time Tarun Vaz smiled. 'You didn't know your father very well, did you? Let me tell you that the evidence and court case were all a huge set-up to malign his name. He was framed. He wasn't selling secrets to any government, or any such nonsense.'

'Well, his actions not only killed my mother but also destroyed all his research in the fire,' Zubin said slowly.

'Not all is lost, Zubin. We managed to salvage most of it,' Vaz said quietly. 'I think it's best you take a look at this in the privacy of your home.'

Zubin reluctantly took the stick and slipped it into his lab coat pocket. 'I'll look at it when I have the time.'

The man gave a long sigh. 'Your father was part of a very powerful organization. You should forgive him,' Vaz attempted, but got a stony response from Zubin.

'Give him my best wishes,' Zubin said icily, and headed to the door.

'Zubin!' Vaz called out. 'You have to meet him. He is dying!'

Zubin didn't look at him. 'It's too late,' he said, and left the room, leaving Vaz standing there in the empty room.

Zubin strode purposefully back to the lower level. He didn't wait for the elevator, taking the stairs instead. Irritated with the meeting, he felt the ghosts of his past shadowing him. He'd thought he had moved on, let go of the old memories—the famous Dr Ghosh, from a well-

respected scientist at the most prestigious hospital in the
world, had been reduced to a nobody. Dr Ghosh had
discreet meetings with a Russian man. There was an
exchange of papers, some phones had been tapped and
some pictures were evidence enough to accuse him of
espionage. The court case that proved his father was a spy
had ruined him. Conclusions were drawn that Dr Ghosh
had brought shame to the foundation. It was embarrassing
for the whole family, including his grandfather who had
been a well-respected politician. Their circle of friends
had diminished drastically and so had their wealth. They
moved away from Rochester and, soon after, Zubin sensed
the strain between his parents. The silent resentment
consumed them. Zubin hated his father, his grandfather
called him a bad seed and hoped Zubin wouldn't turn
into him. So had Zubin.

It was one giant downhill roll after that. His mother
died from a bad liver, and that strengthened his anger
towards his father, who had turned into a quiet man,
living in his room with his shame. He hadn't even had
the decency to talk to his own son, to explain his actions.
Maybe Zubin would have understood. Maybe he would
have taken his side. But the infamous Dr Ghosh spurned
him. Zubin left home as soon as he could. The seniors at
the foundation took care of him. Later he learned his
father had been moved to an old people's home.

He walked back to his lab, lost in the very past he had
struggled to forget.

'So you lost your job, eh?' Barry asked, reading his morose expression.

Zubin shook his head, glad to be back in familiar territory, in the present, amongst the dead and a cowboy lookalike friend.

'Nah, there was an immigration officer. He needed to personally check on all Americans of Indian origin. There's some fake identity scam going on. Needed to make sure I was a living, breathing human being with brown skin,' Zubin grinned.

'Aw shucks! You cost me twenty,' Barry declared and slapped this thigh.

'Okay then, drinks on me tonight,' Zubin said.

'That's great, we leave in an hour,' Barry said as he jumped up and sauntered out of his cubicle. He returned to the autopsy room, pulled on his eye goggles, picked up the electric saw and switched it on. His cadaver was ready.

*

Back home, Zubin felt good. The drinks and the company of his friends had eased the tension from his neck and his mind was abuzz. He hit the light switch in his living room and froze. There was a young girl sitting on his sofa, legs crossed, watching him eagerly. Zubin felt the sting on his knee when he banged against the table. 'Where did you—' his question was frozen midsentence.

'I've been waiting for you, Zubin,' she said in a gentle tone.

'Who are you?'

She looked vaguely familiar, as if he had met her recently. She looked hurt. There were bruises on her face, and her hair was matted with blood.

'Shall I call an ambulance? You look like you need a doctor,' he said hesitantly.

'You are a doctor, aren't you?' she smiled, revealing blood-stained teeth.

He picked up the receiver and began to dial, his fingers trembled and he tried to focus. Her stare was disconcerting.

'We met today, Zubin. Don't you remember me?' she asked sadly.

Then it hit him like a sledgehammer.

She was the dead girl from the dumpster! The one with the head bashed in, blood and brain everywhere. 'Dead' was the key word here, and it was ringing in his ears. His head spun, and he thought he would throw up. He tried to hold it together. One lesson that stuck to him from his memory of his father: face fear in the face.

He regarded her objectively, clinically, shutting out all the emotions that were crowding his thoughts.

Sitting up in a chair, she had one glassy eye focused on him, the other swollen shut. Her left leg hung at an odd angle.

His father's lesson was losing its sense. Damn it! A dead person was here, speaking to him, how can fear not grip him? And he felt panic return and slowly creep up his spine like thin feelers of ice. He tried to reason—he had had too much to drink, not enough food, not enough sleep, and he was hallucinating.

'I'm Naomi. You wished me a peaceful death. Thank you.' She smiled and it didn't help—she looked even more gruesome. 'And now I wish you a good life.'

'Thank you,' Zubin said automatically. 'How can I help you?'

'You work with the dead, but it's time to move on and work with the living. Your father was an intelligent man in his time, he was conned by evil people. They are all around, you know.' She spoke as if she was chatting on a girl's night out.

'My father? How—'

'He was your hero, wasn't he?'

Zubin was silent.

'It hurt more when he was accused of all those nasty things and in your heart you lost all respect for him. You wanted to be him when you grew up, isn't it?'

He shrugged. Zubin was still trying to grasp the idea of conversing with a dead person. And one who knew about his past.

'You have to start trusting people. Not the dead, but the living. Working in the morgue is your way of dealing with your father losing everything he worked so hard for.'

'Why don't you just leave me alone and rest in peace?' Zubin said mildly.

She looked hurt and then there was regret in her voice. 'It is difficult to let go of life, and now that I've lost it, I wish I had not said those nasty things to my mother.' Tears of blood rolled down her cheeks.

Zubin advanced from the back of the sofa and went to sit by her side. 'It's time to let go, Naomi,' he said. Zubin was sure she would disappear the moment he touched her. She was an illusion, and would be gone. But he could smell the strong odour of flesh and blood. There was a lingering aroma of roses and his mind screamed she was real. Her fingers curled round his neck—to Zubin it felt like a string of ice circling and filling his body with cold air. A shriek caught in his throat.

Zubin shot out of his chair. He stood for a moment taking in his surroundings. His heart galloped in his chest. All seemed normal. There was no one around. He relaxed a little, logic got the better of reality—it was just a crazy nightmare! And as he sighed in relief, his breath caught in his throat. On the table was a slim ring with a tiny red heart-shaped stone.

That morning, it had been on the dead girl's finger.

9

Amsterdam, Holland

Lise chewed gum noisily. Her reddish-brown hair was streaked with purple. A small stud shone on the side of her nose and two more on her ears. Dr Halvor knew about the other piercing when she had stuck her tongue out the first time he met her. He was shocked more by the sight of metal in her mouth than by her rude behaviour. Three years later, her oddities didn't bother him.

They were watching a television show and Lise made regular sounds of disbelief.

'You believe in that mumbo jumbo—spirits and the New Age stuff?' She returned to the kitchen, but she could watch both Dr Halvor and the television screen from her vantage point by the island table. 'The body is lifeless—that means nothing's functioning in the brain,' she added.

Dr Halvor narrowed his eyes, highlighting his bushy brows in a single row. 'In a coma, the body is not lifeless. See the hair and nails, how they grow,' he said, pointing to the TV that beamed the National Geographic show *Is It Real?*. 'The man's heart is beating, his eyes move. All this is life, and you don't know what makes all this happen?' He didn't wait for her response. 'It's vital energy, a universal energy that connects all of us.'

'You mean God? Well if there is God then there should be no suffering, right? And besides there's no proof that there is such a vital energy,' Lise responded sceptically. 'By the way, that energy inside me that's so pure and connected with all God's creatures makes me want to smoke. What shall I do about that, Doctor?' she said, chewing vigorously on her gum and giving him a little pat on his shoulder.

Dr Halvor chuckled. The girl had verve, and Lise knew he liked her brutal honesty. He couldn't resist continuing with the debate, 'You are a prisoner to your senses, but you are doing a good job controlling the urge. You have beaten your drug addiction, what's one more for a strong person like you, eh?'

'Strength is not the only thing I need right now. I take each day as it comes.'

'You are the first youngster I have met who has not mapped out a future, and yet I know you will go far. You just wait and see, my dear,' he reminded her.

'Thanks. I'm just working for you to impress the social worker,' Lise muttered, sipping coffee from a mug on the table while she attended to the dishes. 'If I were you, I wouldn't be so optimistic,' she added in the same breath. Her back was turned to him and although she didn't want to admit it, Dr Halvor came closer to a father figure than any other man in her life.

Three years ago her mind was nothing more than a haze waiting for the next hit. She needed the money and she had sunk to the worst possible state of slavery. She did whatever it took to get what she wanted. A small privately funded group pulled her out of her hellhole and helped her beat her addiction. They even arranged for a job for her—working for Dr Halvor. He was a retired professor, had suffered a stroke and needed assistance around the house. The seventy-five-year-old man took a liking to her. Odd man, she thought. Her abrasive personality didn't seem to irritate him. Most people were out to change her. Her mother didn't think much of her. She had just left her. But that was the past, and she should quit thinking about it.

Dr Halvor's attention was focused on the small screen. 'Special arrangements have been made for his care and for him to be kept alive. Aren't you the least bit curious about that?' he asked.

'Yes, very. I'm curious to know whether this guy has lots of money and whether he can leave some to me,' Lise said. She leaned against the sofa, and studied the green varnish on her short nails, a recent fetish she had developed after the streaks of purple in her hair: it made her look unapproachable and she liked it. 'It costs at least a million a month for this kind of special care. Let's face it, why would anyone want him alive? He is old, has lived a full life—they should let him go peacefully,' Lise frowned.

Dr Halvor gave her a lopsided smile. 'So, it is better off for me to be dead too?'

'Not you. I wouldn't mind if you lived to be a hundred. I'm talking about that guy in a coma— doesn't seem he's coming out of it.' Lise glanced at the screen and then shifted her attention to the kitchen. She washed the dishes and placed them on the stand. 'What do you want for dinner?' she called out as she placed the cutlery in the drawers and wiped the countertop in wide, sweeping motions.

'Soup, soup is good,' he replied, distracted by the flickering images on the screen. 'If I left you lots of money, would you do something for me?' he asked suddenly.

Lise nodded absent-mindedly, 'Of course.' She hummed as she took out some vegetables from the refrigerator. Placing them on the island table in the centre of the kitchen, she began grating and chopping. She had a clear view of Dr Halvor's profile. His face had taken on a pasty texture, and he wasn't blinking, as if his mind was somewhere else. 'Lise, it will be the strangest thing you will have ever done in your life. But you will keep an open mind. Yes?' he asked, turning towards her.

'Yes. But what are you thinking of? Not asking me to go to the moon, are you?'

'Maybe something as crazy as that,' he replied softly. Sometimes the doctor went off on a tangent, and rambled about strange places and people. She didn't know much about him, but she knew he had travelled extensively.

Lise got worried. The doctor was gaunt and appeared weaker as each day passed. She noticed his haggard face and that his body had turned to skin and bones. It was as if only his hair and his nails absorbed all the nutrients, like the coma patient on TV. He had been to the clinic but they said it was age, he would die eventually. She knew that life would be different for her after that. There was nowhere to go.

Lately, he had been acting strangely. She felt a twinge

of regret and wished that he would be alive forever so she could stay in this house, cocooned from the world, following the predictable day-to-day routine.

She shifted her attention back to the discussion. 'Crazy things cost a lot of money!' she laughed, and noticed the familiar smile spread across his face.

'Money no problem!' he chuckled.

'Dr Halvor, don't you worry,' she whispered as she peeled the potatoes. 'I will fatten you up and everything will be all right.' She didn't expect him to hear what she said.

Gurgling laughter emerged from Dr Halvor. 'You will, my dear. I know you will.'

*

It was late at night when she heard the sound of glass breaking. Lise was out of her bed in an instant and headed towards the direction of the sound. The house was in darkness but in the kitchen, straws of moonlight from behind grey clouds filtered through the window. The refrigerator door was ajar and shards of broken glass glittered on the tiled floor. She could make out Dr Halvor's shape, slumped against the kitchen cabinet.

Lise hurried to his side, kneeled down and felt his pulse: it was racing. 'Doc, what happened?' She tried to help him up, but he was too weak to move. Then she saw the blood spreading rapidly on his chest.

'No!' She grabbed a few kitchen towels and pressed

gently on his chest. The blood seeped out in seconds and turned the towels red.

She rushed to grab the phone. Then with cold dread, she saw that the kitchen window had been broken, the latch bent out of shape. A burglar! The doctor must have come to the kitchen at precisely that moment, and the burglar had stabbed him.

'It's too late . . .' he whispered, clutching her hand.

'Let me call an ambulance.' Lise hurriedly pressed the keypad. His cheeks were pale and his lips were turning blue. 'Don't die on me, please, please,' she whispered.

'It's too late,' he repeated. 'I should have known this was going to happen. You have to protect—' he gasped and took deep rasping breaths.

'No, no!' she screamed desperately. His hand was gripping hers. 'Don't give up. You have to hold on. I'll call for help.' Lise picked up the receiver.

'No!' he said, and it seemed to take most of his energy. He was panting. 'I want you to do something for me. Come here. Listen to me, this is urgent. You have to contact someone. I have vital information,' he rasped.

Lise tried to steady her breathing: there was no time to waste. She tried again to reach for the phone. 'First we need to get you to a hospital,' she insisted.

The air in the kitchen was distinctly dry and the refrigerator's fluorescent lamp flickered, reflected in the shards of glass on the floor. Shadows moved. Lise felt a shiver of fear raise the hair on her arms. Whoever did this

meant business, the attack on the old man was brutal—
his blood was everywhere.

The doctor took deep gurgling breaths and held on to
her hand with a steel grip. 'You have to keep secret the
keys of the Nine. You have to do this for them, the
protectors of this earth . . .' He spoke in a rush as if he
was counting his breaths.

'I don't understand.'

Dr Halvor was a professor of Asian Studies and knew
much about eastern cultures and their philosophies. He
told her stories about these places and he always made it
sound magical and beautiful. 'You will understand . . .'
he whispered. 'You have to, it is the only way. The monk
will guide you.'

Monk, what monk? She had only seen one long ago. An
elderly bald-headed monk wearing burgundy robes had
come to visit the doctor. It was the dead of winter, yet the
cold seemed to have no effect on him. One shoulder and
arm were completely bare. He appeared immune to the
freezing temperatures, standing in the softly falling snow.

'He has control over his senses and powers to regulate
the mind,' the doctor had told her after the monk had
left. And he had also told her they had to travel east—to a
place called Little Tibet in the heart of India. It was a trip
that took a lot of planning, application forms, supporting
documents and then finally, when she got the visa to
India, it made Dr Halvor a very happy man. The journey
to India had been uneventful, but when she landed on

Indian soil, it was as if she was an infant, experiencing everything for the first time—the whole atmosphere overloaded her senses. She walked around with a perpetually dropped jaw. And when they returned home, all Dr Halvor said was that it was good she had finally got the stamp on her passport that she had visited India— easier for next time. *Next time?*

'Just let me call the police. We'll get the guy who hurt you, Doctor!' Lise said, anger filtering her panic. The doctor was losing his grip on reality. She tried to extricate herself from his grip but he held on tight, as if she were his lifeline. And Lise was afraid he would die if she let go. 'Lise,' he said with such force, that instead of kneeling down, she sat down hard by his side. 'You will listen to me and listen carefully!' he whispered heavily.

'Let me . . .'

'Shut up, Lise, and listen. There is magic in the Nine,' he repeated. Then he spoke haltingly, 'It exists in the physical . . . powerful stone . . . not of this earth. Chintamani fragments.'

Lise pressed his hand and moved closer to his mouth. 'What?'

He turned to her and whispered, 'Nine. The soul of the Nine.'

'Nine what? Let me go,' she said, a sinking feeling in her stomach that he was losing his mind. 'I'm calling the ambulance.' He still clutched her, begging her not to move.

Moments passed and Lise waited for him to speak. She was about to dial but he stopped her again. 'Come closer,' he whispered. She did, and then, he pressed his forefinger and thumb on her forehead.

*

Lise was lying on her side when she woke up. She shifted and felt a sharp stab of pain in her left leg. For one frightening moment she thought she was back in the horrible rehab centre and any minute the girl with the matted hair and cat eyes would lean down and trail her sharp pointed nail on Lise's cheek. She was disoriented, trying to place herself but that awful dripping was distracting her. She turned to look and noticed that the leak was from the fridge door. She sat up quickly, and banged her head on the handle of the kitchen drawer. She massaged the bump and looked around her. Her mind drew a blank.

Sunlight brought tears to her eyes. *Why was she here on the kitchen floor? And Dr Halvor?* A flash of memory and she understood. He was still lying there—his face now a grey mask. Blood pooled around him—Lise didn't need to check his pulse. She clutched her knees to her chest, a fear had frozen her. 'I should have just called the ambulance last night,' she said bitterly. 'Why didn't you let me?' she cried out at his motionless body. Lise rocked back and forth, back and forth. She would be blamed for negligence. The people from the rehab centre would not be nice to her any more. It was always the same. Her past was like a shadow, always following her and then suddenly popping out in the spotlight.

Lise recalled from her rehab days the matted-haired girl with slit marks on her wrist. The girl occupied the top bunk bed. She had a bad habit of repeating a line in Lise's ear. *Once an addict, always an addict,* she would say over and over in the dark cold nights when sleep seemed as distant as the stars. Then one night she was silent. In the morning Lise discovered the girl had found a protruding screw from the bedpost and used it to cut her veins. Lise realized the only way out of the rehab prison was to survive. And she did. The doctors were optimistic. Lise was offered a place to start a new life. And she took it. If things did not work out, she could always take what she wanted and sneak out in the middle of the night. That way she would be free. This thought made her feel good. But then she met Dr Halvor, and he seemed to know what she was thinking. Once when she was sneaking out, he was sitting in the dark by the door. He held a kitchen knife and offered it to her—she could end her misery once and for all, or she could start chopping vegetables. He hadn't had one good meal since he came home from hospital, he said. There was something about Dr Halvor's challenge that made her smile, and she stayed.

From then, Dr Halvor had given Lise the security, the routine of a normal life, a simple existence where desires could easily be controlled with the power of the mind.

He'd said the mind was a secret powerhouse for everyone, they just didn't know it yet.

She closed her eyes, squeezed out the tears and then turned to him. 'Can't stay,' she whispered and reached out to touch his face. At that moment, an entire scene unfolded in her mind and she saw strange places in countries she had never visited before. The cities were named, and her mind mapped the jigsaw puzzle in a kaleidoscope of images. Lise jerked back and, almost by instinct, understood what had to be done. 'Goodbye Doctor, my saviour, I'll do the best I can.'

With trembling fingers she unlocked the bottom drawer of his study table. The money was in an envelope, folded and bound together with a rubber band. She slipped it into her pocket. She dashed to her room and threw a few clothes in a knapsack, divided the cash and hid it in her inside coat and trouser pockets. Little snippets of information were starting to filter into her mind. The doctor was a parapsychologist, and in her opinion, a mind controller, a hypnotist. He didn't like the term but now with the strange pictures emerging in her mind, she knew he had placed it there, in fact, positioned the information so carefully that she wouldn't be shocked by the revelations.

Lise could only repeat the four-letter word every time an image in her head fit into the puzzle. This could only be expected in a haze of drugs and alcohol and she was not on any medication. With a heavy heart and a sense of guilt hovering in the fringes of her mind, Lise left the house for the last time. Calling the police would put her in the forefront as a suspect. She knew she had to leave without alarming anyone. She would place an anonymous call to the police once she arrived at the airport and checked in. *There was no other way, Doctor, especially since you wanted me to get to my destination quickly.*

When Lise boarded the flight to Delhi, she heard his words inside her head: *My existence was purely to hold centuries-old information. I was the human treasure chest, and the treasure is now inside you. Keep it safe for there are many out there who will try to extract it from you. Be careful, for now you are not an ordinary human any more. You are the Knowledge Keeper.*

The soul of the Nine.

10

Tara

'I don't understand,' Tara said, canvassing the blanket of darkness. 'Am I totally disconnected from reality?' The rocky base of the Barabar Hills, a dark mass outlined in the horizon was slightly to the left of her view. She sat in a clearing and leaned against a rock as suggested by Dr Bose—the voice in her head. If her mother or brother discovered she was talking to a non-existent person, they would send her to an asylum. And if the villagers discovered her oddity, they would suggest special rituals performed by their shaman to rid her of evil spirits.

'Please explain, what's going on?' Tara pleaded. How soon the Kala Yogis would reach them she wasn't sure, but they were evil. She could sense it, like a palpable bubbling volcano ready to erupt. Even though an hour had passed, her heart still hopped like she was on an energy drink. Tara heard scraping sounds nearby, the footsteps of an animal. It was probably a deer, she knew there were no wild packs in this area—maybe some domestic animals had strayed from the farm. But then, she thought of snakes and how they might be slithering about at night. One might be right next to her. She shot up and jumped a little.

Can't you just sit still? How can I talk to you if you are so distracted by animals and snakes? he said exasperatedly.

Great, now he reads my mind. 'Okay. I'll be still.'

Tara continued to pace restlessly, a pendulum moving back and forth, back and forth.

Focus on what I'm about to tell you, Dr Bose insisted.

'I want you out of my head,' Tara responded out loud. 'How did you get inside in the first place?'

Power of the mind and my dead spirit. And I'm one of the Nine.

'Great!' Tara said, shaking her hands in the air in frustration, 'Now I'm possessed by a number.'

It's only temporary. I don't want to stay in your mind either. He sounded matter-of-fact, which irritated Tara even more.

'Why? What's wrong with my mind?'

He sighed heavily. *Nothing wrong with your mind, it's just that I'm not used to so much emotion.* He sounded impatient.

'You would get disturbed too if you were possessed by some dead spirit while doing your job as a nurse.' Tara folded her arms across her chest, staring at a rock.

Okay, fine. I would be just as upset and concerned. I apologize, he said in a resigned tone.

Tara accepted his apology. 'Thank you. That was very understanding of you. Now I want the truth,' she said, still pacing restlessly.

I'll tell you the truth. You young people have no patience. Life is not about rushing through everything. Now sit down. All this walking is making me dizzy.

Now I know how to get rid of you. Hope you heard that one, Dr Bose.

I'm sorry to intrude into your mind, but first tell me, have you ever heard about the Council of Nine?

'That's a legend,' Tara replied. 'I've heard about it. But not from my history books. They mention the official story about King Ashoka. He was one of the greatest rulers of the Mauryan dynasty. He converted to Buddhism after he killed a hundred thousand men in a war against the Kalingans. But yes, I have heard about the other stories. The ones that are myths and fairy tales—about Ashoka's secret society to protect the vast reserves of knowledge from evil men.'

It is all true. Not a myth.

'Load of crap.'

Really? And the fact that I sawed through half my foot proves nothing to you? Dr Bose retaliated.

Tara covered her ears and shook her head. 'Will you stop shouting? In case you forgot, you are inside my head.'

Sorry, but this is important for you to understand. The Council of Nine has been appointed as the guardian of all knowledge. Knowledge that is so powerful, so defiant of all that we understand as scientists. That knowledge is kept safe within the minds of the great Nine masters. And also in an object—the Chintamani stone. If found by the wrong kind of people, it would destroy the very existence of the Nine, and this world as we know it. These powerful nine men live amongst us but they carry the most potent knowledge—knowledge that could change the world. Time and again they share that information when the world needs it.

'Yes. Very nice bedtime story.'

A pause, and then Dr Bose spoke again. *There are many Indian scientists who were rumoured to have been among the Nine unknown men, and from time to time, if a Westerner should visit India and then do something astounding, he is considered to have had their help. Like Louis Pasteur, and Pierre Paul Émile Roux who created vaccines for rabies and diphtheria. Jagdish Chandra Bose, an Indian pioneer in radio and microwave optics, was also a member.*

'That's far-fetched and just theories—there's no proof or evidence,' Tara said, dismissing his claims. 'Next you will say that Einstein was a believer and was in contact with the Nine.'

There was silence.

'Come on! You're kidding,' Tara said, hands on hips, staring at the rock.

Dr Bose was serious. *You are now destined to be one of Ashoka's men. Dr Kuruvella, Professor Gupta and I—our identities have been discovered by the Kalingan spirit that destroyed us. This Kalingan spirit in the body of a human is capable of destroying the power of the Nine. You and two other men are destined to take over from us. The other six are alive and well in a safe location.*

The vast expanse of the sky seemed quietly suspenseful. It seemed that any minute a spacecraft would emerge and Tara would believe in the unbelievable. She glanced up and the stars were like a million eyes watching her. 'I don't understand. Destined? Two men? How do you know the future?'

We don't know the future. All we know is that you and two young men from outside India are the chosen ones to replace us. Yes. There are two others. The Council of Nine, six at the moment, has discussed and decided on the three of you.

'But I just happened to be there. How can I be the chosen one?'

Nothing just happens. You are meant to be one of the

Nine. The three, including me, have been killed in body by the spirit of the Kalingan himself and you are one of the replacements. This power is of truth and knowledge. You and the two other men will learn more about the secret society, and carry forward the special knowledge to the next generation. You absolutely cannot let it fall into the wrong hands or it will be the end of the world as we see it today.

Dr Bose became quiet. Tara asked, 'If this was meant to be a men-only society, why don't you find someone else?'

Tara, people change with the times. You have been chosen, you will bring the female shakti element to the power of the Nine. You will be the balance, the nurturing sensitive strength. The Kala Yogis have become more intensely vicious over the centuries. They are hunting us down. I was one of the Nine, and even though we kept our identities secret, they were able to find us. We have been compromised, three are dead and the knowledge may have leaked into the wrong hands. We have to fight to keep the knowledge safe. And the Chintamani crystal that carries the knowledge of the past centuries.

I hand over the responsibility to you. I can see you have a strong spirit, though you are, if I may say so, slightly stubborn. And you will achieve your goals and do what is right. Tara began to say something, but he cut her off. This is difficult, I understand, but it has to be done. The power of hate, revenge and anger is much stronger, more intense in this yuga. The world is not as it used to be. The knowledge is sacred and must be kept safe.

'Knowledge? What kind? Is it a power, and will it make me superior to the rest?' Tara asked.

Don't let your ego get in the way. It will only diminish your energy. Remember, whatever you do from now on is for the benefit of mankind, Dr Bose admonished her.

Tara sat down and waited for him to continue. She had no thoughts to express the impact of his words. Emotionally charged, she felt fear and panic. There was a niggling doubt that she had gone insane. And the other side of her was trying to absorb and accept what he said.

Fear is the most paralysing emotion of the human mind. You will conquer this weakness—the monk will complete you. But you will have to go to him. You are one of the Nine. You have the power of communication, as we are doing right now. It means you have the knowledge of all means of communication, terrestrial and extraterrestrial. You have the gift to read minds, connect emotionally and align with the thoughts of others. This is no ordinary gift, it is the very understanding of the human mind and its thought processes. Use it carefully and you can't even begin to imagine the good you can do in this world, Tara.

Tara sat alone on the rock—quiet for once, her mind still. She knew she had to now plan how to go about her mission.

11

Calcutta, West Bengal

Akash arrived at the airport, and when he disembarked, not only did the malodorous heat hit him, but it also struck him that there was no walkway to the terminal! Akash and Tashi had to board a dilapidated bus. Akash twisted in his seat, he was sitting on stones. The bus jerked harder as if to remind him where he was. India— the land of sadhus.

As if that wasn't enough of a shock, at the exit gate from the airport, Akash experienced his first mob attack. He was surrounded by a dozen dirty faces begging for money. *India—the land of beggars.* He didn't realize he had said it out loud.

As they headed towards the taxi stand, which was across a dusty stretch of road, Tashi admonished him. 'Watch what you say, Akash. Poverty is not the only definition of India.' Tashi moved purposefully forward, as if the oncoming traffic wasn't any of his concern. 'You criticize India, you criticize yourself—after all, this is still your motherland.'

Akash didn't say anything in response, although muttering under his breath had become a habit ever since he had met Tashi. His bodyguard, the monk who got him from his home to the van in the midst of gunshots, then sealed his destiny by taking him to the airport and on to a flight to India, was an obnoxious, over-the-top, cynical and irritating man. Akash was torturously discovering Tashi's traits. Besides being arrogant, self-righteous and overbearing, he was also a patriot.

Akash followed Tashi, pushing the disobedient trolley along the bumpy route towards the taxi stand. He hit a stone: one of the wheels began circling and it stalled. Akash gave it a hard shove, it jerked forward and banged against Tashi's ankle. Akash didn't mean to hurt him, but the monk turned back and glowered at him. Akash apologized, but got no acknowledgement from the angry monk. He continued to lead, arms moving back and forth energetically.

Akash trod carefully behind him. When he made it to Tashi's side, he tried one last line of defence. 'Look, I'm sorry. I didn't mean to make any derogatory remarks. My life's goal wasn't to come to India and fight an unknown enemy. And all this is new to me. If I see something that shocks me, then I have a right to voice my opinions.'

Tashi paused bang in the path of a taxi driver, making him honk wildly and yell obscenities at him. Tashi faced him with menace in his expression, and then turned to Akash. 'I didn't choose to be your bodyguard either. Unfortunately, Jona's death has led me here to be with you, which wasn't my life's purpose,' Tashi said in a clipped tone. 'So if you don't mind, please keep your fancy British opinions to yourself until I get you to your destination.'

Akash didn't respond to his outburst; his first thought was to get out of the way of the taxi, which was inching dangerously close to them. In the nick of time, Tashi turned and strode ahead.

They waited in silence at the taxi stand. Akash turned on his iPod and nodded to the music. Tashi gave him periodic glares and eyed the crowd of people suspiciously. When it was their turn, they hopped into the cab. Tashi instructed the driver to go to the Howrah railway station. The wide-faced driver introduced himself as Raju, and gave them a broad grin. Akash smiled back, while Tashi gave him warning looks, regularly raising his eyebrows. As he drove, Raju furnished a rundown of Bollywood news, and how Bengali actresses were the most beautiful even to this day. Akash enjoyed the bits and pieces of Hindi that he could understand. Taking a circuitous route, with Tashi fuming quietly, they finally reached the station. And the driver asked for Rs 500.

That's when Akash discovered one more of Tashi's traits—he didn't like being cheated. Never in his life could he imagine a monk giving a taxi driver the choicest abuses. 'What are you waiting for?' Tashi yelled at Akash. 'Get the bags before this conniving driver steals them.'

'Yes, boss.' Akash replied and hurried to retrieve their gear from the boot. He didn't notice how much money Tashi finally handed over. He didn't care and wanted to get away from this crazy monk. Akash had a headache the size of a freaking coconut and he could kill for a cup of his espresso, which reminded him of his coffee machine at home.

They bought tickets to Gaya. The early morning commuters were starting to crowd the station. It was eight o'clock and they had over an hour before the train departed.

'Follow me,' Tashi said, folding the tickets and tucking them into his large cloth bag. Akash wanted to retort: *That's what I've been doing for the last twenty-four hours like a faithful dog.*

Up ahead there was a restaurant, more like a coffee house. It was just opening and the aroma of freshly brewed tea and, yes coffee, calmed his nerves. Food was displayed on a plate and despite Tashi's disapproving stare, Akash chose the omelettes. The monk picked a vegetarian dish—Indian puris and potatoes glinting with oil.

Sitting in a quiet corner, rejuvenated by the coffee and the breakfast, Akash leaned back and stretched his hands behind his head. He observed Tashi from across the table, eating with gusto, fingers and all. They had been together for over a day and there were moments when Akash felt like wringing the man's neck. Now he felt differently: the guy was doing the best he could to get a Brit, totally ignorant of India and its gun-toting murderers, to an ancient site in India without losing him. He could see the strain on his face. Tashi was exhausted, there were dark circles around his eyes, his forehead was creased with worry lines and his shoulders were tense.

'You're not really a monk, are you?' Akash asked.

'Geez, what gave me away, Akash?' the man smiled coldly. He called for a finger bowl. 'You're right, I'm not a monk. I'll let you in on a little secret. I'm a trained soldier, ex-Indian army, was on the Pakistan border and fought off a few rebels. I've worked for the anti-terrorists unit in England for countless years, focusing on the Asian cells of terrorist action.'

Akash looked at him incredulously. 'And you're my bodyguard?'

'Unfortunately, yes. Sometimes we have to take up assignments we don't like. I had to play babysitter to you. I'm involved with a special agency of a branch of the government that likes to deny we exist.' With that, Tashi, if that was his real name, paid for the food and got up. His face shone in the scaly light of the restaurant. The burgundy robes and matching sweater hid his muscular physique. Damn, Akash was with a real, live spy. That was something. But Tashi was nowhere near a 007 lookalike.

'What's your real name?' Akash asked as they left the restaurant.

'What's wrong with Tashi?' he smirked.

They hopped onto the train and found their seats by the window. 'Go to sleep, Akash. You need your rest where you're going.'

This time Tashi wasn't being sarcastic. Akash closed his eyes, and fell asleep instantly.

12

Minneapolis, Minnesota, USA

The drive was leisurely. And Zubin would have had a pleasant time with the lilting tunes of Shafqat Ali Khan and his thoughts. But the classified information of his father's work raised a million questions. And mainly it was, *How the f*** did he accelerate his scientific process?* Research took years, and thousands of trials and errors.

But what his father had achieved was entirely different. It was magical! And dangerous.

The more he thought about it, the more Zubin felt a sense of uneasiness weighing on his chest. The history of the secret society was vivid. There were government conspiracies, political involvement, large corporations buying information at all costs, power-hungry terrorists who wouldn't think twice before destroying lives and reputations to gain the secret knowledge. And then there were the Nine unknown men—who anonymously furnished the required knowledge to scientists working on the theories. The knowledge had to be kept safe, just as it had been for over a millennium.

Until now.

He would be at the home in fifteen minutes, and he wasn't sure why, but he knew that after he met his father, his life would change completely. As if on cue, his cell phone rang.

Zubin glanced at the caller ID before he answered his hands-free. It was Tarun Vaz.

'I'm driving.'

'On the way to visiting your father?'

'Yes,' he replied. But the question was a waste of time. Zubin had informed him yesterday. Why didn't he just get to the point?

'You have to hurry. There is a . . . situation. Wait for me at the home, after you have spoken to him. Don't leave the residence; I'm on my way,' Tarun said.

Silence.

'You heard me?' Tarun's voice was hard.

Zubin felt his hands tremble. He gripped the wheel tighter. 'Right. I'll wait,' he said and hung up. He had arrived.

Zubin sat in his car for a few minutes and then stepped out. The Cherry Tree Assisted Living Residence was set on a beautiful stretch of land. It was a sprawling one-storeyed brick building, which spread out and connected to different coloured blocks of residences.

Security was tight, and even though Zubin had called ahead to inform them that he was coming, the guard at the gate double-checked his identification and used a device to look under his car. Another guard in a buggy led him to the visitors' parking area and a designated spot.

The pleasant setting, the flower-lined paths and the mini gardens projected a perfect image for marketing, where caregivers helped and guided the elderly. Some sat in wheelchairs or on benches, and some shuffled; some used walking sticks and some walkers.

The receptionist gave him a warm, professional smile. 'How may I help you?'

'I called yesterday. I'm here to see Dr Ghosh.'

She checked on her computer, asking him for details like his address and phone number. When she was satisfied, she looked up and smiled at him, 'Please have a seat, someone will be here to take you to him.' She used her phone to call someone and then returned to her computer.

As he waited in the plush lobby, he read the large plaque with names of donors etched in gold, prominently displayed on a large wall.

'Mr Zubin Ghosh?' A young woman wearing a neat skirt suit and a gold badge with 'Anne' on it, greeted him.

'Yes.' He turned and nodded.

'Please come with me.' She led him towards a closed door, opened it and walked into a long corridor. Zubin followed her and couldn't avoid noticing the well-lit and brightly coloured walls. The lemony scent of a car freshener hung in the air, but it could not hide the musty smell of old age. A few residents who passed by nodded and said hello.

'All men on this side?' Zubin asked as they turned a corner. They passed portraits of famous scientists and personalities from the past. There was even one of Mahatma Gandhi.

'This block is for our special residents.' Anne didn't explain further. Her heels clacked efficiently as they made their way past a number of doors. Finally, she turned a sharp right and stopped. She knocked on the door, 'Mr Ghosh?'

Someone needed to inform her that he was Dr and not Mr. But Zubin remained silent. She pushed open the door. Zubin stepped inside with her anxiously. He hadn't seen his father in over a decade, and now it was time to face him.

An elderly man with wild grey hair was sitting in an armchair, his back to them. He faced the brilliant view of the hothouse garden just outside his French window. Even though it was winter, the riot of floral blooms was breathtakingly beautiful. The bed was neatly made, and a low side-table had a phone, a notepad and a pen. On the other side stood a floor lamp. The room was impersonal, as if the resident had only lived there for two days, not ten years. The only other décor in the room consisted of a small cabinet of drawers next to the armchair. There were at least ten small black and white photos of Zubin and his mother.

As Zubin walked past them, the frames of tiny pictures—snapshots of times past—jolted him with memories of the bond they had once shared. A deep sense of regret erupted from the well of bitter disappointment he'd kept bottled up.

'How are you today, Mr Ghosh?' Anne said, leaning

towards his father. 'You have a visitor,' she announced in a chirpy voice. Zubin stayed behind her.

His father was still for a minute. Then he slowly turned his head towards her. Zubin caught his profile. That familiar hawk nose and high receding forehead was still distinct. And if Zubin recalled correctly, his father had a piercing gaze. But he was different now. Age and illness had mauled him. There was a pull on his cheek, as if his face had fallen on one side. His eyelid twitched and his voice was muffled. 'Who is it?' he asked, with the same deep resonance in his voice.

'Come and take a look, Mr Ghosh,' Anne said.

The senior Ghosh used his cane to stand up slowly. Zubin wanted to tell her to let him be, he could easily pull up a chair, but he didn't. Part of him wanted to see his father stand tall. He would have preferred it that way.

When Dr Ghosh was steady on his feet and faced Zubin, Anne smiled brightly at them. 'Just press this buzzer if you need me.' She pointed to the button on the floor next to the armchair.

Zubin didn't look at her. 'Thank you, Anne,' he said as he turned to her. 'And one more thing, he is Dr Ghosh.'

Zubin knew she couldn't have missed the waves of emotion between father and son. It was thick with regret and guilt. She nodded and gave them a stiff smile. When she shut the door, silence descended on them like a still winter night.

Zubin's father's lopsided face indicated he had had a

stroke. But it must have been some years back. He had some mobility now. His left arm shook and he grasped it with his right hand to hide the tremors. He peered at Zubin. 'Come closer so I can see your face,' he said.

Hadn't he recognized his own son? Zubin almost felt relieved. He was about a foot away from him when his father said, 'So, you've finally forgiven me?'

Ever the tough guy.

'Yes, father. I forgive you.'

'I was falsely accused. Did you know that?' He indicated a chair next to the window, and limped back slowly to his armchair.

'Yes.'

'Why have you come?'

'You know why.' Zubin almost said Dad, but he held back, he couldn't bring himself to say it yet.

'Are you a religious man, Zubin?'

What had that got to do with anything? He noticed a slight lift of the right side of his mouth, and the single raised eyebrow. His father was smiling.

'No, I'm not particularly of any faith.'

'So do you believe in a God, or the concept of God?'

He wasn't sure where this was going. 'I have a scientific basis for my belief. I don't go to a temple or follow ritualistic worship, if that's what you mean.'

Dr Ghosh smiled again. 'You're not part of some extreme religious group, are you?'

Zubin shook his head. 'A universal energy exists and connects us all.'

'New Age stuff, eh?' His father's eyes twinkled, teasing him.

'If you like to put it that way, but it's actually a code name for God,' Zubin said with a grin.

'That's a good place to be,' his father said. 'But we are not here to discuss religion, are we?'

'No. It's about India,' Zubin said. 'It's about the Nine unknown—'

Dr Ghosh raised his hand. 'I know. The Council is meant to be kept a secret.' His eyes locked onto a distant point above Zubin's head. 'It's been an honour to know Dr Kuruvella. His knowledge was astounding, saved me time and money on research. My work was well recognized; appreciated by the scientific community. But when you fall from grace, no one respects you or all that hard work. Unfortunately, after some men made up stories that I had faked the results, things changed.'

Zubin leaned forward, breathless after learning about the theory, about the secret that men had died to discover.

Dr Ghosh said, 'Electromagnetic force or charge is a fundamental power of the universe. It determines the structure of all atoms and molecules and how they interact. Since all chemical, biological and molecular interactions are fundamentally electromagnetic, there is a technique that has been around for centuries, the power to heal.'

Zubin shook his head. 'This is all a myth, bedtime stories. And about the ancient secret society, there is no proof that it exists today.'

Dr Ghosh's lopsided smile was triumphant. 'That's why it has survived for a millennium, through lost civilizations. The Ancients have maintained the secrecy of this society by avoiding all forms of religious, social or political agitations. Deliberately and perfectly concealed from the public eye, each of the Nine was the incarnation of the ideal man of science: aloof, yet aware of his moral obligations. They live amongst us, interact with us but have a higher responsibility and power. They are, in fact, the perfect guides for modern mankind. You must understand that the human mind is the most dangerous weapon! We would have annihilated ourselves if the world knew who they were. The Council of Nine has maintained the sanity, peace and knowledge required for progress.' He tapped his cane to emphasize his point.

Dr Ghosh got out of his well-worn armchair with effort. His shoulders were hunched, and his hair as messy as Einstein's. Zubin felt a surge of pride in his heart— *This is my father! The strong man, the righteous man!*

He watched his father as he leaned on his cane and moved slowly towards the cabinet crowded with their family photographs. He turned away and picked up one of the smaller photo frames, staring at it for a while. Then he turned to Zubin.

Dr Ghosh's eyes were moist. 'Take this—it will remind you of our bond.'

Zubin took the frame and instinctively leaned forward and gave his father a hug. There was some awkwardness but it felt good to reconnect with him. He was his hero, the great scientist, the father, and the man who had sacrificed everything to keep the truth safe.

They separated. Dr Ghosh patted him on the cheek. 'I have followed your career. I know you have worked hard to be where you are but your destiny lies elsewhere. I am proud that my son will join the ranks of the Nine. You have to uphold this position for the future of mankind.'

Zubin nodded.

Dr Ghosh looked at him long and hard. 'I have to sit down now.'

Zubin waited till he was comfortably settled, then he touched his feet and quietly left the room. Tarun Vaz was waiting for him in the lobby. He led him out of the building, walking at a brisk pace. 'They are on their way here. We will take you to the airport; there's a flight to India that leaves in two hours. You will be on it.'

The cold air was harsh and biting. The wind had picked up suddenly. 'I have to get some things from home. I drove here.'

'You cannot return to your home or place of work.' They reached the car park. 'We will take care of your car.' Vaz directed him to the black van. A black-clothed man with a gun and a grim expression was waiting in the back for him. He watched him intently. There was another similarly attired man in the front with the driver, armed too, Zubin guessed.

'My father . . .'

Vaz smiled, 'Don't worry, we know how to protect one of our own. He will be safe.'

*

A long-range satellite picked up the movement. And a short message was sent to a mobile phone: 'He has made contact. They will take him to India.'

13

Dharamsala, Himachal Pradesh

Lise stood at the very edge of the gorge. The wind was crisp and whipped at her from all sides. Laced with wood smoke, cowdung and the scent of pine trees, the air filling her lungs was a new experience of this strange land. At either end of the north–south valley stretched stunning glacier views. And on the adjacent slope, waterfalls like silver threads glistened in the sun. The precipice dropped a hundred feet but that wasn't as vivid as the sight straight ahead. The snowy mountains formed a backdrop to a scene so breathtaking that she was rooted to the spot. A small village was nestled in the midst of the mountains with a misty glow rising from it like coils of white. She could barely make out a lake. As she craned her neck to get a better view, she drew in her breath sharply—there were a dozen or more women bathing in it, looking like nymphs in paradise. If only she could make it across . . .

'Not planning to take a leap, are we?' She hadn't even noticed the monk standing next to her until he spoke.

There was a warmth in his eyes that touched her heart, and a sense of bliss enveloped her. Or maybe it was the magical effect of the vision that made her all vulnerable and sentimental. She shook off the feeling. 'It's so beautiful . . . heavenly . . .' Lise said, gazing into the distance. Seconds passed; then, aware of the monk's silence, she introduced herself.

The monk smiled benevolently: he understood the effect his land had on people. 'Welcome to our country!' he said with a slight bow and joined hands.

'Thank you,' Lise responded awkwardly. She wasn't sure if she should follow the same form of greeting and bow down with joined hands. 'I need to get to the Monastery of the Enlightened Ones. Can you tell me how to get there?'

'Who do you want to meet at the monastery?'

'I must meet Gedun Rinpoche,' Lise said, trying to pronounce it correctly.

'Why?'

Not used to revealing her intentions to strangers, she felt uncomfortable with his curiosity. She recalled the doctor's words of caution to her to be careful. Lise didn't want to be rude either. 'I have a message for him,' she replied vaguely, hoping that he wouldn't probe further.

He paused, noting her discomfort. 'I see.'

Lise had managed to get this far. It was Dr Halvor's

snippets of information that had helped her get from Europe to Asia and then finally to India. It was difficult enough trying to answer the question 'Why?' in her own head without having another person ask her to explain.

She pointed towards the dusty path, hoping the old man would direct her. A bent sign indicated the way towards a village or monastery, she wasn't sure.

'Yes,' he said, nodding. 'This is the right way.' She started towards the track. The monk spoke again, 'You will need some help to get there—it is a very complicated path that you have chosen.'

Lise turned to him; he was by her side already and she felt comforted by his presence. His smile revealed a gap in his front teeth, and fanning out from the corners of his eyes were deep wrinkles. 'I will show you the way.' *That grin would get him anywhere!*

She nodded and returned a half-hearted smile.

Encouraged, he kept pace with her. His maroon robes swung comfortably around his large, stooped frame. Her jeans and T-shirt clung to her body, making her wish she had worn something lighter, looser. She would change once she arrived at her destination, she thought.

Change. That was what she was going through. It was a simple word—hardly strong enough to define her life, her whole existence. Transformation was what had happened, turning her world upside down. In fact, she felt she was becoming someone else, a different identity in her body. An unusual sense of lightness surged through her, and she felt gratitude for experiencing a renewal of hope. She was determined to fulfil what she had set out to do.

To her right, the slope was covered with shrubs and trees, and to her left, the earth fell away into rolling fields interspersed with brown earth. On the flatter plains, herdsmen, horses and sheep clustered in small groups like small, colourful toys. Lise took a deep breath and her eyes watered, but she smiled instead. For the first time, the air that went deep into her lungs felt like happiness. Every now and then the monk gave her a broad smile, pointed at some idyllic location and waited for her to take it all in. It seemed more important to feast with the eyes and breathe and enjoy the journey rather than rush towards her purpose. As they walked, the sound of the dry crunch of his sandals and of her shoes interrupted the oddly comfortable silence between them.

Following a well-worn sloping trail, they reached a village. The aroma of food being cooked wafted towards her, reminding her of the twenty-four-hour journey she had just made with barely any hot food to sustain her. She felt almost giddy with hunger.

'I will leave you here. My friend's rest house is just around that corner,' he said pointing towards a herd of sheep turning left into a path. 'It's like a hotel, but more homely.'

'Where is the Monastery of the Enlightened Ones? And it is urgent that I meet Gedun Rinpoche.' Lise panicked that he would leave her.

'You are tired and your body must rest before you can meet the Rinpoche. This is a small town, you can find him in the morning.'

'You will not come?'

'No, Lise. I was just making sure you got here and there were no obstacles in your path.'

'But what is your name?'

'I am Wangdak.' He bowed and joined his hands again. This time, Lise did the same.

'Stay well, Lise.'

Lise didn't have the energy to argue. She nodded tiredly. The jet lag was getting to her. She just realized it was 3 a.m. on the other side of the world. She needed sleep, but first, something to eat.

14

Gaya, Bihar

The Rainbow Guesthouse in Bodh Gaya was cheap and cheerful. Tara followed her guide through the main street; off Gaya Road, they continued past the Mahabodhi Temple to the intersection at the end of the lane. Across the road they turned right and there stood Rainbow Guesthouse, justifying its name to a T.

Amongst the rows of guest houses, Rainbow stood out in a riot of bright colours. Tara went inside, relieved to find an atmosphere resembling a city. There was a restaurant bustling with activity. A few tourists hung around a desk where a harried woman tried to organize a tour over the phone. Tara headed towards the reception desk. A young man in an ill-fitting suit welcomed her and introduced himself as Mohan. When she asked for a single room, he licked his thumb and finger to turn the pages of his poster-size thick register. It was yellowing and dog-eared.

'We have rooms on the second floor only. First floor is full. You don't mind walking up the stairs, do you?'

Tara said it would be okay.

'That will be Rs 200 a night, taxes not included,' he informed, handing her a form to fill out. Tara turned to look for her guide. He was standing outside, near the entrance to the lobby. She indicated to him to come inside but he shook his head solemnly.

'He is an assisting monk; he won't enter. The hotel has a rajasic atmosphere, which is forbidden to him,' the receptionist explained.

Tara didn't quite understand and headed towards him. 'Why do you not enter?'

'Too much raja–tama—imbalance of emotions and thoughts—here. I must return to the dharma centre. I am still in training and now is the time for meditation. I will take your leave now,' the young boy said, joining his hands in a namaste.

'Thank you for bringing me here, Kipa.' She joined her hands as well. Tara watched him blend into the crowd of similarly attired young boys-in-training.

She returned to the reception desk to fill out the form.
'You are here alone, madam?' Mohan asked.

'Actually, I'm expecting some friends in a few days.'

Tara wondered if Karan would come and meet her so
that she could explain what was going on. The last time
she'd sent him a message he had sounded upset. And she
couldn't say, 'Oh, by the way, I've got this ability to
communicate telepathically. A scientist killed himself,
possessed me and passed on the gift.' *Definitely not your
ordinary telephone conversation!* Even if she tried
explaining face-to-face, it would take some time for it to
sink in.

The other two chosen ones were on their way. As to
who they were, and where they belonged, she was totally
clueless. It would take them a few days more, she was
told. In the meantime, the monk at the monastery
suggested she should stay there, it was safe in Bodh
Gaya—the land of Buddha's enlightenment. The
Kalingans were powerless here.

With renewed energy, Tara climbed the stairs two at a
time. Yes, she would call up Karan and ask him to spend
a few days with her. That was a good plan.

She dumped her belongings on the bed, turned on her
cell phone and dialled. He picked up on the second ring.
Tara sensed a resistance just from his 'Hello'. 'What's up?
Finally found a reason to call me?' he said by way of a
greeting.

Something wasn't right—she could feel it in her

bones—but she didn't want to analyse it just yet. This was her Karan, her big, strong, handsome Karan. She imagined him on the other side. He loved her and she loved him. It had only been a couple of months since they were apart and although he did try to call, it had been less and less frequent over the last month. Maybe because their conversation had ended on: 'It's not just about spirituality, it's more serious than that.' She needed to explain it to him.

'I'm in Gaya. Bodh Gaya actually. Can you take time off to meet me?' Tara asked.

'Why don't you return to your life, to me?' he retorted instead.

Tara leaned against the window. She closed her eyes, there was a throbbing pain starting at the base of her neck. 'Please, Karan, it's difficult for me to explain everything over the phone. And please try and understand it is difficult for me to leave this place now. I'm at a vulnerable stage. There is a situation . . . I need to see you in person,' she said painfully.

'Why? Are you in trouble? Someone kidnapped you? What's going on?' Her Karan was back. He was anxious, he still cared for her!

'I'm . . . fine, Karan, but I need to see you. Please come here, please—for us. I do love you.'

There was a reluctant sigh. 'Okay. I'll come by this weekend. Tell me where you are staying.'

She told him. Before she could say goodbye, static

interrupted her conversation and the phone went dead. Just as well. She fell head first on the bed and realized how tired she was.

15

Akash

The train screeched to a halt. Tashi waited impatiently for Akash to collect his things. They had two minutes to get off the train, he said. *Why two minutes?* And he repeatedly clicked his fingers at Akash as if to tell him, 'Don't waste time.'

The coolies had already hopped onto the train carrying baggage of various shapes and materials. There were long tin boxes, plastic bags, large bales made out of bedsheets knotted up in the middle. Just standing there, feeling the rush of people assault his senses, was an experience in itself.

But Tashi was all about getting to the destination and not enjoying the journey. Even when he woke up after a restless two hours of pendulum-sleep on the train, and needed the toilet, Tashi went with him and knocked on the door a dozen times to tell him to hurry up. When they returned to their seat, Tashi, the ever-alert spy, was monitoring his surroundings. Akash, the groggy, tired, jet-lagged weakling just wanted to flop down and sleep on a still, warm bed.

'No, the journey doesn't end in Gaya. Akash, what

were you thinking?' Akash thought he heard *stupid fool* at the end of the sentence but the Howrah Express's noisy ride had weakened his hearing. Tashi pointed two fingers at his own eyes and then connected them to Akash's. 'Focus,' he was saying. And after that, Tashi gesticulated with his two fingers repeatedly, in response to which Akash was tempted to use his middle finger! The journey was getting to both of them.

Blocking the exit door was a kid who just wouldn't jump off the train. Tashi yelled at the parents to get him out of the way. Within seconds, the mother got her kid away from the angry monk. Tashi's adrenalin was high, he hopped off and turned to watch his companion. Akash threw his bag down on the platform and jumped off, landing on his feet. He collected his things and they briskly made their way to the exit.

'There's a car waiting for us,' Tashi said. They found the white Land Rover and were on their way to the Barabar Hills. They were 20 kilometres into their silent journey when the driver said, 'We are being followed.' He was wearing wraparound sunglasses that complemented his strong jaw. A perfect face for a bouncer back in England, Akash thought.

Tashi checked the rear-view mirror. 'Lose them.'

The driver turned right, off the main Gaya–Patna road. Both sides of the road were broken by mounds of rock and a vast expanse of tilled land. There were farmers in the middle of the field. 'On this route, it's a narrow

NINE   135

bypass towards the Barabar Hills. The road is potholed and difficult to speed on.' The black car was still tailing them and getting closer.

'They don't seem to care that we've noticed them,' Tashi noted.

The crunching sound of the wheels and the rush of the wind on a scenic route would ordinarily be soothing to the nerves, but Akash felt a strong sense of panic that was only rising.

A spray of bullets hit their car. The windscreen at the back burst and showered them with shards of glass. 'Get down, get down!' Tashi yelled at Akash, pushing his head down. 'Go, go, step on it! Speed it up!' Tashi shouted. The driver stamped on the accelerator but the uneven road was an obstacle course in speeding. They were only a few yards ahead when the next round of bullets flushed them off the road. The driver went off-track, breaking through the green saplings, splashing irrigated mud all around. The black car was now neck and neck with them. And this time, they had a headshot on the driver. The car veered to one side as Tashi tried to control the steering.

'You have to get off the other side!' Tashi ordered. Akash realized what he was saying—jump out of a speeding car. *No way! He wasn't trained for this shit!* 'Do it, do it now, Akash, get off!' Tashi insisted.

Working purely on adrenalin and reflex, Akash pushed open his door, and amidst the rushing green, he jumped out, rolling some distance away until he hit his shoulder against a rock. He stayed low, stunned, his heart hammering in his chest. He saw the Land Rover continue its maniacal course until it slammed into a tree and burst into flames. Three men emerged from the black car.

Some distance away, Akash noticed Tashi clutching a bleeding stomach and crouching in the mud. He crawled to his side. The two-feet-high crops hid them from view.

'Listen, you have to get to the Lomas Rishi cave,' Tashi murmured weakly. 'I can't go beyond here.'

Akash supported his head. 'Don't be stupid, Tashi. We have to go there together. I can't do anything in India without you.'

'Eh, no calling me stupid, that's my line,' Tashi said angrily. 'Look there,' he pointed to the hills. 'The caves are just there. You hide until nightfall and then go. There is someone inside waiting for you. Trust your instincts, everything will be fine.'

'Tashi, I will get help.' He could see the men in the distance, they were looking around.

'No, please go, please don't let me down. I will not rest in peace until I have fulfilled my mission. And now I'm not in any condition to help you.'

'But—'

'Don't be a baby, okay? Just leave me here and go.' There was blood everywhere, and it flowed into the muddy waters clouding it to a dark red. Akash could feel Tashi's life seeping away. He felt an overwhelming sense of sadness and regret. He should have been nicer to Tashi, found out about his family, his plans for them. And while Tashi was protecting him every step of the way, Akash had acted selfishly.

With determined effort, Akash replied. 'I will do as you say.'

'You are the chosen one, and it has been my honour to serve the Nine.' Tashi smiled for the first time since they'd met—he had such a warm and loving expression. Akash felt his throat choke with emotion. And before he could say anything else, Tashi went limp.

Akash heard the rustling and knew the assailants were getting closer. If he didn't leave right away, he knew Tashi's spirit would yell at him for stalling. He snuck through the muddy field, trying to avoid making squelching sounds with his sneakers.

Tiny insects like flies buzzed around him, he felt them in his face, his ears and his hair. Akash ignored them; he kept moving, his mind focused on one goal. Every so often his eyes darted to the back, and then forward at the gentle mounds that were his destination. He stopped at intervals; the fire from the car had subsided and he could see smoke rising in the horizon. Akash should be safe, but he didn't want to take any risks: the men were still searching, even though he couldn't hear them. They must have fanned out. Once they found Tashi, they would know he had escaped and then Akash wouldn't stand a chance.

The air was thick and syrupy as he waded through. He

felt pinpricks around his ankles. Ignoring the discomfort
and the uncontrollable urge to itch, Akash kept moving.
His arms ached and his lips were parched with thirst, but
he kept going. After what seemed like hours, guessing
from the setting sun, he reached a clearing; there were
villagers passing by, some had baskets on their heads,
others tilled the field on the other side.

A young boy stopped to stare at him. When he dragged
himself onto the dry stretch of land, he lay flat, exhausted
from the effort. The young boy patted Akash on the
shoulder and indicated that he follow him. Pain gnawed
at his ankles and felt like spikes. Akash winced as he
stood up on his elephant feet. Each bloody step was a
throbbing ache from tiny razor cuts on his feet. He gritted
his teeth and kept moving, but soon lost consciousness
from the trauma. When he came to, Akash realized he
was being supported by two sturdy farmers. They had his
arms around their shoulders, and were half dragging and
half carrying him. At the same time, a few women were
trying their best to wipe his face with a wet cloth. He
succumbed and lost consciousness once again.

It was night when he woke up. Akash was on a string
cot, staring up at a thatched roof. He sat up immediately,
alert to his surroundings. He was inside a hut. It was
quiet. There was a small flickering lamp in the corner,
and no one around. His feet were wrapped in leaves.
They felt cool and the throbbing had subsided—the
farmers had applied a soothing balm. Whatever it was, it

had helped. His monster feet appeared to be of normal size again and there was only a mild ache. He tried to stand up and found he could. Slowly he took a step. He was wearing fresh clothes, a pair of baggy drawstring pyjamas and a long kurta.

Akash had to get to the caves. Although he felt weak and tired, he didn't want to waste a moment. Outside the hut, there was a family of four eating around a fire. They looked up at him with gaunt faces and bright smiles.

The father jumped up and guided Akash to join them, patting him on the back. He was a tall, emaciated man and Akash guessed it was his clothes that he was wearing. The young boy who had helped him earlier, giggled at him and pointed to his feet. 'Meetha khoon,' he said. Sweet blood. Akash understood and smiled. The mother, just as thin as her husband, covered her head with her sari and scolded the boy, telling him to shut up and eat. Their daughter hid like a kitten pressed to her mother's side.

Akash sat on the ground with them. Besides a few nods and grins there was no communication. Under the star-studded sky, in the open surroundings, Akash finished his watery daal and thick wheat roti and was amazed at how much he enjoyed his meal. He drank water from an earthen bowl, and for the first time, he felt connected to them, to this motherland that Tashi had been so proud of. The warmth spread throughout his body and awakened a deep sense of pride and gratitude. Akash would do what he was meant to do. Life used to be all about him, about his needs and desires, about achieving fame in the world of music. He knew now that his destiny lay elsewhere.

Just like this poor family acted out of humane concern and took him into their home, and cared for him. Just like Tashi had been his bodyguard and died protecting him, and just like King Ashoka, two millennia ago, cared for the souls of this earth. In his own small way, Akash was meant to make a difference and do a good deed, a selfless act that would bring gratitude from the people, right from their hearts.

Akash thanked them and said, 'Lomas Rishi jana hai.'

Their smiles dropped and he faced brooding looks. Akash stood up. He was about to repeat but the father had understood. From his cross-legged position he stood up quickly and led him out of his courtyard and towards the end of the lane. He indicated a straight direction in the darkness.

Akash bent low as a sign of respect and thanked the old man, who blessed him. 'May God be with you,' he said and returned to his family and his hut.

*

The air was thinner, and the night clearer in all its aspects. The horizon, the trees and the hills had taken on distinct shades of grey and black. He inhaled the cool air and felt as if he were a balloon, capable of floating away into the night. There was a lightness in his chest and it reached his soul. The present moment was so beautiful that he knew if he died that very second, he would be content, happy, desiring nothing of this world.

As he walked he felt like he was shedding old skin. He felt a strange kind of energy buzzing upwards from his feet. He focused on putting one foot in front of the other, and with each step, his body felt lighter and lighter. As he glided forward moving, almost running, Akash felt as though he was floating. With a sharp intake of breath he realized he was crossing distances in giant strides. It was exhilarating; the leaves of the trees that lined his path brushed his face. At times, he felt he could touch the stars. He soared high above and then landed gently on the ground.

Akash saw the hills. He moved around them carefully and then found the entrance to the cave. The exterior façade was carved into a fine lattice, its beauty—even if only lit by a slender crescent moon—fascinated him.

He took a deep breath. 'This is it, Tashi. I'm here. Rest in peace.' And Akash entered the gaping mouth and disappeared inside.

16

Zubin was on a flight to Delhi. He had maps and an alert guide, or more truthfully, a bodyguard, with him. There was minimal conversation and the guard, who looked like an ordinary businessman in a black suit and green tie, said his name was Adam and then kept mum for the rest of the journey.

Sounded fake. But it was better this way. Zubin wasn't much of a talker and preferred to delve into *Lonely Planet* and find out exactly where he was going, on the off chance that Adam disappeared. Zubin knew he would find a way to get to his destination. He continued to read:

> Drawing inspiration from ordinary huts, the Barabar Caves are designed to look as if they're made of wood. The facade of the Lomas Rishi cave, which is sculpted into lattice screens, has a doorway designed to resemble an Egyptian form. A large rectangular chamber with a remarkable glass-like polish is located in its interior.

And no further explanation.

The caves were built in the third century, so how did they get a remarkable glass-like polish with primitive tools? Zubin mused. And why didn't anyone want to know? These were obvious mysteries but no one seemed keen on solving them. If he were in charge, Zubin would first do a carbon-dating, analyse the minerals in the rocks and then work out a theory about the kind of tools— other than laser technology—which could get that sort of polish.

He was a forensics guy, his mind worked methodically to find clear-cut ways to investigate an unsolved case. It was how he dealt with situations and problems in life.

Except where it connected to his father. Somehow, the emotions got in the way. He was brooding on the exciting discovery his father had hidden for so many years.

Next to him, Adam stared at the small screen intently. The movie was about an impending disaster that would strike the earth—a meteor. For all the screaming and doom-driven plot, he was watching expressionlessly, hardly blinking—alert as if danger lurked 36,000 feet in the air, amongst dozing passengers and a friendly cabin crew. *Better get some rest*, Zubin thought. After Delhi, there was still a long journey ahead.

*

At Delhi airport, they exited into fierce sunlight. Zubin's senses were on an overdrive. 'Follow me,' Adam said, noticing his distracted movements. He was wearing dark glasses and had removed his jacket and tie. With the ease of a snake, he moved through the dense crowd, guiding Zubin to a waiting car. They hopped inside and the driver stuffed their belongings in the boot. When the blast of the air-conditioner hit him, Zubin realized how much he had been perspiring; it was like an oven outside where people milled about and didn't seem to be affected by the heat. His body too would acclimatize to the city. The human body was a miracle in itself, there was so much about it that we took for granted, he reflected. And so much suffering that we subjected it to.

'Takes a bit of getting used to,' Adam said as he handed

him a few bottles of water. 'You will probably need them all.'

Zubin thanked him and gulped down almost all the contents of one bottle. He put the rest into his knapsack. 'How long before we get to Gaya?'

'This ride is to the train station. From there, we take the Mahabodhi Express to Gaya—about sixteen hours,' Adam replied. 'From there we take a car to the Barabar Hills.'

Zubin felt the strain already. It wasn't just the heat but the uncertainty of what to expect, whether he was prepared for it or not. And there were two other recruits, he was told by Vaz; they would meet him in Gaya after he met the monk. One was from England and the other was a woman, from here. India.

He sighed. He was finally here, on the soil his father had taken a handful of and kissed. It was his mother earth too! His father had told him stories. All that was in the past: the great legends of powerful gods, of culture and the belief and faith that God was the answer to everything.

When in Rome . . .

Everything seemed to be happening too fast. As if there was disaster around the corner. What had his father said? 'It is time to take care of the world before it is destroyed.' *Was that an overreaction? And why was he put in a spot? He didn't want the responsibility to save the world!*

He sighed again. *Take it as it comes, he thought, trying to pacify himself. Let go of the doubts, if this is my destiny then it is best to just surrender to it.* Zubin had explained to Vaz that he wasn't a believer in the quaint word 'destiny'. Life was about choices. And if he chose to opt out, he would. But then he recalled his mysterious smile, as if he knew Zubin would take back his words.

There was the other matter of commitment. He had taken on a responsibility because of his father. Okay, he would see what needed to be done and do it. After that, it was back to the basement, to the garden of the dead. Zubin glanced at his quiet neighbour. Adam, the dutiful bodyguard, was a reminder that Zubin's safety was top priority for the people who supported the Nine. He had to respect that.

The Nine unknown men: mysterious, powerful and almost sacred in this noble cause. Six were safe but three had been compromised. They had to be replaced. He was a part of this. Even if it all sounded bizarre, he had to continue. There were dozens of questions that flitted through Zubin's mind. *How did the oldest secret society in the world survive through millennia, without being acknowledged or noticed?* He pondered. Whole species of animals went extinct in that period of time, so how could anything else survive thousands of years without being on record, except as a myth. And it seemed they were not so secret any more.

The driver pulled into a dusty road, stopping outside a

plain building bustling with activity. They got out, took
their backpacks from the boot of the car and headed
inside, trailed by little children with their dirty palms
extended. Adam meandered smoothly and focused on
his destination—the ticket counters. Zubin was trying
his best, but kept bumping into some of them and
apologizing out of habit. This brought more children in
his way. They giggled each time he muttered 'Sorry'.
Zubin wanted to stop and share some of his money.
Adam looked back and gave him a warning glance. There
was no time. They reached the row of windows where
just two or three of the booths were marked open. They
waited in the queue. 'Why don't they open more
counters?' Zubin asked. 'They can see people waiting.'

'Get used to it. Otherwise, "why" is a word you will use
a lot while in India.' At the counter they bought their
tickets and made it to the platform. 'The train journey is
fairly safe, but it's best to be alert at all times,' Adam
suggested as they hopped onto the train. 'There are bandits
on this route.'

Zubin nodded. *Impending disaster.*

Two meals and ten hours into their train journey, the
lights went out and darkness fell on them like a blanket.
'What's going on?' Zubin was instantly on his feet. Adam
touched his arm, indicating to him to calm down, and
whipped out his gun. Earlier, their pick-up at the airport
had silently passed the weapon to Adam while they were
in the car. Zubin had noticed but didn't comment.
Hopefully, there would be no use for it.

They had a first-class two-tier cabin with two cushioned seats at the bottom and bunk beds above. It was just the two of them in the enclosed cubicle. The toilets, however, were outside.

Adam moved out of his seat, opened the sleeper cabin and looked to the left and right of the dark, narrow corridor. No distinct shapes. It was late in the night and everyone was asleep. 'Stay here, it's probably just a fuse,' Adam said. He slid the door shut behind him.

Zubin waited uneasily. The train hurtled forward in a rhythmic staccato beat. The hum wasn't comforting any more. Ten minutes later, the door slid open and Adam entered. He was carrying a candle. 'The lights have gone out, nothing to worry, the TC is working on it,' he said. He placed the candle on the tray table and sat down.

But Zubin was worried. Adam had dark streaks of black on his hands and his forehead, his gun had disappeared and his eyes—maybe it was the reflection— were red points.

'I'll use the washroom,' Zubin said, making his way to the door.

'Wait!' Adam said. 'They are fixing the lights, let them finish and then you can go.'

Zubin quietly returned to his seat. This time he watched Adam carefully in the flickering candlelight. There was definitely something odd, because Adam actually smiled. Throughout the journey since they left America, he had remained expressionless.

'Adam?'

'Yes?'

'Why are you lying to me?'

'Lying?'

'I can see lights under the door. I will go to the washroom.' Zubin picked up his bag and turned to slide the door open.

He felt the cold metal of a gun on his neck. 'Sit down,' Adam rasped.

Zubin returned to his seat. 'Who are you really?' he demanded calmly, assessing the situation. The windows had rails across them—no chance of escape there. The door was the only way out of their sleeper. But it opened into a very narrow corridor, which led to the next compartment where the exit doors were locked shut. Zubin kept revising his options in his head.

'I'm Adam,' he responded.

'You are not Adam.'

'Shut up.' His eyes glistened red.

'I have something which will be of interest to you,' Zubin said.

'I told you to shut up.'

'First I need to get something . . .' Zubin unzipped his knapsack and searched for the little packet he kept at the bottom.

'What are you looking for in your bag?'

'I'm looking for my cigarettes.'

'Put your bag aside. Don't try anything stupid or

you are a dead man,' he said, aiming at his face with the gun.

'Good point.' Zubin found the cigarettes and let his bag slide to his side. 'You didn't tell me what's going on.' He lit up.

'I am a Kala Yogi.'

'So you're here to kill me, right?' Zubin offered him a cigarette.

The man hesitated and then took one. 'No, first we get the chakra from you.'

'The wheel. I don't have it.' Zubin watched him light his cigarette with the candle flame.

'It's at the Barabar Hills—and they will pass it to you.'

'Who is "they"?'

The man sucked hard. And then he screamed, but no sound emerged. He curled up in pain. Zubin grabbed the gun. He had put three times the accepted amount of formaldehyde in the tobacco; it must be killing his throat.

Now was his chance. He acted quickly. Sliding open the door, Zubin checked the narrow corridor—it was empty. He couldn't see much of the landscape through the windows. They were moving through plains. He made his way to the exit and turned the lever, it squeaked when it budged slightly. He heard shuffling sounds approaching. *More Kala Yogis?* He had to hurry. Zubin used as much force as he could to open the door, the lever shifted slowly.

'Stop!' a man's voice said.

Zubin hid the gun, and turned to face him. He was a middle-aged man holding a tray and looked like one of the pantry guys. Zubin studied him, his hand gripping the gun.

'It's dangerous to open the door while the train is in motion, you could get hurt,' he admonished. His eyes were normal.

'I'm feeling claustrophobic, I need to get some fresh air and have a smoke,' Zubin explained.

He didn't move. Zubin fished out some money and deposited it in his hand.

'Don't tell anyone,' the guy smiled and said. But before he could reach the door, Zubin saw the man sink to the floor. Behind him, stood a tall man. He had black marks on his cheeks and forehead. With his red eyes, he stared at Zubin.

'I suggest you get back to your seat,' he said, following Zubin as he turned to move back in. The man didn't hold a weapon but Zubin could feel the pressure on his back, like the sharp point of a knife. And he knew smudge-face had some kind of psychic powers. Zubin controlled his racing pulse. Now wasn't the time to panic. He wasn't about to succumb to black magic yogis.

'I need to . . .' Zubin said and immediately felt the point press harder into his back. He knew his skin had been slit, the pain was a burning sensation. He relented and was led back to his door. He slid it open and went inside. The cabin was empty.

'Where's Adam?'

'It doesn't matter,' the man said and as the door slid shut, he disappeared. The door was locked tight. Zubin had to get out of there quick.

The candle was still lit. He paced the small cabin deep in thought. They would be reaching Gaya soon. He could see the streaks of dawn in the distance. Then an idea came to him: it would be dangerous but it was the only way out.

Adam's bag was in the corner. Zubin removed the clothes and piled them next to the seat. He placed the cigarettes on top. Then he pushed the windows open, struck a match, and set the pile on fire. Then he quickly took his hand towel, wet it with water from his bottle and covered his mouth and nose with it. Zubin hoped the flames leaping out of the windows would make someone stop the train.

Zubin waited. The smoke was treacherous, the fire wild and roaring out of the window. The railings had turned bright orange in the extreme heat. But the fire was moving inwards as well. It had spread to the seats, and was filling up the cabin, making him cough. He cowered in the corner, struggling to breathe. He was just about to bang on the door when Zubin heard the grating sound of brakes. The train began to slow down. There was a commotion outside his room; someone had unlatched his door. Everyone had to leave quickly. He heard the staff shouting. Zubin stood up slowly, hacking coughs hindering his movements. He slung his knapsack on his back.

The cabin was smoky and he could hardly see. He had to get out right now. Gritting his teeth he gripped the metal door handle and bit back a scream. The handle was burning hot and he hadn't thought of using a cloth. There was no time to waste, his throat was burning and his lungs felt like he was swimming in water. He gripped it with his palms despite the pain and pushed the door open. When he briefly glanced at his hands, he saw that they were beginning to swell and pulse. Bubbles were forming on his palms. Ignoring the injury, he exited quickly. There was panic all around. Passengers were shouting and running helter-skelter. There was no sign of smudge-face or Adam. All the doors to the coaches were wide open as people ran towards the nearest exit. They were throwing their luggage and bags out; some even attempted to jump but didn't, waiting for the train to slow down.

17

Zubin didn't wait. He jumped out and rolled down the incline from the tracks. In a flash he was back on his feet, running like he had never run before—moving away from an unknown enemy that had the power to attack with the mind alone. But he had to try to get to his destination. When he looked back, he could barely see the smoke in the distance. The railroad tracks were not visible either and although he knew he had made it out safe, he still felt vulnerable. The hills stretched in the distant horizon, which he guessed was the location of the caves. All around was flat land and fields. He walked for twenty minutes, using his map as a guide. He guessed he was heading towards a village called Guraru, just one station away from Gaya.

His hands throbbed and he felt pins and needles stretching up his wrists. The three bottles of water and four paracetamols had helped so far but the pain was slowly returning. His hands had suffered third-degree burns. The nerve endings should have been destroyed too, he shouldn't be feeling pain. But his hand throbbed, keeping time with his heartbeat. He wrapped his hands in a piece of cloth torn from his shirt. He needed to find a sterile environment to treat it—or risk infection. He noticed huts. Surely there would be a medical facility in the village ahead, he thought sceptically.

The path to the village was a straight line and all around it, the flat land shimmered. There were a few scattered trees that provided shade for a few minutes when he needed to rest. If he were the doctor, and a patient with third-degree burns came to him, he would hook him up on electrolytes and antibiotics and prescribe lots of rest with nutritional supplements and a high-protein diet. Zubin stayed alert, distracting his mind and keeping up the diagnosis as if treating a patient in his mind.

The early morning sun shone bright. Birds circled lazily in the azure sky. He shouldered his bag and winced at the current of pain ripping through his hands to his bones. He would collapse any minute. No, he wouldn't do that, not yet. Zubin talked out loud to an imaginary patient, explaining the symptoms. He continued until the path curved drastically. There was a vast field of churned-up mud baking in the sunlight, and he could see a ploughing bullock and its lethargic movements as it tilled the soil. He should call out to the farmer.

He fumbled with his map and dropped it. As he picked it up, he saw a pair of bare feet. He stood up and faced a woman. She was carrying a basket on her head, only her eyes and part of her face were visible through the sari that veiled her head.

Zubin showed her his hands. He was shocked at the extent of damage—the heated metal had burned his skin right through the epidermis and dermis to the hypodermis, leaving the skin charred black and red, and a transluscent white in some places. A fluid oozed from the swellings. It must have looked revolting to her, but she just blinked at him. And without uttering a word, she nodded to him to follow her. He did.

The village wasn't exactly promising. There were a few children in torn clothes playing with a stray dog. The houses had thatched roofs and flimsy doors. He couldn't see any overhead wires, which meant there was no electricity. A few women carrying brass vessels passed by, staring at him. There must be a stream or well nearby, he reasoned.

The children were trailing him now. They seemed curious about this stranger in dirty jeans and a faded T-shirt with bandaged hands stumbling behind a woman from their village. The children's muffled whispers and laughter were the only sounds he heard. None of the adults spoke as they went about their work wearing a sorrowful expression.

He passed a small hut where an old woman sat on her haunches. Her haunting eyes were those he had seen on famine victims; flies and tears on their faces. She was gaunt, her cheeks zig-zagged with wrinkles and her razor-sharp cheekbones and chin told a story of starvation and suffering. If she hadn't moved her hand to drag the rag over her head, he would have thought she was a mummified body.

Up ahead, there was a flimsy-looking building, made of untidily placed cemented bricks. The woman pointed, and he noticed the direction of her finger. She didn't wait for his thank you and continued on her way, balancing the weight on her head. Her feet had cuts and he saw dried blood in the cracks of her heels.

The doctor's clinic was small and functional with the barest minimum of facilities. The strong smell of rubbing alcohol hung in the air, and the red cross on the white board with the local black script highlighted the importance of this brick-and-mortar structure. There were five patients sitting on benches on the porch, which doubled as the waiting room. Three of them were mothers who busily pacified their babies, two were bawling and the other had snot running down its nose. Two old men clutched their stomachs, and leaned forward on their canes. The five faces and three babies stared at him wide-eyed. Shell-shocked was the word that crossed his mind. The bawling stopped. Zubin could hear the doctor's voice behind the closed doors. By this time he was mind-numbingly tired and his hands were throbbing masses of flesh. He didn't care about anything but seeing the doctor. He looked for a place to sit, and the old men shifted slightly, giving him just enough space. Zubin sat down and waited. His senses were heightened, he became alive to the sounds, the smells, and the vivid greens on brown earth hurt his eyes. The pain was reaching unbearable levels. He let out an angry grunt, gritted his teeth and leaned his head against the wall. He didn't know it then, but he slipped in and out of consciousness. Each time he opened his eyes, there were fewer patients.

When he opened his eyes next, he was staring up at a stranger. Zubin felt better for some reason.

'It's your turn now and we better hurry up,' he said in thickly accented English. He helped Zubin into his consulting room. The doctor was young, probably in his early thirties. Signs of weariness were evident in his expression. There was a resigned sense of acceptance of human suffering as if healing the poverty-stricken wasn't exactly what he had planned to do in life, Zubin mused as he walked slowly. With great effort, he lay down on a narrow bed. 'You should have told my compounder you were an emergency case—he would have let you in first. You are stupid to wait so long,' the doctor said with an expression of frustration. His mouth was set in an upside-down smile. He was a tall man wearing a white jacket with brown stains, and had a white powdery substance on his fingers.

Zubin felt his hands tremble as the doctor slowly unwrapped them. He saw the mass of pink flesh—he hadn't seen anything like it before.

The doctor pulled on his gloves while the compounder poured some disinfectant into a bowl and placed it on a low stool along with cotton wool. Very carefully, the doctor cleansed the wounds.

Pain stabbed him like fresh cuts. Zubin gritted his teeth and closed his eyes. Tears streamed down his face.

'I would have given you some anaesthetic but it would delay the healing process. Third-degree burns . . . in some areas there's tissue damage. You might need skin grafts, but I'm not a specialist in this field. I'll apply some antibiotic cream and give you some shots. Rest for a while and return to the city and get some serious help. Do you have someone with you? A place to stay?' he asked doubtfully, looking into his face.

Zubin shook his head. He felt dizzy.

'Then you will have to come to my house,' the doctor

said. He must have been used to doing this. In any case, Zubin was in no state to argue.

The compounder helped Zubin out of the consulting room, up a short flight of stairs and into a small apartment. An old woman in a white sari appeared at the door.

'Doctor Saheb's mother,' Zubin heard the compounder say. But Zubin felt his head swim. He was held in the compounder's strong grip. A bed, a cotton sheet over his body and the coolness of a gentle breeze, and he was out.

When he awoke, Zubin stared up at a grey ceiling. He recalled the events of the day. His hands were wrapped in gauze and felt stiff—the slightest movement and it hurt like hell. Zubin sat up, looked around and stared into the rheumy eyes of an old woman. *Oh yes, the doctor's mother.* She hurried out and returned with her son. The doctor was at least a foot shorter than Zubin and offered him a shirt and a pair of trousers. They helped him wash up and changed his clothes. The doctor helped him drink some water from a steel glass. Zubin gulped greedily. A few minutes later, his mother was feeding him. All this was done in silence. Zubin murmured a 'thank you'. The first words he could say since his collapse. This was the most unusual experience of his life. To be chased by yogis with magical powers, and then to reach a village where a doctor and his mother offered their home and fed him like he was family. It would be hard to explain to anyone back home. Home—as distant as the stars glittering in the sky.

Zubin fell asleep again. Hours went by. When he woke up later he felt better. He stared out of the window at the stars from the comfort of a string cot. He wondered about his destiny, his emotions getting the better of him. At the same time an overwhelming sense of gratitude towards the old woman and her son filled his heart.

He stepped outside the room. There was a veranda beyond the simple living area. He headed towards the low wall. There were acres of sun-baked earth and tilled fields.

'That's our ancestors' land and the government, despite politicians changing so many times, did not provide the promised electricity, water supply and health care,' the doctor explained, joining him in the balcony. 'I'm Dr Rathod,' he introduced himself with a smile.

'I'm Zubin. That's a huge piece of property you have there,' he said, looking admiringly into the distance.

The doctor shook his head sadly. 'Yes, it is,' he said and turned away. 'After my father died, I couldn't leave this place. I wanted to work in the city. But now my obligations lie elsewhere. I want to help the villagers. They have no doctors and my father and his grandfather suffered and died because the nearest doctor was in Gaya, still some distance away in an emergency.'

'Sometimes a man has to follow his destiny,' Zubin said. And realized he meant it for himself as well.

Rathod agreed. 'I studied medicine and returned home to treat the villagers. We receive a small grant from the government to cover basic expenses but,' he smirked, 'I work for peanuts. It is very frustrating at times. Especially when there's so much more we can do to improve the lives of the villagers.'

Zubin noticed the twinge of regret, but it wasn't for himself. If there were any demands in Rathod's words, they were for the improvement of the village. It was rare to see that kind of simplicity in someone who had lived in a better world, with all the modern-day conveniences. How could the doctor spend his days in a community where life was like a page from history?

Zubin felt empathic. A sense of responsibility grew in his heart and the desire to help turned intense. It wasn't like him to get this emotional about a poor village and its residents whom he hardly knew. 'Can I have some water please?' he croaked.

The doctor brought a steel glass filled with water and handed it to his guest with a smile. 'You are looking better already. My medicines must be working.'

Zubin drank it, and knew that the water had accepted him just as he had accepted this land, its people and this country.

'Thank you very much,' Zubin said. 'Your medicines and your kindness have made all difference.' Instinctively, Zubin cupped the glass with both hands.

'You better get some rest and you will be fit and fine in the morning.'

Zubin shook his head. 'I have to get to the Lomas Rishi cave immediately.'

'You must rest another day.' Rathod tried to take the glass from him.

'Wait!' Zubin said, closing his eyes. He felt his hands pulsate but it was an oddly comforting feeling. A powerful energy surged through him. He felt better and stronger. He clutched the glass, stared at the emptiness within and then felt it turn warm in his throbbing hands. The glass slid from his slippery palms and fell to the floor with a clang.

Rathod stared at it as it rolled on the ground, back and forth.

'Are you all right?' Rathod asked with visible concern.

'I'm fine,' Zubin said and opened his bandages. His hands were still throbbing and he felt the power still surging through him. He looked at his hands—they were completely healed!

Rathod stared wide-eyed. 'This is not possible ...' Then he seemed to remember, 'But the villagers have talked about the legends of Ashoka. I know who you are—one of the Nine!' He whispered excitedly and then looked around in fear, hoping no one had heard.

'But it's not possible for me to have these powers yet. I have to go to the Lomas Rishi cave first.' Zubin whispered urgently.

They heard the old woman's wavering voice, 'It is your will that makes it happen, Zubin. You are already destined.'

'I thought you were asleep, Ma.'

'I knew the moment he came in that he was no ordinary man. He was destined to pass by our house. There is an old connection,' she said, looking at him with her piercing gaze. Zubin looked at her face, shocked. The face of the old mother-like figure now bore the gleam of a seer's.

'He must go now before the Kala Yogis come,' she spoke in a hushed tone. 'May the power of the Nine be with you!' she said, blessing Zubin.

He smiled at her. 'Thank you, sweet mother. You are a wise, wise woman.'

'Come, I will guide you,' Rathod said.

Zubin's heart raced. 'You are a good man, Dr Rathod. You have a very warm, generous heart. I can see it.'

Rathod looked at his mother. They both smiled. Then Rathod led Zubin out the door. 'It is a straight route to the caves. You see that bullock cart?' Zubin saw a small cart trudging slowly towards them. 'I will tell Kishen bhaiyya to take you to your destination.' Rathod helped him with his knapsack and gave him some fruits for the journey.

Zubin thanked him and hugged Rathod like he was a long-lost brother. The cartpuller was more than happy to help the doctor and agreed readily. Stepping onto the straw-laden cart, he settled back. It was time to face his destiny. He smiled and waved until the doctor was nothing more than a shape in the distance.

18

It was a moonlit night and the dark woods skirting the town lay quiet. Vayu pressed the palms of his hands together; they trembled in pain. He gritted his teeth and pressed harder, the tips of his fingers pressing against each other. The wooded area was secluded and even if people were to pass the stream, they wouldn't notice Vayu sitting cross-legged, eyes closed, inside the shallow arched cave that was adjacent to the *Eleocarpus ganitrus* or blue marble tree (rudraksh). The marble-sized, multi-faced, reddish-brown seeds were scattered around him, symbols of the God of dissolution, the universal force of re-absorption. Sharp spikes of pain shot through the centre of his hands. Vayu pressed harder until he felt the moist sensation of his blood seep, and slowly trickle down the inside of his forearm.

'Welcome, Kalingan master,' Vayu whispered and opened his hands in the shape of a V, from which a small rudra seed fell out. His bare chest glistened in the faint shafts of the moonlight. He smiled. The warrior force filled his being as his muscles rippled along his body that was stretched out in the yoga pose. He had thirsted for this, yearned for the immense energy. The world lived with the power of technology, but he lived with the power of the mind; the consciousness was far stronger. Vayu felt the strength of his pounding heart in the centre of his abdomen. He focused on it until it throbbed with intensity and spread like the rays of the sun throughout his body. He controlled the expanding energy, shuddered and then went still. Vayu opened his eyes and blinked.

The darkness was a shade lighter than black, but he was not afraid. There were snakes, beetles the size of his foot, and other strange creatures in these parts of the woods. He almost wanted to be challenged, attacked. He was alert, ready to face his enemy no matter in what form he appeared. Through the mesh of trees he could make out the vague jagged lines of the mountains in the distance against an onyx-coloured horizon.

'The Guide is here,' Vayu whispered aloud. The Kalingan directed him. And Vayu was as brave and courageous as the great warrior once was millennia ago!

He stood up and headed towards the monastery. Wrapped only in an orange loin cloth, Vayu felt the winds slap against his body. The air had suddenly turned cold. A storm was approaching. Dark clouds rumbled across the sky and to Vayu they sounded like the beating of war drums.

*

Wangdak waited by the edge of the forest. He had met Vayu a few times and shown him around the village. He had been here a week and like all other tourists, Wangdak expected him to leave. But he had settled comfortably in a small house close to the forest. The house was owned by an old man, and Vayu had mentioned him as an uncle.

The uncle died in his sleep a month ago. The house was deserted, and suddenly one day, Vayu showed up with a key. And the stranger became a part of the village. The locals were trusting. But Wangdak felt something wasn't quite right. And Wangdak had kept watch. The man was very interested in the history of the place. Wangdak had introduced himself as the local guide and offered to show him around. The monk guide was surprised that Vayu had asked him to come here, today, in the middle of the night. Vayu had found something unusual but it was to be revealed only in darkness, he had said mysteriously. And Wangdak had agreed to meet him here.

He saw the man approach him. There was a hardness about his demeanour this time—something Wangdak had noticed about him in the daytime too. It was as if he was facing a different person each time he met him. His face was glistening and streaks of dirt covered his clothes. As he came closer, Wangdak saw the look in his eyes and felt uncomfortable. Something didn't feel quite right. 'What was it that you were going to show me?' Wangdak asked without greeting. He felt a chill that was growing more persistent, urging him to get as far away from this man as he could. But Wangdak also needed to know what it was. He stared at the man who now seemed like an enigma.

'Actually, it's more of what you can show me,' he said, looking straight into Wangdak's eyes. 'I have been asked to find the Knowledge Keeper. I'm told he was to arrive sometime today in the village. I know you are aware of the people entering and leaving this place. Do you know if this person has arrived?'

Wangdak began walking towards the village, where there would be people. Vayu, next to him, was breathing heavily, almost animal-like. There was a distinct smell of blood but he knew that the darkness would reveal nothing.

'Who has sent you?' he asked.

Vayu's smile was wide, 'The Council of Nine.'

And Wangdak knew this man was trouble. He didn't say more. He realized that Lise was the person Vayu wanted.

They arrived at the edge of the village where a well, a landmark through decades, still stood. Wooden buckets tied to a rope hung from one end of the pulley. The local women congregated here but it was dead quiet at that hour. The moon's distinct glow cast shadows across the low-rise homes. A monastery stood out on a hilltop and further away, vague outlines of mountains and plains could be seen.

The well was covered with a wooden plank. He stopped next to it and faced Vayu.

'We have a Buddhist saying around here,' Wangdak said. As he spoke, he circled the well until it was between them, 'Believe nothing, no matter where you read it, or who said it, no matter if I have said it, unless it agrees with your own reason and common sense.'

Vayu was silent for a few moments, he wore a hurt

expression. 'You do not understand the purpose. It is noble and requires a simple answer from you. I do not wish to harm you.' As Vayu approached him, his hands were clenched into tight fists, his knuckles bony and white.

Wangdak's gaze was steady. 'I don't trust you and I don't know you well enough.'

'So the Knowledge Keeper has arrived, eh?'

'I have not said that.'

'But it is not in your dharma to lie.'

Wangdak looked resignedly at him. He shrugged and began to walk towards the village.

'Wait!' Vayu said.

The monk didn't stop. His heart was racing, but Wangdak had not realized the serious consequence of what had led him here. 'You cannot leave. You know that I will find and kill this person.' Wangdak stopped in his tracks. 'You might as well join me and tell me the truth.' Vayu latched his arm around the man and dragged him back. He pressed hard. 'Tell me and I will spare your life,' he grunted.

Wangdak saw the beauty of the clouds and the moon. He was beyond caring. He prayed that this man would not harm the woman.

Vayu eased his arm slightly and Wangdak spoke distinctly, 'My life is not worth much. But yours is in a bad state. Pray that you die an easy death.' Those were his last words. The Kalingan grasped his neck and twisted. And Wangdak collapsed, limp.

19

Lise had slept for more than ten hours, interrupted by disturbing dreams of Dr Halvor and monks whispering to each other. It was late morning when she finally awoke to the sounds of tinkling cowbells. After she refreshed herself with water from a plastic bucket in the sparse bathroom, she dressed quickly and went downstairs.

The corner table facing the window was vacant, and Lise was fascinated by the breathtaking mountain view— the sacred Mount Kailash. In ancient times, it was thought to be the centre of the universe. Considered to be sacred, the Himalayas were empowered with God-like energies, capable of transforming anyone who visited the holy mountains. It is believed that pilgrims have experienced great spiritual transformation, a state of bliss that one can only dream of achieving in a lifetime.

Her attention turned to the traditionally attired vendors. They had laid their colourful wares along the street. Some had fruits and vegetables and others trinkets and crystal bracelets. She looked at the wrinkled, eager faces of the locals. Farther in the distance, farm animals loitered and little huts buzzed with domestic activity. Lise's breathing slowed, she felt as though time was moving at a languid pace. All her senses were absorbed in feeling the new atmosphere.

'Breakfast is coming!' the landlord announced, interrupting her thoughts. The big-built man wore a long shirt, loose pants and thick boots. His oily hair shone in the streaming sunlight. His broad face bore the signs of sunburn and a healthy diet of yak butter. His cheeks had a rosy glow and his smile was broad and infectious. He placed a big pot of tea and a cup in front of her. 'Drink,' he said with an enthusiastic nod. He poured the steaming hot brew into her cup, and waited until she took a sip.

It was thick and sweet, with a tangible flavour of spice. Lise took another sip and smiled at her attentive host. 'Thank you, it is very good,' she said, giving him the thumbs up sign.

Then, remembering the incident of the previous day, she asked, 'Yesterday an elderly monk, Wangdak was his name, guided me to this village. Do you know how I could get in touch with him?'

The landlord's face fell. He looked around as if to check that no one was listening. He had an odd expression, and she was convinced there was fear in his eyes. 'It is better you do not ask,' he said and turned to go. 'I will get your breakfast.' He hurried away.

She focused on the chipped cup in front of her. Lise had strange colours in her hair and pale skin—basically, not their type—which probably made them uncomfortable. But this wasn't about her appearance— something about Wangdak had bothered him enough for him to walk away. Lise felt she needed to know where Wangdak was. He seemed the most well-versed with this area, and she felt comfortable with him. She had planned to make him her guide.

The landlord returned, this time accompanied by a short, rotund woman carrying a plate laden with thick pancakes. She placed it in front of Lise and indicated that she must eat it while it was still hot. The woman wore an apron and her fingers were thick and callused. She smiled at Lise.

'Thank you,' Lise said, feeling uncomfortable with all the attention. It was unusual for someone to be so happy just because she was enjoying a good meal. It was divine. Lise was enjoying herself.

The landlord sat across from her. 'I will have some hot tea, and bring a fresh pot for her,' he ordered, and his wife eagerly left to fulfil his wishes.

'Why do you not tell me about Wangdak? He said you were a good friend,' Lise asked. She had tried asking for a fork and knife but noticed that everyone was eating with their fingers, and dug in. It was satisfying.

'Because you are new here. You are not familiar with the ways of our . . . culture or tradition. I don't want you to be afraid,' he responded.

Lise stopped eating. *What was there to be afraid of?*

'I . . . I . . . am here for a reason,' she said impulsively, wondering whether it was the right thing to do. 'I am not a tourist, someone . . . someone sent me here . . . with a message and it must reach its destination. How can I do that if—'

'Wangdak died last night. He is now a spirit guide,' he blurted out. Again, he checked that no one had overheard. The dining hall was empty except for a family with three boisterous children sitting diagonally across from them. 'He was making sure you got here fine,' the landlord replied, wiping his hands on a kitchen towel that was draped over his shoulder. 'He knew that you have a purpose for being here, that's why he came to guide you and he realized there was danger.'

The tea arrived at that moment, and the wife was thanked with a look of irritation and dismissal. She saw the expression on the white face and scooted away quickly.

Lise didn't understand clearly. 'What do you mean he died and became a spirit guide?'

'Someone killed him last night. But he is a monk and blessed by the Rinpoche, therefore we do not mourn, for he is now a soul that will protect our village.'

'But I was with him, and he was very much alive!' She felt a cold shiver down her spine. *How had he died? Did it have something to do with her?* If it did, she would have to be careful from now on or more people would die because of her.

'Don't worry. He is now protecting you in spirit,' he said softly. Then he leaned closer and whispered, 'Maybe forever. He helps people to reach here, but only the good souls, the ones who have a noble purpose—like you.' The landlord's eyes narrowed. 'You are a strange one.'

'You mean . . . Wangdak is a ghost now and you can see him!' Lise exclaimed in a slightly higher octave.

'Shh . . . we don't want to scare people around here,' the landlord said. 'You have to take this seriously and it means that you are being followed by evil. You need to be careful.' He shook his head and said, 'And it's good he sent you here. It is very easy to get lost in the woods. This house used to be home to many lamas five hundred years ago. It is sacred land. And the spirits live here too.' The landlord spoke matter-of-factly as if meeting a ghost was an everyday happening.

A chill crept over her and raised the hair on her arms. She looked outside, the sun hid behind passing clouds. The frost seemed to penetrate the glass and touch her soul.

'Are you making fun of me?' Lise asked half-smiling.

The landlord sipped on his tea and looked at her with kindly eyes. 'No, you can ask around here. We don't make fun of our spirit guides.' He stood up.

'Guides?' Lise asked, looking up at the towering man, who indicated to her to keep her voice down. 'There are more?' she asked in a whisper.

'Plenty, my dear. Plenty. This world needs guidance and there is a lot of heaviness, anger and bad feeling here,' he said, waving his hands around. 'We cannot see, but it is there, it affects us here.' He touched his chest. 'And sometimes people suffer and die because of the negativity in this world,' he said shaking his head. 'Maybe you don't understand. But if you are here, it is better that you accept it as a part of life.' The landlord cleared up, and wiped the table with the handy napkin from his shoulder. He was like a mini giant, his hands were big and the hair grew thick, black and wild on the back of his forearms and upper arms. And at odds were the monks who had no hair at all. There was so much about this place she needed to understand, including why people didn't cry when someone died. The landlord lumbered away. Lise noticed the wife and daughter glancing surreptitiously at her from the little porthole in the kitchen door.

They couldn't begin to fathom her purpose here. Lise recalled Wangdak's weathered old face and his warm smile. And for more than an hour he had shown her the way, stopping at intervals to let her enjoy the scenic views. In all that time, not once did she care to ask him his purpose. She felt a pang of guilt and regret. *I'm sorry!*

The guest house was an old slate-roofed building with many rooms. It had been refurbished to accommodate tourists passing through as well as vacationing families. Lise had noted the ancient carvings on the walls along the poorly lit corridors, and always got the sense that someone was watching her.

The night before, after Lise had checked in, she had walked down the narrow corridor, and as she approached her room, she thought she saw a wispy white glimmer of light just above the entrance. This hadn't alarmed her. She had thought it was the effect of the shadows, but now she was convinced it was one of the ghosts or spirit

guides. Lise had reluctantly come down to the dining hall
for dinner. And when she returned, her eyes practically
half closed from exhaustion, the same wispy cloud had
trailed just above her.

The thought of it made her recall the other oddities in
her room, the strange sound of muffled footsteps,
whispering and then the shadows.

The landlady arrived, placed two small steel bowls,
one filled with cream-coloured balls, and the other with
a white square. 'Eat, eat, sweet,' she insisted enthusiastically.

The couple returned to her table and stood by it,
engaged in a discussion. She received quick sharp glances
from them and therefore assumed that the conversation
was about her. Their daughter, a younger version of her
mother with the bone structure of her father, joined in,
and the three spoke rapidly in the local dialect. Her hair
was combed back and snaked on her shoulders in two
plaits, just like the Dutch milkmaid pictures Lise had
seen on the tins of condensed milk.

'Eat, eat,' the landlady repeated in between her
exchanges with her family. Seemed like the only English
word she knew. Lise couldn't guess the woman's age, but
she had a warm loving smile, heavy jowls and rosy cheeks.
Motherly was the word that came to her mind. She
smelled of something sweet, like warm milk. It was a
strange feeling but Lise realized things were changing
within her. It was as if she was turning more human in
some ways. Back home these feelings had been battered

and bottled up, but this place seemed to pull them out. Her eyes misted up as she looked at the small family. They smiled at her and when she received a raised eyebrow from the mother, Lise turned to her plate.

'Thank you very much,' Lise said, but they were too busy talking. Hesitant at first, Lise gorged on the delicious sweets after tasting the first mouthful. Their presence felt more comforting than intrusive.

When she was stuffed, she returned to her room and checked the address she had scrawled on the paper. She felt drowsy and lay down. Jet lag was overtaking her but sleep didn't claim her immediately. There was a bunch of puzzle pieces in her head, circling around like birds looking to nest. Countries, cities, places and hidden caves, strange interlocking triangles and circles all crowded around in her mind. They seemed important but she couldn't piece them together. Finally, she fell asleep.

Her dreams were vivid. So alive and so close that she was startled awake. She felt alone. The room seemed to be closing in on her. Everything was strange and unusual. And everything was happening too fast! Lise wasn't ready for this. She needed a smoke, a drink—anything to deaden the panic squeezing her middle. *Were there ghosts around her?* Knees to her chest, she wondered if this was normal. The dreams seemed to be taking effect. Tall men with knives, holding skulls dripping blood, flashed before her eyes. She trembled as the fear rose in waves. Suddenly, she wanted to return to where her life began, to her home

in Amsterdam. To technology and phones. Television
and canned laughter, frozen foods and insulated homes.
This was too much to deal with, too much to understand.
She wanted to go home!

Conversations with a wispy spirit guide, and then this
ancient guest house with odd people . . . it was all alien to
her. She needed familiar territory. Lise jumped up and
starting packing her things. She checked her handbag. It
contained her passport and other papers. She had enough
money to fly back, she was ready to go. Taking a deep
breath, hand on the door handle, she pressed down.

'Are you sure you want to do this, Lise?'

She froze. That voice was familiar but a little deeper, a
little ephemeral even, as if it were coming from a shadow.
She felt a shiver down her spine. Somebody was right
behind her! Slowly, she turned around. There was a
shadow. And even though she couldn't make out the
lines of his face, she knew it was Wangdak. He was
standing in the middle of her room!

'You are not real,' was her first reaction. She knew it
could be a hallucination, or she could still be dreaming.
The landlord had put enough in her mind to make her
think like that.

'What is real and what is an illusion?' She could feel his
smile, warm and comforting. It was real—this apparition,
this shadow!

'I cannot do this. I am not one of you and—'

'And this is not the way life was supposed to be?' There

was a silence. 'Everything we experience has a purpose. It might not be what you thought it would be but you know you can handle it. If you were not who you are, if there was the slightest doubt that you were incapable, then you wouldn't have been here. You have a reason to be here . . .'

Lise took a tentative step closer. 'You speak in riddles. And I repeat, you are not real.' And her hand went through him. He was air! She snatched her hand back as if she had touched a live flame, and stepped away from him. Wildly, she looked around, feeling fear pressing her pounding heart.

'Please don't be afraid. We spirits have a purpose too. And it is to lead you, to guide you to your destiny.'

Lise looked at him again. She had questions. 'But I don't want people to die and I don't know how to get to where I have to go.'

'You will know. This place provides the answers you seek. Sometimes they are not the ones you want but it is necessary.'

'What do you mean?'

'Life's lessons are hard but they make us strong. You will go to the monastery to meet the Rinpoche. He knows you will come. And remember, there is nothing to fear. All of our experiences are interlinked to achieve a purpose. Think of it like that. I am here with you, to guide you. Don't run away from yourself. It is not possible to escape from yourself. And remember, stay away from the dark force in human form called Vayu . . .'

The end of the conversation was as if a candle had been snuffed out—soft, wispy and mildly scented. Instinctively, she knew he meant for her to stay and face her fears. She felt emboldened. If she had tolerated the pain of addiction, she could do anything! There was no job, no home and no father figure waiting for her. Nobody, nothing left in her life worth living for. She might as well make the best of it here.

20

Tara waited expectantly at the station for Karan's train to arrive. She was having second thoughts about asking him to come. In fact, she searched her soul for a feeling that resembled love for him. It had to be there somewhere! They'd made wild, passionate love and dozens of promises to each other. *Surely that counted for something!*

The train screeched to a halt. Coolies boarded the train while people emerged—some monks, some families and a few lone figures with a lost look on their faces. They all came to Bodh Gaya to find answers.

Karan carried a small bag. He looked around confused, but when he saw Tara, his face broke into a smile. Like always, that smile melted her heart like butter. She ran towards him as he approached her. It was all very filmy in her mind, but this is the way love was meant to be, she felt. They hugged, talking about how much they had missed each other.

As they walked to the Rainbow Guesthouse, Tara
explained a simple version of what had happened to her.
She was kidnapped and now she had to meet a Tibetan
monk because her life was in danger.

He nodded quietly. 'Do you realize this isn't a normal
occurrence? Are you still hiding something from me?'
Karan asked. 'Why would your life be in danger? And
what do the Kala Yogis you keep mentioning have to do
with you, anyway?'

She didn't want to answer questions, not yet, so she
just smiled. Thankfully, the business of booking a taxi
diverted their attention. Karan seemed to be eager to
hear what she had to say but didn't quiz her on the way to
the hotel. They held hands.

Back at the hotel, they made love. It was sweet and
passionate and comfortable. And Tara wished they could
stay this way forever: in love, in each other's arms, and
without interference from the outside world. He smiled
down at her, taking in the soft curves, 'Feeling good?'

Tara smiled back. She had the warm, after-sex fuzzy
feeling. 'So good. And you?' She caressed his cheek and
nuzzled close to him.

'Wonderful!' He lay back, staring up at the whitewashed
ceiling. 'Why do you want to leave your life behind?' he
asked softly.

'I have a responsibility towards . . .' Before she could
complete her sentence Tara heard words.

She is going insane.

She couldn't ignore the sentence that crept into her mind—it sounded like it was Karan's thought.

'Towards?' Karan glanced at her.

'Towards a certain cause.'

Yeah, right!

'I'm a man of science. And I'm tolerant of others' religious beliefs. I can accept it if you have them and you want to indulge in your faith. But I cannot understand if it disrupts lives, Tara.'

So you are insane just as I suspected! Aarti is solid, reliable and marriage material. Why would I want to settle for someone unpredictable like you?

So those were Karan's real thoughts?

Tara felt as though someone had ripped her heart out and then prodded it with an electric wire. The pain she felt was so strong, she wanted to scream at him. She wanted to ask him why he had deceived her. But she also knew why she had questioned it all along. The fact that she could read his mind was a clear indication that she was far deeper into things than she'd cared to admit. This power of the Nine was both a blessing and a curse. It was meant to isolate her. Loneliness was her destiny. Tara should just surrender to it.

The dam of tears was building and the only way to distract herself was to move away. She began dressing, her clothes were strewn all over the floor. He was still lying down, and he watched her with a bemused expression.

She kept an even tone. 'It's like this. I need six months to sort things out here. If you can accept it, that's fine. If not, I understand.'

Karan sat up. Clearly, he was suddenly confused about her change in mood. 'Please understand my situation. I need you; I love you! Let me show you how much I care about us and then you can take a decision. Come back to bed. Let me make you feel good.'

One for the road and I'm out of here.

Tara ignored the voice and looked stoically at him. 'How about we go grab a bite? And then I can drop you back to the railway station. There's an express that should be here in about two hours.'

Something in her demeanour made Karan get up and pull on his pants. 'So should I consider that it's over between us?' He seemed to be keen to have a decision. She gave him a cold stare. *How dare he put it on her!* He didn't wait for a response as he entered the toilet.

You just called me here for comfort sex. What a bitch!

Tara sank to the floor and covered her ears. It didn't help. She wished she couldn't hear the damn thoughts streaming in like a radio channel. She hugged herself as tears streamed down her face. She had to control her mind.

He was in the toilet for a while and when he emerged he saw Tara's expressionless face.

They ate in the restaurant downstairs. Amidst the noisy diners, Karan made small talk about his work. Tara listened quietly.

They walked to the railway station. Karan and his complaining thoughts and Tara listening to every word: but she was immune to them, they bounced off her and she felt nothing.

Tara hugged him before he boarded the train. A cold, distant hug that seemed to say it all. The station master blew the whistle. 'Thank you, Karan, for a wonderful time and I will always love you. It's too bad it didn't work out. Wish you a good life with Aarti,' Tara said.

As the train moved forward, she saw his shocked expression and heard the question that fell from his lips. 'Aarti? How—'

Tara gave him a sad smile.

21

Tara waited by the Bodhi tree. She paced restlessly, occasionally staring up at the spreading fig tree where Lord Sakyamuni had meditated and attained enlightenment, becoming the Buddha. It was the appropriate place to meet her new partners, forming one third of the Nine.

She was curious about the senior six. Currently, they were not living normal lives, working and sharing knowledge in their respective professional capacities. They had been transferred to a safe location. If a famous scientist or philanthropist suddenly disappeared, it would arouse suspicion. But apparently, they had 'alter selves' to take their place.

It sounded as far-fetched as aliens but then, so was hearing other people's thoughts. Here she was, with a skill that she couldn't even imagine existed. She ran the tips of her toes up and down the grassy line that had pushed itself through cracks in the concrete steps. A thought struck her: just like these weeds, nothing can stop what is meant to happen. Even the extraordinary!

Now that she was in this position and the two others would be joining her soon, they had to prove themselves. That much she knew. But she wanted to meet the senior six to understand what was expected of them. The power to communicate telepathically wasn't something she expected would happen just like that. The scientist had chosen her. *But was it really her destiny to be one of the Nine? Had there ever been any women on the Council, she wondered. What if she wasn't able to fulfil this destiny?*

Monks and nuns were performing their seated or standing meditation around the tree and its surrounding stone stupas. One was bestowed with powers if one focused on God long enough. Tara was fortunate to have achieved this state without long disciplined hours of meditation and controlling of the mind.

Monks clad in colours specific to the countries they belonged to—robes of brown, yellow, red and orange—walked around the temple peacefully. Countries like Japan, Myanmar, China, Sri Lanka, Korea and Nepal, where Buddhism is an important faith, have built their respective monasteries and temples in Bodh Gaya. These monasteries and temples reflect the varied architectural styles of the countries. Nuns in pure white, their shaved heads a stark contrast to those of female tourists, meditated a few steps away from their male counterparts.

Soon she saw a young monk move purposefully towards her. He informed Tara that the other two were on their way and that they should meet at the main temple. Nervousness wouldn't quite describe how she felt at that moment. There was anticipation, and the awareness that the future depended on the three of them not just getting along, but also connecting. She would try, and hoped they would too. She sat down on the raised walkway that faced the Mahabodhi Temple built by King Ashoka. His name in Sanskrit meant 'without sorrow', she recalled. As the third monarch of the Mauryan dynasty, he was regarded as the emperor of the ages. He was the first emperor in human history who preached unity, peace, equality and love. After two thousand years, the symbol used by Ashoka had become India's national emblem; the Ashoka chakra also found a place at the centre of the Indian flag, signifying the cycle of time and how the world changes with time. She looked up at the fifty-metre-tall pyramidal tower crowned with a bell-like stupa; beautiful carvings on its exterior depicted the life of Buddha. The beauty of the monument was breathtaking, and from what she had read, back in the fifth century, people used ingenious methods of construction. Built of bricks, the temples were considered architecturally advanced for those times.

A ceremony was in progress under the Bodhi tree. Pilgrims were handing over new robes to one of the monks. A group of monks chanted and meditated in the background. It was beautiful to watch and she could feel the calming energy touch her heart. Only briefly, though—the peace was soon shattered by a cell phone going off. She saw a middle-aged man stand up, and instead of looking embarrassed, as most people would, he answered with a loud 'Kaun?'

Tara wanted to snatch the phone from his ear and throw it into the Phalgu River. But that would go against Ashoka's doctrine of staying calm and accepting change. She turned away and returned her attention to the Mahabodhi Temple.

She saw them arrive and recognized them instantly! The energies they radiated matched with hers. She smiled. They were walking uphill towards the grand structure and looking at it with awe. Tara found Akash a good-looking man. He was tall and rugged, with features that wouldn't be out of place in an Indian film, Tara noted. But there was an odd humility in his gait—which she imagined hadn't existed before. Right behind him was Zubin. Tara noticed a round plump face topped by wind-swept hair. She sensed that a frown and a morose expression were a habit from before he arrived here.

Their journeys had changed them. Just like it had changed her—they'd suffered—and in that intensity they had rediscovered themselves and what was important in life. They had been transformed. But she also knew that they would carry the pain in their hearts as a reminder of what they had become. It brought with it the humility to do what was right.

'Tara,' she offered, as they faced each other. The monk who had informed her of their arrival stood aside and watched their awkward introductions. The men said their names and shook hands. And then they were ushered into the temple to seek the blessings of the Buddha.

Inside the temple was a large gilded bronze statue of Sakyamuni Buddha in the earth-touching mudra, robed in yellow silk that gleamed in the dim lighting. Hesitantly, they made their way into the quiet sanctum.

'Why does he hold his hand like that?' Akash asked, referring to the posture of the statue—its right hand facing down, placed upon the right knee.

Their guide answered in a soft whisper, 'It is said that when the Buddha-to-be was to attain enlightenment there was no one to witness it. He touched the ground and summoned Mother Earth to bear witness, which is what the mudra refers to.'

Another monk joined them. 'The statue is over a thousand years old and the serenity of enlightenment is visible in Buddha's expression. Facing east, seated under the Bodhi tree, it is at this very spot that Buddha found his bliss. In the early days of Buddhism, it was not Buddha's image but the Bodhi tree under which he achieved enlightenment that was worshipped. Later,

Buddhist disciples started worshipping the stupa where Buddha's relics were interned. The worship of Buddha's statue requires explanation. The statue is not an idol; rather, it is the artist's creative attempt to make one's mind focus on the teachings of Buddha rather than on Buddha himself. He was a teacher who preached that eternal bliss resided within oneself to be discovered by the self.'

'That means that we are all Buddhas—if we can discover ourselves. Cool!' Akash retorted.

Tara frowned at his casual remark. Zubin chose not to comment.

The three were led into a small square room. It was bare except for floor mats and low tables. There was a prayer wheel in one corner and Tara detected the subtle fragrance of juniper. There must be incense burning somewhere. Light filtering through the slatted windows reminded her of the prison-like clinic she had left behind. It felt like a lifetime ago that Dr Bose had disappeared, changing the course of her life. But her heart palpitated at the slightest sound, as if he had left his imprint behind. Oddly enough, she missed him. He had explained things in a way that had helped her accept what was happening. She fiddled with the chakra that hung from a black string around her neck.

Everything that she had experienced was too bizarre to explain. It had been the weirdest experience with the pyramid-like object. After she pressed it to her forehead, she'd felt different— changed—but she wasn't sure how.

If she was to believe any part of the legend, then being a woman among Ashoka's chosen men would be a challenge, she thought. It was a secret society carried down through thousands of years and she was probably the first woman to be given such powers. She had always wanted to make a mark in the world, to be recognized for some great achievement.

Never in her wildest dreams could she have imagined this was it.

The Lomas Rishi monk didn't seem surprised at her presence. But then he was a monk—acceptance was part of the fundamentals of Buddhism. Plus he was a superior being, if that's what they call people who've gone through years of meditation. An amazing magician—one minute he was there, and Dr Bose had shared all the information with him, and the next minute she just knew what she had to do. Everything was communicated in silence. It was as though a transmission wave had extended into her mind, connected with her cerebral cortex, linked neurons in her brain, and when a thought flashed through her mind, the information was there.

Was that a power she possessed or did Akash and Zubin experience a similar bizarre transformation inside that cave?

And now the three of them were here. The three that were linked with the power of the Nine. Ashoka's men and one woman. Akash and Zubin knew nothing about India, its culture or its history, and here they were, preparing to be a part of the greatest national secret of the ancient world. They were confused, she could tell by their awkward style of talking. How would they be able to work together? she wondered. They first had to understand each other, and till now, they had barely communicated. She noticed them sitting quietly like her, waiting for the next instruction. They looked uncomfortable sitting cross-legged on the straw mat.

Tara didn't want to start a conversation with the boys yet, even though she felt her energies intermingle with theirs. It was better to wait and see what was meant to happen next.

22

Lise left her room the next day wearing loose cargo pants, a T-shirt, a light sweater and sneakers. For good measure, she threw on a scarf and made her way to the ground floor, humming softly to ward away the ghostly spirits. The family of three, the two rosy-cheeked ladies and the father, were having a late lunch. They beckoned to her to join them. No, she said, pointing to her tummy. 'Still full from breakfast,' she said as she neared their table.

'I need to find Gedun Rinpoche,' she explained to the landlord. 'He is at the monastery somewhere here.'

'Come with me,' he said as he got up and walked her to the main gate outside the guest house.

'Not easy to find. You must follow the road to the big

hill and ask there,' he said, pointing to the left. 'You need to walk for ten to fifteen minutes.'

'Thank you,' Lise replied and headed down the street. The air was crisp and she felt energized by its coolness. How difficult could it be to find the monastery? This place was small. She held a map and glanced at it every now and then. But it seemed outdated and not exactly specific with details. She could see a quaint little village in the distance, nestled in the midst of hills and undulating plains. Tiny paths branching out from the main street led towards a thick wall of trees and a forest-like area to the north.

As Lise walked on, she passed a busy marketplace with stalls laden with strawberries, cabbage and other colourful fruits and vegetables, and paused in a corner—if only she had a camera to capture the beauty and simplicity of this cradled land! The walk had been pleasant and she wasn't sure if she had been on her feet for over half an hour, pausing at various places, taking in the ambience of an eastern culture. There was so much that was unusual, so different from what she was used to.

Lost in thought, she didn't notice a stranger approach her. 'Need any help?' the young man asked.

'I'm . . . not sure . . .' she said, glancing around and offering her map to him.

Lise noticed his hands as he gripped the edge of the paper. He had thick fingers streaked with scars that looked like thin cuts. His nails were crested with brown as if he worked with soil. *And stay away from the dark force in human form called Vayu.* 'Do you have a particular destination in mind or are you just wandering about and don't know how to get back?' he asked.

She narrowed her eyes, appraising him. *Could this man be the dreaded Vayu?* She couldn't just ask him. His face was wide, John Lennon glasses sat on his flat nose, bridging oriental eyes that were a soft shade of brown, the colour of earth. He had a pleasant smile that brought crinkles to the corners of his eyes. A crew cut and a solid build added toughness to his soft round face. 'I'm not sure if this is the right way to the monastery,' Lise said.

'It is,' he said, quickly adding, 'I'll walk you.' He slid into step with her, then after a momentary silence, he said, 'I'm from Hong Kong. And you?'

'From Amsterdam,' Lise replied, slowing down at each little shop or stall as she walked, hoping her pace would throw him off her track.

'Here to study . . . ?' He waited patiently with her, watching her with an amused expression.

'The culture,' Lise said, transferring her bag to her left shoulder and adding, 'for a travel magazine. And sightseeing, of course. I'm researching age-old customs, symbolic rituals, something unique.'

He was wearing a long-sleeved T-shirt pulled up to his elbows and jeans that seemed too baggy for him. He walked with a strong shoulders-back military bearing, Lise noticed. He stood with his hands behind his back, attentive to her movements.

'You a tourist?' Lise asked.

'You could call me that.' He shrugged those broad shoulders. 'I'm staying here for a few months, working for my university, researching the sites in this area. Training to be an archaeologist. Just like my uncle who was famous for having unearthed a lot of ancient fine pottery in China, and for having discovered a whole new clan of people that is now extinct. He was always digging around, nose practically to the ground.' He smiled. And his oriental eyes met hers with a wink. It was too long a speech for a stranger. He was trying too hard.

'What kind of research have you done so far?' she asked cautiously.

'There are many aspects of Tibetan, Bhutanese and Nepalese culture and history that are intriguing, and, of course, there are many sites in these border regions that have been left unexplored,' he said, and they walked single file as they made their way past a row of fruit stalls. 'I'm aiming to research these remote areas.'

Lise smiled at the sellers, but many of the locals seemed shy and turned away.

'By the way, I'm Steve,' he said once they were on a quieter stretch. 'Steven Chan.'

She sighed with relief. *Not Vayu. Why would he lie to a total stranger?* But what if he knew? She let the thought disintegrate. He wouldn't hurt her in broad daylight and in the midst of a crowd.

'Lise,' she replied. The aroma of burning paper and

sweetish incense rose in the air. And the monastery came into view. It loomed up suddenly like a fort atop a hill dwarfing the surrounding area and structures. Perched on a slope, the Buddhist Monastery of the Enlightened Ones sat majestically with lush green hills in the background. The place was busy with lamas, Buddhist monks, robed in rich maroon. A few steps from the entrance was a large lavishly carved stone shrine. On either side were similar but smaller places of worship. 'Why do all these temples have mountain-shaped roofs?' Lise asked, fascinated by her first close-up glimpse of a monastic complex.

'They represent the shape of Mount Meru, a mythical place considered to be the abode of the gods and the centre of the universe. Everything about a temple is symbolic,' Steve answered.

'So the structure and columns all mean something . . .' Lise gazed up at the intricate designs created thousands of years ago. 'And monks live here too?'

'Yes. There were over four thousand monks living here but now there are only about six hundred,' he replied as they made their way around the curve. Steve's eyes were on the monks as they exited the side gates of the monastery. He skirted the concrete walls surrounding the holy area. Lise ran a finger along the walls as they walked. Then he continued, 'The carvings depict the everyday life of Buddha. It means that the daily activities were relevant to Buddhism and made it easier for the followers to understand the symbols. These monasteries are large areas that consist of open courtyards, a big stupa, sanctuaries and small rooms for the monks.'

They arrived at the main entrance of the monastery and Lise bounded up the few steps to the main gate. Steve stayed behind, his pulse was racing, he felt perspiration roll down his back and the sides of his face. The Kalingan within him was swirling, pressing on his mind to snap her neck. He imagined it, heard the delicate bone crack, saw her head roll and her body fall to the ground. He looked hard at the sunlight, letting his eyes water, and clenched his fists in his pockets.

*

Noticing he wasn't beside her, Lise spun around and looked at him questioningly. From this distance, she could see his hard black eyes boring into hers. It made her slightly suspicious but she brushed her uneasiness aside.

'Aren't you coming, Steve?' she called out. 'I really want to know more.' There was so much to explore! What seemed ordinary to most was new and mysterious to her. She climbed further up. The ringing bells and cymbals were a welcoming sound. Her attention was drawn elsewhere. 'Look at all these sculptures—so intricate and beautiful, as if they were carved of wood and not stone. Isn't it?'

Steve removed his beeping mobile from his pocket. 'I have to take this,' he said and turned away from her.

Lise sprinted towards the steps marked with a dozen animal symbols.

He stood outside. 'What's up?' she called out. He had hung up and was watching her with narrowed eyes. A few monks turned towards her. She gave an embarrassed smile for raising her voice and skipped back down towards him.

'I've got to make an important call home,' he tapped his watch.

'Okay, then. Thank you for showing me the way. And telling me all the interesting stuff left out of the tourist books.'

'You're welcome!' Steve forced a smile.

*

A group of monks passed them and entered their domain. Steve shuddered—it took all his strength not to lash out at them. He waited until they had gone. 'I was wondering if you would like to meet again? And if you're not doing anything tonight, I can show you around, tell you about the legends of this place,' he said, looking a little beyond her head. 'And there's a nice little restaurant where you can try some local delicacies. That is, if you are free.' He shrugged, hands in his pockets.

*

Lise's heart tapped excitedly. 'Yes, that would be wonderful! Let's meet here.'

'About 8 p.m. then?' he asked, backing away slowly. A group of monks was headed in his direction. She nodded absently, her eyes already on the shrine, all suspicion about Steve, if she had any, getting washed away in her fascination. She turned around, and he was already a smallish figure receding into the distance.

23

Lise entered the sprawling grounds that surrounded the Monastery of the Enlightened Ones and the smaller dome-topped temples. Monks moved in groups of threes or fours, and farther away she saw a few of them seated cross-legged on the hard ground, meditating. They were still, and in that stillness, Lise felt the serenity of time in its element, while the world moved about. They looked like a family of birds, contemplating in silence.

The monastery complex was an ethereal experience. The moment she entered she felt an unusual stirring within. Tears pricked her eyes and she blinked them away. She felt like she was suspended in mid-air, enjoying a slice of heaven with the lush mountain view surrounding her. She had climbed five hundred steps to reach this level. And there was another level further up, where a small temple stood, carved out of the hill itself.

She took off her shoes and entered the monastery. The

monks glided by when they saw her. They kept their distance. A boy with a shaved head and burgundy robes blocked her from entering further.

'I'm looking for someone,' Lise explained.

'Then you must ask,' the young boy with wide brown eyes said seriously. 'Women are not welcome here.'

'Oh, I'm sorry!' she said in a respectful whisper. Then she asked the young monk for Gedun Rinpoche.

'Wait outside.' The boy ran inside the crowded temple.

Lise was surprised that Steve hadn't mentioned this crucial fact to her. Lise sat down on the steps facing the mountains and waited.

A few minutes later, an old monk approached and led her via a circuitous route to the recesses of the complex. It was quiet and deserted. The air seemed thinner and cooler. And it reeked of a heavy sweet incense. She was feeling slightly breathless. The monk showed no signs of discomfort. He led her to a corner cell, a dome-shaped structure, and she noticed that it housed a single person. He grunted and gestured to her to enter and wait quietly. It was not stuffy but the enclosed space made it seem warmer than it was. The stone walls added to the cave-like atmosphere. There was a man seated on a mat with his eyes closed; he looked as weathered as an ancient manuscript. It was him, Lise understood instinctively. Gedun Rinpoche was in a meditative pose. She sat tentatively resting her back against the wall. Gedun was so old, at least a hundred, she thought; his robes of burgundy practically enveloped him. A reddish-brown string of beads hung around his neck.

Lise waited and waited. Then she shifted uncomfortably. Sitting on the hard ground for fifteen minutes was giving her cramps. She stood up and looked around the small enclosure. The walls curved, forming an egg-shaped oval with the ceiling rising into an apex. An incense stand held a pungent stick that let off greenish smoke. Two standing lamps with three cotton wicks each were lit creating large wavering shadows. The flickering flames had a hypnotic effect on Lise, washing over her like a warm jacket on a winter's day. She had come across a number of sculptures and etchings in the monastery and mentally check-listed the bunch of questions she would ask Steve.

'You will do no such thing!' The sudden burst of words in the serene atmosphere was like the first blow of a hammer on a nail. Lise was so startled, she spun around and almost tripped on the floor mat. The old man glared at her. His eyes were not black or brown but grey, hard, steel-like. The focus of his stare was so intense that Lise felt momentarily disoriented.

'What . . . what?' Lise asked confused.

'You took the name of the evildoer. Ashoka's enemy!' For a thin, visibly weak old man, he had the voice of a lion. Lise gaped stupidly. He spoke in English, yet she had no clue about what he was referring to.

'I don't understand what you mean,' she approached

cautiously and sat facing him. He hadn't shifted the slightest, except for his wild eyes keenly watching her.

'The man you met outside, before you entered our terrain—he is evil. You will not think of him in this holy place. It's sacrilege!' the livid monk exclaimed.

Again she gaped. 'But I didn't say anything,' and then with a chill, it dawned on her. 'You can read my thoughts?' This was as crazy as the guy who performed magic stunts in her country, the one who swallowed a sword and made coins appear out of people's ears. First ghosts, now a mind-reader. *He must have heard that.*

Gedun gazed stonily. 'You think I am doing magic, eh?' A half-smile played on his lips, and his skull-mask face looked scarier than before. His bald head shone. 'You have come here for a reason. So tell me what you have to say, otherwise leave this place. You are nothing but a worthless being, living your life through your addictions and ego. Instant gratification, that's what you seek, isn't it? But that is not my problem. Only take heed of my warning: that fellow is the enemy!'

As far as she could tell, Steve was kind and friendly and knew a lot about the culture. Was this attitude part of the decorum with regard to male–female friendships? She wasn't sure, but his ferocious behaviour was a little overboard. With his mannerisms like that of a drill sergeant, she thought it was better that she just pass him the message and meet Steve before she returned home, to her country.

He spoke again. 'Do as you wish, your soul needs the life lesson before it can begin to practise. And besides, your destiny does not lead you back home, my dear. You must confront suffering.' It seemed to Lise that he took pleasure in knowing she would suffer. 'But don't reveal the secret to this man. Or bed him. Remember you are a treasure chest, a receptacle of precious gifts, and you have a higher responsibility—do not abuse it.'

She didn't understand a word of what he was saying. *Bed him? Now why would she bed Steve?* A little voice in her heart told her that she was attracted to him, but sleeping with him sounded a bit much. She focused on the purpose of her visit. 'Dr Halvor is dead. He said I must see you and tell you that—'

'I know everything. The minute you walked in here I understood. He has transferred the information of what he held secret for over half a century and the crazy guy picked you!' Gedun Rinpoche wasn't hiding his impression of her. 'You' was spat out with disgust.

Lise felt a spark of anger. 'I had not planned to be the holder of his secrets. And Dr Halvor wasn't crazy. He was . . . he was like a . . . father to me,' she said with a quiver in her voice.

'Ah, you have a sense of loyalty! Very good. Then perhaps the good doctor wanted to transfer his knowledge to a person least likely to be suspected. But you are still young. I judge your mind—so easily trusting of the physical—so easily manipulated by the illusions of this

world. You think with your senses, not with your heart,'
Gedun said, raising one skeletal hand to his chest, and
Lise felt all this mumbo jumbo was turning her mind to
mush. The fragrance from the incense was giving her a
headache and she was tired of being criticized. Lise looked
at him reproachfully. In the twenty-four hours she had
spent in this land, she had warmed up to it, and wanted
to bond. But Gedun Rinpoche was treating her like she
was evil personified.

'I have come all this way in search of you. To give you
the message. Now that you have sensed it and I have
done my duty towards the doctor, there is no reason for
me to be here. I shall leave this place,' she said, standing
up.

Gedun Rinpoche's steely eyes gazed in rapt attention.
His eyebrows shifted from a crooked bush to a wide-eyed
straight line. 'You are feeling sorry for yourself, eh?' In a
swift smooth movement, he stood up too. For a man his
age, his limbs were nimble. 'Come with me, young lady,'
he said, turning towards the back wall.

In the gloomy interior she hadn't noticed a small
wooden door. He opened it and walked in, then stopped,
waiting for her impatiently. She followed him. Lise
wondered absently if he too were a ghost like Wangdak,
the spirit guide.

'Don't compare me to that guide. He likes to show
off!' Gedun murmured.

How does one protect one's thoughts?

'Think of one thing and that's all,' he advised. 'Try *Om Mani Padme Hum*—the chant of the Buddha.'

She knew one thing she wanted to think about, but decided to avoid it or the Rinpoche would . . . She recalled the first sight of this land that touched her heart, before Wangdak had appeared. She focused on the breathtaking scenery in her mind.

He led her through a narrow tunnel-like corridor. It was dark and the only light there was the one Gedun carried with him. He barrelled forward as if he could see what was ahead. It was pitch black and cold, like a cemetery. Lise had to trot to keep up with him.

'Where are we going?' she asked in a wavering voice that echoed around her.

'To protect you from your destiny.'

His answer didn't help, she was as confused as before.

They reached an ornately carved door. And he stopped abruptly.

The door creaked and the sound echoed around them. They entered a large circular chamber. There was no light source, yet the room was lit up as if the walls were made of crystal and glowing from within.

'Here we shall test your mental strength. Go to the centre,' Gedun pointed to the ground, which had concentric circles of light that seemed to be buzzing with energy. In the middle was a pulsing orange glow.

'Why? And why do I have to do this?'

He gave her an impatient look and said, 'Do you have to question everything? The first step is to learn to accept.'

'Just tell me what is going on, okay?' Lise said with irritation.

'We have to know if you are who you say you are.'

'Can't you read my mind?'

'Yes, but the Kala Yogis have mastered the art of creating falsehood. We have to protect what is left of the knowledge. They will come after you and split your mind open like a coconut and scoop out all that is relevant and you will be left a blubbering idiot if this is not done.' He paused when he noted Lise didn't react, then said, 'The doctor has given you a very important secret to keep. I need to know that it is for real and that you are not a tool that has been sent to sabotage our cause. Whatever you possess within you is the most potent secret of our time, not even the Council of Nine is aware of it yet. You let it out to these evil beings, and the secret society to which the many scientific breakthroughs are credited, will be non-existent. That's been their evil plan for centuries. You serve a higher purpose and we don't want to deal with infiltrators weakening our position.'

He spoke with such passion and conviction that Lise couldn't think of doing anything but what she was instructed to do. Standing on the glowing circular segment she thought of all that had happened. Life was racing ahead, every step presented a choice to be made, and the future held some treacherous paths. *Was she capable of choosing the right one? And how would she know which was the right path to follow?* This was one of the oddest days of her life, which would bring her nothing positive except the satisfaction of having done her job well. She was sure that when it was all over, and if she lived to a ripe old age, she would talk about it and people would call her senile.

The minute she stepped on the mysteriously lit floor, a sharp tingle passed through her like an electric current. The back of her neck and her ears felt hot, a burning sensation closed in on her, and her eyes watered from the heat. Her head began to swim and she gasped for breath. But before she could do anything, Lise felt another burst of energy hit her. This time she fell unconscious.

24

Dharamsala

'Right on time,' Lise said, standing in a corner some distance away from the monastery. She felt a strange excitement race through her at the sight of him. *What was this? Was she destined to be attracted to all that was not good for her?*

'You've been here all this time?' he asked, greeting her with a handshake. Steve looked relieved to see her, as if she may have changed her mind. 'Let's go, there's so much I want to tell you.'

'That's great. What is it?' she asked, moving ahead of him. The monks were giving them odd looks. She felt uncomfortable, as if she was cavorting with the devil. She wished Gedun hadn't coloured her mind. Steve deserved the benefit of the doubt. He had such a harmless appearance. He didn't have a hard edge to his face or his demeanour. True, he looked strangely at her, but that didn't prove anything. Even when he spoke he had a soft grit to his voice that was hypnotic. 'So, did you meet the monk you were looking for?'

'Yes, there was so much I had to learn in there.' Lise pointed a thumb back at the receding outline of the holy structure.

'Whatever you want to know, just be careful. Monks are, well, monks. They have a different view of the world. A little too harsh, a little too self-righteous and intimidating for outsiders.'

'Maybe. But they seem least concerned with the outside world.'

She stepped lightly beside him. His hands were in his pockets and he shrugged his shoulders as if nothing really mattered to him.

'It gets dark and deserted quite early around here,' Steve said. There was a stillness in the air. The sun had lost its strength and was an orange globe shimmering in the distance. Lise felt fear radiate from the pit of her stomach. It was unnerving—this sudden connection with her emotions. There was a clarity of thought which she had not experienced before. Emotions had never come to her with such focused intensity. For her they'd almost always arrived in a packaged desire for alcohol or drugs.

What she was feeling right now was a clear 'stay away from the evildoer!' sign but Lise was not one to follow rules or old bald men wearing burgundy robes. She dismissed her fear.

They walked quietly, enjoying the view. 'It's so peaceful here . . .'

Steve nodded. 'Yes, it's very different from city life, there are no street lights and one needs to remember that we are outsiders; typically not much policing. You have to be careful, especially if you are here for the first time.'

'You are a tourist too, aren't you?'

'Yes, but I have been in these parts quite often. And I understand the culture.'

'I see,' Lise said, and folded her arms, trying to push the odd feeling away.

They walked together in silence for a few minutes. Then Steve broke the silence, 'You seem different.'

'I am different.'

'No, I mean compared to earlier, before you entered that monastery. There is something different about you.'

Gedun Rinpoche had warned her about Steve. He didn't look like an evildoer, she wished he hadn't created this doubt in her mind. The monk wanted to protect her from her destiny. Odd thing to say. He seemed to know what would happen in her future. Even she didn't know where she was headed. 'Yes, too much happening too fast. Life is not as it seems. Sometimes we have to face situations we were not meant to face. You're thrown into the sea and expected to swim . . . I don't know if I can,' she said, her voice dropping to a whisper.

He paused and gave her a sideward glance. 'You have turned philosophical all of a sudden. Being thrown into the deep end is the only way to learn,' Steve said insightfully.

'Yes, that is true. But if someone else had been in my shoes and experienced what I'm going through, it would be good to learn how to . . . deal with it.' Lise sighed and turned to him. 'You must think I'm crazy, speaking in this way. It's just that I'm faced with a situation that is a little difficult.'

His expression softened, as if he understood what she felt. 'There is a deep-seated hurt within you,' he said. Steve was so sensitive, he could sense her confusion. She didn't mind when he took her hand gently and held it in his. 'Do you want to tell me what's really on your mind? I am all ears. I don't mean to pry, but sometimes a stranger's ears are more accepting. I think you are here in search of . . . I don't know . . . answers. People come here when their life loses its purpose and meaning. They come looking for spirituality, for the reasons of their existence. Sometimes their questions are answered.'

'And other times . . . ?' She didn't draw her hand away. He had a soothing touch.

'They return, dispirited, even more disillusioned than before. It's hard to live in a mind like that,' he said, staring away into the distance behind her head. She felt his hand turning warm and his gentle repetitive caress was beautiful, inducing a deep sense of contentment. His words were like a balm compared to her experience with the monk earlier.

Even though she had been unconscious, she was able to recall her unusual experience in the middle of the strange electrical field. Snapshots of her life zipped through her mind. The monk was inside her head, judging her. Lise had to face the painful memories coming at her like a waterfall. The sensations, the feelings of hurt and happiness, all bunched up and coursed through her as if she were reliving her past. She fought it, but couldn't bear the emotional pain. She cried out. Then the monk's hard voice filled her head: 'The Knowledge Keeper chose you because he had faith in you. You are a coward if you cannot face yourself, your mistakes and the emotions. Face them, experience the pain courageously, brave the shame, and then surrender, let them all go into nothingness. Your mind will become strong and will weather any storm. But if you wallow in the shallow layer of your conscious mind, using worldly pleasures to avoid the pain, you will lose yourself again and again. Do it for Halvor, the man you call your father. Do it to protect the ancient knowledge.' Lise shook her head. The monk's eyes bore into her. 'Then know this, weakling, I will stop you from sharing any information with that evil spirit. You will reveal nothing or suffer dire consequences!' The monk's warning voice reverberated from deep within her as she moved closer to Steve. She couldn't resist his charm. He was a friend in this land of strangers.

Steve stopped at a bridge. A small stream flowed underneath and, in the horizon stood the mountains, glowing gold in the setting sun. He faced her, his eyes were molten, drawing her into them like a magnet. She felt it, the sense of something deep and ancient within him. He spoke with an ability to understand her. No man had ever tried to understand her feelings. Frissons of fear lurked just beyond the sense of happiness. She ignored it, and very slowly Steve took her other hand. He pressed gently and the sense of alarm disappeared.

Lise was rooted to the spot. Her heart throbbed in anticipation. She felt both an attraction and an intense need to speak her mind, to tell him everything. Her life story, her addiction, her struggle to break that horrible dependency, about Dr Halvor and finally, the real reason she was here. She wanted to let it all out, and it didn't matter what else happened. *Who could see the future? What is meant to be would be. And wasn't this her destiny?* It wasn't love, but a deep sense of wanting surged through her. Love. Why did that word even pop into her head? Love at this inopportune time, and with this person of all people. No it was not love, it was just . . .

'There is some connection between us . . .' Steve whispered. He stepped closer, their faces inches apart. 'Do you not feel it, Lise?'

Her lips parted, and she felt his breath on hers. 'Yes,'

she whispered and very tenderly his lips pressed against hers.

Lise pulled herself away. 'This is very strange, not something that happens to me.'

'I feel that way as well,' Steve responded.

'I'm not ready for this,' Lise said unsurely.

They strolled down the street again. Lise's heart pounded in her ears, she flushed. Sweat broke out on the back of her neck.

Steve spoke, 'It could be that we are soulmates. And we can sense the connection between us. In the city our senses are bombarded with so many things that we get caught up in them. We don't focus on one single thought for long enough before another takes over and that messes up our brains. Here it is easier to connect. With people from a past life.'

'Past life?' Lise giggled softly. 'You believe in a past life?'

'You think that after we die, there's nothing left? That is such a naive viewpoint! The way you look at it, you live, you die and shit happens, ha!' And he stopped as if to get a grip on himself. 'Our souls are pure energy, they don't just disintegrate to nothingness, Lise. They carry on their journey until they attain the purity to join with the universal light. In this part of the world it is a common belief that souls are reincarnated to ultimately become pure and become one with the light. That is why we have the ability to introspect.'

Lise didn't know how to respond. This was a belief system she had not bothered to delve into. If God did exist then there would be no suffering in this world. It was that simple. She didn't think there was any purpose to life, except to exist and then when the heart stops, you become one with the earth. *Souls? No one knows what they are and where they go. How could he know what happens after death?* It was her belief that bodies carried electrical impulses, and just like a light bulb goes off, we go off. Full stop. And there was no other way to come alive again. Eastern philosophies were riddled with legends and stories but for her they were just that—legends and stories. From the way Steve explained, the only conclusion she could draw was that if a man speaks of God, he could not be evil.

They stopped in front of a dimly lit restaurant. Not exactly a restaurant, it was more like a little square space without a door, resting just above the sidewalk. The back wall had a glass centre, revealing the tiny kitchen. The place seemed to be no more than a thousand square feet, consisting of four tables that could barely seat four each. It was a shop converted into an eatery. Looking at the three bright cooker flames blazing in the kitchen, Lise wondered about fire hazards, and whether they even had permission to have a fire. A thin couple were the only other diners inside. The middle-aged proprietor was a big man with keen eyes. He was sitting behind an old-fashioned cash register, chewing on something that made his lips and teeth all red. When he saw them, he jumped up. Steve and Lise climbed the three stone steps, entered and were greeted eagerly by the man. He pumped Steve's hand as if they were old friends. 'Welcome, welcome,' he said, giving him a hearty back slap, speaking in the local lingo.

'This is Mr Harinder. He has lived here for many, many years,' Steve said, introducing them. Noticing her husband's guests, Harinder's wife, a short squat woman with flushed cheeks emerged from the kitchen, wiping her forehead with her apron. Her hair was tied up in an untidy braid, and Lise noted that she wasn't wearing a scarf or net to protect the food from hair strands that might fall into it.

'This is my friend from Holland. Her name is Lise,' Steve introduced her.

Harinder was friendlier than his wife. The woman nodded and managed a tight smile. She quickly returned to her place in the kitchen, while her husband continued to chat and ushered them to choose a table. 'We'll take the one nearer to the entrance, the air is cooler.' They sat down on wooden stools and Harinder left them alone with the menu.

'Seems like you come here often,' Lise noted.

'Yes, the only place where the food is good,' he said loudly and smiled at Harinder, who responded with a hearty laugh and translated the words to his wife. She gave him a warm smile.

'I'll order the local food,' Steve said, beckoning the young waiter. 'Hope you don't mind trying something different.'

'Not at all!' she said, without feeling any enthusiasm. Lise asked for bottled water. They didn't have it, so she settled for a cola.

'Try something different—you probably drink coke all the time.'

'I know, but I've been craving some caffeine.'

Steve grinned. 'How about coffee later at my place? I've got good old-fashioned Nescafé. Try the lemon tea here. It's good.'

Was that an offer for a sleepover? He was moving fast. 'Okay.'

Steve placed the order for drinks and food and leaned back against the wall. He had an amused expression on his face.

'What?'

'What's with the tattoos and the black nail polish and the piercings?'

Lise spread her hands on the table. 'Why? What's wrong with it?'

He shrugged. 'I don't mind, it's interesting. Common in big cities, but here things are a little different. People believe in ghosts and strange symbols,' he said with an odd expression. Taking a big gulp of his drink, he continued, 'Just a piece of advice, though—the locals don't like black markings and funky tattoos, especially on women's bodies. They are more inclined to religious and protective symbols. And if you are going to interview people you might not get a good response.'

Lise sipped her lemon tea. 'Hmm . . . I understand. People could have been a little stand-offish with me because of this.' She wondered if the landlord's wife and, more recently, Gedun Rinpoche felt the same way. She shrugged and drank some more tea. 'Where I come from, this is not such a big deal. But I suppose there's always a reason to change.' Lise pointed at the object dangling from his neck. 'But what is the meaning of that thing round your neck, with the red stone? Is it something religious?'

Steve touched it reverently. 'It's a talisman, a symbol of an ancient warrior clan.'

'Why do you wear it?'

'It is my loyalty to the Kalingan.'

'Kalingan?'

Her reaction was immediate. The world seemed to close in on her, and her knees trembled. The word had raised the hair on her neck. The sudden fear alarmed her. She took a large gulp of her lemon tea and coughed violently.

'Are you okay?' Steve stood up quickly, eager to help.

'I'm fine,' she rasped, gesturing to him to sit down.

He ordered another drink for her. It was an irrational feeling. But it lurked uneasily at the back of her mind. Before she could ask anything more, the waiter arrived.

He gave them wide friendly smiles and placed before them a plate of tomato broth with dumplings.

'Those are momos, a Tibetan delicacy,' Steve explained. *Why did she feel that danger lurked in the vicinity?* She wasn't sure she could eat. Then they began talking and things seemed to settle down a bit. Lise was so overwhelmed by the happenings around her that she decided to put everything out of her mind till she could process it. Right now, she was in no danger and could afford to relax.

To help take her mind off things, a plate of thick pancakes arrived, they looked like they were deep-fried. 'Balep—Tibetan bread,' he said, helping himself to the dumplings and dipping the bread in the tomato soup.

Next to arrive was a dish with white rolls that wobbled like jelly. Lephing was an all-time favourite street food, Steve explained. It was a spicy moong bean gelato flavoured with chillies and garlic.

'Hope you haven't ordered more,' Lise said. She was nibbling on the momos and bread, mimicking the way Steve ate. It was all very delicious and filling her up very fast.

A middle-aged man with slick hair and greying side-burns entered. He sat down and ordered immediately without bothering with the menu. His food arrived instantly and he began slurping from a bowl of soup. As he ate, he gave them surreptitious glances.

It must be her appearance—the black nail polish and

purple streaks in her hair—that made people uncomfortable. Steve seemed totally unaffected by the way she looked. She heaped some more food on her plate. The company was good, the atmosphere warm and enticing. Initially, she had been a bit antsy but now she was beginning to relax. She looked at Steve and her eyes fell on his talisman. The red stone was beautiful, stunning even—she couldn't help staring at it. Everything was fine, she was just overreacting.

Lise turned her attention to the large picture of a monastery on the wall above them. It reminded Lise of her question.

'You mentioned the stupa earlier. I've read about it, but I want to hear you talk about it.'

'A stupa represents the Buddha,' Steve explained as he spooned some of the lephing on to her plate. 'He is crowned and sitting in meditation on a lion throne. So the architecture of the stupa was designed to have a metaphoric context. The top of the spire is the crown, Buddha's head is the square at the spire's base, his body is the vase shape, his legs are the four steps of the lower terrace and the base is his throne. The five components of the stupa also constitute the five elements—earth, water, fire, air and space—the fabric of physical existence.'

The monk was wrong—Steve was a good guy, not evil personified as he claimed—Lise mused as she smeared the last bit of red sauce on her bread and ate it. There was nothing about him that spelled nasty. He just seemed to have a deep knowledge of history, almost as if he was living it and there was no danger in that. The Rinpoche was probably reacting to his attachment to the Kalingan.

'There is something very poetic about the way you explain it,' Lise smiled.

Steve smiled back and they ate in silence. There was too much food and they couldn't finish all of it.

As they relaxed, Steve threw a question in the air. 'How would you like it if you were the most powerful person in this world?'

Lise was caught by surprise. 'What do you mean?'

'You know what I mean, to have the power to do, be and get anything you want. Change destiny. Live a life of luxury, have so much money that you don't know what to do with it. Do you not want all that and more? What if you could have the power to fulfil all your dreams!'

'Power to fulfil dreams, change destiny! Tell me more, Steve, sounds interesting.' She saw his face turning red, and he asked for water. 'But I must warn you, I have come here to write a travel story, based on reality. I'm not here . . . for legends and fables of the past. Your story sounds quite bizarre,' she teased.

Steve didn't smile. In fact his face was turning a deeper shade of red, as if he had had too much beer. 'We do different things for different reasons. I'm sure the real reason you have come to this corner of the world is not just to write about it.' His voice was gritty.

The same dread raised its head. Lise began feeling

nauseous and the dumplings floating in red sauce weren't giving her pleasant thoughts. She wiped her mouth. 'I think we are both tired. And I would like to return to my guest house,' Lise said, standing up.

Within seconds, Steve lost his angry edge. 'Please sit down. I'm sorry. I was doing some research and there is something about this place—it's magical—and I guess I got carried away. I just wanted to share it with you. You seem to understand me. We have a connection, don't you think?' He looked at her with an apologetic expression. The redness was decreasing as he waited for her response.

She didn't sit down.

Steve sighed and got up. He paid for the food and moved out of his seat. With a courteous gesture, he thanked the owners of the restaurant, while Lise waited outside.

His guest house was just down the road, he explained. 'If you are not in too much of a hurry, can I please make it up to you over a cup of coffee? I would like to explain.' He saw her wavering expression. 'No, I promise, no more outbursts! And the coffee is not the local kind, it's good old-fashioned instant stuff. I picked it up from one of my treks to the city.'

Lise tapped her feet and turned away from the direction that would lead her back to her guest house. 'A cup of instant coffee sounds like a great idea!'

They walked in silence. The full moon, visible behind

wispy clouds, cast greyish shadows on the stone sidewalk. It wasn't the atmosphere that bothered her as much as the stirring within her. Steve was attractive and his alternating personality was enticing. But a part of her was also aware of her odd tendency to get involved with unstable men. She recalled Bernard—he was one of the odd characters. He was an exchange student studying in Amsterdam and Lise had met him at an art exhibition. It wasn't love at first sight—they had opposing views on the paintings and as the evening progressed, their animosity towards each other converted into something almost animal-like. The memories made her shiver. They met often to discuss art, but their physical relations were intense. It was soon after that they both got hooked on drugs. The sex filled a void but it was never enough. She turned her mind away from that crazy time of her life. She shouldn't be thinking about getting into a physical relationship. But, Lise thought, this place helped her open her heart to someone, to feel and to touch another human being in that way. To be able to trust again, love again. *What was wrong with that?* She would let emotions be her guide.

The coffee was good, and his small apartment was simple and clean. After she returned to her hotel, Lise decided to spend a few more days in the village. She met Steve a couple of times after that. He would take her sightseeing, followed by more local food and coffee in his room. They would chat for hours. She told him about her past in Amsterdam and then, about more recent things like Wangdak, the monk's warnings, and how she didn't think Steve had an evil bone in his body. Steve listened with a sympathetic ear, telling her about his martial arts training, and skimming over his near-death experience. Lise was falling in love. This man was next to perfect for her! The only odd behaviour she noted was that he didn't enter monasteries. 'It's all that smoke from their incense. It affects me, I'm allergic to it.'

She accepted his reason and let it go. About a week later, while travelling on a bus to a small village, Steve mentioned a cave they should visit.

'Sounds good.'

And just like that the next thing he whispered in her ear was, 'I want to make love to you.'

Lise was startled. She didn't even know how to respond. Why was she behaving like such a prude? Ordinarily, she would have responded with an equally bold statement.

'Don't say anything. It will be beautiful tonight. You are so beautiful.' He pressed her hand, before he let go. She was nervous for no reason.

The bus stopped and they stepped out. Lise couldn't concentrate on the beautiful pastures and the scenic view. Over the past few days, she had wanted to return home, but she kept delaying it. There was no reason to stay back, but now she knew. It was because of Steve. She was hooked to him, and she needed closure. The physical attraction was holding her back.

Lise had removed the black nail polish; her tawny hair was no longer painted in artificial colours, it had faded away after three shampoos. She styled her hair so that it framed her face, giving her a softer, feminine look. She had deliberately done all this to please him. A sense of panic clutched at her heart: *Was she an addict all over again?* First Bernard, then drugs and now a stranger in a strange land.

*

At 6 p.m. she went directly to his guest house. Steve had picked up some food from a restaurant; he had a bottle of chilled orange juice which he blended with some vodka that he had managed to buy from tourists. She had an odd sensation in her stomach: pleasant, like champagne bubbles. Every time she thought of Steve, her heart leaped and her skin broke into a sweat. There was an animal-like aura about him—a suppressed energy—and she wanted to know what would happen if he unleashed his wild side. She was ready to play with fire, and get singed if she had to. Life wasn't only about staying sober and within boundaries, and being controlled.

They clinked their glasses. He took a large swig, while she sipped hers slowly.

'Don't look so nervous! I don't bite, unless that's what you like.' He had an amused, thoughtful expression. 'You want to do this as much as I do. I can see the hunger in your eyes.'

Lise felt her cheeks burning. She sipped her drink and turned away from him. The window was curtained. She slid it aside and noticed the distant valley with a few herdsmen and goats. The sun was slowly sinking in the horizon. She could feel him behind her, breathing on her skin, and she wanted to respond. The suspense made it exciting, the air crackled with their heat. She let go of the curtain and darkness fell on them.

'I should turn on the light.'

'No,' she whispered. He pushed her against the cool glass. And she felt her skin react to his touch. He smoothed away her silk top and slid his fingers under it, caressing her skin. Her mind closed, and her emotions took over. They didn't make it to the bedroom, as they ripped their clothes hungrily, exploring each other. Lise felt she had unleashed all her pent-up emotions. She wept hot tears while they lay naked. Later, they sipped on their drinks, studying each other with narrow eyes until their breathing settled, and they eagerly ate the cold food.

And then they made love again.

'I have been with other women, but none as white and angelic as you . . . ' Steve whispered as his eyes moved over her bare skin.

She didn't know whether to accept his compliment or to feel offended at being compared to other women. She chose to feel flattered.

Much later, when the moon was high, and they were in bed, their breathing quietened and regular, Lise spoke. 'I know where the soul of the Nine lies.' She didn't know why she said that but she suddenly didn't want any distance between them. Steve's legs were entwined with hers, and she felt his muscles tense up. Lise turned to face him and in the semi-darkness she saw the red pinpoints of his eyes.

'Where is it?' he asked hoarsely.

'It is . . . ' she waited for the fact to emerge, but it didn't. 'I . . . I . . . can't remember!' she said, feeling like an idiot. 'For some reason my mind is all a jumble,' she said, pulling away. Steve moved closer, trying to fathom her expressions. She looked confusedly at him and said, 'It feels as if the secret is buried deep in my mind. And I feel as if there is a dark heavy blanket covering it. I keep trying to lift the blanket but I can't.' She let out a sigh. Here she was, ready to give the love of her life all she had but her mind was failing her!

Steve shifted away and slipped out of bed. He was breathing hard, avoiding her stare.

'Are you all right?' she asked concerned. *Was she going to lose him?*

'I'm fine,' he said as he sat down for a moment. Then abruptly, he stood up and headed for the bathroom.

Lise found her clothes and put them on quickly. A sense of dread rose again in her beating heart. She was about to leave when he emerged, looking agitated and restless. He gripped her by her arms and pushed her back on the bed. Without a word, he was on top of her, kissing her hard. Pushing her long skirt above her legs, he found her skimpy nylons and ripped them away. His eyes were predatory and he didn't hide his desire. It drew her in and she let him. She wanted to feel the pain from his grip, his gyrating pressure and the flooding relief when nothing else mattered in this world. *Was this love? Or was her past haunting her again? Was it her destiny to be with tortured men, and let them torture her?*

When the moment of release came, she readily gave up, in complete surrender. He was lying on her thigh, his fingers caressing her skin. 'You have no fear of me?' He pressed her flesh harder.

There was admiration and confusion in his voice.

'Is there any reason to be afraid, Steve?' Lise felt nothing, as if the dread had lost its edge, and in its place was a temporary lull. Her heart was a lonely place again. She knew what he wanted. But the monks had blanketed her mind in that electric chamber. Gedun was a smart monk, he knew her better than she realized. She was playing out her little game of self-hurt, of addiction to pain.

'You have no idea,' he said, sliding up until they were face-to-face. His eyes were like molten gold. What was it about him that made her want to sink into those mysterious pools?

'I know what you want from me, Steve. But I can't give it to you, because I can't seem to remember a thing.'

He turned and was lying by her side. Lise turned away, her eyes focused absently on the fake flowers in a chipped vase on a plastic table. His voice had a hypnotic effect. And his hand slid across her bare shoulders and rested gently on her breast. 'Lise,' he said with a lazy stretch of her name, 'you and I are the same. We both have our reasons to fight the injustice in this world. We are good people, you and I. We have suffered at the hands of others, and they are heroes while we look like villains.' *What was he talking about?* He continued, 'You must join me. I can give you everything you could ever dream of and more. I will have the ability to make things happen'— he waved his hand in the air with the flair of a magician— 'and we can win this battle together. We can become more powerful, more of everything if we are together.'

Lise turned to him. 'I didn't come here to fight anyone or to become more powerful or for anything of the sort. I am a messenger. I have finished what I came here to do. And I will return home, I have already overstayed.' She turned to face him and was swept by the intensity in his eyes. A sharp intake of breath, and her expression betrayed how she really felt, 'It is because of you that I am still here.'

'Yes. We are destined to be together. Think about it— you come from halfway across the world, and we just happen to meet. How unexpected, how unusual and how impossible! Yet it happened. Clearly, the universe is telling us something, we are destined to be together,' he insisted. There was so much truth in his words . . . Lise was lulled by what he said. It was all so magical! Lise felt the possibility of a 'happily ever after' scenario. 'The world, as you see it, is all an illusion,' he said as his hand waved out in an arc, and returned to her bare body, touching her in places that made her tremble with longing. 'I want to break that illusion and be master of our universe. We will have access to such powerful knowledge. It will give us the power to defeat the Nine.'

Finally, he spoke the truth. She stopped his roaming fingers. 'You need vengeance? I don't understand!' she said with a bitter laugh. 'You don't really need me for that? I'm sure you can manage on your own. But I'm curious, why do you want to defeat the Nine?'

Steve was eager to share the story. 'You have to know the truth of this piece of history before we can move forward with our relationship. Everyone praises the great King Ashoka for doing what he did. For having changed completely from the savage he used to be to a monk. Everyone forgave him his sins but he had blood on his hands. He murdered thousands, destroyed millions of lives before he turned all noble. He fooled everyone but us!' He shook with emotion, his voice turning tremulous. 'We, the Kalingans, fought a brave war against him. Our army was destroyed—more than a hundred thousand lives lost in a single battle. The victor was Ashoka, and he repented and turned to dharma—decided it was a sin to harm another. Hah!' Steve trembled with anger. 'One minute he destroys a whole clan of people and the next he converts. That is the most ridiculous way of repenting.

First you kill, and then you think it's over by saying sorry. The man cannot go unpunished! No one goes unpunished for murdering a hundred thousand people!' His voice was a seething whisper. 'I will exact revenge from all those who serve him. I am the Kalingan link on this earthly plane. I will complete their goal and bring peace to my clan of restless spirits.' His breath was hard and fast. And the talisman sparkled around his neck. It seemed to be feeding his anger.

Lise moved closer to him, sliding her palms in long wide strokes down his back. He was hot as if a fever burned inside him. Instinctively, his muscles tightened, as if he was braced for attack—any sudden movement and he would leap and attack her out of sheer frustration. Lise spoke without fear. 'So you are the Kalingan scapegoat, their puppet . . . '

Steve turned and was on top of her in an instant. He pinned her wrists down. 'You are stupid to speak to me this way! Others will grovel to do my bidding! I will have power and knowledge of all the secrets of this universe. I will be a king, not a puppet.' And she could see in the depths of those eyes, where the hot seething fire of resentment burned. 'You do not speak to me like that. I have killed three of the Nine and it will not be difficult to snap your little neck! And then I will find the rest and destroy Ashoka's men.'

'Thanks for letting me live, Steve.' She held his gaze steadily. Her heart pounded with the excitement of

knowing he wouldn't hurt her. 'You will not get anything
from me once I'm dead. You need me, Steve. Don't mess
with me. You want something, don't rope me into your
agenda. Mine is different and you cannot control my
choices.'

He let go of her arm. Lise eyed him wordlessly.

'I love you, Lise.' His words were so pure in their
simplicity and yet so dangerous, she felt her eyes burn.
Savage one minute and so tender the next, she was on the
same roller-coaster ride. Those damn eyes . . . he was
intoxicating! 'We are so good together. Made for each
other . . .' he whispered in her ear, his soft breath caressing
her ear lobe.

She tried to focus. 'I thought you wanted to kill me,
and now you suddenly love me?' she asked pointedly. He
shifted.

She got out of bed. She needed the distance to get up
and get dressed again. The incident had hit her like a
tornado. *What was she doing here? So close to getting her
neck snapped!* Lise began shivering uncontrollably, but
she maintained an outward appearance of calm. 'Maybe
I want what you want: money, power and control, but I
don't think I can trust you. One day you'll stick a knife in
my back or kill me in my sleep.' She went to the door and
opened it. The outside air was cool. 'Destiny may have
other plans for me. But I do care about you, Steve.
Feelings have come in the way, and you know what, I will
consider your offer. But I need time to think.'

Steve was sweet again. He bounded towards her, held her close and kissed her softly. 'I understand. We will talk soon. I will call you tomorrow.' She turned away from the heat, into the cool night air and walked briskly back to her guest house. Gedun Rinpoche was right, Steve was pure evil and she was lucky to be alive. But she would find out more and maybe she could change him and stop his fanaticism. Maybe she wasn't that weak after all. Tonight had proved that!

25

Vayu dropped the spoon in his bowl of porridge with a loud clatter. The sound startled the young woman at the registration desk. She looked up at him questioningly.

'Sorry,' he murmured. He couldn't stop thinking about Lise. To her, he was Steve, but he was now sure that even if he had told her his real name, she would still be attracted to him. He now knew that she was the Knowledge Keeper he had been looking for. No one else could have spoken about the secret of the Nine in third person. He was just surprised that this role was now being played by a woman. However, this had only made his job easier. He smiled wickedly at what had gone on between them. He'd had to use the Kala Yogi's ash to influence her. The ash of a cremated human had powerful magical properties. Each time Lise had come to his place he had added a pinch of ash to her coffee. She was totally enchanted by him. Even then, she'd been easy. But there was one more thing that was bothering him, and it was in this very hotel . . .

'Do you need anything?' the woman at the counter asked, abruptly butting into his chain of thought.

'No, thank you!' he replied curtly, wanting to be left alone.

She sighed and turned her attention back to her work.

Outside, just a stone's throw away, goats grazed lazily in the lush green pastures. The small dining room felt like a box with two glass walls and he could experience the sumptuous mountain view and vivid-coloured scenery in all its glory. The snow peaks shimmered in the sunlight. Time seemed to slow down. Vayu felt the stillness seep into his core. There was a hypnotic lull in the air, it made him want to go into a trance.

Seconds ticked by and when he felt the woman's stare bore into his neck, he turned to face her abruptly. He glimpsed the quick turn of her head, as if she'd been caught with her hand in the cookie jar. She stood behind a desk which doubled as a reception counter where guests registered. A voluminous book with dog-eared corners and light-green pages was spread open. The hard cover seemed glued to the desktop. It had seen better days and clearly hadn't been moved for years. A thought struck his mind.

Vayu smiled at her. 'Not in the kitchen yet?' He knew there was no chef, and the family members cooked the main meals for the guests. He got up and faced her with a friendly smile. 'By the way, what is your name?'

She blushed and smiled stiffly. 'Mita,' she said, twirling the ends of her long scarf. 'We will start to cook later; my brother and father have to finish cutting all the vegetables first. Can I get something for you?' She swayed slightly, side to side.

'Mita, do you have a painkiller?' he asked, pressing his forehead. 'I have this maddening headache.'

She looked concerned. 'You need a doctor? My uncle, he is one.'

'No, it's not that bad. Just some medicine for the pain, if you have any? Would save me the trouble of going to the village centre to look for a drugstore.'

'My father has something like that,' she said. 'Wait a minute.' She headed into the back office. Vayu glanced down at the large register on the desk. It was upside-down, but the writing was large and childlike. He flipped a page, and found the room number. There was a suspicious-looking man who had been watching him for the past few days. He was working for the Nine, Vayu was sure about it. But he had to find proof.

A few minutes later, she returned and handed him a strip of medicine. 'I can make some tea and bring it to your room,' Mita offered.

'Thank you, Mita. That would be very nice of you,' he smiled. She seemed to glow every time he said her name. Whistling softly, Vayu sauntered down the corridor. He could sense her eyes on him, and he was pretty sure she would make the tea with special spices and that nauseating yak butter.

Before he got to his door, he made a sharp right and headed towards Room 11. It wasn't difficult to enter. In his hand was a piece of metal that looked like a nail. He pressed it in his palm, muttered a few words, and slipped it into the hole. He waited for a minute for the metal to mould itself into the space. Then he turned it, heard the click and pressed down the handle. It gave. He pushed the door open and closed it behind him.

Once inside, he paused, letting his senses take over. It was a compact room; the bed was neatly made. It was very quiet in there. Vayu sensed a stillness in the air, as if it was too sacred a place to be disturbed. He moved swiftly, methodically searching through the sparse furnishings. Last, he picked up a camping bag. It had a dozen pockets and was still stuffed: the spy had not unpacked.

He unzipped the bag. A whiff of the sanitized interiors of an aircraft hit his nose, reminding him of his own journey to get here. He searched quickly. There was nothing in particular he was looking for but the man hadn't come here to enjoy the view. He was here for another reason. Vayu checked the side pockets; inside the smallest zippered section he found a piece of crumpled paper. He unfolded it. He smiled and put it in his pocket.

Placing the backpack exactly as he had found it, he looked around, making sure nothing was amiss. He completed his search in less than ten minutes. When he exited, he sensed someone had seen him, but there was no one around. After searching around a bit, he returned to his room and hooked up his laptop to the Internet with a secure device. Just then he heard a tentative knock on his door.

Mita entered self-consciously, carrying a tray with a teapot, a cup and a saucer. He also noticed a plate of biscuits and a tiny vase of purple flowers. *How sweet!* He was now getting a bit irritated with her clinginess but he could not afford to get angry with her.

After she'd placed the tray on the table, she just stood there, hands clasped together, swaying slightly.

'Thank you,' he smiled. She didn't leave. Maybe she was expecting a tip. He turned to get his wallet from the table, when suddenly he felt a sharp blow to the side of his head.

'Wha—'

He fell against the chair. Another blow that felt like a sledgehammer had landed on his back. He was on the ground, crawling away from this thing. *The very woman who had been smiling naively at him! What the hell was happening?*

She reached down and turned him over. Mita had transformed. This wasn't the docile cook, the waitress-cum-receptionist he'd seen half an hour ago. Her eyes were as hard as polished pebbles, her empty grin had disappeared. *Hell, where was that other sweet female?* She gave him a cold hard smile. 'Thought I was some stupid village girl interested in you, eh?' The side of his head was still throbbing with pain from the blow.

'No, I know you are more than that. Got the message loud and clear. What do you want?' he asked through gritted teeth.

He felt her knee dig into his stomach. 'Yes. You stay away from that room, you understand?' she said menacingly.

Under her flimsy pink pants, she had strong legs. Her elbow jabbed at his neck like a plank of wood. He was finding it difficult to breathe, or even move.

But this wasn't over. Nothing was over till Vayu had had his own way. 'It's none of your bloody business what I do!' Vayu rasped, returning her threatening demeanour with his menacing, icy stare. While he spoke he focused his anger inward, his breath, in and out, was energizing. He visualized the black Kalingan aura and it made his skin feel like pins and needles, which meant she had broken a bone. If this female was some trained fighter, he was no spring chicken.

Before she knew it, his arm darted out and the base of his hand connected with her jaw. She fell backwards, but he didn't miss the shock in her wide eyes. He was on top of her this time. 'Who has sent you? Come on, tell me!' He gripped her wrists.

She struggled to break free. Vayu felt her strength, but he could also sense the fear sapping her energy. 'Don't worry, I will make this easy for you,' he smiled. 'Just tell me a name.'

She began to cry. Large drops of tears trailed down her

eyes. Her body turned soft: her firm muscular build melted away into a feminine gentleness. The transformation was visible. She was nothing more than a puppet on a string. *Someone had sent him a message!*

He stepped back, thinking. The Nine were fighting back. But he knew that they were too weak to last. The new recruits could easily be manipulated. Their power at this stage would be like that of a newborn coming to grips with its existence. They wouldn't know how to apply themselves mentally and control or use their strengths to overcome him. It would take them years to be able to shed their egos and detach themselves from this materialistic world. He could easily bring them down and embarrass King Ashoka's men for generations to come. This time, victory would be his—his to rule the world!

'Don't . . . misunderstand . . . me. You slipped . . . and . . . and fell. I'm just trying to help you up,' Vayu spoke hesitantly. She looked a little dazed, batting her eyelids as if she had been caught in a very bright place. Vayu was sure she didn't remember a thing. He had to be more careful. As she shuffled out of the room, she looked suspiciously around and then at him. There was no warm smile or blushing shy gaze. When she slammed the door behind her, he was left with an accusatory glance.

Deal with that later. Vayu returned to his laptop and jiggled the mouse to reactivate the screen. The aroma of the tea, though unattractive to him, was enticing. He went into the bathroom, poured the tea into the saucer and left it for the lizard hiding in the ceiling vents in his room.

He typed in his username and password, the 'K9' was online.

'The white woman has arrived.' Vayu typed. 'Finished the new three?'

There was a pause, and then the word 'Negative'.

'Explain,' Vayu typed. He wanted to reach through the laptop and shake the minion until his head fell off. These guys had been hired by the Golden Group. He would upbraid them for their lackadaisical ways. He had given these assassins specific instructions on how to go about disposing of the three. He had taken down the old fogies, and these newbies should have been a piece of cake. They were uninitiated, ordinary people. Now it would become harder. On Indian soil their strength awakened and strengthened with each passing day.

'They had help and managed to escape. We just managed to kill the handlers.'

'Where are they now?' The least they could do was monitor them.

'In Bodh Gaya.'

Shit! Kalingan power had no effect there.

'When they leave, use your powers to make them vanish. I will take care of the Knowledge Keeper.'

'You made contact?'

'Yes, she trusts me.'

'It will be easy to find the locations of the crystals.'

'Not so easy. I will have to use force to extract the knowledge from her mind. The monks have pushed it deeper. Even she doesn't know what she knows.'

'We will be in Gaya by tomorrow.'

And they went offline.

Vayu was burning with anger. The coiled beast within him was more than eager to deal with the three fresh recruits. Actually, the Kalingan would have liked to slice them in half and feed them to the dogs. But he curbed the warrior instinct. Now wasn't the time to draw attention to himself.

*

In the Western-style coffee shop overlooking a busy street, Lise was seated across the table from Vayu. The woman thought she could outsmart him. Just because the secret was suppressed in her mind, didn't mean he couldn't access it. He had other ways to dig up information. It wasn't pleasant and would seriously affect their relationship, but it didn't really matter. She was dispensable.

He invited her to breakfast for a chat and then a trek to the unusual place he had talked about. The air was so crisp and clear, you could feel it flood your lungs with its minty freshness. Around him, kiosks selling food and clothes lined the streets and noisy shoppers milled about. There was much haggling going on.

Lise had made an effort to change her appearance and now she had natural hair and normal-looking nails. She had removed all her piercings, including the one from the tongue. He kind of liked that.

Vayu sat back and drummed his fingers on the table. He wanted to say something but held back. Lise seemed to have sensed it.

'What?' she asked.

'There is a way to find out what's lost in your subconscious mind.'

The few tables around them were filled with families and tourists. They were having light-hearted conversations about their trip, taking pictures with their digital cameras. Their expressions were comfortable, positive, eager and happy. Lise felt like deadweight in comparison. She wished she were seated at the other table where the couple laughed every minute. She wanted to be that carefree person again. There were so many serious decisions to be made. Their table faced the roadside and there were a few pedestrians who glanced at them, smiled and waved before moving on.

'How?' she asked sadly.

'Through a very simple hypnotic method. Hypnotherapy has helped many people overcome their addictions and deal with personality disorders. It's nothing to fear.' Vayu leaned closer. 'I can arrange it for you.'

Lise flicked a crumb from the table. 'I'm not sure.' She

glanced at his suspicious expression, sipped her coffee and grimaced. 'I need more time to think about it. And anyway, what's the hurry?'

'The Kalingan knows that it is time to hurry. I've told you everything I know—about the Nine, the Kalingan army and the Mauryans. And the Nine are getting stronger and learning new information. We have to act quickly. The power of immortality is the knowledge that will be transmitted next. The Kalingan knows it, he wants it. And with you by my side, we will be the most powerful people on earth.' He was staring at her with those wild eyes.

Lise's knees quivered and she felt like throwing up. Despite the turmoil within, she maintained a poised expression.

She took a deep breath. 'Okay, I'm in. But I need to do this tomorrow.'

Vayu smiled, his expression returned from wild eyed to normal. He patted her hand. 'Good, good.' He paused for a few minutes. The locals seemed to observe her more than they did him. Her milky skin worked against her. 'I will arrange for it tomorrow then,' Vayu smiled benignly. 'I have some more news that might interest you. This place I was talking about . . . Some elders talk about it as if it were filled with ghosts of the past. It's a small cave full of ancient symbols. The locals say it dates back to the Ashokan era.'

Lise's eyes lit up. 'That's very interesting. I would like

to take a look at this cave, but I need to use the washroom first.' She stood up and left. In the tiny toilet, she splashed water on her face. Her cheeks turned pink at the touch of the cold water. She stared at her own reflection, then took a deep breath, pulled out her mobile and dialled a number. She was in contact with the assistant monk at the monastery. She told him about her plans and he promised to pass the information to Gedun Rinpoche. She sighed with relief and sadness. Even though she was falling for Vayu, she had no doubt that he was dangerous. Gedun Rinpoche had said they would protect her.

26

Vayu and Lise followed a trail through thick undergrowth. A slight incline began soon after they reached a clearing. A few minutes of rest, and they continued on a narrow path. They had to walk in single file and Vayu led the way. Lise stared at the back of his head, strands of his hair shone gold in the sunlight. She was falling for him. This evil, twisted megalomaniac was making her heart soft. Perhaps because a part of her didn't believe he was possessed by a Kalingan spirit. It sounded unreal, but to him it was as real as the world around him. Lise saw herself in him—a split personality—and her heart went out to him. But they were both operating at a level which was beyond them, so Lise went along with what he said. He talked about the Golden Group, to which he was attached. They seemed to be a dubious group that was experimenting with strange concoctions of serums and chemicals to mess with his mind. He was open to it and, psychologically, it worked. Lise was aware of the power of belief—it was enough just to think, feel and have faith in something, and it happened. The mind was such a powerhouse. In her case, it was her strength to push herself to change that had worked. But Dr Halvor's belief in her had been the much-needed fuel that propelled her to overcome her addictions permanently.

The wooded path began to get constricted with snake-like roots and twigs embedded in the ground. Overhead, the trees converged into a canopy blocking out the light— darkness descended on them abruptly. There was an eerie silence, the birds and insects had stopped chirping. A cold dread made the hair on her arm stand on end. Vayu suddenly turned to her and towered over her on the incline. 'There is one question that has been bothering me about you,' he said.

There was something sinister, a fire blazing behind those molten eyes. He seemed to be holding back, his fists tight by his side. There seemed to be something desperately wrong with him. Lise knew she couldn't run. Not with the tall trees draping that pall of sinister darkness. With the thick undergrowth all around them, she wouldn't be able to find her way back. With a quiet determination, she moved closer to him.

'What is your question, Vayu?' she asked, hiding the fear that was slowly turning her insides to liquid.

He took a step back and hesitated. Taking a deep breath, he closed his eyes and opened them again. 'Do you trust me? Do you love me?'

Lise felt her hands grow clammy, a trickle of sweat slid down her back. Yes, she had made some wrong choices in life but this was not going to be one of them. 'I do love you. But I do not trust you,' she blurted.

'I have killed men,' he said, his eyes narrowed with interest.

'I know.'

'Spit out the truth, Lise! You know I'm a murderer, and yet you want to be with me?' He gripped her wrist. 'The Nine. You work for them. You lied that you would tell me the secret, when you are in it with the monks!' He reached down to her jeans, pushed his hand inside her inner pocket and found her mobile. He threw it away.

Lise looked at him expressionlessly. 'You're crazy. Oh, by the way, there was no network connection.' Then she seized his hand, unclasped his fingers to release his grip on her, and moved away a few steps.

Vayu laughed out loud, releasing an echo akin to an animal sound. 'You've got spunk, you dare to defy me— a warrior like me—I like that.'

Be careful whom you trust! Professor Halvor's words popped into her head. A bit late for that, she realized.

Vayu put on a wide grin that made him look even more dangerous—and attractive. He turned and walked ahead. Lise followed the trodden path. She had to find

out what he was hiding. There was a definite Dr Jekyll
and Mr Hyde act going on here. Deeper in the woods,
there was no room for light: it might as well have been
night, but for the needle-like rays that strained through,
shining on the dense undergrowth. She shivered in the
odd cold and warm slivers of light.

Walking carefully, she berated herself. She shouldn't
have taken up Vayu's offer. The monk at the monastery
had warned her that he could easily dupe her. She should
have listened to the wise old man and just stayed away.
Before she knew it, she tripped over a vine and landed
face down in the muddy soil. Vayu was beside her in an
instant, helping her up, pulling her to her feet. 'Are you
all right?' he asked with deep concern in his eyes.

'Fine, thanks,' she said, recoiling from his touch. She
was covered in mud. 'I'm okay.' Lise pulled herself up,
feeling irritated. She wished she could be back at her
hotel, sipping on yak butter tea, reading the *Lonely Planet*
guide and making plans to take the bus to the nearest
city.

As if reading her thoughts, he spoke, 'We're almost
there, and you might be able to wash up.' He led her
forward. 'There is a shack up on this hillside I was told,'
he said, pointing somewhere in the distance. Then he
looked at her with apprehension. Glancing around, Lise
realized she had no choice but to follow. 'You hadn't
mentioned anything about a shack before. I thought we
were going to see a cave full of Ashoka symbols,' she said,
irritated with the sudden change of plans.

'I thought we could freshen up first. And it's a nice place, isolated. Just you and I. And no one to bother us.' Vayu slipped his hands around her waist and massaged up and down her back, pulling her closer until she was moulded to his body. 'What do you think?'

'Sounds like fun!' Lise smiled, feeling her body respond. She was experiencing nothing less than Jekyll-and-Hyde emotions herself. They were supposed to return by evening. But she didn't think it would be possible. *How long had they been walking?* She had lost track of time. There was an indistinct hum in the air. She became aware of the sound after the sudden stillness of the surroundings. Sounded like a refrigerator's white noise—there but not really there.

'Where are we exactly?' Lise asked anxiously. She had stopped walking, tired and irritated. Sweat trickled in steady streams, her head felt hot, her skin hurt. There was too much happening—she needed to wind down and sleep. 'I'm not moving until you tell me why we are here,' she demanded irritably.

'Where do you want to be, really?' Vayu's burnt-copper eyes were level with hers, three crease lines formed on his forehead. And she felt his hot stare in the pit of her stomach. He was smiling, making light of the moment, but there was a heavy weight behind that question.

'I want to . . . go back to . . .'

'Look around you. . .' he interrupted, pulling her arm. 'Where is "back"? Which way will lead you home, Lise?'

He was close, too close for comfort. His face was inches from hers, and she could smell his sweet heady breath on her cheek.

'What do you want from me?' Lise asked, backing away slowly. She almost tripped.

'You,' he gripped her wrist gently, and stopped her from falling. Very softly he traced her jawline with the tip of his finger. 'I want to know what's inside that deep dark mind of yours.' Lise's heart thumped in anticipation. Vayu's eyes were pools of intense hatred. Instinctively, she tried to push away. But he held on. 'And I want to know every little secret locked behind those blue, blue eyes.'

Lise shook her head. 'I don't like being pushed around. I've told you, I'll let you know what I know when I'm ready.' Now what? Despite the frisson of fear, Lise wasn't going to give in. *She would fight the crazy bastard if she had to. How could she have felt any love for him? Was it his doing?* But then she realized with a sudden dread, he was probably capable of hypnotizing her. There was no way she could contact the monk. Vayu was smarter than the rest of them. He had figured what she really was all about.

Vayu dragged her forward, then paused. 'Don't think I'm a fool.' It seemed to Lise that they were the only two living beings in this strange forest. Everywhere she looked was foliage: wild creepers surrounded her legs, branches burst with thin green leaves at her eye level, and fat red ants trailed up the tall trunks of trees above her. She shielded her eyes from the sharp points of sunlight filtering through the canopy and she realized the chill on her arm where Vayu gripped her tighter. They moved up the incline. 'I'm tired. I need to rest. My elbow hurts, I think I landed on it when I fell,' she said.

'We're almost there.' Vayu was moving faster, his arm clamped like a shackle on her wrist, and Lise struggled to keep up, stumbling over the uneven earth.

'Let go of me.' She tried to escape from his grip.

They reached a clearing before he let go of her. Lise was panting, her heart raced and a weird sensation in her legs made her feel weak. The stench of dried mud on her clothes irritated her. Beads of perspiration trickled down her face.

'You look pale. Not used to this kind of heat, eh?' Vayu was smiling. He passed a bottle of water to her and she drank in thirsty gulps. They walked no more. Soon things began to get tougher for Lise. She couldn't focus her eyes and mind; Vayu's face grew fuzzy. A buzzing sound seemed to envelop her. Lise tried to take in big mouthfuls of air but her chest felt like a tight band that wouldn't expand. She bent low, breathing heavily and fell down unconscious. The water he had given Lise was spiked with a drug.

Vayu heaved Lise onto his shoulder like a gunny bag and walked the few steps up the porch of the shack. He fished out his keys and unlocked the door. Once inside the wooden shack, he surveyed the room. He was pleased with the arrangements. Vayu dragged her on to a flat rectangular board of wood.

As if on cue, he heard a knock on the door. Without a word, Vayu let the four mantriks in. Then he locked and barricaded the door.

They were ready for the ritual.

'Everything she knows, I want to know. Invade her mind and find the knowledge. I want the soul of the Nine and once I have that, not only will I tear out every single shred of the Mauryan clan from this era, I will also have the power to control the world for centuries to come!' Vayu's voice was guttural.

The four men, with black-kohled eyes and garlands of rudraksh beads around their necks, nodded. Wrapped in robes of black, their foreheads smeared with white ash, they looked like sorcerers.

'We will do as you wish, Kalingan master,' one of them said as they took up their positions in the four sacred directions. With thick ropes, they bound her wrists to the legs of the wooden table. They cut out segments of her clothing and placed small earthen bowls containing ash and salt on her body.

'She must be awake for the spell to work,' the tallest and oldest mantrik said. 'Her mind cannot be manipulated otherwise.'

The first one lit a fat candle inside a coconut husk. He chanted, 'I am I, and I seek your knowledge,' and sprinkled rice on her.

The second lit his candle. 'I am you, and I seek the truth,' he said, showering her with mustard seeds.

The third one did the same. 'I am we, and the knowledge is ours,' he said, throwing fistfuls of red vermilion powder on her.

The fourth one held a tiny knife and placed the tip on her forehead. 'Awaken mind to unite with us,' he said. The others repeated the words, chanting louder and louder until Lise's eyes flew open.

She looked up to see four ghoulish faces peering down at her, and one of them held a glinting knife slicing the air above her. Lise let out a piercing scream.

27

'If you stop struggling, it will be easier on you,' Vayu said coldly as if the words would relieve the terror. The room was dark, hot and oppressive. She still struggled to free her bound hands and feet. A sense of dread picked up in her gut when a distinct odour of metal and burning wood reached her.

'Let me go!' She winced as the bounds bit into her skin.

Vayu leaned close. 'It's pointless to struggle. If you let your mind relax, I get what I want, and then you are free to leave—go back to your civilized country and live your antiseptic life. I knew all along you were lying to me— you can't fool the Kalingan warrior, and you will pay for this deceit.'

'Your crazy mumbo jumbo won't work on me. I don't believe in your nonsense and these crazy magicians. You think I'm afraid of you and your cronies? Bloody hell, the last thing I will do is give you any information!' she spat angrily while the yogis circled her, ignoring her rant. 'And besides, the Rinpoche has blocked that part of my mind. You will get nothing. And trust me, when I'm out of here, I'm going to get you and your damn witch doctors for this.' Despite her brave words, only one thought ran through her head—she was utterly helpless. 'Tell your zombies to stop touching me!' she yelled.

Vayu grasped her hair. 'What courage!' He laughed in her face and said, 'After these yogis are done with you, my dear, I can make sure that you will not even remember your name. So watch your tongue, woman, and I will spare some part of your memory.'

She breathed in violent rasps as she writhed angrily against the restraints. The cabin had poor lighting, but from what Lise could see, there were two shuttered windows and a door. Off to the left, was a makeshift kitchen and all she could see was a countertop. To her right was an open space, with four folding chairs and a rickety table at the centre.

The drone of the yogis began. Lise controlled herself, holding back, trying not to get caught in their hypnotic spell.

'The mind is mysterious and holds so much more information than you can digest. You are not meant to be a carrier of such knowledge. You have no strength, no willpower. You have never controlled your mind. You've been a slave to your addictions.' Vayu's smooth smile was as ugly as the glinting knife. *How could she have been in love with him!*

The tall mantrik pressed his fingertips on her forehead. She struggled but it was a futile attempt, her wrists and ankles were bound tight. A band of pain extended around her head, made her squeeze her eyes shut; tears rolled down the sides of her face. The other mantriks continued their droning mantra. The sound filling the room seemed to seep into every corner and held her captive in its monotonous hum. Lise felt something strap down across her forehead. They were holding her down, she wasn't even able to turn her head.

'Let me go,' she pleaded. *Vayu was so loving, so sensitive. So kind! How could she have been fooled into thinking they could be together?*

Vayu stood near her head, within her line of vision. 'Then join me, Lise. I've wanted you to be a part of my mission to destroy the Mauryan clan. Open your mind to me and it will be easy for us to retrieve the information.' He was speaking to her in that same tone—the one that made her love him so much. She felt a heavy weight of sadness rest in her heart. He wasn't real. He was faking it again, he was using her. He didn't really care about her or he wouldn't have put her in this position. She wanted to weep at her own foolishness. Of falling for a liar. It hurt

so deep she wanted to let them take whatever she had.
She was nothing. And she wanted to feel nothing.

His voice was still messing with her mind and heart.
'Lise, don't resist. The pain comes because you resist.
Once we are done, you will be free. The Kalingan wants
the location of the Chintamani. If you let us take it, then
we will let you go with your sanity intact.'

'No,' Lise said. But her voice was a soft whisper. It
drowned in the chants of the mantriks.

The mantriks surrounding her waved peacock feathers.
The heavy odour of camphor filled the air. Her head felt
like it weighed a tonne, and her body was like lead. She
couldn't move.

Sweat broke out from every part of her body. It made
her shiver. She wanted to hold back the fear, the buzz was
getting louder, her head seemed heavier. This time she
couldn't even open her eyes. Hope of escape was a distant
dream. Lise was swimming in and out of consciousness.
She saw Dr Halvor, she heard him whisper strange words
in her ear. It was as if time was being rewound. Panic
took hold of her and pressed on her chest. She blinked,
and the mantriks circumambulated faster and faster,
waving their strange objects over her, making her dizzy.
Their words were energetic, and the ash that they so
eagerly showered on her blurred her vision. There was
more—Vayu was turning into the evil warrior he had
spoken about. His face was a mask of red. She saw his
eyes blazing with rage. *This was not the man she loved!*

The cold fact sunk in that once they got what they wanted there was nothing to stop them from chopping her up and burying her in the woods. No one would know. The thought made her weak, and Vayu's will became stronger because of it.

The mantriks stretched their hands out.

Then suddenly there was absolute silence. This was more terrorizing than before. Lise strained her head, moving her eyes as far as she could see. Terror tore through her and the sight was like nothing she had ever imagined. The mantriks were doing something strange and horrific. Lise eyeballed their every move. They waved a black object across her body and she felt a warm liquid dripping over her bare midriff. Its sticky thickness came as a shock: it wasn't water. Her breathing became erratic as the black object came closer. This time she saw what it was: shiny black feathers from which dripped drops of blood.

'What are you doing to me?' she rasped. 'Let me go, please. Steve, didn't you ever love me?' she whispered. The drone of mantras started up again and turned into a rhythmic chant. It washed over her in waves, making her body tremble.

'We are helping you remember,' Vayu's mouth was by her ear, his hot breath was revolting. 'I did love you. But you are the one who betrayed me.'

'Let me go, for the sake of the love we shared. It was real, didn't you feel it too?'

'Love is an easy word to throw around. Did you think of love when you thought of trapping me? It doesn't matter any more, Lise.'

The tall mantrik—the head priest—held a curved blade in his hand. Lise struggled wildly but her wrists were red and bloody, still tightly bound. Life wasn't supposed to be this way, end this way. There was so much more she wanted to do. 'What . . . is he . . . doing?'

'Very gently he will cut the flesh from the tips of your toes.'

No, shit! Lise's brain buzzed with the strain, trying to think of a way out, trying to understand. Nothing came to mind. 'That's crazy! Why? No, please tell him to stop. Stop! Stop! Stop!'

Vayu covered her mouth. 'It has to be done, Lise. Just relax. This will distract your mind and when you are focused on your pain, we can take anything we want from your mind. You don't want to make the Kalingan angry now, do you?' he said, his red-rimmed eyes blazing down at her.

Very slowly, Vayu released his hand. 'Now listen to me. The monks have locked the secret in your subconscious mind. These friends of mine will release the memories. It's not painful, believe me.' Vayu held her left hand and gently caressed the tips of her fingers. 'You are so beautiful, almost angelic . . . I hate to ruin this lovely body. But if I don't get what I want, then there are other parts of the body that we will work on. You don't want that to happen, do you?' He was caressing her hair.

'No!' Lise cried as her shoes and socks came off. Lise writhed violently, but couldn't move her legs. Coconut shells filled with camphor were waved over her. The aromatic smoke infused the air and turned the room hazy.

Lise squeezed her eyes shut. She was back in her bunk bed at the rehab centre. The whispered words of the girl on the upper bunk sank into her, *Once an addict, always an addict.* Lise had beaten the monster, the drug addiction, but the world looked at her as if she was handicapped. She would slide down the slippery slope again. Maybe they were right—fear was back in full force. It was an uncontrollable animal, she needed a fix. Now. She was being tested, tormented by the puppet master who was having fun with her, playing with her mind. The world was a terrible place, fate wasn't on her side. She was fed up. Dying, giving up was so much easier.

She was on a roller-coaster ride, sinking and rising. Thoughts were crashing against each other. Lise was making love to Vayu, he was sweet. And then she felt hate with so much force it left her bone-heavy, miserable. Death would be a wonderful release. Lise opened her eyes again, craned her head to see the face of the man she had loved. Vayu was watching, he looked even more evil then the crazy priests who muttered their strange poetry. There was no control and she couldn't win this abnormal game, this insane ritual. She was going mad.

The cold metal was a shock. The mantrik traced her

toes one by one. She was panting, tears and sweat rolled down her face. She waited for the inevitable pain to take over.

Her mind raced. And then, just as abruptly, it stopped. She was sinking deep into a hole at a dizzying pace. Let them take what they want. There was a reason for everything, for being here, for meeting Vayu, for loving and then hating. There was purpose in every choice.

If this knowledge was in Vayu's destiny, than who was she to stop the process? And if she was meant to suffer . . .

Lise let her mind go blank. When the tip of the knife cut into her toe, she let out a hollow scream.

28

Bodh Gaya

A tall monk entered the room. He looked at each of them. 'Welcome to our humble abode.' He had a strained expression, as if he wanted to get somewhere urgently but had to get over the pleasantries first.

Tara joined her hands and greeted him, 'Gratitude and obeisance to your grace.'

Akash and Zubin mumbled a hello and bowed awkwardly with their hands joined together.

'Come with me, but first wear this,' the monk said. He pulled out two chakra pendants and handed over a green one to Zubin and a blue one to Akash. Tara showed off the red chakra that hung from her neck.

The monk continued to look at each of them with a serious expression. As soon as they started walking, he spoke with urgency, 'There has been a situation. The Knowledge Keeper is in danger.'

Outside the chamber, they turned left into a maze of corridors. He walked at a brisk pace and the three followed close behind.

'I didn't know there were secret passages that went this far. The temple didn't seem that big when we entered,' Zubin observed softly.

'Maybe we are going round in circles,' Akash smiled hesitantly.

Tara didn't like his choice of words but kept silent. They entered a cave. The walls had been hewn out of rock. Butter lamps in small alcoves offered poor lighting.

'Looks like we are back in the Barabar Hills,' Akash said. His voice echoed in the narrow curved passage.

After another ten minutes, the granite corridor opened up into a wide circular area with mushroom-shaped rocks emerging from the ground. It was a temple, but instead of deities, ancient rock-cut sculptures of lions and elephants stood out in a frieze on the walls. Closing her eyes, Tara could sense the history hidden deep in the crevices of the stone cave—they were dripping with blood. She blinked, but there was nothing other than a dull grey all around.

The elderly monk stood in their midst, silently waiting for them to focus. The three of them found the air humid and thick with an animal-like smell. They breathed heavily, while the monk stood poised and calm, his hands joined together under his burgundy robes. Garlands of beads hung around his neck and seemed to weigh him down. Then he smiled benignly at them and said, 'I know you have a thousand questions.' As he led them towards the mushroom-shaped stones, he continued softly, 'But unfortunately, you do not have the luxury of time.' The nine flat-top rocks were positioned in a circle. They seemed to have risen from the depths of the earth. Zubin was on his hands and knees, searching for a crevice of connection. At the centre of the nine seats was a squat round plinth. There was nothing on it.

Studying the intricate engravings on the plinth, Zubin looked more like a detective than a scientist. 'This looks like it was cut with a laser,' he pointed out, tracing the fine etchings.

'What are we doing here?' Akash muttered, looking around.

The monk looked at him quizzically. 'That is a deep question, son. But not until you have become an ascetic can you answer it.' His grin was wide. A joke, the monk had cracked a joke.

Tara smiled appreciatively. Akash didn't look happy with his answer. He tried again impatiently. 'No really, what is the purpose of being inside this cave? I'm feeling claustrophobic.'

'Feelings are all the work of the mind,' the monk said

seriously. Tara knew he was baiting him. Zubin was too busy inspecting his surroundings. If he wanted scientific and logical answers, he might have to search harder.

The DJ from London was about to ask another question.

'Don't bother, Akash, you will only slip deeper,' Tara suggested. 'He will tell us when the time is right.'

'I don't get—'

The monk interrupted him. 'You have already felt your powers. Now the elders will guide you to your destiny, and the spirits of the departed ones will be your shadow.' That didn't really answer any of Akash's questions. 'Kalingan energies have increased their collective strength. As you are aware, the single warrior soul has harnessed the black gunas and destroyed three members of the Council of Nine. You don't have much time. Each of you has a segment of a chakra.' He pointed to the plinth and said, 'Place them in the centre and you will understand what needs to be done.'

'But why have we been chosen?' Zubin asked, looking at the elderly man with confusion in his eyes. 'My father is the one who understands this better than me.'

'Because it is your karma that you are the chosen one, son. It's not a fact of today, or hasn't happened because of today. It is the culmination of centuries of history. This is your destiny. Don't fight it,' he said, but Zubin didn't appear satisfied with the answer. The old man drew out a small bag from the folds of his robe, poured its contents on his palm and offered it to them. 'Here, eat this jaggery: it is sugar from the palm sap, blessed with the Buddha's teachings.' They each took a piece and chewed on it. The monk placed his hand on each of their heads. 'You will learn to accept. Don't resist. Feel from your heart. And you will understand that everything happens to mould you to be one with the universe. The three of you coming together is no accident of nature, it was all meant to be. There is much that you need to learn—you are young at heart and impatient in spirit. The recent suffering has taught you patience and acceptance, the Buddha knows this. With his blessings you will do well.' He looked deep into their eyes. Tara sensed his admiration, and then she sensed nothing. He bowed to them and left, turning into one of the passages.

'Wait!' Akash called out. 'How will we know our way back?'

Tara removed the chakra from her neck and placed it in the centre. 'We will know from within, he says.'

'My mind is off limits, don't go reading it,' Akash said. He removed the chakra from his pocket and placed it on the plinth. Zubin did the same. They sat on the stone stools. The chakra segments began to glow with red, green and blue light, and then, like magnets, the pieces slid together and melded into a single circular white disc with a hole in the centre. Akash reached out to touch it.

'Don't!' Tara said, breathlessly. 'Something is going to happen, I can sense it,' she murmured.

Nothing happened for five seconds. 'You have a tendency to overreact, Tara,' Akash smirked. He was about to reach for the crystal when a blast of clear white shot out of it. He withdrew his hand quickly. The great shaft of bright light fell on the smooth curve of the cave. It adjusted itself—lighter and darker—until it became a distinct picture just like on a computer monitor. They were surrounded by a glow of soft light, the epicentre was still the chakra. As their gaze widened, Akash murmured a repeated 'what the . . . what the . . . ', and Tara's jaw fell—the shadowy images turned into distinct shapes. Six men took their seats, and the scene played out before their eyes as though they were in a modern-day office, having a conference call through a wide LCD screen.

Holy shit! It was the Senior Council.

Zubin had trouble assimilating the science and the magic of this unusual journey. To reach here had been no less than an experience out of an adventure reality show. The holographs were amazing, and to think that they existed inside a primitive cave with no visible technological gadgets! It was practically unbelievable! If he were to tell his American friends that he was sitting next to a holographic image of a Nobel-winning physicist inside a centuries-old cave, he would be laughed at! He would probably be sent off to a psychiatrist for therapy before he was allowed to return to work.

These were the ranked men of science, religion and politics. They were the ones who had made a difference.

Their inventions, ideas and discoveries had influenced the world. People knew of their existence. The six seniors with the secrets of the all-powerful knowledge—knowledge that could change the destiny of every living being on earth.

'Greetings, and welcome to the society of the Nine.' He was a short squat man with a generous moustache, and was dressed in a three-piece suit. There was nothing extraordinary about him and yet the surroundings made him and the rest of them look like an enigma. 'As you know, a few of our colleagues have been martyred protecting the powerful secrets that have led this world forward for centuries. You are here to replace them and each of you has the power to do so. There is, however, one difference—you are young and physically able. Hence, you form the action force of the Nine—the Trinity. The circle of Nine cannot remain broken. We have waited a long time to have you here. And now that the threat from the Kalingans has become so palpable, so close, and so human, you have to ensure his destruction.' He fell silent as he looked at them. Perhaps he wanted to see what effect his words had had on the three now that they understood the gravity of their mission.

Then he spoke again, 'Since I have started first, let me introduce myself. I am Dr Dongri. I have the power of light.' He raised his hand, palm up, to show the same blue light through which the holographic images were getting reflected.

'Yes, he is the reason you are able to see us,' the tall, stooped, bearded man said. He looked older than all of them combined. 'I'm Dr Lamba, alchemy.'

'Tara, you met Dr Bose,' the youngest-looking of the six said. 'You have been chosen to replace him.' Tara nodded.

'Akash takes the place of Dr Kuruvella.'

'And Professor Gupta had been replaced by Zubin.'

Rewa Khem, who introduced himself as an expert in psychological warfare, looked at them with a serious expression. 'We are gathered here to meet you. To let you know that we are in this together. To fight the Kalingans who have been trying for centuries to destroy us. As much as you may dislike the situation we are facing, we have to accept, not fight it.'

'I'm Joshi, the sociologist,' another of the six said, turning to Rewa. 'If we are terminated one by one, the power of the Nine diminishes with each of our deaths. Remember, we were initiated very carefully and in secrecy. We cannot unleash our powers, else the Kalingan will find us in a second. He has spread his wings through the Kala Yogis. This is serious. We have to salvage our millennia-old society and protect the powers.'

'How do we do all this?' Akash asked.

'With the powers that you possess. You use your combined force to destroy the Kalingan,' Dr Kapadia explained. 'In every yuga, the Nine unknown have faced the enemy and warded off their destructive forces. In this yuga, the enemy's power has increased because evil has increased and humans have become weak.' Dr Bhosle piped up, 'Therefore, the Kalingan has killed three of us. We cannot let them destroy any more of us. Ashoka's legacy must live on. Your destiny is to live in the world as one of the Nine unknown of the great King Ashoka's army. You have the power of the Trinity, and with our guidance, you will destroy the Kalingan.'

'But we don't know what he looks like or who he is.'

'You will know when the time comes. Believe me, "you" will. For everything else, Tara is your link. We will communicate through her,' Dr Lamba said decidedly.

'Zubin you have the power to heal. Use it wisely—it will affect you, weaken you physically with each healing experience,' Dr Kapadia warned.

'And Akash, you are the youngest in experience and spirituality. We do not judge you, for you have been chosen. Do justice and respect our ancient society. And your colleagues.'

'The first and foremost task for you three is to find the Knowledge Keeper.'

'The Knowledge Keeper?' they chorused.

'Yes.' And Dr Lamba told them about Dr Halvor and Lise.

Then, just as they had become visible, the image of the six men faded. The monk entered the cave again. The light was still a bright, single shaft. The monk guided Tara, Akash and Zubin to circle the chakra with their hands joined together and their faces turned towards the bright light. They understood deep within their subconscious minds that they were being connected and that this communication wasn't just verbal, but far more subtle.

Then under the monk's guidance, they took their oaths.

'Give me guidance, great king, for I am the body,' Zubin said.

'Give me guidance, great king, for I am the mind,' Tara said.

'Give me guidance, great king, for I am the spirit,' Akash said.

They raised their eyes upwards.

Their hands connected and soon enough the circumference of the chakra began to glow. They felt light drift through them and they understood that they were bonded for life.

The monk waited. A wall of light grew out of the ground and the three were hidden from view. When it was over, the light ceased to be.

'You are now the Trinity, the power of the three, the perfect awareness of the universe, which has existed from time immemorial. You have the knowledge of the final frontier: the integration of spirituality and science,' the monk said. He indicated that they should follow him. He led them back through the narrow corridor towards the monastery.

Zubin spoke first. 'We have received communication

that the Knowledge Keeper has died. Before he breathed his last, he gave his caregiver the information. She is a young woman, a recovering addict, and unstable of mind. She has become the Knowledge Keeper.'

Akash responded, saying, 'We must find her before the Kalingan does.'

Tara squeezed her eyes tight. 'She has already been taken. I can see her. There is some sort of ritual being performed to weaken her mind by inflicting pain on her body. The Kalingan has called the mantrik yogis, their black magic is extremely powerful. He will be able to extract the information from her mind. There is great suffering.' Tara spoke as if she were present at the scene. She heaved and faltered. The other two supported her. The monk directed them towards a chamber where food and water were laid out on a small wooden table.

Tara sat down heavily and lay her head down on the table.

'Are you okay?' the monk asked.

'Yes,' Tara looked at the warm concerned face. She smiled. 'I'm better. It is the Knowledge Keeper's suffering that makes me weak.'

'Where is she?' Zubin asked.

'Dharamsala.'

'We need to rescue her now. I'll go ahead and take the lead,' Akash said, closing his eyes and summoning the power of air.

'You will need some sustenance before you start your mission,' the monk suggested.

29

'According to the famous Kalyani inscription, a thirteenth-century Burmese monk took advantage of the psychic powers he had developed through meditation to levitate and travel to Bodh Gaya each day and sweep the temple courtyard. You would think that such special abilities were unusual, but it was the most natural progression for those ascetics. They had complete control. The powers of the mind are immense and harnessing them gives us more than we could ever want in life,' the monk told them after they had eaten a warm meal fresh from the monastery kitchen. It had been an all-vegetarian fare, but delicious nevertheless.

'Centuries ago people believed in ghosts, in miracle-healing and incidents that defied logic. But in this era, the intellect has taken over and the most basic sense, the instinct, therefore remains suppressed. Science is king, all else falls by the wayside.' The monk's story was fascinating and all three listened in silence.

'There was one other person who did not use any form of transport to make the journey from Tibet to Bodh Gaya. It was Sherof Thamse. He prostrated his way, face down, singing hymns, all the way to India. It took him one and a half years. He arrived in time for the 2550th anniversary of the passing of Lord Buddha. Sherof Thamse did it for world peace.'

The monk looked at Akash and gave him a teasing

smile. 'Your mission is the same—world peace, though you are going to do it differently.'

'Yes, I suppose we will.'

Tara and Zubin agreed.

The monk then guided them to a deserted area behind the monastery. The moonlight glinted on the rooftops and splattered dark shadows on the stone floor. The monk indicated to them to close their eyes and pray. He murmured a few words and then smiled. 'You must be respectful of your powers. The ego may prove to be an obstacle. Be careful.' With those words, he gave them a broad smile. 'I wish you luck in your mission,' he said and bowed his head. Then he returned to his domain.

Akash was ready. Tara spoke first, 'You don't even know where to go. Wait, we need to establish our link.' With that she pressed her fingertips on his forehead, just above his nose bridge. Akash felt the warmth of energy coursing through him but it was soon over. 'We will be in communication at all times.' Taking off her scarf, she tied it around his neck. 'This is a reminder that we are connected, be aware.'

'Yes, darling, we are all aware.' Akash grinned, pulling at the scarf playfully.

'You must learn to take things seriously,' Tara admonished.

'Yes, but where's the fun in that, eh?' He closed his eyes and concentrated on the power of the air. Soon he was swirling above their heads. Tara watched him with a scowl, hands on hips. He floated down and stood facing her. 'Chill, okay?'

'Don't patronize me, Akash. This is not England, and just because you don't know the ways of Indians, doesn't mean that you can act disrespectfully. In this case, we don't have a choice, we are stuck together. So, let's get this over with.'

'Don't give me that "don't-know-the-ways-of-Indians" shit. I know your double standards, just as I know your hypocrisy. Don't judge me—you look at yourself first, acting but not really meaning a damn thing. I can see right through you.'

'You are such an arrogant fool!' Tara hissed.

'Stop it, guys!' Zubin came in. 'We are all here for a common purpose. Let's not lose sight of that fact.'

'Yes, and you are Mr Smart Scientist from America. Tara seems to have taken a liking to you, but what do you know about Indian culture?'

'I keep my opinions to myself,' Zubin responded in a calm voice. 'I don't go around telling people to chill. People are who they choose to be.'

'Yeah!' Akash said, 'tell that to li'l Miss Stuck-Up here.'

'Yes, and you are vain, arrogant Mr Congeniality. I don't even know what the Council saw in you!' Tara snarled.

Akash gave her a hard look, and his fists were tight with anger. 'You don't know a damn thing about me, so don't judge.' He spoke softly, controlling his voice with effort.

'Okay, guys, enough!' Zubin said. 'We're not in a school yard—let's try and get along, okay?'

Silence. Akash and Tara were fuming in each other's faces.

'Okay?' Zubin repeated.

Tara took a step back and paused after a deep breath. 'Okay.'

'Now shake hands,' Zubin said, looking back at the monastery. 'This would be so embarrassing if one of the monks were watching us. The Trinity indeed!'

Akash guffawed. 'Yeah, that would turn their robes green.'

Tara gave him an icy glare.

'Sorry—their robes are a darker shade of blood!' And Akash laughed at his own joke.

Zubin snickered. And Tara's accusing glance was on him. *You too?*

Zubin stuck out his hand. Akash clasped it with both hands and shook vigorously. They nodded at each other. *If we can't joke in front of her . . .*

Tara read his mind. The two had bonded.

'We will leave by train immediately. And make contact in Dharamsala,' Tara said, interrupting their camaraderie.

'Will do,' Akash saluted and took to the skies. He soared above treetops and appeared only as big as a bird when they looked up at the dark sky.

You will reach the mountainous region, winds will be cold and severe. Keep yourself warm. Tara's voice was so clear he felt she was right next to him. Her tone was metallic and cold.

'I am adequately attired,' he responded.

The night air was crisp, and the moonlight glinted off his watch. He was guided by Tara's telepathic ability. She communicated the route to him. *You have to hurry,* she said as she guided him over hills and valleys. *The woman is giving up.*

From this high up it looked like nothing he had ever seen before.

'Understood.'

Soon Akash landed on a soft slope. Like a transmitter, Tara guided him towards his goal.

You seem to be close, possibly about 500 metres from your destination, she said in his head. *Look for a closed space, like a house or a hut.*

He crept forward, shivering slightly from the adrenalin rush that rocked his body. The partial outline of a shack was visible beyond a cluster of trees. His footsteps were soft but clear and it surprised him that there was not even a murmur of night insects or the hoot of an owl, even the rustling of leaves wasn't audible. Akash took a deep breath. Senses alert, he bent low and moved cautiously but quickly through the winding route that was choking with undergrowth. The darkness helped, he was alert to his surroundings. Then he stopped suddenly. It was a human voice. He paused. There it was again, it came in bursts: cries of pain. He moved faster. Then a long piercing scream, as if an animal was being gutted. His breathing was loud and shallow as he paused at the door of the shack.

*

Zubin felt uncomfortable. Recently, at every word, at the hint of any link to ancient primitive beliefs, his scientific training took over. His most natural impulse was to analyse and investigate the scientific reality behind the paranormal activity he had witnessed. Cutting right down to muscle, bone and pumping heart, man should not be able to fly and defy gravity. It violated the most basic law of physics that what goes up must come down. *But then, wasn't there a clause in every rule book that there are exceptions?*

The religious cult—he considered the Nine a cult— was essentially saying that the mind could control every aspect of the human body, every disease could be denied, every fantasy could become reality and every thought had energy. Einstein had more evidence in that direction. But this was bordering on . . . New Age stuff. He had read and heard about it, scoffed at it and at times had a good laugh over it. But . . . now, it seemed the joke was on him. He himself had healing powers. *Did he imagine all that? No, it happened, it was happening.* The world had turned upside down, his world, everywhere it was the same. He began to doubt his sanity. There is only one way to be of this world and not go insane, and that is to accept every new experience as if it was meant to be. This too was meant to be, his father would have said.

The only reason he was still sane was because Tara and Akash were with him and going through the same emotions. They had all been given unusual powers and thrown into the deep end of the ocean, entrusted with the responsibility of preserving the most sacred of repositories of knowledge. They were all so different in character and personality. Tara and Akash were both strong-willed and hated each other. Akash was frank and idiotically honest, he was in tune with the craziness of the world, and found some cheer in it. Tara was all business, practical—always wanting to do the right thing.

'We must move now, Zubin, the train leaves in half an hour,' Tara said, interrupting his reverie. She gripped his hand for comfort, and he knew she was trying to understand. She was just as confused, and telling him in her own way that she understood how he felt.

'Yes, Tara. We must hurry. Akash should not be left alone.' They raced out and reached the station just in time for the train. The Rinpoche had sent his monks and organized tickets for them. The train hooted its impending departure, they climbed in and found seats close to the exit. Panting heavily, Tara looked pale. She pressed her arms to her stomach.

'What's going on?'

'The Knowledge Keeper is in pain . . . she is losing it. You need to take this down. I'm trying to connect directly with her thoughts.'

Zubin tapped his mobile device to record her voice. Tara began reciting some sort of information. A name and places he didn't know about. Tara was talking in a trance. She seemed to be lost in another realm. Her eyes were looking straight at him, but were not focused. And then she snapped out of it.

'You got that?'

'Recorded everything,' he said, showing her his mobile and turning it on for her to hear.

'The secret of the Nine is the Chintamani crystal. It acts like a transmitter. It directs and transmits the knowledge of this world and all its sciences. In the wrong hands it is deadly. But in the hands of the educated and worthy it will benefit mankind. The Council of Nine regularly updates its understanding of these fields with the help of the Chintamani crystal. At the Barabar Hills and certain other specific areas, where it is possible to link with the Chintamani, the Nine receive their knowledge. If the Kalingan gets it, he will use it to declare victory overruling the millennia-old war that King Ashoka won. The Kalingans had died with burning revenge in their hearts. It was this infamous battle that turned Ashoka from a ruthless, bloodthirsty, ambitious king to a peace-loving ruler. He preached the path of dharma, becoming a follower of the Buddha. It is believed that Ashoka, through his travels and meetings with great monks, was bestowed this gift and the great responsibility of keeping the Chintamani crystal safe. Over the years, many people have tried to get their hands on it, and so the Council decided to divide it into three parts. No one except the Knowledge Keeper knows of the location of the three pieces. He or she is never a member of the Nine. Whenever the Council needs to meet, the members connect with the Knowledge Keeper to find a location. Once their work is over, all Nine members and the Knowledge Keeper split up. The fact that the secret location of Chintamani crystal lies with the Knowledge Keeper makes it easier and safer for the Nine to carry on with their work.

'This soul of the Nine is what has kept the society alive for millennia ever since it was started by King Ashoka. If the Chintamani is destroyed, the knowledge that has been collected over these centuries will also be lost and the Council of Nine as we know it will be finished.'

'I don't understand! How can the Kalingan destroy the Nine by learning its knowledge?'

'It can. Once the transmitter is linked to the Kalingans on their frequency or energy waves, there is no more progress. The Nine have done great things for the world. You think the sudden spurts of scientific inventions have occurred without help? There is more knowledge that is being transmitted. And eventually, the ultimate secret will be revealed—immortality.'

Zubin wasn't sure how to digest this information. Science involved a specific method of research and analysis, and here was knowledge emerging out of crystal? Hard to believe. 'Where is this knowledge coming from?'

'From everywhere. Scientists, philosophers, educationists and thinkers have been connected for centuries, putting together the vast repository. The earth is not young itself and has witnessed many civilizations flourish and fall and start again. This knowledge has passed through it all. I hear all this from the minds of the elders; I am connected telepathically. I know what they must keep a secret—even from themselves. That's why the Knowledge Keeper must be protected, she knows the location.'

'How can we protect her? We are not as experienced or knowledgeable as the elders of the Council.'

'It is faith that makes the difference. Do you believe you can stop the evil? Then you can. Any ordinary man can. That's why King Ashoka wanted his society to be defined as the Nine unknown—they were not special, not superheroes, and yet the unknown few have changed the direction of the future, introduced revolutionary inventions and pioneered scientific discoveries. All in the name of the unknown—the protectors of the future of this world as we know it. They must remain anonymous for their own safety.'

The train reached a sleepy deserted town, a few kilometres from Dharamsala. They stepped out; in the darkness, they saw a car waiting, the driver waved at them.

*

'She has already spoken: the warrior spirit knows too much. He will start his search and get what he wants. We just have to beat him to it,' said Akash.

'Be careful, they know you are close,' Tara said. Akash circled the place, half running, half soaring. All the windows were boarded up. There was no way but to try the door, the moans were coming in shorter intervals. He had to do something, and now. *The woman will die if you don't stop them,* the voice in his head warned.

'Make up your mind, do you want me to go in or hold back? Wait, let me decide!' Akash snapped.

Akash didn't heed Tara's repeated warnings. He kicked the door, hard. It didn't budge. An eerie quiet suddenly settled upon him. No more screaming. And then the door was being unlocked. It sounded like three arms of steel were removed before it was pulled open.

He came face-to-face with an Asian man of medium height with slanting eyes and jet-black glossy hair. There was no hint of distress or anger on his face. He looked like he was just out camping. Then his face broke into a wide smile. And Akash saw the crazy look in his eyes.

'You're late, mister!' the man said with a wide grin.

'Late for what?' Akash responded. He heard the moaning and peered inside the partially opened door.

'The Kalingan knows the truth!' the man said, and Akash felt a powerful blow in his stomach. It sucked the air out of him, sharp pain clouded his brain and he went down. Before he knew it he was being dragged inside the house by his ankles. As he tried to focus, he saw two blurry figures wearing black robes and strings of beads around their necks. They had strange markings on their foreheads. Then, suddenly, something hit his head and Akash lost consciousness.

Vayu laughed at him. 'What an idiot! I don't even want to waste my time killing him. These three new recruits of the Nine are particularly useless.'

*

'He's hurt, the fool!' Tara whispered, staring into the darkness from the window of their speeding car.

'He will be all right. I'll heal him.' Zubin looked at his hands as if they belonged to a stranger.

'Yes,' she said in a regretful tone, 'but the Kalingan is ahead of us. He is already on his way.'

'We can still make it in time. The Knowledge Keeper will survive and we will know where the warrior is headed.'

The car came to a halt at the edge of a dense forest. They asked the driver to wait for them. 'We are close,' Tara said, getting out of the car. Without waiting for even a moment, she went in blind, walking slowly and then speeding up through the undergrowth. Zubin was close behind her. 'Careful!' he called out when she stumbled.

They trudged through muddy ground towards the shack dimly illuminated by chinks of light through its windows. The door was open when they arrived. As they entered, their eyes watered at the distinct fetor that hung in the air. Inside, Akash looked dazed. He was on the floor nursing his head, and the girl was shivering on the wooden plank. Still strapped, she looked stricken, her haunted eyes vacant and her body trembling. Her feet were a bloody mess and the tips of her toes looked like they had been flattened, crusts of dark red had formed on them. Her wrists and ankles had streaks of blue–black. Her moans for help were feeble. Tara helped her first.

'There was this crazy guy—he almost killed me. I'm telling you he really looked like he belonged in an asylum. His eyes were bloodshot and really crazy-looking,' Akash spoke excitedly. Slowly, he got to his feet with Zubin's help.

'You should have been more careful,' Tara admonished as she worked on the straps on Lise's forehead. She appeared dazed. 'At least to help this poor girl. All you can think about is yourself. Look at what she's been through, you idiot!' she hissed angrily.

'I . . . I'll be okay . . .' Lise mumbled weakly, trying to sit up, wondering what the argument was all about. Zubin patted her arm.

'Oh, just get over your self-righteous attitude, Tara. I got here in time to break up their little black magic party. You should at least say thank you. I didn't think I was expected to jump and fly and then fight off fiendish evil magicians. And what kind of directions were you sending me? You didn't exactly help, confusing me with your warnings.'

Zubin moved around the room, checking the sinister objects that were strewn around. He saw the makeshift bed and bare kitchen. 'These guys must have been planning this for a while,' he said, picking up a coffee jar and showing it to them.

Lise was crying softly. 'I'm sorry,' she repeated over and over. Tara ignored them and focused on the young woman. She looked so white and frail, it seemed like the blood had drained out of her. *Such a vulnerable being, carrying such a heavy burden!* Tara caught fragments of her past, of her feelings, and Dr Halvor. Instinctively, she held her close. 'You will be fine. We are here to take care of you.' Lise shifted slightly and wiped away her tears. 'My name is Tara, that's Akash and that's Zubin,' she said, pointing at the men. 'And you are?'

'Lise,' she said softly. 'I didn't think Vayu would do all this,' she said, wiping her face with the back of her hand. Ash was everywhere and so was the red lead powder. She was covered in it. Tara grabbed the scarf from Akash's neck and used it to gently wipe away the dust from Lise's face and arms. 'He was so kind and loving, and said such wonderful things. The monk had warned me but I didn't listen. And it was all destiny!' she was sobbing and Tara couldn't understand what she meant.

Akash was by her side. 'That conniving cheater!' he said. Akash took Lise's hand in his. 'His name was Vayu, was it? Well, we will get him. That's Zubin, he's the healer. He has powers to heal.' Flicking him a look, Akash pointed to the swelling on his head. 'Well?'

'That's a nasty bump,' Zubin said, pressing his hand on Akash's head wound.

'Wait!' Tara looked at them exasperatedly. 'Don't you think Lise needs to be healed first?'

'We'll get her out of here first,' Zubin suggested, and removed his hand. The contusion had disappeared.

'Thanks, man!' said Akash, amazed. 'Now her?'

'Can't do this right away. Her wounds seem a lot more severe than yours. I need to gain back my energy.'

'There was no need for you to have used your powers on him,' Tara said, looking at both of them reproachfully, 'but I guess the London boy can't handle a little bit of pain.'

'Back off, Tara!'

'You are an obnoxious—'

Zubin noticed that Lise had a curious expression on her face.

'You are the three new members?' She looked at each of them.

They nodded.

She managed a small smile. 'Good of you to come and save me,' she said. Her eyes were filled with tears. 'You will have to hurry and find Vayu. He knows too much and is on his way to getting the Chintamani.'

Akash smiled at her. 'You're welcome,' he said and shot an accusatory glance at Tara. *See, at least someone appreciates me!*

'Lise, we need to get out of here first! And then we need to know what you know,' Zubin said, frowning at the candles, the burning smell of camphor and the bloody ritualistic items strewn around.

Tara helped Lise up. She shivered uncontrollably. 'They did crazy . . . things to me.' Lise murmured. Tara noticed dark circles around her eyes; her complexion had taken on a pale grey tinge.

'Black energy fills this place,' Tara said, eyeing the surroundings uneasily.

'Who the hell would do something so outrageously barbaric?' Zubin said, listening to Lise's moans of pain. 'I can help her.' He bent down and reached out his hands, but when he tried to heal her wounds, he saw that the tips of her toes were crusted with blood, and her feet were red and swollen. Standing up would be sheer agony for her. He tried to heal her, but immediately felt as though a barrier had formed, blocking his energies. He tried again but just couldn't reach her feet. 'It's not working. We have to get you to the monastery first.'

Zubin had a first-aid kit in his knapsack and handed it to Tara. The best she could do was to disinfect and bandage her wounds and hope that she could make the short journey. They helped her to her feet. Immediately she screamed. 'I can't!' she said, tears rolling down her face. 'I'm sorry, it hurts too much. Vayu, what did I do to hurt you? I loved you!' she cried.

Akash put a comforting arm around her shoulder. 'You'll be fine. Zubin will heal you. Don't you worry, we'll get that asshole and he will never hurt you again.'

Tara grimaced at his abrasive style. He had only just met the woman and was already all over her. But his physical proximity seemed to calm Lise down and she gripped his hand tightly.

With their help, and mostly clinging to Akash, Lise managed a few steps and staggered. They half carried her out of the suffocating room. Outside, in the cool stillness of the woods, she seemed to regain her balance and some of her strength. Zubin took out a bottle of water from his cloth bag and helped her take a few sips. She wasn't able to swallow, the water dribbled down the sides of her chin and her stomach heaved. They sat her down under a tree. Very gently, Zubin coaxed her to keep trying, holding her hand and patting her back. She took a few more sips and this time she was able to drink. Her bandaged feet had turned red; her wounds were bleeding again. He tried to heal her again, but couldn't.

'Damn it, I don't know why I'm not able to connect with you!' he said.

Akash was pacing restlessly. 'We should get going, you can try again later.'

Tara nodded in agreement, 'Give her a chance to settle emotionally.'

Zubin said, 'Take deep breaths, Lise. We have to get out of here. You will feel much better when we leave this terrible place.'

The car was waiting for them at the edge of the woods.

'Rinpoche . . .' Lise whispered, crying and laughing, as the car raced through the muddy path towards the bend of the hills. 'He had warned me about Vayu. But I didn't believe him, I didn't believe him. . . .'

The monastery appeared like a small house from the outside; inside, it was festooned with dozens of handwoven and stitched silk hangings depicting the life of Buddha and his followers. The hallway was softly lit with candles and the aroma of frankincense scented the air, bringing a sense of calm to Lise. Zubin and Akash supported Lise, guiding her slowly. Weak and faint with pain, she stopped and slid to the floor, unable to move further, sobbing violently and cursing Vayu. Akash was experiencing the beginnings of guilt. 'I should have come sooner,' he said, trying to pacify her. 'Please calm down, we will get this guy. He will not win this and whatever he did to you, we will make sure he regrets it to his dying day.'

'No!' she said suddenly. 'Revenge will be all mine.'

A resident monk wearing a red robe approached them. His voice was soft. 'We do not speak of such things here.'

'She has been through a traumatic experience,' Akash argued. 'I think she deserves to vent.'

The monk was silent, hands folded in front of him. He

didn't look upset and spoke in the same calm voice. 'Like I said, this is not the place to vent. Please come with me.'

Akash was about to counter him, but Zubin stopped him. Tara helped Lise stand up.

'We can carry her,' Zubin said. And Akash lifted her, supporting her back, one arm under her thigh. Zubin followed suit on the other side and they walked behind the monk down a narrow corridor. He stopped outside a corner room and let them in. They helped Lise on to a low bedding, into which she sank with relief. She was still whimpering.

'Let her rest here,' the monk said. 'You three can follow me.'

'Shouldn't someone be with her?' Zubin asked.

'Someone will attend to her shortly. Please explain to her that she must calm down.' He flicked his gaze at Akash but didn't reveal his emotion.

Akash muttered under his breath, 'I'll do it.'

As the three were leaving Lise, a bespectacled young monk walked in carrying a tray with water, fruits, a bowl containing a yellow paste, and some fresh bandages. The monk explained, 'He will treat Lise's wounds and remove the negativity with a healing chant. She needs to calm her mind and spirit before you can heal her body.'

'Why does Zubin's healing energy not work on her?' Akash asked.

'We cannot use the healing energy until the negativity has been eliminated. With the herbal wrap that has been blessed by the invocations of the Buddha, we will remove the yogi's black power and later, after she is rested and her mind is stronger, Zubin can heal her,' the monk said, leading them into another corridor. Tara was beginning to feel dizzy and wondered when they could actually sit down and have a meal. She suddenly realized how hungry she was.

'Didn't realize there were so many rules,' Akash retorted softly.

'You should learn to respect them,' Tara admonished.

'Yes, mother.'

'You two should just go outside and have a punch out,' Zubin said with irritation.

They were silenced and embarrassed. The monk watched them with an amused expression. 'Come with me, we must talk,' he said to the trio. They made their way through a maze of passageways. Without the monk, Tara doubted if they would be able to find their way around. When she looked back, she couldn't tell which way would take her to Lise's room. Finally they stopped, and the monk led them into a large empty room, clean and quiet. It was bathed in a soft golden light. In one corner was a giant statue of the Buddha; cushions were placed on the floor. There was no furniture. The ambience was hushed and reverential, as if the spirit of the Buddha meditated there.

'Sit down.'

They did as they were told, realizing how tired they were. The monk sat on the bare floor.

'Close your eyes and meditate.'

'I thought we were going to talk, I—' Akash said.

'Close your eyes and meditate for a few minutes. Then we talk,' the monk said sternly.

The moment they closed their eyes they were transported to another place.

30

A lone man waited for them in the centre of the room. He was attired in a traditional burgundy robe. The tall monk, despite a sturdy stance, appeared at least a hundred years old, and gave each of them a piercing gaze. Then he spoke in a gruff booming voice. 'Awaken young souls! I am Na-khi, the ancient one, who lived away from the rest, protecting the Bon sect. We have been blessed with psychic powers and most importantly, we possess the link to the Chintamani stone. Focus and follow me!'

Na-khi walked as if he had a metal spine, moving soldier-like, ramrod straight. He was completely unlike the other monks they had met: he didn't look Asian, his eyes were a light blue and his hair, now white, must have been blonde. He looked more like a wizard from Europe than a Buddhist monk.

Tara was the first in line. Akash joined her, irritated, and Zubin seemed unaffected by what was going on, just going with the flow. The man was a saint in the making, Akash guessed. In the West, he could make tons of money with his healing powers and live in the lap of luxury for the rest of his life. Akash would be considered a freak if people found out he could fly—he would be in some secret science lab hooked to machines. He couldn't milk millions with his ability, he would have to keep his knowledge secret. Tara had her telepathic gift and if she used it wisely in casinos, there's no telling how much money she could make! These guys were set for life. Akash, however, would have to go back to DJing.

'Move faster!' Na-khi hollered. He turned and tapped his cane impatiently on the wall—it slid open. There was a small square doorway, cleverly hidden behind a large wall hanging. They followed him inside. It was cave-like, and the walls were made of rock.

The old man's voice echoed in the dark recesses. 'To keep your energies contained, you must learn not to transmit highly sensitive brain impulses, the Kala Yogis are on the lookout. They have become so strong, they can create . . . obstacles.' The monk paused briefly for effect.

'Obstacles?' Zubin asked. They continued through a narrow corridor and reached a circular chamber. The monk didn't respond. Instead, he lit fat red candles and thick stems of frankincense and placed them in the alcoves. He directed them to the centre.

They moved towards stone seats covered with red ornately stitched mats and sat down in a circle. In the middle was a wooden table with a world map stretched out on it. Tara's attention was drawn to it and she began tracing her finger along it.

'Yes, obstacles,' Na-khi explained. 'Like the way you talk to each other, without respect. The way you have created a dislike for each other, especially the two of you,' he said, pointing a crooked finger at Tara and Akash. 'Your negative energy drains me.' Tara looked up briefly, but preoccupied with other thoughts, she returned to the map. Na-khi stood up with a jerk. He clasped his cane— its polished top carved into a lion's head—and leaned on it, as though without it, he would topple. Despite his seemingly wobbly stance, his gaze was fierce. Tara could feel his presence inside her head, he was communicating with her. 'Explain to these foreign boys,' he told her aloud.

Compelled to do as she was told, Tara focused on Akash and Zubin. 'You are aware of black magic, aren't you?' she asked, looking intently at Akash. 'And different cultures have a dark side: voodoo rituals and other primitive methods of making wishes come true. This can be achieved by invoking dead spirits. Desires rule the mind, and when we become slaves to those desires, there's nothing we won't do to get what we want.'

'Rubbish!' Akash hissed. 'I don't believe in that nonsense. And you can't get things done by waving a joss stick and poking needles into dolls.'

The monk turned a sharp eye on him. 'You doubt my word, imbecile?' He raised his cane and pointed it at him. 'You are arrogant, a small-minded fool. Your ego hangs around your neck like deadweight and you are unable to let it go!'

Tara stared in horror and Zubin shifted uncomfortably. They saw Akash's face take on a purplish hue. In seconds, and without so much as a movement from Na-khi, Akash's nose began to drip blood. The drops fell like tears from his eyes and ears, soon it was gushing out of his mouth, then his hands trembled and more blood flowed. He choked and panicked and gesticulated till Tara came to his rescue.

'Stop!' Tara called out. 'He understands, he begs you to stop.'

A wizened finger was in his face. 'Believe what is happening! Believe in your powers! And believe that you have a responsibility!' the monk said in a voice that boomed and echoed in the cave. He lowered his cane and the blood stopped. Akash wiped it away.

'Are you all right?' Zubin asked anxiously. Akash pushed him away, he wasn't ready for pity or anything else from these crazy people.

'This is not right. I wasn't meant to be here. And everyone is messing with my mind. I can't handle this sort of a ... thing,' he said lifting both hands and retreating. 'I want to go home to my normal world and normal life. I can't deal with this.'

'Coward!' Na-khi said and laughed heartily. 'You want to return to your world, and you think it is normal. Nothing is normal in your life and never will be. Accept it. Be courageous and accept your fate!'

'Who are you to tell me what to do?' Akash hissed in anger.

'It's not right to talk to him like that!' Tara whispered.

'Why?' Akash asked loudly, aggression getting the better of him. 'Because he will make me bleed again? Or kill me? Or show off his powers? That's fine, he can go fight the Kalingan himself. Why does he need us?'

'Listen carefully,' Na-khi said. 'We don't live in your world any more. And we use this time to strengthen and protect you. Don't think our power is limited. You are alive and standing here today because of us!'

'I don't believe you,' Akash retaliated.

'I don't care what you believe. But you are fighting with yourself and wasting your powers by not accepting who you have become. You are not the same person any more. You think you can go home to your normal life?' He waved his stick like a wand. 'It will not work, nothing will be the same. Your mind will direct you to your destiny. It is here and you have to follow it. Fight it all you want, but you will not win.'

There was silence. And it carried weight. What Na-khi said was true. To Akash, they were like puppets handed special powers, and they had not yet fully grasped the importance or the all-encompassing meaning of this new ability. If it were explained on a science-fiction level, they had been genetically modified. *How?* That was another question. Zubin and Tara seemed better able to accept their fate and responsibility.

'Let's just do what needs to be done and get this over with. Let's not dwell on matters that we don't understand scientifically,' Zubin suggested calmly.

'You of all people, Zubin? A scientist, a doctor—you of all people are letting their beliefs take over you? We are altered, modified—like clay dolls we have been moulded into something we are not. How did they do this? Why do you not ask these questions? Why are you so accepting of this destiny?' countered Akash.

Zubin shook his head. 'No. It's not true. I have questioned and thought about this matter endlessly. But now that we have already crossed that bridge, the "why" and "how" is not the point any more. If we are altered, then it is for a reason. We have been chosen because we have something in us that can handle this power. Akash, if you retaliate, and you question and you are angry, maybe that's one of the reasons you are the chosen one. I cannot scientifically explain the healing powers I possess, or your ability to defy gravity, or Tara's telepathic powers. I cannot disprove their beliefs because we are proof of its existence. Akash, the best way is to stop resisting. And when we have done what needs to be done, we can lead our lives eventually. Find our way back to where we came from.'

The way Zubin explained, it all seemed so easy. And in a flash, Akash sensed that, in fact, it was that simple—they had the powers because they were meant to have them. Their bodies were designed for this purpose. Now they were complete. Whole. He was staring at the floor and when he looked up at each of them, he was sure they could see the change in him.

'We have to get out of here,' Tara said suddenly. 'The Kalingan is already on his way to steal the segment of the Chintamani. It is in a museum in America. The Knowledge Keeper is awake—she wants to fight back. She knows where he will be next.'

Akash responded, 'We will do what needs to be done.'

Zubin suppressed a smile, and gave Tara a knowing look. Akash had embraced his destiny.

'Even if you fail to find the Kalingan, but can protect the three segments of the Chintamani, the power of the Nine will be safe. But once he gets his hands on it, there is no telling what can happen. He can do anything he wants.' Na-khi whirled around and pointed to each one of them. 'And you will be the reason for millions of deaths. So stop feeling sorry for yourself and go stop the enemy—the Kalingan.'

The words echoed. 'Leave right away and return with the news that the Chintamani is unsoiled by the Kalingan's sinful hands.' Na-khi tapped his cane and just like that, he disappeared.

'What did you mean by America?'

'The three segments of the Chintamani are in different parts of the world. Once the two are found—in New York and in Siem Reap, Cambodia— he will have access to the third location. Without the two he will never be able to find the city of Agartha,' Tara explained. 'The city of Agartha exists in another realm. Only those who are destined for it will experience it.'

'From what I can understand, Lise's mind has revealed the details. Agartha is a mythical place, and many have heard of it, seen the people who have emerged from it. But its exact location is still a mystery. All I know is that it is near the mountains, I see snow-capped ranges . . . somewhere there beyond the valleys. I can't access any more than that,' she said.

'The information is buried deep in the Knowledge Keeper's subconscious mind,' Zubin said.

'Possibly, but she may not be aware of it. It's just flashes of light. The other two locations were clear and vivid—that's how Vayu was able to get it out of her,' Tara said, returning her attention to the map. 'He is headed to New York. We better get going.'

'Are you able to connect to the Kalingan?' Akash asked.

'He is challenging us, telling us to come find him, fight him so he gets the pleasure of . . . killing us,' Tara said, her eyes closed tight. 'He is communicating with me. He knows I can hear him. But the warrior spirit is very strong: he can control his thoughts, so I get only what he wants me to know.'

'Then we should get this guy and shut him up for good.'

31

The incident stayed with her, and she relived it again. Vayu had sliced off the tips of her toes, and now he was pulling out her nails one by one. She cried out in agony. He disappeared and the three appeared. She recalled the moments when they freed her. Lise was shivering uncontrollably, crying for help. Her head hurt where the Kala Yogi had placed his hand, and the awful camphor smell still lingered. The two, Tara and Zubin, untied her from those awful leashes. They were so gentle, soothing her with kind words. Her skin chafed and bled. When she tried to sit up and the whole room seemed to swim, Tara supported her. The dream moved in slow motion and then it speeded up. Where every movement of her body hurt like hell, the images slowed down and Tara's whispered words helped the panic subside.

The other man, the brown-skinned one, Akash, the one who arrived first, had interrupted the torture; he was kind to her. Vayu had let him in and then knocked him out. He spoke with an English accent.

In the car, she had fainted, and didn't quite remember how long it took to get to the monastery. When they arrived, Lise was so weak she couldn't move. Her feet throbbed with pain and any movement sent excruciating knife jabs up her legs. She wept and cursed Vayu. They helped her quietly, supporting her in silent connection and calming her mind. She was restless, delirious, drifting in and out of sleep as she relived the torture.

A monk had led the trio, who hauled her feeble body through hushed dimly lit corridors. They carried her into one of the empty rooms. It was bare except for the thin cotton bedding in the corner. She fell on it. Surprisingly, it was extremely comfortable. They managed to get her to drink a few sips of water, and as she listened to the distant drone of chanting, she fell unconscious. Then she awakened, with a vague sensation of someone tending to her feet. She felt something cool and it eased the pain almost immediately.

Just as she was sinking into a secure slumber, Vayu's raging voice and red-rimmed eyes slammed into her mind. Lise woke up drenched in sweat, her body quaking with fear. Her temples were throbbing with pain. She sat up and crouched in the corner of the mattress. The pulsating pain in her feet timed with the throbbing in her head. She noticed the bandages—her feet were wrapped up like a mummy's. She wasn't sure how much time had passed since she had been brought in here.

Replaying the sequence of events in her mind, she let her thoughts turn to Vayu. She had trusted him. Vayu had seemed so normal, so nice, and she had fallen for him. At the back of her mind, she knew he had wanted her for one reason only. Yet she let him take advantage of her. He knew she was the Knowledge Keeper. Her past relationships had been based on pain and she had been subconsciously playing out the same emotional trip. She wanted more and then she wanted to feel it lessen. It was her crazy way all over again. She was stupid, stupid, stupid! Vayu had emptied her mind and taken the secrets, stolen Dr Halvor's information, snatched it from the very depths of her consciousness. She felt used, dirty and broken down, and she knew she had failed her mentor. Vayu was a thug and an evil monster. The warnings of the Rinpoche echoed in her head. Lise curled herself into a ball: she hated the feeling that was building up inside her and thought of ending her life.

The elderly monk had said something about destiny. She couldn't remember exactly, but there was another piece of the puzzle that didn't fit in her mind. There was a jumble of questions. And no answers.

Then she thought of Dr Halvor. He was so good to her, he had helped her through her worst times. As much as it hurt, she wasn't giving up so easily. *Dr Halvor hadn't given up on her, how could she?* She straightened up. Vayu was headed to America. He may have sucked the knowledge out of her but it had also come to the surface from her subconscious to her conscious mind, and she understood his intentions. She knew the locations of two fragments of the Chintamani crystal. The location of the third was like an illusion—it was there, at the back of her mind, just as if a word was at the tip of her tongue but wouldn't surface. Lise had to ask someone about this. The Rinpoche.

As if in answer to her question she heard a soft knock and the door opened slowly. A young monk popped his head in, and smiled when he saw she was awake. He opened the door wider and entered. He watched her and waited for her to stand. 'You look better, a little stronger than before. You need food. Come with me and refresh yourself.'

She took a step, but collapsed on the floor. Pain gnawed at her from her ankles to her toes, and jabbed its sword with every movement. The monk helped her up and ran out of the room. He returned in a moment with wooden crutches. With the aid of the sticks, he led her out to the back of the monastery. Every step was like stepping on broken glass. Her head bowed, she focused on simply lifting her foot forward and setting it down again, gritting her teeth to hold back the tears. A walk of two minutes took them fifteen. The monk was patient, ever so gently supporting her, letting her catch her breath until she could take the next step. When they finally reached the end of the corridor, she saw a bathroom and a small adjoining toilet. It was rustic but clean. He handed her a towel. 'Wash up and take the same route, it will lead you to the main hall.'

'Will you wait for me? I cannot go back alone.'

The monk smiled wisely and said, 'You have come this far unsupported. I was only here to show you the way. Now you walked all by yourself. And you can do it again. Trust in yourself.'

He patted her and turned, walking away briskly. As his back receded from view, she leaned against the wall and felt a sense of loneliness grip her. She was suddenly alone in this vast alien world. It made her angry. She threw the crutches to the floor and went inside the bathroom. Then she sunk to the floor, sobbing.

Zubin was waiting for her when she emerged. 'Feel better?' he asked, helping her balance on her crutches.

'Not really,' she said, gritting her teeth. 'The pain is like spikes driving into my bone.'

'I understand how you feel.'

'No, damn it, you don't understand how I feel!' Lise's eyes blazed with anger. 'I've travelled halfway around the world. And been royally screwed by some possessed man who was after my secret, the one Dr Halvor trusted me with.' She continued, 'And you know what? I'm glad I have this physical ache to keep my mind off that man.'

Zubin folded his arms and waited for her to finish her rant. 'So do you or don't you want to be healed?'

'What?'

'You heard me. I can make the pain go away. Your physical wounds will heal completely.'

'You are so matter-of-fact about it.'

Zubin smiled. He helped her sit down with her back against the wall. Then he kneeled down and held her feet in his hands. He closed his eyes. 'Focus on the good things,' he said to her. It took a few moments before he could feel the palms of his hands turn hot; the wounds were deep. His hands began to sweat. In a few minutes it was over. He opened his eyes and looked at her. 'It's fine, mostly. You will have to do the rest,' he said, letting out a sigh and sitting next to her. 'It takes a lot out of me.'

'This is a miracle!' Lise said, unable to grasp the reality of what had just happened. Her feet didn't look completely healed but there were only minor scars. Very slowly, she stood up, and put pressure on her feet: it felt fine. 'I can't believe this!' she cried, taking a few steps. Zubin watched her move around and then she jumped, up and down, up and down. She laughed gleefully. And the next thing he knew, she was on top of him, hugging him tight, thanking him.

Zubin pulled away. 'So, are you going to help us find Vayu now?'

He saw the determination and the new enthusiasm in her eyes. 'Yes, and then . . .' she looked away, but not before he caught the hardness in her expression.

32

Lise was captivated by the view from the monastery. Her heart beat rapidly, as if a gift was coming her way, and she revelled in the excitement of receiving it. But in fact there was nothing coming her way. Her state of mind was such that thinking was becoming a conscious effort. She was aware of the movements within her mind; her floating thoughts, like clouds, turned heavy with emotion and weighed on her. And slowly she was facing it, staring at the cloud from a distance, letting it disappear into wispy nothingness. She wasn't afraid to face her feelings any more, and therein lay the secret of confronting her fears head on. As she fought every emotion like a person in combat, it drained her completely, but it was cleansing. And she fell silent, like the stillness that descends after heavy rain. The world looked washed clean and full of hope.

Sitting on the steps, staring out into the gently sloping hills and the monasteries that dotted them, there was no need to think. What she was experiencing was the feeling of 'being completely in the moment,' she imagined. *Was this some sort of enlightenment? Was this what mankind searched for—the ability to be still for a moment?* Her whole perspective had changed and the question of the meaning of life was beginning to nibble at the fringes of her still mind.

The garden surrounding the monastery was a riot of colours, a blend of wild and carefully tended plants. Tall trees, shrubs, a vegetable patch, a section for flowers and a sprawling lawn surrounding a small pond—the grounds seemed to be the wild yet creative work of an inspired gardener. Then she spotted him: he was a short, scruffy man and his hair was a spiky mess. Wearing a T-shirt and shorts, his bare feet squelching in the wet mud, the gardener held a watering can and appeared to be completely absorbed in his work. He seemed to be talking to the plants.

Lise stood up, her curiosity drawing her towards the gardener. *Was there someone he was talking to?*

There was no one in the vicinity. He saw her watching him. Lise waved, he hesitated for a moment and waved back awkwardly.

'Nice garden.'

He continued to water the bed of flowers and smiled shyly at her. He looked very young, perhaps still in his teens.

'Have you been here long?' Lise asked.

He shrugged. 'A few years.' He put down the can, picked up a shovel, and headed towards the pond. He began to dig up a bare patch of mud.

Lise leaned against a tree, watching him. A gentle breeze rustled. After a few moments she said, 'It's so peaceful here.' The boy-man looked at her and shrugged. He pressed a bare foot on the shovel head and dug deeper. The unearthed soil formed a mini hill. Streaks of sweat ran down his brown skin. His T-shirt was frayed around the neck line and torn in places. His shorts were actually trousers rolled up. 'My name is Lise. And yours?'

'Bala,' he replied without looking up.

'You like it here?'

He shrugged again, a habit, Lise noted. She waited for him to answer. Realizing she wasn't going to leave, he responded. 'Yes, I like it here. Three meals, a roof over my head, what's not to like? And I tend the garden. It's what my father did, and his father before him.'

'You are content. Happy. No other desires? To go out into the world and see what it's all about? Maybe you would like to try another kind of work, and not just be a gardener like your forefathers.'

'This is my world and I like it here.'

'That simple?'

'Yes.' And he stooped to feel the soil. Then she saw the little saplings, each of them in bundled soil. He was transplanting.

'Who were you talking to earlier?'

He eyed her suspiciously. 'No one.'

'I saw you talking to someone.'

He looked at her boldly. 'I talk to the plants. Sometimes they bother the others, like naughty children. I tell them to behave themselves. And to learn to share the space.'

'And they listen to you?' Lise asked, following him towards a tree.

'Sometimes. They like to think that they are in control. But it is this tree that is in control. It is the oldest one and it deserves respect around here.'

The massive tree with its thick canopy of branches dominated the scenery, vines clung to its trunk and snaked around it like eager lovers.

'You mean this tree?' Lise asked.

'Yes.' He shifted his weight from foot to foot nervously. He looked embarrassed talking to her. 'Are you that woman with a special power?' Bala asked.

'No, I don't have any special power.'

'You do. You have some power, otherwise you wouldn't be here. Only those who are special are destined to come to this part of the world.'

There was something odd about him. He looked wizened and old all of a sudden, or was it the way the soft light of dusk fell on him? She wondered if he was another spirit guide like Wangdak.

'I am here to help the others,' she replied, watching him through narrowed eyes. She wasn't afraid, but she wanted to know. 'Did you see the three?'

'Yes, I saw them.'

'They are here for a purpose. When did you die?' she blurted.

'I'm alive, just like you,' he smiled. 'See! I knew you are special. You can see ghosts. Only the pure at heart can see them.'

'You are not real,' she murmured to herself.

'We are all illusions,' he said, caressing the tree with rough dirty hands.

'What happened to you?'

'I lost my way, that's all. But now I'm here, I'm happy and content.'

'I'm not afraid any more, Bala,' she said, reaching out. He took her hand, and held it against the tree. The bark was rough and uneven.

'Fulfilment.' Bala smiled mysteriously. 'The little plants survive despite the grand king of trees taking up so much space; the vines are selfish, living off the tree; the flowering shrubs are there just to look beautiful. Why do you think everything still exists within its space?' He let go of her hand and circled the giant trunk. She followed.

'Because they are unique? Or is it their destiny to be where they are?'

'Because it just is. There is no mystery. There is no reason to overthink. It does not matter whether you are big or small, or as beautiful or as ordinary as the other plants. It just exists within itself, within its little world within a world. And similarly, we do what we need to do, because it just has to be done. Within our own little self-created world.'

'So we all have to exist just because we have to?' Lise asked, dodging a bee that buzzed around her. 'And there has to be a purpose to living—to do what we have to.'

'Exactly!' He looked at her and then turned to the garden again. 'This is my kingdom, my world,' he said as he spread his arms out wide and looked up at the sky. Lise saw the joy in his face reflect like an aura. 'Everything that I've ever longed or wished for is here. This is my purpose—to be the gardener.' He turned towards her and shrugged. 'It's really quite simple.'

'And what if it all goes away, and there's nothing left?'

He came close to her and gave her a victorious look. 'Then I will be grateful for having experienced it!' He laughed and ran in circles around the patch of blooming petals. Then as if something came over him, he plucked one of the yellow flowers and handed it to her. She took it and smiled. 'Thank you, Bala. You are as wise as the monks who live in the monastery.'

He picked up his watering can and continued to water

another segment of his garden. 'I'm just a gardener. Just a gardener.'

Where Lise stood under the evening sky, the leaves of the giant tree rustled and an odd stillness enveloped her. Within that moment, she heard him whistle, as melodious as a bird and as touching as the words of a saint. She closed her eyes.

Lise wasn't sure why her heart was heavy but it was ready to unburden itself through her tears. And in the middle of that beautiful garden, she'd found what she had been looking for.

33

Vayu paused in the midst of the rustling trees and the ghostly quiet of the night. Small pools of moonlight filtered through the thick foliage; in places, the leaves were so smooth and waxy that the refracted light glittered like diamonds. Swiftly, he made his way through the thick undergrowth; serrated leaves and sharp twigs made small cuts on his body. He ignored the pain. The Knowledge Keeper didn't realize the power of what she had stored within her mind. There was a twinge of guilt on how he had manipulated Lise. He felt something for her, and that's why he had let her live. Ordinarily, she would have been nothing more than an obstacle in his path to achieving his goal—the Golden Group's goal. They respected him and, he knew from what they understood, feared him. He wasn't a beast that they could control with their chemicals. He had his own power. The Kalingan had been with him, empowering him with such immense strength of body, mind and soul that ultimately the Golden Group would bow to him. Whatever he needed, he could get. And what Lise had given him, it was his knowledge now. If he wanted, the Golden Group would have to give him carte blanche on its power. Ancient knowledge required a balanced mind, faith and, most of all, a belief in the subtle world of ghosts and demons that controlled the lives of the living. Vayu knew there was more in the world than met the eye. The living lived in an illusory world—little did they know that good and bad energies were living out their unfulfilled desires through them. Only when one's desires were within one's control, when the galloping horses were reined in by a strong grip, only then could one be the ruler.

Lise had given him the key to that power but first he had to find the crystal fragments—the power of the Nine—believed to be not of this planet. Even they didn't know the secret of its origin. Ha! The Nine were vulnerable fools who had chanced upon something that gave them a pool of knowledge. Its location had to be kept secret even from them. *King Ashoka, you couldn't even trust your own men!*

Vayu raced down the hillside buoyed by a fresh surge of determination. He was heading for the West again, this time with a renewed purpose. The first place to look for the Chintamani fragment, one of three, was the American Museum of Natural History in Manhattan. He would retrieve it, and in less than forty-eight hours he would hold one-third of the power of the Nine in his hands.

Vayu caught a slight movement from the corner of his eye. It was an animal, its eyes red in the refraction of the moonlight. It slipped away, seemingly afraid of what it saw. Vayu laughed. The world should be afraid, very afraid of him. It knew not what the Kalingan could achieve.

He arrived at the remote guest house where he was staying. As quietly as he could, he entered and made his way to his room. Without wasting a minute, he packed his sparse belongings in his rucksack and sat down. He needed to plan every step of the way, he couldn't risk any hurdles. He wanted to be absolutely prepared. Turning on his laptop, he clicked to start a conversation on the restricted access site. The Golden Group was online. He reported the latest situation. They gushed and offered any help he needed.

'For now, I need information,' Vayu responded, cautioning them that there was not a single moment to lose. He gave them instructions to meet in New York. It would take him twenty-four hours to get there. And by then, they should gather as much information as they could find about the museum. He needed to get inside it to steal the Chintamani artefact, he needed to know its exact location in the sprawling museum. He could make it look like a terrorist attack if the place was protected like a vault. No one would suspect anything was missing— for a few days at least.

As he left the guest house for the last time, Vayu felt a draught of cold air envelop him. Lise's mind had been rich with knowledge and he had been able to break through the lock that the monk had imposed on it. Vayu had offered the Kala Yogis anything they wanted. They wanted more of their kind, they wanted to expand their clan, recruit people to learn how to manipulate the human mind through their knowledge. Vayu promised them they would get their wish.

Closing his eyes, he turned his face up to the sky, grateful for being the chosen one. Vayu had the power to change many lives. The fragments would combine to form the ultimate treasure—the Chintamani crystal, the wish-fulfilling stone. It was the point of power, a non-technological quantum vortex, the key to all knowledge. Anyone who held the two parts in his hands would glimpse where the third fragment was hidden.

Vayu knew the Nine would use all their powers to hunt him down and stop him. He had to get as far away as possible. A quick exit from the country and finding the stone in New York: that was his first plan of action. Eventually, killing every single member of the Council of Nine would be an added bonus.

34

New York

The information counter was deserted at the opening hour. Vayu bought a ticket and calmly entered the museum lobby. He had instructed his men to wait outside. They were obedient, conditioned by his power to control their minds. They knew that working for the greater good required patience and sacrifice. They were ready. He was ready. The purpose of his existence was directing him to his fate. He knew that only he could hold that power, that control. The Nine were an overhyped group. Show-offs. And if they had indeed protected mankind from itself, then why was there war, global warming, pestilence and disease? Why could they not have prevented the inevitable and eventual destruction of the earth? Vayu had the power to create a better world. And he was ready to accept that power.

He surveyed the vast, open foyer to plan his move. He could not afford to waste even a moment. One of his men was strapped with explosives—the minion was prepared to die for the Kalingan cause. The commotion and fire would cause enough of a distraction for Vayu to be able to get the Chintamani fragment and escape before anyone discovered the theft.

Vayu had to check the layout of the museum before he timed the bomb. The building was old, with high ceilings. The halls were enormous and Vayu guessed he would have to pass through several corridors with exhibits in glass displays. He was aware that the museum was deserted at this time of the day. In fact, other than schoolchildren who would follow their teacher through the various displays and exhibits, he would see no one of consequence. The guards and museum attendants didn't give him a serious glance. Vayu was dressed like an ordinary tourist: jeans, T-shirt and a sports jacket with a knapsack on his back, a map in his hand and a look of confusion on his face. Vayu noticed a few young girls walking in a cluster, slightly behind their group, giggling excitedly. They were more interested in the Facebook newsfeed on their mobile phones than the ancient artefacts of the museum.

'May I help you?' a friendly voice offered when Vayu paused.

Vayu smiled at the pretty lady, his eye wandered to her badge. 'Laura', it read. She was wearing a light-coloured skirt and silk blouse. The museum representative sported a plastic welcoming expression.

'I'm looking for the display of crystals, ancient stones and similar artefacts.'

She nodded, sighed and smiled wider, pleased that she understood his accent. 'Follow the directions to the Rose Centre, then turn right down the corridor and you will see a sign.' She pointed to the lift and handed him a brochure which gave details of the sister building. 'It's up on the fourth floor in the east wing. Enjoy.'

'Thanks, this is useful,' Vayu said and headed towards

the bank of lifts. No one was waiting for the lifts. He entered and pushed the button for the fourth floor. The lift lurched upwards. When it reached the destination, the doors parted slowly to reveal a marbled corridor extending on both sides and straight ahead. He turned right, and made his way past groups of tourists admiring a window display of volcanic rocks. They glistened under the halogen lights.

He slipped past and found the hall he was looking for. He saw it immediately. The beauty, the intricacy of such an ancient, unearthly piece struck him at his core. He couldn't believe it—the stone was labelled as a trapezohedron, placed amongst ancient stones, including zircons, feldspars, rubelites, malachites and dozens of amber-coloured crystals with fossilized bones or whole insects trapped in them, frozen in time.

This was a treasure, the king of all crystals, the past and future of mankind, the secret of all existence—and the museum had shoved it with the rest of the ordinary earth crystals!

Vayu felt a stabbing pain of the past deep in his soul and the warrior in him wanted to smash the glass and snatch the stone from its velvet nest. But he closed his eyes and took deep strong breaths. 'Not yet, not yet,' he whispered, calming his spirit.

His job was easier than he had imagined: no one would notice the loss of a three-inch curved crystal that was only one of many. As Vayu left through the Rose Centre exit, he realized he had hardly taken fifteen minutes to find what he was looking for. And it would take less than ten from this side of the museum entrance, where guards were few. And cameras were nowhere in sight. He noted that the museum would close at five. The explosives would be timed to go off five minutes before that. The four young men who had taken on the job of becoming martyrs to the cause were not afraid.

Vayu exited the building and led his four men to a coffee shop round the corner. One last meal and then they would find victory at last.

*

Akash felt the heat of the blast. Tara warned him again and again to leave it alone. It was dangerous to enter a burning building. But she knew he wasn't going to listen. 'Back off!' he had snarled at her. 'Let me do what needs to be done,' he had said. She simmered in frustration and gave Zubin accusing glances.

'He's always been like that, we can't stop him,' Zubin shrugged.

'Don't think you can heal him that fast if his injuries are serious,' Tara said, arms folded.

'Yes, so we hope that he does not get hurt,' Zubin replied. His eyes reflected the fire burning wildly.

'Where are those damned fire engines?' she muttered.

Amidst the confusion of screaming people running helter-skelter, Akash had already made his way into the inferno. The sounds of the fire-engine sirens were still

some distance away. He leapt above a burning beam and
narrowly dodged another one that came crashing down.
The smoke was getting to him, it clogged his throat and
his breathing came in bursts. He felt dizzy, disoriented.
But he kept moving forward. If he could just get to the
Chintamani fragment first . . .

He saw the shape of a man ahead of him. It was the
Kalingan and he had something in his hand. Akash faced
him.

'Give me that,' he shouted over the raging crackle of
the fire.

Vayu laughed cruelly. 'You are as stupid as you appear.'

Akash approached him, ready to fight. His heart burst
in rapid beats. The smoke seemed to have no effect on
the Kalingan. He was breathing evenly.

*

'Akash is taking a huge risk facing the enemy,' Tara
murmured. They were right outside the museum. The
police had pushed back the onlookers, putting up the
yellow tape and barricades. Some crazy fanatics had
managed to blow up a part of the museum despite the
heavy security. Water gushed from the firemen's hoses.
The black oily soot seemed everywhere and the water
sprayed across it, turning everything in its path black.

'He can take care of himself. Give him a chance, trust
his instincts,' Zubin responded, looking as worried as
her.

The fire had reached the extended part of the museum. The smoke surrounded them and made it hard to see.

'I hear there are bodies inside,' Tara said.

'What's Akash up to?' he asked.

*

'That does not belong to you!' Akash shouted over the blazing furnace.

'It belongs to whoever takes it,' said Vayu, holding the Chintamani up in his hand, as if in victory. 'So you are one of the Nine.'

Akash ran towards him and rose into the air, ramming his leg into Vayu's chest. The stone fell out of his hand. Akash made a dash for it but Vayu was too quick. He was on his feet in an instant and his fist got Akash, but not where he had intended. Akash swerved and only felt a slight impact of the punch, his attention on the gleaming crystal. It was a few hundred yards away. He could grab it.

The fire licked the ceiling. Smoke filled the room. Akash raced for the crystal but Vayu landed on it first. He grabbed it and smacked Akash in the face with it. The impact sent Akash reeling and he tasted blood: a sharp pain erupted in his ribs. The Kalingan was on his way out of the window. Akash didn't give up. He chased Vayu and grabbed his legs, thrashing him on to the ground. His grip on the crystal loosened again, and it bounced some distance away.

Vayu roared, twisted his body and slammed his elbow into Akash's back. The pain was excruciating. Akash tried to move away but a large exhibit table blocked his way and Vayu came down on him again. Hard. Akash found a long shard of glass, he gripped it and turned to Vayu.

'You have no claim on this stone,' Akash said weakly. 'Give it up and we will spare your life.'

'Don't think you can win,' Vayu said, leaning closer to give Akash a final blow, when Akash, using all his energy, slammed the glass into the man's neck. He missed, but got him in the shoulder.

The Kalingan screamed in pain and fell backwards. The fire was blocking his exit path. The smoke was getting thicker, making it harder to see. Akash tried to move, dragging himself to where the stone had fallen. But Vayu was already there, searching frantically. The stone lay against a glass wall that looked ready to shatter. Vayu scooped it up from the floor as Akash watched weakly, barely able to move. And without so much as a backward glance, the Kalingan disappeared from view.

Akash tried to walk. It was sheer agony. He should have listened to Tara. They could have chased the Kalingan even after he had stolen the Chintamani. But no, he wanted to prove he was this big strong hero. Akash felt like an idiot. *What was he thinking?* Just because he could fly and Zubin could heal didn't mean he was invincible.

With great effort, he shifted one foot and then another.

There was a single doorway that wasn't consumed by the fire. He began crawling towards it. The ground was burning into his skin, he gritted his teeth and kept moving. 'Please find me, Tara,' he said as the smoke got to him, filling his lungs like oil, clogging his throat. He saw the fire lick his arm and singe the hair. In seconds, he smelled his skin burning and closed his eyes.

'I'm sorry, Tara,' he whispered.

*

'Someone is still inside, he's in there. He's hurt, you must save him!' Tara yelled at the firemen.

'Ma'am, stay back. There's no one alive in there!'

'There is—he is in the room with the crystals. Please believe me. He is there! Send someone quick! He's alive! I beg of you!' Tara cried.

'Please,' Zubin said. Tara had gripped his hand tight. She was sensing Akash and it was making her weak with panic. She was hysterical and attracting attention. Two uniformed officers were looking at them with interest. Forget racial profiling, this time they would be right to arrest them, and question later.

'Tara, please calm down,' he said, holding her firmly by the shoulders. She was crying as though Akash was dead. 'Stay focused. The police are all over the place. The firemen are inside, they will find him. But you must calm down or they will suspect us.'

'I can feel his pain but I can't sense him any more. He's

NINE   317

unconscious. How are they going to find him?' She yanked
his hands away, anger and desperation in her voice. 'You
know what your problem is? You think too much. Not
enough action. At least Akash just goes and does the
craziest things but he faces it head on. Wants to get it
done.' She sobbed, falling to her knees. 'You just want to
think and think and think. Both of you are nuts and I'm
stuck in between.' Tara clutched her stomach.

A police officer was approaching them.

'Get up, Tara, let's get out of here,' Zubin looked
worriedly at her.

She waved him away. 'I can't move, there's too much
pain!'

'We will be arrested. How are we going to save Akash
then?' He helped her up and they started moving. 'Tara,
disconnect from Akash for a few minutes, then we can
decide what to do. Let's get away from here at least.'

'Hey!' the policeman called out, jogging towards them.
'Stop! I need to talk to you.'

At that very moment, a Mercedes Benz drove up to the
sidewalk. Two men dressed in black emerged from the
car and hurried towards them. 'Come with us, we know
who you are; you will be safe,' one of them said.

Zubin eyed him suspiciously. 'We have to get our
friend out of there. We have to help him.'

'You cannot help him from prison. It's better you
come with us.' He jerked his head at the waiting car.

Tara saw the look in their eyes and knew they were
right. 'He's telling the truth.'

The policeman had almost caught up with them. 'Stop or I'll shoot!' the young pimple-faced youth said. He looked like he was just out of the police academy, and Zubin guessed he would shoot carelessly.

Zubin and Tara froze. The men in black addressed the uniformed officer. 'If I were you, I would put that away,' one of them said. They walked towards the cop, unfazed by his pointed gun. They waved government badges and without waiting for him to react, led the two to the waiting car.

'Damn! The CIA gets everywhere!' the confused officer muttered and lowered his weapon. Before he could place it back in its holster, there was another explosion. Instinctively, they ducked. The fire was now raging through the roof. It had spread viciously across the two main buildings and had erupted in a fiery blast. The policeman dashed towards the burning museum. He yelled at the crowds to stay back, while more police cars arrived. Sirens blared, fire engines unrolled their snake-like hoses and connected them to the water hydrants. The water erupted suddenly, its gush drowning all other sounds. Crowds were surging along the cordoned area. Newshounds arrived with camera crews in tow. Words such as 'terrorist attack' and '9/11' were being repeated by newscasters using the burning building as the backdrop of their coverage.

Zubin and Tara watched the display through the tinted glass of the Benz. The sound was muffled but it didn't diminish the horror of what had happened over a fragment of stone. The orange fire from the museum had taken on a harsher tint, burning wildly in the streaked sky. The black smoke rose higher, giving a clear idea of the damage from miles away. As the car headed farther and faster, they left behind the riot of sounds and the desperate attempts to extinguish the blaze.

The two turned their attention on their host. Tara couldn't get a fix on him. Warily, she waited for the middle-aged gentleman sitting across from them to introduce himself. He was dressed immaculately in a well-pressed expensive grey suit, his shiny black custom-made leather shoes gleamed. He had the confident air that hinted his life—and maybe those of others—were in his control. Money was clearly his power. The two guards were in the front seat facing forward; a sliding glass panel ensured the three had privacy. The car glided as if on air, its interior was leather-lined and smelled lemony like it had been freshly polished.

'So you finally made it to the land of opportunity,' the silver-haired man said with a small smile.

'Not any more. It's the land of disappointments. Who are you?' Zubin asked, sipping on a bottle of water that he had been handed by the man. 'And what do you want from us?'

'Ah the forensic expert speaketh!' He pressed a button on his armrest and spoke into it, 'Turn right and head to the district.' The driver responded with a 'yes sir'. How high up in the CIA was he?

'Akash is badly hurt and we don't know if they found him,' Tara said desperately, turning back to glance out of the rear window. There was nothing except empty streets. 'I know he is alive. I can feel his pain. You have to take us to him. Please.' Tara squirmed in her seat, worry written all over her face. Her bottle of water remained untouched.

The man flicked a nonchalant glance at them and answered a phone call. They caught snippets of the conversation.

'. . . In the hospital . . .'

'. . . Third-degree burns . . . in the burns unit . . . other injuries . . . hm. Good, keep me informed.'

They gave him questioning looks.

'Your friend Akash is in safe hands. He has third-degree burns and some cracked ribs but he will live,' he said as he checked his other mobile.

'We need to get to him,' Tara said. She leaned closer and pleaded, 'Please! We need to save him.'

'Who are you?' Zubin asked again.

'People call me the Seer.' He smiled, but it didn't soften his expression. 'I work in the special branch of the CIA. We know about the Nine because we handle odd assignments. The kind no one else will handle.'

'How did you know we were here? About us?'

'The Nine have connections in high places. We know what they are capable of achieving. Technological and scientific advances can be credited to them. We know the Nine have contributed in many fields over the last century.

It's just that they like their privacy. We do what we can for them. It is an honour to be chosen to protect them.'

He exhaled deeply, and then seemed to sink further into the upholstered seat. 'But you haven't had the chance to learn the ways of the seniors. I will guide you, protect you and assist you, but you must take responsibility for your powers. Understand its strength, live with it, accept it and behave like normal people.'

'When can we see Akash?' Zubin asked. The Seer had a point, he realized: the sooner they got their act together, the sooner they could get out of here and deal with the crazed Kalingan.

'When the time is right, you will meet and heal him. Now we will go to a safe house where we have to wait till the chaos has died down. You will have to plan your next course of action. Please make sure that this time you do not call attention to yourselves.'

Tara slid back and closed her eyes while Zubin looked out of the window with glazed eyes. This mission was proving to be a roller coaster for them—both physically and emotionally.

35

The skin on Vayu's legs and hands was a mass of bloody tissue. With every movement, the burning pain bored into him like a hot prodding rod. The smell of charred flesh wouldn't leave his nostrils—it was coming from his own body. As he struggled forward, he glanced down the dark alleyways. Pain made him tremble, a soft roar emerged as he gritted his teeth and pushed himself to keep moving. Next stop: Cambodia. He needed to stay focused.

Staggering, leaning against walls, he kept up the pace. The street was deserted but there were a few late-night pedestrians who hurriedly moved out of the way when they saw the hooded man approach, walking like a drunk. Clutching the talisman around his neck, Vayu felt the weight of the Chintamani fragment in his inner jacket pocket, safely zipped up and close to his chest. It made him feel victorious and an inner strength gave him an extra spurt of energy. There was hope, he had time to make a safe exit. Everything had gone as planned. His followers had served him well. Their martyrdom had not been in vain. All was fair in love and war.

Love brought to mind Lise and he mentally thanked her for her generosity: her physical expression of love and her release of information. She would have been a good partner. If only she had the warrior instinct.

He turned a sharp left at the end of the block and tried as far as possible to keep away from the street lights. The van would be waiting. Vayu had instructed the yogis to wait five blocks away. The journey that had seemed effortless before, now felt like torture. The screams of the fire sirens were still audible but he was at a safe distance. He needed to rest. Leaning against the wall, his legs gave way and he fell down. In the semi-darkness, he saw his shredded trouser-legs and the charred skin on his shin. It was the escape through the burning window that had injured him. The metal was molten, and when he climbed through it, he had to use his hands to break the fall. Then, he had run away from the building with every shred of strength he could muster. That young and reckless member of the Nine had tried to stop him. The ability to defy gravity was a gift, but the boy had not learned how to use it to his advantage. He had been deadbeat on the ground, Vayu had given him a dose of his power and knocked him out completely. But that had delayed Vayu and his exit route had been compromised. Still he had managed to escape. If he chose to, he could kill all three: they were here and giving him chase. Their deaths would make the Nine weak, and with the Chintamani finally in his grasp, it would completely demolish them. The Kalingans would regain their power. Forever.

Vayu stood up again, but he stumbled over the uneven path and a sharp spike of pain shot through his leg. He kept going, taking deep ragged breaths. Tears and sweat mingled and rolled down the sides of his face. He felt the stinging drops fall on his hands and legs. He pushed his mind away from the suffering and tried to distract himself. It was possible that Lise had come with them. She would recognize him and that would be stupid. But it was too late now: he knew they were on to him and she must have told them his next stop.

Vayu was ready to collapse when he finally saw his contact vehicle. Some men emerged quickly and helped him inside. Vayu took a deep breath, and before he lost consciousness, he sensed the van pick up speed and heard the yogi bark instructions to a chemist. They couldn't risk taking him to a hospital.

36

From Newark, Vayu arrived at the Thai capital, Bangkok. Directly from the airport, he took a ride to Siem Reap, the home base for Angkor Wat expeditions. Once in Siem Reap, he wasted no time and hopped on to a tuk-tuk. He was tired, but he knew that the quicker he got to his destination, the easier it would be to be in control. The last two weeks had been a gruelling experience. There was no way that the chemist's medicines alone would heal him. He had third-degree burns, wounds and a broken rib that required hospitalization. But the Golden Group had invested in enough pharmaceutical companies researching other forms of medicine for Vayu to have got the best treatment. They were his support system, his backbone and his financiers. And they needed him. Vayu was the only one who could give them the power they wanted, and he knew it.

A Golden Group representative once told him, 'Don't underestimate the power of the Nine: if you have us, they have twice as many and thrice as smart people ensuring their survival. You watch your back, boy, we cannot be there for you all the time.' Yes, they would be. Once they found out he had the fragment, they would watch his back, his front and every part of him.

'Take me to Angkor Orange,' Vayu told the driver. Once he checked in and got to his modest room in the budget hotel, he hung the 'Do not disturb' sign outside his door. Within minutes he had shed his clothes and ordered room service, instructing them to leave the tray outside the door. Vayu took a steaming hot shower, ate his sandwich and went to sleep. Eighteen hours later, he woke up. When he checked the time, he realized it was not dawn yet. After washing up, he meditated for fifteen minutes. It calmed his breathing and his mind. The Kalingan warrior was eager, sometimes Vayu wished . . . and he stopped himself from thinking further. He went down to the reception desk to rent a bicycle. It was a good time to ride to Angkor Wat.

When he started his journey, the sun was still not visible in the horizon. No one was around on the potholed path they called a road. Even the street vendors' carts were still covered with cloth and tied with rope. After about twenty minutes of pedalling, he reached the ticket office and bought a three-day pass. It was 5.30 in the morning. On the ticket was a picture of him—he didn't even realize that his picture was being taken, he should have been more careful. Hunger pangs and a distinct throb in the back of his neck reminded him that he needed food. A small kiosk selling day-old buns and fruit was open. He ate the bread and washed it down with coffee. Then he bought some oranges and bananas for the journey. A bottle of water was offered, and Vayu bought that too.

Securing his bag on the pillion, Vayu got back on the bicycle and reached Angkor Wat just before six. It was bustling with a cluster of tourists and locals setting up stalls.

Finally around 7 a.m., they were rewarded with the glorious vista of the sun coming up from behind one of the towers of Angkor Wat. It was captivating and the serene sight almost made him forget about his mission. He wandered around with the tourists, admiring the carvings on the temple walls. The sun was a bright orange and the surroundings were ablaze with light. Angkor Wat was breathtaking! The huge structures that were hewn into temples, idols and enclosed giant caves were festooned with thick vines that circled the stones in the most artistic manner. Even man couldn't be this creative!

He bought more coffee from a vendor outside one of the popular temple ruins. There was a niggling discomfort about the fact that there was no one around. *What about the Nine? Their men must be here already. Where were the three new recruits? And why weren't there any protectors? It didn't seem right.* He should just keep moving, he realized. Vayu got on his bike and pedalled further to Angkor Thom and the Bayon temple with its crumbling towers and high walls. The place was half covered by the jungle and was in ruins, which had earned it a special heritage site status from the UNESCO.

Finally, Vayu arrived at the Ta Prohm temple; it had been taken over by massive strangler fig and silk-cotton trees like leeches sucking the life out of the monument. It was as eerie as the pictures he had seen all over town. Roots of trees grew out through the temple grounds. Five rectangular enclosing walls surrounded a central sanctuary. He waited impatiently for a party of Japanese tourists to finish clicking photographs. Eventually, they moved on.

When he was alone, he stepped over the warnings and entered the dark doorway. Certain areas of the temple were closed to tourists.

Inside, it was dark and dank. Vayu pulled out a light stick from his knapsack and flicked it on. It was so quiet that the only sound he could hear was the steady trickle of water: a gentle stream must be nearby, he thought. The temple opened up into a large circular cave, it housed Prajnaparamita, the goddess of 'perfection of wisdom'. The statue of Prajnaparamita was surrounded by over two hundred lesser divinities, housed in their own sanctuaries. Above, on a balcony, monolithic stone statues of half-human, half-animal creatures were carved on the walls. They were the dvarapalas or temple guardians. Dozens of statues had fallen off their perches, where the roots of trees had prised apart the gigantic stone heads of

ascetics or the Buddha. The upper platform had ominous-
looking statues with weapons. They followed him with
their stone eyes. The tree roots snaked throughout the
cave and added an unusual ambience of stone and wood,
or earth, to the energy of the cave. The other three
elements could exist and there would be perfect harmony.
Water—he could hear it—and then it would be space
which existed, and fire.

He continued inwards and stopped at the centre, facing
the grand deity. Vayu focused on the sound, which was
nearby. He circled the cave holding the light outwards to
check for water. There was nothing: it was bone dry, yet
there was a distinct smell of wet walls and the air was
humid. He went further inwards. A large statue of the
Buddha in a meditative pose, eyes half-closed, lay fused
with the stone wall of the cave, as though watching his
moves silently. It rested on a podium on an upper reach
of an incline. He would have to climb up to get closer.
Vayu turned away from the idol as a sensation of being
watched came over him and he swirled, his hand on a
dagger attached to his belt. There was no one around. He
looked up at the platform—it would be easy to hide
there. He couldn't see in the darkness and went up the
stone steps cautiously. There was a rock platform, it
seemed solid enough as he stepped on it. The veranda
extended along the arc of the cave. More statues, but
these were human images, and they held out their hands,
palms cupped. And there was the water: it dripped from

their outstretched hands. There were dozens of statues
fixed to the walls. *Where was the water coming from?*
Vayu stepped closer to check. He shone a light into the
hands of the statues but couldn't figure out the source. It
seemed as though there was an endless supply of water
flowing from their hands. Must be a spring underneath
or behind the statue, he thought. From the corner of his
eye, Vayu caught movement. He turned to check. He
looked down at the lower level, and all he could see was
the Buddha in repose. There were dozens of pillars and
tall structures—anyone could be hiding behind them.

He had come for a purpose, he would find the
Chintamani and leave. As the thought hit him, his eyes
fell on a statue embedded in the wall, taller and more
skilfully cut then the rest. It was of a woman, and from
her outstretched hands, water dripped down in a gentle
cascade. He approached the statue and shone his light
stick into her cupped palms. There was water, yes, but at
the bottom, resting on her palm was a glittering stone.
Without thinking, he slipped his hand inside. The cool
water felt soothing in the oppressive and humid heat. He
tried to pick up the stone but it wouldn't budge—it was
stuck to her hand. He took out his dagger and used the
sharp end to chip at it. The stone didn't move.

Vayu had a torch, he removed it from his bag and
shone the bright light on the stone. The water had tiny
bubbles of air, and even though it streamed out over her
palm, it was continually replenished. The stone was

jammed near the wrists of the stone figure. Again, he attempted to prise it away with his dagger, but the stone remained firmly embedded. Vayu looked up at the benign expression of the statue and felt as if she were mocking him. 'Damn it!' he muttered. And felt anger rise—he would need dynamite or ten men to move the statue. He paced restlessly thinking of the next step. There had to be a way.

'There is a way.' A voice echoed through the cave. Vayu swirled around, peering into the semi-darkness. Then he looked down and saw a monk standing there, hands clasped together, as if waiting. His orange robe stood out in the grey–black interior.

'Who are you?' Vayu asked as he came down the stone steps, keeping his eye on the monk and his hand on his dagger.

'I am the resident guard here, the gopura. I see you want the stone. But only the one who is entitled to it can get it. That is Goddess Tara,' he said pointing to the statue, 'and she will not just give it to you.' He smiled, showing no concern at the weapon in Vayu's hands.

'So who is the entitled one?'

'My fellowman, you know who it is! Why would you be here otherwise?'

Vayu went closer and glared at him. In a flash, he put his blade to the monk's throat and threatened, 'Tell me who it is and I will spare your life.'

The monk smiled. 'Who are you to spare lives?' Vayu

let go of him. He wasn't worth killing. 'The one we speak of is the Nine—any of Ashoka's men can use the stone. Not you, Kalingan warrior.'

'How do—' Vayu saw his smug expression and changed his tack. 'Which one?'

'Pick any one.' He gurgled lightly, it was laughter. 'This is a fight worth watching.' He walked over the stones as if gliding, and kneeled in front of the Buddha. Bowing low, he prayed silently.

Vayu felt a barrier within himself when he got closer to the inner sanctum. It was like a pressure on his chest. He stayed back. 'Who are you?'

'Possessed by a spirit, and knows not what a spirit looks like. That's funny,' the monk said and glided away to stand on a stone. He was at least three feet above Vayu, looking down at him. 'Tell the Kalingan warrior to stop his ancient rumblings of revenge. It is time to rest in peace. And if you want him to leave this body, go to Kushinagar. That is the place where Sakyamuni entered Mahaparinirvana. When Lord Buddha reached his eighty-first year, he gave his last major teaching there. You will benefit from that place. And the Kalingan will disappear.'

Vayu gripped the monk's leg and pulled, he fell with a cry. Vayu was on top of him with the dagger, he felt the Kalingan pushing him to plunge the blade into the monk. There was a split-second of hesitation, and Vayu saw the monk's face: he was smiling. 'There is hope for you, boy,' he said. And as the dagger came down hard, it hit stone.

Vayu stared wide-eyed—where he had felt solid flesh and a breathing human in his grip, there was nothing, absolutely nothing! He ran out of the temple, his heart palpitating wildly. There was no one around, the place was as silent as a tomb. Crumbling stone structures and huge faces of Buddha silently watched the man and his weakness. It wasn't a new sight. Doubts were crowding his mind. Vayu had not wanted to kill the monk; it was the Kalingan, the crazy warrior, turning him into a murderer. 'What have I done?' he cried and fell to his knees.

Don't be afraid, Vayu. We have reached this far. Don't be a weakling. You are here for a higher purpose. Don't destroy the Kalingan spirit before it achieves its glory.

Vayu stood up and smiled. He knew what had to be done.

37

Tara and Zubin were taken to a house in the suburbs. It was a quiet area, isolated and cleverly concealed at the end of a narrow street. The house was compact, basic and contained enough for them to lie low. A slim metal wire framed the floor and ceiling, it criss-crossed the windows. The Seer stood by the door stoically and watched them look around the room.

'I will leave you guys now as I have work to do. It is your duty to make sure your identities stay hidden as your lives are in danger after Akash's confrontation with the Kalingan warrior. Please make sure you maintain a black zone of communication. The wires will block out the access of probes. You do not, and I repeat, do not contact anyone. Have I made myself clear?'

Zubin nodded. He realized that their being new to the scene was causing the Council a great deal of anxiety. 'But what about Akash? How will we know . . .' he spoke up.

The Seer had raised his hand. 'That is my responsibility. You are in my territory and I will ensure that nothing sabotages the Nine. You will be informed as soon as the coverage of the fire has died down. I will contact you.' He handed them a device that looked like a remote for the garage door. It had a single push-button. 'This is an emergency device. You press it if there is trouble. For now, you just need to know that Akash is in hospital and in good hands.'

'I can heal him,' Zubin said.

'No, you cannot at this stage. Think before you do anything that will call attention to yourselves. Besides, he is vulnerable because the enemy has seen him. We have our own security keeping an eye on him. He is a weak target and if you go to the hospital, it will make matters worse. Wait until I give you the go-ahead.'

'How long will that be?'

'Give me twenty-four hours and I shall give you an update of the situation.'

'We can't just sit here and do nothing!'

'Plan your strategy. Think carefully before you jump into any situation. That is the power of the Nine—they are humble, organized and anonymous in their approach. It's a lesson to you newcomers. Also, there's a file on that table. Read it carefully.'

With that, the Seer shut the door. They heard the key turn in the lock.

'What's the matter with you? Why couldn't you be a bit more aggressive?' Tara demanded. 'How can we be completely sure if this guy is on our side or not? For all you know, he could be one of the conniving Black Yogis. He might kill us, and Akash might be dying out there.'

'You think the Seer is lying?'

'Yes!' Tara fumed and then hesitated. 'I mean we have no proof of either except a gut feeling. Why couldn't you just tell the guy off? Why didn't you tell him to take you to Akash?'

Zubin smiled at her. 'You know what, Tara? The Seer makes more sense than you right now. You get carried away by your emotions. You never give them the benefit of the doubt. Can't find one good thing to say about anyone. And the real problem is that you just don't trust people. Been hurt bad, isn't it? Someone ditched you, Tara? Is that what it is? If you think you are so smart . . .'

She turned suddenly and strode towards Zubin. Without thinking, she slapped him hard across his face.

Zubin grasped her wrist. 'Someone hurt you real bad,

huh?' He held her gaze and the anger slowly dissipated. He let her go when he saw her eyes glisten with tears.

'Take your time, Tara, and get over it. But don't take it out on your friends,' he said and walked out of the room.

The next day, Tara found Zubin having breakfast and reading the thick file. The kitchen was well stocked and there was even some fresh food in the refrigerator.

'Zubin, I'm sorry about last night,' Tara said.

'It's okay.'

'Please let me explain.'

'You don't have to.' He was still looking at the file.

'I want to.' She touched his arm, and he turned his attention to her. 'The truth is that you were right. Someone hurt my feelings and I guess I hadn't got over it. You are right, I find it difficult to trust people now. I shouldn't have taken it out on you.' Tara reached over and touched his cheek. Zubin gave her an awkward smile and took her hand in his. 'Please stick a post-it note to yourself—we are friends and we look out for each other. But we are different and cannot behave in a synchronized manner,' he said.

'Yes, got it.' Tara smiled and picked up a slice of toast from his plate.

Zubin nodded, looking through Vayu's file. 'And now to plan our action while we wait.'

They spent their time wading through the papers. The Kalingan powers were written about in great detail. Over the centuries there had been many failed attempts on the Nine.

'This has happened before, and the Nine have survived it. We cannot let them down,' Tara said.

'We not only have to fufil the mission, Tara, we also have to prove that we are worthy to be among the Nine.'

'So true. And we have to prove it to ourselves as well,' Tara responded with a sigh.

*

Five days later, the Seer arranged for them to visit Akash. They had to go through security clearance before they were allowed into the Burns Unit, a separate wing of the hospital. When no one claimed responsibility for the museum attack, security slackened and other motives behind the bombing were being explored.

As they walked through the hospital corridor towards his room, Tara felt Akash's suffering and sensed his willpower failing him. *Shut up!* Tara said in her mind. *You will get better, and we will fight this Kalingan. Zubin is with me, he will heal you. It is not the time to give up. Pain, there's so much pain,* he had responded. *Leave me alone, let me die in peace.*

The doors of the Burns Unit slid shut behind them with a hiss. They were dressed in protective garments. The patients had vulnerable immunity, Zubin explained. They went through another set of double doors. It was quieter in this part of the unit. Even the nurses spoke in soft whispers. Following the nurse, they made their way through the corridor, and right at the end of it, they were led into a corner room. An officer sat outside reading a magazine. He checked their ID and registered their presence before allowing them inside.

'Akash is in no mood to see us,' Tara whispered to Zubin, she grasped his hand and entered.

Akash was wrapped in gauze. *Like a mummy*, he said mentally, *and that's why I didn't want you to come.* Tara smiled. His pain was sharp. Zubin heard it too. She had opened her mind to him so that the three of them could communicate. The part of his face that was visible was bruised black and blue, and there were stitches across his right cheek.

'You're not so pretty any more, pretty boy,' Tara teased. Akash tried to shift but was constrained by the various tubes and the neck support. He winced at the effort. *Heal me, Zubin, the pain is bloody awful even after all the drugs they are pumping into me. They don't last very long*, he said.

'We must be careful not to arouse suspicion,' Tara said, noting Akash's weak state.

Zubin placed his hands along the bandaged areas. 'He is in a bad shape. It will take me time to get you back on your feet. I will heal your back first. Tomorrow we will work on the rest of your body. That way we will be able to take care of you and yet not arouse too much suspicion.' He felt the brace that supported the length of Akash's spine.

The sooner the better, can't wait to get out of here. The

asshole gave me a real bashing! Excuse my language, Tara,
Akash said, looking at her. *I want to get even with that*
bastard!

'We have to do this now, Tara. The more we delay, the
easier it will be for the Kalingan to get the Chintamani,'
Zubin agreed.

'I wanted to share this new piece of information. Lise
has informed me that even if Vayu finds the Chintamani,
he will not be able to remove it from its location. Only
the one worthy, which is one of us, can retrieve the
Chintamani. He will have to wait for us,' Tara said.

Akash jerked. 'What happened? Are you all right? Shall
I call the nurse?' Tara asked anxiously.

No, no! I was just laughing. The poor bastard must be
fuming and pulling out his hair. Aargh, it hurts to even
laugh. And tears rolled down the sides of his face. *Tara,*
don't make me laugh, it makes me cry!

'I'm sorry, Akash. We'll get you out of this torture
soon. I'll go get some coffee.'

While Zubin stayed with Akash, Tara went out in
search for . . . she wasn't sure what. There was a restless
urge that pulled her. She stood uncertainly. The security
guard looked at her questioningly.

'Need coffee,' she said.

He pointed to the left.

'Okay then, I'll be back soon.' She removed the
protective garments.

Tara headed down the corridor. She arrived at the

nurse's station where there was a rush of activity and hurried voices—some emergency case. Tara paused. A faint voice called out to her, 'Help me, Tara . . .'

Weak yet distinct, clear words in her head. *Who else would know her name here?* It was not Zubin or Akash. This was different. The hospital corridor was a typical linoleum-floored, white-walled, disinfectant-sprayed place. The nurse's station was like an island in the middle, a place to ask questions or just wait for updates on patients. It wasn't as noisy as a market but there were enough people bustling about to make it seem like one.

Tara checked if anyone was looking directly at her. No one was, and in the rush and bustle she noticed one slow patient: an elderly man in a robe clutching a metal pole that carried his drip, its tube snaked up his arm. He shuffled slowly forward and didn't seem to notice her, his eyes were to the ground. The cacophony of hospital sounds, of doctors, nurses and visitors didn't affect what she heard and she followed instinctively. She heard it again and turned the corner. It was quieter and the corridor was long with rooms on either side. She walked slowly, trying to figure out who was calling out to her. The further she went the quieter it became and when she got to the end, she was the only one standing there. Two doors on either side seemed ominous.

Tara felt doubt cloud her mind and, all of a sudden, she knew she should leave. This was a trap! She strode away, almost running, and this time she heard the words distinctly. She stopped dead in her tracks. It sounded so much like Karan, her boyfriend, or rather, her ex-boyfriend. Tara waited for the voice and as if on cue, she heard it again. It came through the door on the left. Tara was aware that she shouldn't go in, logic warned her to stop. She gripped the handle, cold steel in her trembling hand. Panic clutched her pulse, but she had to know, had to see that it wasn't Karan suffering inside. She pushed open the door and entered.

38

Zubin was fumbling with the adjustment lever of the bed when the nurse, a petite woman with bird-like movements and a name badge that read 'Jane' came in breezily. She checked Akash's vitals. 'And how are we today?' she asked cheerfully. Then, with an enthusiasm that didn't match the atmosphere, she said to Zubin, 'I think you'll have to step outside for a while. We have to change his dressing and it's not going to be very pleasant.' Jane smiled at Zubin, and as if on cue, two nurses joined her.

'Okay,' Zubin said. He turned to his friend. 'I'll be right back,' he said, and patted him gently on the arm. Tara hadn't been communicating for the last ten minutes and it was like an empty space in his head. She was a little chatterbox, with constant updates of her feelings about what was happening to them and why. And how, if it wasn't for her, they wouldn't have a clue about Vayu's location and how, despite their powers, they would be powerless. She had headed out in search of coffee, he knew that much. And then she said she thought she heard Karan. After that, nothing. He had a vague idea of who Karan was. But the sudden silence was worrying.

'Which way did she go?' he asked the guard. He pointed in the direction he had seen Tara walk off. 'She said she would be back with coffee. Should be here any minute.'

'I'll go check,' Zubin said, peeling off the protective plastic hurriedly.

He sprinted towards the end of the corridor and headed right. No one at the nurse's station had noticed her. But he couldn't blame them. They faced a bank of elevators and a constant flurry of visitors, doctors and hospital attendants. Zubin knew it was unlikely that anything would happen to Tara—she must have gone off to find some cakes or something else. He waited, wondering what to do next. A gurney with a patient passed by. He didn't take notice as the orderlies quickly wheeled it away. Then, as if in slow motion, Zubin felt an intense vibe, like an aura. Of Tara. He swirled around and looked at the stretcher that was halfway into one of the elevators. 'Wait! Stop!' he called out and raced towards the wide door, but they were too quick and pulled the stretcher in. The doors slammed shut in his face.

'Damn it!' Zubin found the emergency exit staircase and raced down two steps at a time. This didn't make sense, nor did the sudden disappearance of Tara and the feeling that she was in danger. He had caught a glimpse. The two orderlies were bulked up under their white uniforms, their hair a neat military crop. One had stared at him with cold eyes, while the other had viciously pushed the button to close the lift doors. One had even put on a small smile of victory as the doors slid shut before Zubin could prise them apart. Tara, if it had been her lying on the gurney, was covered from neck to toe with a white sheet, her mouth and nose hidden behind a paper mask. Her eyes were closed. *What the bloody hell was going on?* Without Tara as a conduit, he couldn't even communicate with Akash. And if Zubin went back, he would waste precious time.

He made it to the ground floor and pushed the emergency exit door. It opened into a basement car park. It was empty. *How could they have—*

A black van careened past him; it was the kind they used at funerals. It screeched and turned the corner at full speed up the sloping ramp leading to the exit. 'Hey! Stop!' Zubin called. He caught a glimpse of the number plate. *Shit!* He returned to the hospital and dashed to Akash's room. They had to get out of there immediately. Forget what it would look like, Akash was about to be healed completely. Zubin clenched his fingers into a fist and tried to focus his mind on Tara. Nothing. The slate was wiped clean, the screen was blank.

39

Zubin's frantic call made the Seer sit up. After pacifying the distraught Zubin, he listened carefully to the sequence of events leading up to Tara's abduction. 'I think they got the crucial link, Tara, because she was the connection amongst all of you,' the Seer reasoned.

'Yes, but where have they taken her?'

There was a silence, then Zubin's eyes lit up. 'It has to be Angkor Wat!' he cried. 'They need one of us to retrieve the second fragment of the Chintamani crystal. By taking Tara they've accomplished two things at once—got a member of the Nine and derailed the communication amongst ourselves. What I fail to understand, however, is this: how have they stopped Tara's mind from communicating?'

'Well, from what we've learned so far, the Golden Group has developed a serum which, when injected into the body, completely blocks the mind's impulses to communicate with thought. These are controversial experiments, covert trials on humans, and so they never surface. But they must have succeeded.'

'Hmm . . . This means we need to leave for Cambodia at once?'

'Yes, I will organize that, but what about Akash? I don't think he is in a position to move.'

'I'll take care of that. Just help me secure his release

SHOBHA NIHALANI

from the hospital,' Zubin said, an emptiness surrounding him.

*

Akash was horrified when he learned about Tara. 'How could you let her out of your sight?' he mumbled angrily through the oxygen mask.

'Shut up!' Zubin said. 'I cannot heal if you keep complaining. I'm not a magic wand. Keep still.'

The healing process wasn't difficult, it was just that Zubin couldn't concentrate. The nurses kept interrupting them. 'What are you doing, love?' chirped one of them.

'It's called ayurveda,' Zubin said, trying to paste a smile on his face. 'It's an ancient Indian healing method, helps ease the pain as well.'

The nurse checked Akash's vitals. 'Your pulse rate is high and your blood pressure has tipped upwards. Nothing to worry but you need to rest.' She tucked the covers around Akash, where Zubin had slipped in his hands to heal him. She eyed Zubin curiously. 'You look drained! Let your friend rest. He's not going anywhere any time soon. Go get yourself some coffee,' she said, giving him a smile and almost a frown.

'That's okay, I'll just sit here by his side,' Zubin replied. 'He said he wanted me to stay.'

The nurse shrugged, her buzzer vibrated and she left them alone.

'She suspects something,' Akash mumbled. He shifted

slightly, removed the oxygen mask from his face and sat up slowly. 'I do feel a lot better.'

Zubin was out of his plastic chair. 'I'll call the Seer. Hopefully, by now he would have figured out how to get you out of here.'

And he had. It was difficult but the Seer had thought of a way that Akash could be released even though it wasn't advisable. His position had helped again.

Zubin paced the floor while the Seer signed a bunch of release forms.

'We have to leave right away. Tara is in trouble,' Akash said in an agitated whisper. 'I can't wait to get out of these bandages and lay my hands on that beast!'

'Slow down, Akash. You have a habit of leaping into things before you think them through,' Zubin said, watching him as if he were an errant child. 'We have to plan our strategy. First priority: save Tara,' he said, pointing with his forefinger, 'and second, we get the Chintamani stone.'

'Third, we kill the bastard!' Akash said, punching his fist in the air.

Zubin sighed. He couldn't wait to take upon himself the responsibility of controlling the impulsive Akash.

40

Tara smiled as she linked her arm with her companion's, walking through immigration like newly-weds. The flight had been uneventful. Peter was such a wonderful man and so perfect for her! She recalled all the moments they'd shared, and how they'd met—at a medical conference. Dr Peter Gregoire was a psychologist and she was just out of medical school. Their wedding was just like a fairy tale and he had promised he would take her somewhere exotic for the honeymoon. And here they were in Cambodia! She felt a sense of euphoria.

Ten hours later, Peter gave her one of his melt-the-heart smiles. 'Almost there, my love,' he said, fastening his seatbelt.

'Can't wait!' Tara said ecstatically. Her arm ached and she stretched it to ease the discomfort. She must have slept at an odd angle. There was a split second sense of disorientation.

Tara held her head and bent low. She shook her head and when she looked up, she stared around her as if she was not quite sure where she was. Peter watched her curiously.

'Are you all right?'

'It's . . . just my arm . . . it hurts. And my head feels heavy. I slept well but I'm feeling tired.' She grimaced as stretching her left arm brought fresh pangs of pain. She started to pull up her sleeve but Peter stopped her. 'Let me massage it for you,' he said softly.

NINE   347

She dropped her arm as if it were deadweight and looked confusedly at him.

He calmed her, taking her arm in his hand and gently rubbing it. 'Don't worry, everything will be all right. I'll ask for some water,' he said and buzzed for the flight attendant. The fresh-faced young woman was by their side, and instantly left to get them their refreshments. He fished out a medicine bottle from his holdall and shook out its contents—two round white tablets landed on his palm. 'Take these. They will ease the pain,' he said and placed his hand on hers, stroking it gently. Tara felt as if a warm calming blanket fell over her. It was so soothing that she drifted into a half sleep until the attendant reappeared with the water. She swallowed the pills under Peter's watchful gaze. *He was so wonderful! She was lucky to have such a caring husband.* She sighed gratefully and he took her hand again. She fell asleep dreaming of colourful fish in a tank, swimming back and forth.

The plane landed with a gentle bump which woke her with a start. Again that sense of disorientation. Her head felt heavy as if it held more than one brain. Peter was attentive as they exited the plane and boarded the bus to the airport terminal. 'Let me get the bags, you just hold my hand, okay? How's that arm of yours?' he asked. His voice soothed her nerves, which, she realized, felt suddenly very raw. She wanted to snap at someone, she was angry about something but didn't know what. And then Peter made everything all right. 'Everything is going to be all right,' she repeated to herself and the weight lifted miraculously.

'I'm feeling so much better,' Tara said, clinging to her husband's arm.

41

Zubin and Akash were at the airport. The Seer had organized things very quickly. Within twelve hours of Akash getting out of hospital, they were on a plane out of New York. They arrived at their seats. Akash dumped his bag in the overhead compartment, sat down and clicked his seatbelt in place. Zubin shoved his bag under his seat after he removed a book and a pen. He wasn't in the mood for conversation.

They were quiet, contemplating their past and future actions.

The Council had communicated with them. They were concerned about the situation and wanted to use their powers to help. But Zubin and Akash suggested that they would venture out and that the seniors should remain invisible. If they needed help, the Council could guide them. It was important for them to stay in hiding until the Kalingan warrior was destroyed. But that would be later, after they had saved Tara and got hold of the two fragments of the Chintamani.

'Meditate, Akash, you need to concentrate and build your strength.'

Akash grunted. Zubin knew it was difficult, especially now. But he too needed to stay calm. Zubin recalled Na-khi who had taught them many things and one of them was to focus on a chant or mantra when quiet. The chanting method wasn't just religious, Zubin had discovered, there was a scientific effect, a physical reaction. A mantra worked on the mind, but its effects were felt throughout the body.

He understood why. The mind works in two ways: linear thinking and associative thinking. IQ is associated with linear thinking and emotions with associative thinking. And a repetition of a chant breaks both these circuits and allows the mind to be in a state of rest and awareness. The Ancients understood each chant as complete in itself in both meaning and feeling, and were aware of its effects. When a mantra is chanted either verbally or mentally, it vibrates in the brain and connects new neural circuits. Zubin was open to it simply because it was scientifically explained. He wasn't a ritualistic person and couldn't understand the restraints observed in the ritualistic worship of gods. The monk had taught him the power of the mind. And the phrase 'what can be imagined, can be achieved' took on a different meaning.

Na-khi had explained that the mind in an intuitive state directly understands all the higher laws. One who grasps these higher and subtler laws unknown to the five senses is called a scientist in the modern world. In the ancient world he used to be known as a rishi, a seer—one who sees and knows.

But the Kalingan had access to another kind of power, the modern science of chemicals. With the backing of some super-rich men, their covert research on mind control had continued in secret locations. And they had discovered a formula so potent that effectively, they had erased Tara's memory. To affect someone with psychic abilities was a feat. His thoughts went back to Tara. She would be at Angkor Wat, and they were going to find her.

Zubin flipped open his book and studied the information on one of the largest temple complexes in the world. He noticed the number nine mentioned in several places. The relevance of the number nine was significant in religion and astronomy. He nudged Akash.

'Listen to this, I got this from the Tourism Cambodia Facebook page,' he said and read from his notes:

> At the temple of Phnom Bakheng there are 108 surrounding towers. The number 108, considered sacred in both Hindu and Buddhist cosmologies, is the sum of 72 plus 36. The number 72 is a primary number in the sequence of numbers linked to the earth's axial precession, which causes the apparent alteration in the position of the constellations over the period of 25,920 years, or one degree every 72 years. Another mysterious fact about the Angkor complex is its location: 72 degrees of longitude east of the Pyramids of Giza. The temples of Bakong, Prah Ko and Prei Monli at Roluos, south of the main Angkor complex, are situated in relation to each

other in such a way that they mirror the three stars
in the Corona Borealis as they appeared at dawn on
the spring equinox in 10,500 BC. It is interesting to
note that the Corona Borealis would not have been
visible from these temples during the 10th and 11th
centuries when they were constructed. And Ta Prohm
is the terrestrial counterpart of the star Eta Draconis
in the Draco constellation.

Zubin didn't get a response from Akash, who seemed
lost in thought.

'Once upon a time, in another life, I had one of those
long-range telescopes and I would spend hours studying
the stars,' Akash said, looking out of the window. A
mattress layer of white clouds was below them. In the
distance was the shimmery sun's final curve in the horizon.
Soon the stars would be out. 'I looked forward to it, spent
hours gazing up at the sky. But I never imagined that
mankind could have built structures to honour these star
systems. Amazing!' He turned towards Zubin. 'Makes
one feel insignificant in the face of such ancient intelligent
cultures.' Akash seemed older, wiser even.

Zubin glanced at him. 'I'd never have imagined that
you would be interested in cosmology!' He noticed
Akash's softened expression, his eyes were neither
arrogant nor judgmental.

'Yes I understand,' he sighed and then smirked. 'I am
just a lowly DJ turned birdman, who couldn't even use
his powers properly.' He shook his head and turned
away.

'We will find Tara and get her back. By the time we get there, your body should be completely healed and strong enough to take giant leaps. You are good at that, Akash. Taking action, impulsive even in the face of danger. Like a superhero, not caring about the consequences,' Zubin said, trying to make light of the situation. Akash was looking defeated.

'Tara hated this side of me. She said one day I would regret being so rash and careless. And I do regret it. If I hadn't gone inside the museum to face Vayu alone, which resulted in the chain of events that led to her being taken, we wouldn't be in this position today.'

Zubin felt like telling him that it was all true. But destiny was a higher force than 'what ifs'. More often than not, thought processes resulted in the action that was destined. It was all very simple, the monk had said. 'Regret is not something you can live with and we should focus on what it is we can do from now on to create a situation that is in our control. Let's plan.'

A few hours later, they felt the tug of the descending plane. In the blackness of their oval window, they could see rows of tiny orange lights on the runway, like diyas on Diwali, welcoming them to an unknown destiny.

42

Vayu waited for them. He had felt like a fool at first, but after a discussion with the Golden Group, he realized that he was actually in the lead. And his actions had been fruitful. Locating the second fragment of the Chintamani was an amazing feat and he was commended generously for it. To ensure that his goal was achieved, the Golden Group had arranged the kidnapping of Tara. Tremendous progress had been made in the research field of mind-control drugs. They had successfully created a new personality. And Tara didn't know who she was any more. It served their purpose. All they needed was for her to be alive and well so that she could retrieve the crystal from the statue. She could live the rest of her life in her mind hell, and that would make for perfect revenge. And those poor replicas of the Nine would be able to do nothing. The Kalingan warrior was ready for them.

*

A blast of warm air greeted the two men as they disembarked from the aircraft after a twelve-hour flight. The city was hot and the humid air weighed on them. It was crowded and difficult to move quickly. They waded through immigration and baggage claim before they could finally get to the greeting area. And as Akash and Zubin looked for a placard with their names, a familiar face peered back at them with a wide grin and an enthusiastic wave.

'Guess who's here?' Zubin said. They passed people pressed against the metal fence. Uniformed men held up large placards with names of passengers printed on them. Some announced their five-star hotel status, and looked the part of a chauffeur; others nervously appraised each passenger, raising their boards each time, in case they missed someone.

Akash dragged his trolley bag with effort, searching for the face. 'Who's coming for us?' he asked.

'Lise,' Zubin pointed. They had reached the arrivals area where they were face-to-face with her in a moment.

'What are you doing here?' Akash asked, surprised.

'I heard about Tara and had to come and help,' she said, leading them away from the bottleneck of passengers and greeters and directing them to a waiting car. 'A lot has happened. Get in and I'll fill you in.'

The driver was a morose elderly man with greying sideburns. He briefly explained their destination and that it would take them an hour to get there. With that, he popped a piece of gum in his mouth, turned up the aircon, stepped on the pedal and hit the highway.

Lise handed them mini water bottles. 'You both look as red as lobsters and I'm the white one here!' she joked, laughing.

'Thanks,' Akash said appreciatively. 'Still adjusting to the heat.'

Akash removed his sweatshirt. In his T-shirt he looked thinner and his skin was blotchy despite the healing. He looked tired.

'What happened to you?' Lise asked, staring at him as if he were a different person.

'Let's just say it's Vayu's fault.' Akash saw the immediate change in Lise's expression. Her jaws tightened. 'Yes,' she said, facing both of them with a determined expression. 'That's why I'm here.' She held out her hand. 'We get this guy, okay?'

'Yes, we will get him.' Zubin placed his hand on hers.

Akash gripped both their hands and said, 'No one messes with us.'

Lise told them, 'Tara was drugged using a neutralizer. It induces retrograde amnesia, and combined with a 100-volt shock, it causes a complete blackout of the mind. She has a new identity and is married to a man named Refaq, or Peter as she thinks his name is. Refaq, believed to be a highly evolved individual with a background in parapsychology, is the chief of the Kala Yogis. He knows how to keep Tara under his spell.'

'Married!' Akash said, emerging suddenly from his lethargic state. 'She thinks she is married!' he repeated as if he needed to say it to believe it. 'How are we going to get her out of *that* state of mind?'

'There is a way. Dr Bhosle has sent a serum antidote for Tara's condition. But it's risky business with the yogis surrounding her ... plus their energy field is blocking our entry either through telepathic or other means.'

'What about Vayu?'

Her tone was hard. 'There are people monitoring Tara's

movements but no contact has been made yet. We expect that when they do, they will lead us to Vayu and the Chintamani.'

The rest of the journey was made in silence—the three of them went over the sequence of events in their minds and weighed their options.

43

Angkor Wat was a sprawling area teeming with ruins. To Akash, it represented death and decay—an awesome sight with sculptures seemingly leached by cascades of vines from gigantic trees. Their roots had encircled the temples in a stranglehold. The stillness in the air was eerie, as if energy had been suppressed and unplugging that hole would unleash something other-worldly. He shook off the feeling of being watched. They had been informed by the Council that Tara and Refaq had been spotted in the area, and knew that Vayu would not be far away. They trudged through the undergrowth where a path had been cleared for tourists.

The entrance to Angkor Wat was clogged with a crowd of excited tour groups and he wondered how he could levitate without creating a stir. Finally, after they moved inwards, they reached a deserted area not so popular with tourists. Lise had headed off to find Tara. She knew she would blend in easily with the tourists. Besides, Refaq didn't know her. Soon enough she spotted the duo.

Tara was clinging to her husband's arm. Peter to her, Refaq was being charming, holding her hand and playfully whispering something in her ear that made her laugh. He was a handsome man with a chiselled jawline and aquiline features. His hair was combed down neatly with a side parting, and it gave him an honest appearance. *How far had Tara been led in this lie?* Lise was at once filled with sadness for Tara who had helped her in her hour of darkness, and rage at those who had put her in this condition. What a simpering fool Tara looked like! This intelligent, intuitive girl had been reduced to a brainless imbecile. She wanted to drag her friend away from these monsters who had dared to mess with her mind. Tara was giggling and whispering in his ear. Lise wanted to puke. Vayu was responsible! Just as he'd conned her, he was doing the same with Tara.

Lise clutched the small hypodermic syringe in her hand tightly. It was the antidote that would break Tara's spell. Zubin and Akash had one each; they too were looking for her. Angkor Wat was so vast that even a whole day wouldn't be enough to visit all the monuments and structures. Lise was lucky that she had been able to spot them so soon. She did not, however, tell Akash or Zubin. She wanted to try and work this out herself.

The obstacle was Refaq: he wasn't leaving Tara's side. Lise couldn't just walk up to Tara and stab her in the arm—no matter how small, the needle would sting. But if she could just slide past and jab her thigh or hip, it might work.

Where were they headed anyway? If only she knew.

Lise edged closer, following them but keeping a safe distance, making sure they never left her line of sight. She was trying to communicate telepathically. Tara was more sensitive than the average human, and she should be able to pick up her voice, like she had before. Damn it, she wasn't responding and was glued to her 'husband'!

A large group of German tourists appeared behind them. Lise joined in, mingling and looking like she belonged. The path was narrow, and Lise saw that Tara was just ahead on the same route. She was standing by the temple. Lise wished she would unhinge herself from the man, and that would be the perfect timing to inject the serum. She got closer, stepped to the side and stood next to Tara. It was a crazy thing to do but there was no other alternative. Besides, Lise was dressed like a tourist, she had coloured her hair blonde and the piercings had returned. The one on her lower lip was new and painful.

Lise smiled enthusiastically at both of them. 'Imagine! These temples were built thousands of years ago!' she exclaimed. Tara returned her friendly smile but showed no signs of recognition. 'Looks so magical,' Lise said as she turned towards the left entrance. 'Wow! Look at that statue, isn't it amazing?' she tried again, half circling the two lovebirds. Refaq was watching her movements with keen eyes, and his hand slid into the crook of Tara's elbow with the intention of guiding her away from Lise. They started moving. It didn't affect her stride and Lise continued her effervescent admiration, following the two, but looking at the structure. 'Don't you want to go inside?' Lise gave Tara a friendly smile. *Remember me? Your friend? Come on, Tara, trust your instincts—it's me, Lise.*

A pause. And then Tara went pale. Refaq gripped her arm and supported her as she seemed unsteady on her feet. 'Are you all right, dear?' he asked, his voice was a soothing timbre. 'Maybe you should sit down for a while.'

'Please carry on, it's the heat—it's getting to her. She needs to rest for a few minutes,' he addressed Lise with a hard look. He helped Tara to the low crumbling wall of the temple ruins and murmured gentle words.

Lise took out a bottle of water from her backpack. 'Here,' she handed it to Tara, 'this should help.' *Om Mani Padme Hum*, she repeated in her head.

'No!' the man said, pushing the bottle aside. 'We have our own.' He took out a bottle from his bag and handed it to Tara. *Om Mani Padme Hum*, Lise repeated. Harder and stronger with all her mind and breath focused on the words.

Tara took the bottle but didn't drink. She gave a feeble smile. 'I'm feeling better,' she said, eyeing Lise's bottle.

'She needs time to herself,' Refaq said, throwing a stronger hint that Lise should leave them alone. 'Please go, she will be fine,' he said firmly. Lise felt an overpowering sense of hate. She wanted to bash his face in.

'That's okay,' Lise said, sitting next to them. 'I'll just be with her for a while—woman stuff maybe. Would you like to go to the toilet? There's a ladies' loo just around the corner.'

'No!' he said, raising his voice. This time both the women stared at him.

'I would like to go,' Tara said, standing up with quiet determination. 'I'll be back. This kind lady will accompany me. Don't worry, dear.'

'I'll come with you,' he gripped her elbow tight.

Tara had an odd expression: a mix of sadness and anger. 'You worry too much, my dear. I'll be back. Please wait for me here.'

'I'll join you,' he said, standing up and grasping her hand.

'Not in the toilet, I hope!' Lise's tone was light. But Refaq gave her a steely glance.

Lise trailed as Tara walked supported—held in an iron grip, rather—by her husband, in case she bolted. Lise continued her chant silently. She was convinced it was having an effect. Tara was looking confused and exhausted and Lise knew it was the pressure of the black magic pulling her away from her real self. They followed the directions that led them down a path to a small concrete structure that housed the toilets.

44

Vayu was watching them from some distance away. Lise had changed her hair colour again. It suited her complexion. She shouldn't have taken the trouble to come all the way here. Life would have been easier if she had just left, returned to her country. He didn't think she would have the gall to come chasing after him. *What was her purpose? Was she aiming for revenge or helping Tara on humanitarian grounds?* He entered a small sheltered part of the temple ruins. A huge tree with roots that snaked through, splitting the earth and cracking ancient stone, enhanced the eeriness of the haunting scenery. A beautiful place to die—and Lise deserved it.

Vayu noted how easily Tara was led away into the ladies' toilet while Refaq waited impatiently. Tara was heavily under the spell of her husband and she wouldn't do anything to contradict him—else she would suffer. Her skin would erupt into painful lesions, her limbs would ache as though she was afflicted with arthritis and she would have headaches that would make her want to bang her head against a wall. Lise could try her luck but it was a futile attempt and would prove to be deadly. It was best to take the direct approach. He headed towards Refaq. Just knowing that Tara was here, within five kilometres of the temple, and would soon help him extract the sacred Chintamani fragment, was energizing. He gleefully rubbed the first piece he had acquired from the museum. It was strapped to his chest. Safe, until he got the second one. The two melded together would give him the knowledge of the third piece hidden in the kingdom of Agartha—mythical but definitely in existence in another form or by another name. The Kalingan was ecstatic.

*

Akash and Zubin searched feverishly. Lise wasn't in touch. Akash's frustration at not being able to take giant leaps was resulting in a spate of swear words. 'Just shut up!' Zubin muttered as they entered another part of the ruins with a temple at the centre. 'We are doing the best we can. Okay, there's no one here. Why don't you get to the top of that tree? You will be hidden in the branches and can see if you can find somebody. I'm surprised Lise hasn't contacted us.'

'She's obsessed with getting her revenge. And she wants to do this alone.'

'Yes, but our purpose is to find Tara and save her. Let's focus on that first.'

Akash hopped onto the wide curve of a brick wall encircling a protected mammoth of a tree. Its trunk could be hugged if five people stood around it, interlinking their outstretched arms. He checked to see that no one was around and jumped up to a higher branch. Zubin was watching him like an anxious parent.

Zubin had been great with the healing but he was just

so annoying at times, thought Akash. Never really learned to chill. And the combined mentality of him and Tara was such a dampener that he wished he could go back to being an ordinary guy with a string of girlfriends and the best job in the world. He missed his music and his MP3 player had crashed. All his favourite stuff had disappeared. His life died the day he met that woman on the street in London.

'Be careful, I hear someone approaching,' Zubin called out, breaking his reverie. Akash stayed put. He could make out four people painstakingly studying the sculptures. Zubin pretended to be fascinated by a towering Buddha head. *Big face and small face.* From his angle it looked almost comical—Zubin wore an intense expression as though he were communicating with the stone.

Suddenly Akash spotted Lise—her hair colour was vibrant and had caught his eye. Then he saw the other two—Tara and Refaq. 'Found them!' he called out.

Zubin looked up. 'Which direction?'

Akash was screening his face and peering in the distance, he didn't say anything.

'What's happening, damn it?'

*

Inside the toilet, Lise didn't waste any time and plunged the serum into Tara. It took a few minutes to take effect and Tara looked dizzily at her. Then she stumbled back as if in shock. 'What's happening? What's going on? Shit, where am I? I was with Akash . . . coffee . . .' She pressed her temple. 'And then I don't remember anything,' her voice was rising.

'Listen, Tara, we don't have much time. You were hypnotized. More like part of your personality—your memory—had been wiped out. Replaced with one that made you think you were married.'

'Married?' she stared at her in horror.

'There's a man outside—you address him as Peter—but his real name is Refaq. He is waiting for you to come out. He thinks I'm a tourist but I wanted to get you alone so that I could inject the serum.' Tara was staring wide-eyed as if she could not register any of this information. Lise gripped her by the arms, 'Tara, please focus, you have to pretend that you are still under their spell.'

'I can't . . . I don't know . . .'

'You were smiley, giggly and clingy so keep up the pretence. You were sick and then you had to go to the toilet and I helped you. Okay?'

Tara was still staring, wide-eyed.

'Okay?' Lise gripped her harder and shook her slightly, trying to snap her out of her reverie. 'We don't have time. They've done this to get you here, to Angkor Wat, and Vayu will use you to get the second Chintamani fragment. Do you understand?'

'We are not in New York any more? How did that happen?'

They heard an impatient male voice, 'Are you all right, darling?'

'Oh shit, I feel like I know that voice!' Tara exclaimed.

'That's him!' Lise said hurriedly. 'That's supposed to be your husband. You have to play along so that he will lead us to Vayu and the second Chintamani fragment.'

'Okay, okay. I understand. I'm still dazed, though, and I feel extremely weak. But where are Akash and Zubin?'

'They are around here somewhere, looking for you.' Lise looked at her desperately. 'Please, Tara, we have go outside now or he will get suspicious.'

Tara took a deep breath, 'Okay.'

'Respond to him, tell him you're all right.'

'I'm fine . . .' Tara said and saw Lise mouth the word 'darling'. '. . . Darling!' she called out and grimaced.

'Smile!' Lise said and they went outside.

*

Akash managed to make his way down the tree without arousing suspicion. 'Let's go, I'll tell you on the way.' He would have preferred to leap but Zubin insisted he pretend to climb down. You never know who's watching.

Zubin followed him exasperatedly, 'What's going on?'

'I saw Vayu. Lise must have injected the serum while they were in the bathroom. When they came out, Tara was acting like she was still under Refaq's control. It didn't seem to work. Vayu emerged from behind the temple wall. He had been watching them all this time. He has a dagger pointed in Lise's back. They're taking the girls towards his destination, he's heading in the direction of . . .'

'Ta Prohm temple,' they said in unison—Tara was communicating with them.

Welcome back, Tara, Akash said.

Glad to have you back. Are you feeling all right? Zubin asked.

Just a massive headache, other than that I feel like my old self . . . except for the few days that are blank.

They dashed through and while Akash occasionally rose in the air to keep track of their whereabouts, he would still keep pace with Zubin. They were silent, Tara was doing the talking. *Lise is taking risks, she's antagonizing Vayu. I can't stop her. She will get hurt. You guys better have a plan for when we get there.*

*

Refaq held Tara in a firm grip. They moved along the path that led them towards the temple. Vayu prodded Lise with his dagger. She moved slowly and defiantly. 'Acting all hurt and irritated, Lise?'

'You conned me. Took advantage of me.'

'And you were not doing the same thing?'

'I fell in love with you, Vayu.'

They were simple words and the way she said them made Tara pause to think. She heard the pain and the depth of emotion in her voice. Lise might do something irrational.

'Let it go, Lise. He's a monster and he doesn't understand the meaning of love,' Tara said. Lise was edgy, gritting her teeth and clenching her fists.

Vayu laughed aloud. 'Thank you for the compliment, dear woman, one of the Nine. It will be such a pleasure to slice you in half and demonstrate how much of a monster I am.'

All of a sudden, Lise let out an angry scream. Tara turned and saw a dagger in her hand. 'Oh my God!' she whispered as Lise raised the dagger, aiming it at Vayu.

*

Akash stopped suddenly and stood as still as a statue. Then he rose in the air and balanced on a rock. Zubin looked up at him, a questioning look on his face. 'What's going on?' he murmured aloud.

Shit, shit, shit! they heard Tara cry.

What's going on?

Lise tried to stab Vayu, he was too quick and turned the dagger on her. Lise is hurt, bleeding like crazy! Come quick!

*

Vayu didn't want to hurt her but the Kalingan got the better of him. Damn, it wasn't easy to get a grip on the monster now. He had to get them out of there before someone saw them and called the police. They made it inside the temple. Outside, the grounds were deserted. Tourists wouldn't enter the temple, and anyway, it was almost closing time. He didn't want any intrusions. Lise was weeping, crying out to him. She heard his words, and it did affect a deeper part of him, but there were the immediate, more urgent, details to take care of.

Very gently, he laid her down on one of the large tree roots that grew aggressively and intrusively throughout the temple. She pulled him close—the familiar tug in his chest brought the guilt back. 'I forgive you if you let go of this crazy plan of yours,' she whispered. Blood seeped through her clothes and pooled on her stomach. Tara pressed it with a cloth and stayed close to Lise. 'They are on their way,' she said, holding Lise close. She wiped away the cold sweat that streaked her pale face. 'Zubin will heal you.'

'Shut up! Shut up!' Vayu shouted. 'You come with me.'

'No!' Tara shouted. 'I will stay with her.'

Vayu extracted a gun and pointed it at Lise. 'Come with me or she dies right now!'

Where are you two, damn it?

Close, very close.

Reluctantly, Tara stood up. She removed her jacket and placed it under Lise's head. She had lost consciousness. *Zubin, she's dying, you better hurry.* Vayu gave his gun to Refaq. 'Stay here and watch the white woman. If she so much as coughs, shoot her,' Vayu instructed Refaq.

Refaq nodded, 'Yes, boss.' He smirked at Tara. 'Too

bad our marriage didn't last,' he said, licking his lips. 'It would have been a pleasure.'

'You're a sick bastard!' Tara yelled, as Vayu dragged her into the sanctum.

*

Akash and Zubin looked at each other. Tara was furious. They'd never heard her swear before. In less than three minutes, they arrived on the temple grounds. Zubin climbed over the entangled roots and stones, while Akash jumped over. Refaq was in their line of vision, but Zubin didn't seem to care and hurried in his direction. 'Wait!' Akash warned but Zubin ignored him. Then, he saw Lise, bloody and pale, lying unconscious on the ground. 'Shit!'

Yeah shit! they heard Tara say.

Refaq was watching over her . . . Vayu must be inside the temple.

'I'll make myself scarce,' Akash said and swooped into the darker recesses of the cave. Before Zubin could kneel down to check on Lise, Refaq slammed a fist in his face. 'Stay away,' he snarled. Zubin staggered back but maintained his balance.

Anger flashed in Zubin's eyes as he turned back to face him. 'Don't do that again,' he said and edged forward. Refaq blocked him menacingly.

'What are you going to do, weakling?' Refaq prodded him. But before he could raise his hand to punch Zubin again, he felt a rock slam into his face. Akash had been hovering overhead with a stone and had flown full force at Refaq, smashing into him. The impact threw Refaq to the ground. Groaning in pain, he tried to lift himself up, turning to see what hit him. 'You son of a bitch!' he murmured through his bloody split lips.

Akash was above him, ready with another block of stone. 'Not so handsome any more, eh?'

Zubin rushed to Lise's side and he checked her pulse. It was faint. Blood had collected in a pool around her midriff, and spilled through her fingers and down her sides. She looked as white as a ghost. Life was slowly seeping out of her—he had to act fast. He placed his hand on her chest. She turned weakly to look at him and managed to smile. 'My guardian angel is here,' she rasped and shifted slightly.

'Don't move,' he said, supporting her head on his knees.

Tears were streaming down the sides of her face. 'Save your energy for Tara. I don't want to live any more.'

Zubin glanced at Akash, who was walking towards them. He held Lise's hand and gently wiped away the tears. 'You are a tough woman, and you can't let him get away with this, Lise. You are a survivor, you've made it through tough times,' Zubin said. Akash caught the emotion in his voice. He sat down and waited while Zubin worked his magic on Lise.

'It's going to take a little longer,' Zubin murmured, his eyes closed. 'She's hurt bad.'

*

Without wasting time, Vayu dragged Tara towards the leaning statue with the outstretched cupped hands. 'Dip your—'

He felt a hard shove before he realized that it was Akash, hovering above him like a bird. Vayu lost his balance and fell but rolled onto his back, aimed and fired his gun. Akash wasn't quick enough to react, the bullet smashed into his shoulder. The impact rammed him against the wall, and his body slid to the ground. Still.

'No!' Tara tried to run towards him.

'Come here, you bitch, and get me my Chintamani!' Vayu shouted, clutching at her leg. She fell forward and tried to scrabble in the opposite direction. But Vayu was too strong for her.

I will try and stall him, she communicated to her friends. She was dragged to the foot of the statue and hoisted up by Vayu's strong arms. The black pool of water in the woman's cupped hand had held the secret through centuries: how was it possible that she could get hold of it and not Vayu? Zubin had said that they were genetically modified. It was a half-baked scientific theory.

'Let me go, you stupid fool!'

'Fool? You call me a fool?' he slapped her hard. 'Once I get the Chintamani, you will be on your hands and knees bowing to me.'

Despite the sting of his slap, she turned to face him courageously. 'Why do you have to do this, Vayu? This is not really you.'

'Why?' he chuckled. 'And this is me, all me.'

'I asked, why you! Not that spirit,' Tara said softly.

'Show some respect, woman!' He grabbed her hair and pushed her to kneel. 'The Kalingans are a superior warrior race. They have suffered disrespect for centuries because of what the Mauryan ruler did to them. The Kalingans are a strong and courageous people, they don't deserve the disrespect heaped on them, while a murderer who destroyed a whole clan of warriors is still being called the greatest king. He was nothing compared to the Kalingan!' Vayu's voice echoed and Tara felt his anger like a red hot skewer burning in a live flame. Vayu's face was grotesque—he was turning into the monster that had possessed him. His grip was so tight, she felt the pressure close in on her bones.

Vayu dragged her up on her feet, pushed her hand inside the black pool of water. 'Give it to me now,' he growled in her ear. He aimed his gun at Akash, who was stirring.

Thank God you're not dead.

The water was cool and her fingers searched in it: there was nothing in the smooth base of the stone palms. Tara closed her eyes, dipped her whole hand in the water and flattened it against the sculpted palms. Immediately, she could feel the difference in one part of the water—the metal underneath felt different. She tugged gently and it came away with a sucking sound. She pulled it out. Vayu was about to claim it from her, when Tara said 'Oops,' and dropped it to the ground. The object was as large as a five-rupee coin but much heavier. It fell, bounced and landed at Akash's feet. Vayu leapt for it. But Akash had already picked it up. Vayu aimed his gun at him but before he could pull the trigger, Akash was in the air and behind him. Vayu shot at him wildly.

Lise and Zubin were already on the circular stone steps. Refaq had taken a bullet and had fallen. Vayu had got his own guy with his wild shots. 'Save me!' he called out to Zubin.

'Sorry,' Zubin shook his head and turned away saying, 'my friends first.'

Lise was ahead, racing up to the next level. She bounded towards Vayu who was still distracted by Akash, and pounced on him from behind. Hard. Zubin grabbed the gun that fell out of his hand. 'No!' Vayu yelled. And with a violent, vicious grunt he heaved Lise off and grappled with Zubin. In the scuffle the gun fell away.

Lise took hold of it and aimed. 'Stop right this minute or I will shoot,' she said in a calm voice.

Vayu paused and then, in the blink of an eye, he twisted his arm and caught Zubin in an elbow grip. 'Shoot, Lise. I thought you loved me.' He smirked and edged back slowly. 'Kill me and your saviour dies too.'

Tara searched for Akash. He was nowhere to be seen. *Where are you? There's a problem.*

In the dark corner of the ceiling. I can see what's going on. What should we do?

'Let him go, Vayu,' Lise said, her finger steady on the trigger.

'Give me the Chintamani and I will let him go.'

'Give me the first fragment and I will give you the second one.'

Vayu looked at her suspiciously. 'Tell your bird to come down here, where I can see him.'

You better come down here, Akash.

Akash emerged from behind a stone sculpture and landed gracefully next to Tara. He moved towards Vayu.

'Stay back, you idiot, or I'll jump off this ledge and take your boy with me,' Vayu shouted.

'That's a stupid plan for someone who wants to destroy the Nine,' Lise smiled. 'It's the warrior inside you that's making you behave this way. Remember, there are many who can replace the Nine but none to replace you, Vayu.'

She has a point.

'Give me the fragment,' Vayu roared at Akash. 'Or I twist his neck.'

The change was significant, they saw his eyes glow animal-like as his grip around Zubin's neck tightened.

Give it to him, Akash—he's going to do something stupid.

I have a plan.

Oh shit!

Everything played out in slow motion. Tara stared in horror when Akash hurled the crystal towards Vayu. In his eagerness to grasp it, he lunged forward, pushing Zubin over the ledge, and Lise fired. She hit Vayu square in the chest. Tara raced towards Zubin who was holding on to the edge with the tips of his fingers. Akash flew to him and buoyed him upwards. Tara and Akash managed to get him safely back on the ledge. Akash noticed the crystal gleaming inside an entanglement of roots and stones. Before anyone noticed, he glided down and picked it up.

Vayu was on the ground, bleeding but not dead yet. Lise was searching for the other fragment. 'Where is it, Vayu?'

'You . . . can save me . . . save us,' he whispered. 'Give me the Chintamani and we can escape together. You and I are meant for each other.' His voice was raspy.

She found it strapped to his chest. Pulling off the thick tape he had used, she extracted the bloodied crystal. It was still intact.

'No . . .' he said weakly. 'It belongs to the Kalingan.'

Lise moved away. 'It is not for me to decide who this belongs to.' She handed it to Tara.

At that precise moment, Na-khi, the blue-eyed, white-haired monk, appeared. He stood by the large stone gopura, leaning on his lion-headed staff, watching them with his piercing gaze.

Akash, Tara and Zubin gaped at his sudden appearance.

'Who is that man?' Lise whispered.

'He's one of the protectors of the Nine,' Tara whispered.

Na-khi's tone was raw with anger. 'You!' He pointed a crooked finger at Lise and said, 'The Knowledge Keeper, you deserve to die with this worthless Kalingan. It is the mercy of the Nine that you live. Go, get out of here, go back to your life!'

Lise gaped in horror. 'I helped . . .'

Na-khi aimed his staff at her.

'Don't hurt her, she protected us!' Akash shouted. 'After all we've done, this is the thanks we get?'

Na-khi smiled. 'The ego still lingers in you, boy!' His voice was a soft hiss. He strode towards the three, then stopped in his tracks. He looked down at where Vayu's body lay. He was alive, barely. He moaned for help. Na-khi placed his staff on Vayu's chest.

'No doubt, you three have proven your worth to the great Mauryan leader,' Na-khi said in a condescending tone. 'It was your dharma, so don't think you've done any one any favour. What you do benefits you; you will receive your rewards through your karma.' Na-khi extended his hand. 'The Chintamani fragments are no longer safe. We must keep them in another location, away from the powers of the Black Yogis and the evil men. And you.'

Tara came forward and placed her fragment in his hand. Akash hesitated until Tara prodded him, *It is best we let it go. It does not belong to us.* He reluctantly handed it over.

'What now?' Zubin asked.

'Go home, go back to your lives,' Na-khi smiled. 'We will take care of this Kalingan, enemy of Ashoka,'

Na-khi's voice boomed. And as if by magic, orange-robed monks emerged from the stone statues. The monks surrounded Vayu's body, chanting deep resonant sounds that seemed as ancient as Angkor Wat.

'What's going on?' Lise whispered.

Tara pulled her away. 'We must go now. They will imprison the Kalingan spirit inside this temple. Forever. I hope.'

Zubin and Akash glanced at the orange-robed men swarming over the body like bees. 'This place is no longer safe,' Zubin murmured. 'Let's go.' They could sense an ominous darkness loom above as the chanting rose to a crescendo.

They reached the doorway that led out of the temple cave. Just before they exited, Tara paused: she felt a tug. She turned and saw the Kalingan spirit—like a dark vapour it hovered above the monks. She saw his form, a warrior from centuries past. He looked at her, his eyes blazing. 'Our spirit will never die! I know who you are—Tara, Akash and Zubin—be warned. I shall return to destroy you.'

ACKNOWLEDGEMENTS

I am deeply grateful to my editors at Penguin. Vaishali Mathur gave me keen insights and generous counsel in the completion of this book, and Arpita Basu contributed perceptive editorial inputs.

With her brutally honest advice, Sharvani Pandit of Red Ink Literary Agency taught me how to take my storytelling to the next level.

I would like to thank my family, Bhagwan, Heenu and Nitin. They have been my source of strength and inspiration.

I owe a special thanks to the Legend of the Nine unknown men. I don't know if they exist amongst us, but I know that there are many silent unsung heroes in this world. They have overcome their own obstacles in life. These men and women are intuitive and sensitive to others and their troubles. They have the innate ability to motivate, transform and help people on the path to a better life.